SELECTED DOG STORIES

Also Edited by
ERA ZISTEL

A TREASURY OF CAT STORIES

SELECTED CAT STORIES
(Illustrated by W. Martin)

DINAH

Selected

Dog Stories

Edited by
ERA ZISTEL

Illustrated by
ERNA PINNER

LONDON
HAMMOND, HAMMOND & CO., LTD.
87 GOWER STREET W.C.I.

COPYRIGHT

Printed in Great Britain by
William Brendon and Son, Ltd.
The Mayflower Press (late of Plymouth)
at Bushey Mill Lane Watford, Herts.
9.49

CONTENTS

v

vi CONTENTS

ACKNOWLEDGEMENTS

The publishers have to acknowledge their thanks to the following for permission to reprint in this edition:

To Albert Payson Terhune *and* Harper & Bros. *for* 'The Coward'.

To the Exors. of Hugh Walpole *for* 'A Dog Has His Day'.

To Eric Posselt *and the* Arrowhead Press *for his translation of* 'Fritzi' *by* Carolin Lorentz.

To Samuel Arthur Derieux *and* Doubleday & Company, Inc. *for* 'The Comet' *from* 'Frank of Freedom Hill'.

To Frank Buck *and* Jarrolds Publishers (London) Ltd. *for* 'Tiger Bait' *from* 'Fang and Claw'.

To Joseph E. Harry *and* Appleton-Century-Crofts, Inc. *for* 'The Dog of Montargis' *from* 'Dogs and Dogs'.

To A. A. Milne *and the* Proprietors of 'Punch' *for* 'Enter Bingo'.

To John Taintor Foote *for* 'Dumb-Bell's Cheque'.

To Ilya Ehrenburg *for* 'Jo'.

To Arthur Train *and* Charles Scribner's Sons *for* 'Old Duke' *from* 'Mister Tutt Comes Home'.

To Dan Russell *for* 'Two Friends'.

To the Exors. of James Oliver Curwood *for* 'Wapi the Walrus'.

To Don Marquis *and* Doubleday & Company, Inc. *for* 'Blood Will Tell' *from* 'Revolt of the Oyster'.

To William Heinemann Ltd. *for* 'The Black Godmother' *from* 'Caravan' *by* John Galsworthy.

To the Exors. of Booth Tarkington *and* Brandt & Brandt *for* 'Fox Terrier or Something'.

To the Trustees of the Estate of the late Mark Twain *for* 'A Dog's Tale'.

To Zane Grey, Inc. *and* Harper & Bros. *for* 'Don'.

To Mazo de la Roche *and* Macmillan & Co. Ltd. *for* 'Reunion' *from* 'The Sacred Bullock and Other Stories'.

To the Exor. of Emma-Lindsay Squier *for* 'Czar of the High Sierras'.

To John Lane, The Bodley Head Ltd. *for* 'Riquet' *by* Anatole France *from* 'Crinquebille'.

To Dorothy Cottrell *for* 'Tiddlywinks and the Train Wrecker'.

To John Held Jr. *and* Vanguard Press, Inc. *for* 'S.P.C.A. Case 280,141' *from* 'John Held Jr.'s Dog Stories'.

To the Estate of Jack London *for* 'Brown Wolf'.

To B. W. Chandler *and the* Proprietors of 'Punch' *for* 'The Dog That Knew Too Much'.

To Walter A. Dyer *and* D. Appleton Century Company, Inc. *for* 'The Strike at Tiverton Manor' *from* 'Gulliver the Great'.

To Colette *and* Jacques Chambrun, Inc. *for* 'Absence'.

To R. G. Kirk *for* 'The Mugger and the Shadow'.

To the Exors. of Stefan Zweig *for* 'Jupiter'.

To the Exors. of Ernest Thompson Seton *for* 'The Making of Silly Billy' *from* 'Wild Animal Ways'.

To Eric Posselt *and the* Arrowhead Press *for his translation of* 'The Pedlar's Dog' *from* 'Ruf der Wildnis' *by* Paul Vetterli.

To Walter D. Edmonds *and* Harold Ober *for* 'Moses'.

To W. E. Hadaway *and* Donald Allen *for the frontispiece.*

Introduction

AS far away and long ago as the days when man first began to
put down his thoughts and impressions in writing, his 'best
friend', the dog, figured in his stories. And even before that,
when tales were merely handed down by word of mouth, even
then the dog slipped in as an occasional character. There is, for
instance, the age-old Arabic legend that tells of Adam after he
had been driven from Paradise, sitting dejectedly on a rock,
feeling something soft and warm nuzzling against the palm of
his hand and looking down to meet the gaze of a dog, silently
pleading with him, consoling him, offering his companionship.
And when Adam rose to go into the dark, unknown and terrifying future, the dog followed, to become the devoted friend of
man from that time on, to share his burdens as well as his
pleasures, to share hunger and thirst and misery and even
death, if need be.

To share. In that word 'share' is, I think, the secret
strength of the bond that has ever since the days of Adam tied
dog to man and man to dog, throughout history, from ancient
to medieval to modern times. To share implies a giving and a
taking. The dog does not give without taking something in
return. If he did he would be merely a servant, a slave, and not

a companion. He gives his undying love, his boundless devotion, his undivided loyalty, his sometimes ill-advised admiration and respect (occasionally also ill-advised), plus food and lodging and comfort and as much security as any of us are offered in this insecure world.

In fact, I have a suspicion (ill-founded, I dare say, and quite slanderously false) that he may take even more than he gives. Or—let us be fair and amend that—more than he has a chance to give. He will give up, for his master, his food, his comfort, his well-being, his life. Beyond that he cannot go. There is no more for him to sacrifice. But his master? What a wealth of delicate nuances there can be in the sacrifices he may make for his dog!

Or there is even the subtler, even harder to make, sacrifice re-books, in what has been called the oldest dog story in literature, a king mounts to heaven alone—all his human companions having failed to accompany him up the steep slope—except for his faithful dog following close at his heels. But when at last they reach the gates of heaven, and the dog is refused admission, the king himself also declines to enter, protesting that 'to desert a faithful friend is as great a sin as to slay a priest.'

Can there be any greater love than this: that a man should give up even the kingdom of heaven for his dog? If such love as this were weighed against a mere life, any kind of a life, human or canine, would the scales be balanced?

Or there is even the subtler, even harder to make sacrifice recorded by Shakespeare in his *Two Gentlemen of Verona*. Here it is, in Shakespeare's own words, which I shall not attempt to improve upon:

'When a man's servant shall play the cur with him, look you, it goes hard: one that I brought up of a puppy, one that I saved from drowning, when three or four of his blind brothers and sisters went to it! I have taught him—even as one would say precisely, Thus I would teach a dog. I was sent to deliver him as a present to Mistress Silvia from my master; and I came no sooner into the dining-chamber but he steps me to her trencher and steals her capon's leg. O, 'tis a foul thing when a cur cannot keep himself in all companies! I would have, as one should say, one that takes upon him to be a dog indeed, to be, as it were, a dog at all things. If I had not had more wit than he, to take a fault upon me that he did, I think verily he had been hang'd for 't; sure as I live he had suffer'd for 't; you shall judge. He thrusts me himself into the company of three or four gentleman-like dogs under the duke's table: he had not been there—bless the mark—a pissing while, but all the chamber smelt him. *Out with the dog*, says one; *What cur is that?* says another; *Whip him out*, says a third; *Hang him up*, says the duke. I, having been acquainted with the smell before, knew it was Crab; and goes me to the fellow that whips the dogs: *Friend*, quoth I, *you mean to whip the dog? Ay, marry do I*, quoth he. *You do him the more wrong*, quoth I; *'twas I did the thing you wot of*. He make me no more ado, but whips me out of the chamber. How many masters would do this for their servant? Nay, I'll be sworn, I have sat in the stocks for puddings he hath stolen, otherwise he had been executed: I have stood on the pillory for geese he hath killed, otherwise he had suffer'd for 't: thou thinkest not of this now!—Nay, I remember the trick you served me when I took my leave of Madam Silvia; did not I bid thee still mark me and do as I do? When didst thou see me heave up my leg and make water against a gentlewoman's farthingale? didst thou ever see me do such a trick?'

Can any man have greater love than this, that he take upon himself even the burden of his dog's worst faults?

I have often wondered whether my dog Muff would sacrifice her life for me. Fortunately there has never been an occasion for such a test of her love. But I have a suspicion, loath though I am to admit it, that she wouldn't; not because of any shrinking cowardice or fault in her devotion, but simply because it wouldn't occur to her that it was the proper thing to do. She would no doubt sit, trembling and bewildered, watching me suffer and die, and would continue to sit, bewildered and faithful, through the hours and even through the days, waiting for instructions.

I, on the other hand, have been tested. More than once have I run out in front of the cars (that she is conceited and trusting enough to think won't hurt her) to risk my own life, to face the driver's legitimate curses, to yank her out of the way. And the time I was under the impression, fortunately erroneous, that the apartment overhead was being consumed by fire, and that any moment the ceiling would come crashing down on our heads in a mass of flaming debris, did I desert her? No. It was then that I made the decision I know would be the same no matter what crisis confronted us: we escape together, or we perish together, Muff and I.

But does that make my love the greater and hers the less? I don't think so. She gives me all she has, a dog's love. I give her all I have, a human's love, which only seems the greater because of the particle of reasoning power that has been added to it. In many other ways, true dog ways, she proves her devotion to me. My friends are her friends. My enemies are her enemies. Let me show a liking for a particular dog and, no matter what sort of an unpleasant pest he may be, she accepts him and likes him, too. Let me show a distaste for another and, regardless of how attractive he may seem to her, especially at certain seasons of the year, she growls and drives him away. Cows? She hates them because I do, and will not allow one near the house. Goats? Horrid creatures, confusingly similar to cows, but I seem to have an utterly incomprehensible fondness for them so, doggedly patient, she accepts them by turning her back on them, her early overtures toward friendship having been brutally rebutted.

Cats? When she first came to me, they were things to be barked at and chased. Until she learned that I loved them, that I worried over them, that I suffered when they died. Then they became not only her friends, but her special charges. Let one of them scream in fright or pain and she turned into a cannon ball of avenging fury. Even now, when her eyesight has grown dim and her body prefers the lethargic comfort of the fireside, she will, at the slightest sound of terror from them, rush out into the night that she dreads and fears, to bump her poor black nose against the tree trunks and stub her toes on jutting rocks, still valiantly on the job.

Thus, in a hundred small ways, she proves her love for me.

Throughout this book, in most of the stories assembled in it, these two streams run side by side: the love of man for dog, and the love of dog for man. One is as great as the other, as wide, as deep and as powerful. In Terhune's *The Coward*, a little boy's devotion saves a puppy's life, to earn, in return, a puppy's devotion strong enough to conquer cowardice and save his life. In Walpole's *A Dog Has His Day*, a lonely man and a lonely dog find in each other's company the perfect happiness. In Zane Grey's *Don*, a man earns the friendship of an aloof dog by saving his life; the dog reciprocates in kind. And in Moroso's *Cinders*—well, nothing can separate Cinders and his fire-fighting master and their great white friend King, not even the advent of modern fire trucks.

Then there is Edmond's charming tale of *Moses*, a fool of a stubborn hound dog trying to get into a delightfully unorthodox heaven, harking back to that earliest of all dog stories in the Indian *Rig Veda*—only now it is not a king willing to wander for evermore with his dog in that terrifying nothingness between earth and heaven, but a group of tobacco-chewing, plain-spoken commoners, including Saint Peter himself. Here, there can be no such simple solution as having the dog suddenly turn into a god, as in the earlier tale, but a manœuvre closely resembling a modern walkout gains him admittance, nevertheless. And glad I, for one, shall be to meet him there some day (God willing), in the land where licence tags are made of gold!

In only one story among these presented here does the dog prove himself to be infinitely superior to his master. Stefan Zweig's *Jupiter*, consumed with hatred and jealousy, offered an opportunity for perfect revenge, shows a magnificent contempt for his erstwhile master by rescuing instead of destroying his dearest possession and then calmly walking away, disdaining the praise and proffered friendship of the fool and hypocrite he had once loved.

Most of the dogs are good. It is difficult to find an arrant dog among the short stories written about him, although the study of a canine malcontent and the causes leading up to his defection would be interesting, and in the hands of a master, exceedingly powerful. Two such studies are presented here: Paul Vetterli's *The Pedlar's Dog* (to my mind one of the most moving stories in the book); and the absorbing psychological analysis of a dog's changed personality that unfolds almost like a detective story, Mazo de la Roche's *Reunion*.

In selecting the stories, an effort has been made to offer the reader his choice of as many different varieties of dogs as possible. There are collies, bulldogs, dachshunds, pointers, setters, Alsatians, greyhounds, Pekinese, Airedales, Dalmatians, cairns, fox terriers, Saint Bernards, police dogs, shepherds, plenty of just plain pooches—and one Presbyterian.

There are hunting dogs, lap dogs, watchdogs, sled dogs, fighting dogs, work dogs and completely useless dogs. There are aristocrats and proletarians. There are dogs worth a lot of money and others worth nothing at all who are, nevertheless, priceless. There is one, Chandler's *The Dog That Knew Too Much*, who, in my opinion, is worth ten times his weight in gold, for he should put an end for all time to the persistently and brashly extravagant tales about dogs' super-intelligence.

Like Terhune, I feel there should be a limit.

'My dogs can read my mood, to a nicety', Terhune says. 'They can work out problems which call for genuine reasoning powers—there is no possible doubt of that . . . But—

'I never yet knew a dog that had sense enough to unwind his own chain when he had tangled it around a tree, or gotten it snarled in the brambles. I never knew a dog with the simple brain-power to lay a stick on a hearth-fire when the blaze flickered low—although such a dog loved the fire and had seen it replenished in that way a thousand times. I never knew a dog with sense enough to cease worshipping a human fool.'

I also agree with G. K. Chesterton when he says: 'I always like a dog so long as he isn't spelled backward.'

There, in the words of two wise masters in the art of writing and good judgement, I found the prescribed limit beyond which I myself would not go in making my selections. Thus certain stories were automatically eliminated, the one that just barely squeezed through being Mark Twain's *A Dog's Tale*, because it seemed to have enough appeal to offset its obvious extravagances.

Others were put aside because they had previously appeared in anthologies and therefore should already be familiar to the reader. Still others were without any hesitation whatsoever tossed into the discard (and may they remain there for ever) because of their cruel or flippantly libellous treatment of my friend and Muff's friend, the cat. We like cats, Muff and I, and think there's no earthly reason, within sanity, for other people and other dogs not liking them, too. And some stories were left out—simply because there wasn't room for them. Any book must have a beginning and an end not too many miles away from the middle, and since the number of dog stories runs into the hundreds, no reader should take it amiss if his favourite is absent. Perhaps at some other time, in some other book, his patience will be rewarded.

The stories in this one were all originally written and printed *as stories*. Not all of them are masterpieces of literature, but they are good, sturdy, authentic, absorbing dog stories. Most of them have, in their own field, passed the test of time. With a few exceptions, they cover the period from around 1910, when Moroso, Dyer, Foote, Hines, Derieux and Terhune started the avalanche, down to the present day, with John Taintor Foote's *Dumb-Bell* still in the running, and going strong.

There are no excerpts from books, great though the temptation was to include a chapter or two from some of the most beloved volumes on my own shelves. There are, for instance, Elizabeth Barrett Browning's *Flush*, Roosevelt's *Falla*, and the brave little dog who accompanied Admiral Byrd through the iceland wastes and the city traffic. There is Oliphant's *Bob, Son of Battle*, Ouida's *Dog of Flanders*, Strobl's *Rex*, London's *Call of the Wild* . . . but again, perhaps at some other time, in another book. . . .

ERA ZISTEL

The Coward

ALBERT PAYSON TERHUNE

IT began when Laund was a rangily gawky six-month puppy and when Danny Crae was only seven years old. Danny had claimed the spraddling little fluffball of a collie as his own, on the day the boy's father lifted the two-month-old puppy out of the yard where Laund lived and played and slept and had a wonderful time with his several brothers and sisters.

On that morning Ronald Crae ordained that the brown-and-white baby collie was to become a herder of sheep and a guard of the house and farm. On that morning, seven-year-old Danny announced that Laund was to be his very own dog and help him herd his adored bantams.

Now, Ronald Crae was not given to knuckling under to any-one. But he had a strangely gentle way with him as concerned this cripple son of his. Therefore, instead of the sharp rebuke Danny had a right to expect for putting his own wishes against his sire's, Ronald petted the wan little face and told Danny jokingly that they would share Laund in partnership. Part of the time the puppy should herd the Crae sheep and do other

farmwork. Part of the time he should be Danny's playfellow.
And so it was arranged.

A year earlier, a fearsome pestilence had scourged America,
sending black horror to the heart of ten million mothers
throughout the land and claiming thousands of little children
as its victims. Danny Crae had been brushed lightly by the hem
of the pestilence's robe. He did not die, as did so many children
in his own township. But he rose from a three-month illness
with useless legs that would not move or bear a fraction of his
frail weight.

Quickly he learned to make his way around, after a fashion,
by means of double crutches. But every doctor declared he
must be a hopeless and half-helpless cripple for life.

Small wonder his usually dominant father did not veto any
plan of his stricken child's! Small wonder he skimped the
hours of herd-training for Laund, in order to leave the puppy
free to be the playmate of the sick boy!

In spite of this handicap, young Laund picked up the rudiments and then the finer points of his herding work with an
almost bewildering swiftness and accuracy. Ronald Crae was
an excellent trainer, to be sure; firm and self-controlled and
common-sensible, if a trifle stern with his dogs; and a born dog-
man. But the bulk of the credit went to the puppy himself. He
was one of those not wholly rare collies that pick up their work
as though they had known it all before and were remembering
rather than learning.

Crae was proud of the little dog. Presently he began to plan
entering him sometime in the yearly field trials of the National
Collie Association, confident that Laund would be nearer the
front than the rear of that stiff competition.

Then, when the puppy was six months old, Crae changed his
opinion of the promising youngster—changed it sharply and
disgustedly. It happened in this wise:

Of old, Danny had rejoiced to go afield with his father and
to watch the rounding up and driving and folding and penning
of the farm's sheep. Now that he was able to move only a little
way and on slow crutches, the child transferred his attention to
a flock of pedigreed bantams his father had bought him and
which were the boy's chief delight.

Like Ronald, he had a way with dumb things. The tame
bantams let him handle them at will. They ate from his

wizened fingers and lighted on his meagrely narrow and uneven
shoulders for food. Then it occurred to him to teach Laund to
herd and drive them. Luckily for his plan and for the safety
and continued tameness of the little flock of chickens, Laund
was as gentle with them as with the youngest of his master's
lambs. Gravely and tenderly he would herd them, at Danny's
shrill order, avoiding stepping on any of them or frightening
them.

It was a pretty sight. Watching it, and Danny's delight in the
simple manœuvres, Ronald forgot his own annoyance in having
to share a valuable puppy's valuable training-time with his son.

One day Danny and Laund sat side by side on a rock, back of
the barnyard, watching the bantams scramble for handfuls of
thrown feed. Among the flock was a tiny mother hen with a half
dozen downily diminutive chicks. Anxiously she clucked to
them as she grabbed morsel after morsel of the feast, and tried
to shove the other bantams aside to give place to her babies
where the feed was thickest.

As the last of the flung grain was gobbled, the flock dispersed.
Most of them drifted to the barnyard. The mother hen and her
chicks strayed out toward the truck garden, some fifty feet in
front of where the boy and the dog were sitting.

Of a sudden the tiny mother crouched, with a raucously
crooning cry to her children, spreading her wings for them to
hide under. As they ran to her, a dark shadow swept the sunlit
earth. Down from nowhere a huge hen hawk shot, like a brown
feathery cannon ball; diving at the baby bantams and at their
frightened dam.

'Laund!' squealed Danny, pointing to the chicks.

The six-months puppy leaped to them. He had no idea why
he was sent thither or what he was supposed to do. He did not
see the swooping hawk. Never had he even seen a hawk before,
though hawks were plentiful enough in that mountain region.
But he noted the flustered excitement of the hen and the scurrying of the golden mites toward her and the alarm in Danny's
loved voice. Wherefore he bounded alertly into the arena—to
do he knew not what.

As a matter of fact, there was nothing for him to do. As he
reached the hen, something dark and terrible clove its way
downward, so close to him that the air of it fanned his ruff.

A chick was seized and the hawk beat its way upward.

Instinctively, Laund sprang at the bird, before its mighty pinions could lift it clear of the earth. He leaped upon it right valorously and dug his half-developed teeth into its shoulder.

Then, all the skies seemed to be falling, and smiting Laund as they fell.

A handful of feathers came away in his mouth; as the hawk dropped the mangled chick and wheeled about on the half-grown puppy that had pinched its shoulder.

The drivingly powerful wings lambasted him with fearful force and precision, knocking him off his feet, beating the breath out of him, half-blinding him. The hooked beak drove a knife-gash along his side. The talons sank momentarily, but deep, into the tender flesh of his under-body.

It was not a fight. It was a massacre. Laund had not time to collect his faculties nor even to note clearly what manner of monster this was. All he knew was that a creature had swept down from the sky, preceded by a blotty black shadow, and was well-nigh murdering him.

In a second it was over. Even as Danny yelled to the bird and as he gathered his crutches under him to struggle to his feet, the giant hawk had lurched away from the screeching and rolling puppy; had snatched up the dead chick, and was beating its way skyward.

That was all. On the recently placid sunlit sward below, a frantically squawking hen ran to and fro amid five piping and scurrying chicks; and a brown collie wallowed about, waking the echoes with his terror yelps.

In all his six months of life Laund had known no cruelty, no pain, no ill-treatment. He had learned to herd sheep, as a pastime to himself. He had not dreamed there could be agony and danger in the fulfilling of any of his farm duties.

Now, while still he was scarcely more than a baby—while his milk teeth were still shedding—before his collie character could knit to courage and tense fortitude—he had been frightened out of his young wits and had been cruelly hurt and battered about; all by this mysterious and shadow-casting monster from the sky.

Through his howling he was peering upward in shuddering dread at the slowly receding giant hawk. Its blackness against the sun, its sinister sweep of pinion, its soaring motion, all stamped themselves indelibly on the puppy's shocked brain.

More—the taste of its feathers was in his mouth. Its rank scent was strong in his nostrils. Dogs record impressions by odour even more than by sight. That hawk-reek was never to leave Laund's memory.

The pup's wails, and Danny's, brought the household thither on the run. Laund was soothed and his hurts and bruises were tended, while Danny's own excitement was gently calmed. The doctors had said the little cripple must not be allowed to excite himself, and that any strong emotion was bad for his twisted nerves.

In a few days Laund was well again, his flesh wounds healing with the incredible quickness that goes with the perfect physical condition of a young outdoor collie. Apparently he was none the worse for his experience. Ronald Crae understood dogs well, and he had watched keenly to see if the pup's gay spirit was cowed by his mishandling from the hawk. As he could see no sign of this, he was genuinely relieved. A cowed dog makes a poor sheep-herder and a worse herder of cattle.

Crae did not tell Danny what he had feared. If he had, the child would have given him a less optimistic slant on the case. For more than once Danny saw Laund wince and cower when a low-flying pigeon chanced to winnow just above him on its flight from cote to barnyard.

It was a week later that Laund was driving a bunch of skittish and silly wethers across the road from the home fold to the first sheep-pasture. Outwardly it was a simple job. All that need be done was to get them safely through the fold gate and out into the yard; thence through the yard gate out into the road; thence across the road and in through the home-pasture gate which Ronald Crae was holding open.

It was one of the easiest of Laund's duties. True, there was always an off-chance of the wethers trying to scatter or of one of them bolting down the road instead of into the pasture.

But the young dog had an instinct for this sort of thing. Like the best of his ancestors, he seemed to read the sheep's minds— if indeed sheep are blessed or cursed with minds—and to know beforehand in just what direction one or more of them were likely to break formation. Always he was on the spot; ready to turn back the galloping stray and to keep the rest from following the seceder.

To-day, he marshalled the milling bunch as snappily and

cleanly as ever, herding them across the yard and to the road. On these wethers he wasted none of the gentleness he lavished on heavy ewes or on lambs. This, too, was an ancestral throwback, shared by a thousand other sheep-driving collies.

Into the road debouched the baaing and jostling flock. As ever they were agog for any chance to get into mischief. Indeed, they were more than usually ready for it. For their ears were assailed by an unwonted sound—a far-off whirring that made them nervous.

Laund heard the sound, too, and was mildly interested in it; though it conveyed no meaning to him. Steadily he sent his wethers out into the road in a grey-white pattering cloud. Through the yard gate he dashed after them, on the heels of the hindmost; keyed up to the snappy task of making them cross the road without the compact bunch disintegrating; and on through the pasture gateway where Crae stood.

As his forefeet touched the edge of the road, a giant black shadow swept the yellow dust in front of him. The whirring waxed louder. Frightened, gripped by an unnameable terror, Laund glanced upward.

Above his head, sharply outlined against the pale blue of the sky, was a hawk a hundred times larger than the one that had assaulted him. Very near it seemed—very near and indescribably terrible.

A state forest ranger, scouting for signs of mountain fires, glanced down from his aeroplane at the pastoral scene below him—the pretty farmstead, the flock of sheep crossing the road, the alert brown collie dog marshalling them. Then the aeronaut was treated to another and more interesting sight.

Even as he looked, the faithful dog ceased from his task of sheep-driving. Ki-yi-ing in piercing loudness, and with furry tail clamped between his hind legs and with stomach to earth, the dog deserted his post of duty and fled madly toward the refuge of the open kitchen door.

Infected by his screaming terror, the sheep scattered up and down the road, scampering at top speed in both directions and dashing anywhere except in through the gateway where Ronald Crae danced up and down in profane fury.

The plane whirred on into the distance, its amused pilot ignorant that he was the cause of the spectacular panic or that a fool puppy had mistaken his machine for a punitive hen hawk.

After a long and angry search, Laund was found far under Danny's bed, huddled with his nose in a dusty corner and trembling all over.

'That settles it!' stormed Crae. 'He's worthless. He's a cur —a mutt. He's yellow to the core. If it wasn't that Danny loves him so I'd waste an ounce of buckshot on him, here and now. It's the only way to treat a collie that is such an arrant coward. He—'

'But, dear,' protested his wife, while Danny sobbed in mingled grief over his collie chum's disgrace and in shame that Laund should have proved so pusillanimous, 'you said yourself that he is the best sheep dog for his age you've ever trained. Just because he ran away the first time he saw an airship it's no sign he won't be valuable to you in farm work. He—'

' "No sign", hey?' he growled. 'Suppose he is working a bunch of sheep near a precipice or over a bridge that hasn't a solid side rail—suppose an airship happens to sail over him, or a hawk? There's plenty of both hereabouts, these days. What is due to happen? Or if he is on herd duty in the upper pasture and a hawk or an airship sends him scuttling to cover, a mile away, what's to prevent anyone from stealing a sheep or two? Or what's to prevent stray dogs from raiding them? Besides, a dog that is a coward is no dog to have around us. He's yellow. He's worthless. If it wasn't for Danny—'

He saw his son trying to fight back the tears and slipping a wasted little arm around the cowering Laund. With a grunt, Ronald broke off in his tirade and stamped away.

More than a month passed before he would so much as look at the wistfully friendly puppy again or let him handle the sheep.

With all a collie's high sensitiveness, Laund realized he was in disgrace. He knew it had something to do with his panic flight from the airship. To the depths of him he was ashamed. But to save his life he could not conquer that awful terror for soaring birds. It had become a part of him.

Wherefore, he turned unhappily to Danny for comfort, even though his instinct told him the boy no longer felt for him the admiring chumship of old days. Laund, Danny, Ronald—all, according to their natures—were wretched, in their own ways, because of the collie's shameful behaviour.

Yet, even black disgrace wears its own sharpest edge dull, in time. Laund was the only dog left on the farm. He was imperatively needful for the herding. He was Danny's only chum, and a chum was imperatively needful to Danny. Thus, bit by bit, Laund slipped back into his former dual position of herder and pal, even though Ronald had lost all faith in his courage in emergency.

A bit of his faith was revived when Laund was about fourteen months old. He was driving a score of ewes and spindly-legged baby lambs home to the fold from the lush South Mowing. There was a world of difference in his method of handling them from his whirlwind tactics with a bunch of wethers.

Slowly and with infinite pains he eased them along the short stretch of road between the pasture and the farmstead; keeping the frisky lambs from galloping from their fellows by interposing his shaggy body between them and their way of escape, and softly edging them back to their mothers. The ewes he kept in formation by pushing his head gently against their flanks as they sought to stray or to lag.

Even Ronald Crae gave grudging approval to strong young Laund coaxing his wilful charges to their destination. Try as he would, the man could find nothing to criticize in the collie's work.

'There's not a dog that can hold a candle to him, in any line of shepherding', muttered Crae to himself as he plodded far behind the woolly band. 'If he hadn't the heart of a rabbit there'd be every chance for him to clean up the Grand Prize at the National Collie Association field trials, next month. But I was a fool to enter him for them, I suppose. A dog that'll turn tail and run to hide under a bed when he sees an airship or a hawk will never have the nerve to go through those stiff tests. He—'

Crae stopped short in his maundering thoughts. Laund had just slipped to the rear of the flock to cajole a tired ewe into rejoining the others. At the same moment a scatter-wit lambkin in the front rank gambolled far forward from the bunch.

A huge and hairy stray mongrel lurched out of a clump of wayside undergrowth and seized the stray lamb. Crae saw, and with a shout he ran forward.

But he was far to the rear. The narrow by-road was choked

full of ewes and lambs, through which he must work his slow way before he could get to the impending slaughter.

Laund seemed to have heard or scented the mongrel before the latter was fairly free from the bushes. For he shot through the huddle of sheep like a flung spear, seeming to swerve not an inch to right or left, yet forbearing to jostle one of the dams or their babies.

By the time the mongrel's teeth sought their hold on the panicky lamb, something flashed out of the ruck of the flock and whizzed at him with express-train speed.

Before the mongrel's ravening jaws could close on the woolly throat, young Laund's body had smitten the marauder full in the shoulder, rolling him over in the dust.

For a moment the two battling dogs rolled and revolved and spun on the ground, in a mad tangle that set the yellow dust to flying and scared the sheep into a baaing clump in midroad.

Then the two warriors were on their feet again, rearing, tearing, rending at each other's throats, their snarling voices filling the still afternoon air with horrific din.

The mongrel was almost a third larger than the slender young collie. By sheer weight he bore Laund to earth, snatching avidly at the collie's throat.

But a collie down is not a collie beaten. Catlike, Laund tucked all four feet under under him as he fell. Dodging the throat lunge he leaped up with the resilience of a rubber ball. As he arose, his curved eyetooth scored a razor-gash in the mongrel's underbody and side.

Roaring with rage and pain, the mongrel reared to fling himself on his smaller opponent and to bear him down again by sheer weight. But seldom is a fighting collie caught twice in the same trap.

Downward the mongrel hurled himself. But his adversary was no longer there. Diving under and beyond the larger dog, Laund slashed a second time; cutting to the very bone. Again he and his foe were face to face, foot to foot, tearing and slashing; the collie's speed enabling him to flash in and out and administer thrice as much punishment as he received.

The mongrel gained a grip on the side of Laund's throat. Laund wrenched free, leaving skin and hair in the other's jaws, and dived under again. This time he caught a grip dear to his wolf-ancestors. His gleaming teeth seized the side of the mongrel's lower left hind leg.

With a screech the giant dog crashed to the road; hamstrung, helpless. There he lay until Crae's hired man came running up, rifle in hand, and put the brute out of his pain with a bullet through the skull.

For a mere second, Laund stood panting above his fallen enemy. Then seeing the mongrel had no more potentialities for harming the flock, the collie darted among the fast-scattering ewes and lambs, rounding them up and soothing them.

In his brief battle he had fought like a maddened wild beast. Yet now he was once more the lovingly gentle and wise sheepherder, easing and quietening the scared flock as a mother might calm her frightened child.

'Laund!' cried Ronald Crae, delightedly, catching the collie's bleeding head between his calloused hands in a gesture of rough affection. 'I was dead wrong. You're as game a dog as ever breathed. It's up to me to apologize for calling you a coward. That cur was as big and husky as a yearling. But you never flinched for a second. You sailed in and licked him. You're *true* game, Laund!'

The panting and bleeding collie wagged his plumed tail ecstatically at the praise and the rare caress. He wiggled and whimpered with joy. Then, of a sudden, he cowered to earth, peering skyward.

Far above flew the forest-ranger's aeroplane, on the way back from a day's fire-scouting among the hills. With the shrill ki-yi of a kicked puppy, Laund clapped his tail between his legs and bolted for the house. Nor could Crae's fiercest shouts check his flight. He did not halt until he had plunged far under Danny's bed and tucked his nose into the dim corner of the little bedroom.

'Half of that dog ought to have a hero medal!' raged Crae, to his wife, as he stamped into the kitchen after he and the hired man had collected the scattered sheep and folded them. 'Half of him ought to have a hero medal. And the other half of him ought to be shot, for the rottenest coward I ever set eyes on. His pluck saved me a lamb, this afternoon. But his cowardice knocks out any chance of his winning the field trials next month.'

'But why? If—'

'The trials are held at the fair grounds—the second day of the Fair. There's dead sure to be a dozen airships buzzing around the field, all day. There always are. The first one of them Laund sees, he'll drop his work and he'll streak for home, yowling at every jump. I'm due to be laughed out of my boots by the crowd, if I take him there. Yet there isn't another dog in the state that can touch him as a sheep-worker. Rank bad luck, isn't it?'

So it was that Laund's return to favour and to respect was pitifully brief. True, his victory prevented the Craes from continuing to regard him as an out-and-out coward. But the repetition of his flight from the airship all but blotted out the prestige of his fighting prowess.

The sensitive young dog felt the atmosphere of qualified disapproval which surrounded him, and he moped sadly. He knew he had done valiantly in tackling the formidable sheep-killer that had menaced his woolly charges. But he knew, too, that he was in disgrace again for yielding to that unconquerable fear which possessed him at sight of anything soaring in the air above his head.

He lay moping on the shady back porch of the farmhouse one hot morning, some days later. He was unhappy, and the heat made him drowsy. But with one half-shut eye he watched Danny limping painfully to the bantam-yard and opening its gate to let his feathered pets out for a run in the grass.

Laund loved Danny as he loved nothing and nobody else. He was the crippled child's worshipping slave, giving to the boy the strangely protective adoration which the best type of collie reserves for the helpless. As a rule he was Danny's devoted shadow at every step the fragile little fellow took. But at breakfast this morning Crae had delivered another tirade on Laund's cowardice, having seen the collie flinch and tremble when a pigeon flew above him in the barnyard. Danny had seen the same thing himself, more than once. But now that his father had seen and condemned it, the child felt a momentary disgust for the cringing dog. Wherefore, when the little fellow had come limping out on the porch between his awkward crutches and Laund had sprung up to follow him, Danny had bidden him crossly to stay where he was. With a sigh the dog had stretched himself out on the porch again, watching the child's slow progress across the yard to the bantam-pen.

Danny swung wide the pen door. Out trooped the bantams, willingly following him as he led them to the grassplot. Supporting his weight on one of the two crutches—without which he could neither walk nor stand—he took a handful of crumbs from his pocket and tossed them into the grass for his pets to scramble for.

Laund was not the scene's only watcher. High in the hot blue sky hung two circling specks. From the earth they were almost invisible. But to their keen sight Danny and his scuttling chickens were as visible as they were to Laund himself.

The huge hen hawk and his mate were gaunt from long-continued foraging for their nestlings. Now that the brood was fledged and able to fend for itself, they had time to remember their own unappeased hunger.

For weeks they had eaten barely enough to keep themselves alive. All the rest of their plunder had been carried to a mammoth nest of brown sticks and twigs, high in the top of a mountain-side pine tree; there to be fought over and gobbled by two half-naked wholly rapacious baby hawks.

To-day the two mates were free at last to forage for themselves. But food was scarce. The wild things of woods and meadows had grown wary, through the weeks of predatory hunt for them. Most farmers were keeping their chickens in wire-topped yards. The half-famished pair of hawks had scoured the heavens since dawn in quest of a meal, at every hour growing more ragingly famished.

Now, far below them, they saw the bevy of fat bantams at play in the grass, a full hundred yards from the nearest house. True, a crippled and twisted child stood near them, supported by crutches. But by some odd instinct the half-starved birds seemed to know he was not formidable or in any way to be feared.

No other human was in sight. Here, unprotected, was a feast of fat fowls. Thrice the hawks circled. Then, by tacit consent, they 'stooped'. Down through the windless air they clove their way at a speed of something like ninety miles an hour.

One of the bantams lifted its head and gave forth a warning 'chir-r-r!' to its fellows. Instantly the brood scattered, with flapping wings and fast-twinkling yellow legs.

Danny stared in amazement. Then something blackish and huge swept down upon the nearest hen and gripped it. In the same fraction of time the second hawk smote the swaggering little rooster of the flock.

The rooster had turned and bolted to Danny for protection. Almost between the child's helpless feet he crouched. Here it was that the hawk struck him.

Immediately, Danny understood. His beloved flock was raided by hawks. In fury, he swung aloft one of his crutches; and he brought it down with all his puny strength in the direction of the big hawk as it started aloft with the squawking rooster in its talons.

Now, even in a weak grasp, a clubbed and swung crutch is a dangerous weapon. More than one strong man—as police records will show—has been killed by a well-struck blow on the head from such a bludgeon.

Danny smote not only with all his fragile force, but with the added strength of anger. He gripped the crutch by its rubber point and swung it with all his weight as well as with his weak muscular power. The blow was aimed in the general direction of the hawk, as the bird left ground. The hawk's upward spring added to the crutch's momentum. The sharp corner of the armpit crosspiece happened to come in swashing contact with the bird's skull.

The impact of the stroke knocked the crutch out of Danny's hand and upset the child's own equilibrium. To the grass he sprawled, the other crutch falling far out of his reach. There he lay, struggling vainly to rise. One clutching little hand closed on the pinions of the hawk.

The bird had been smitten senseless by the whack of the crutch-point against the skull. Though the force had not been great enough to smash the skull or break the neck, yet it had knocked the hawk unconscious for a moment or so. The giant brown bird lay supine, with outstretched wings. Right valorously did the prostrate child seize upon the nearest of these wings.

As he had seen the first hawk strike, Danny had cried aloud in startled defiance at the preying bird. The cry had not reached his mother, working indoors, or the men who were unloading a wagon of hay into the loft on the far side of the barn. But it had assailed the ears of Laund, even as the collie was shrinking back into the kitchen at far sound of those dreaded rushing wings.

For the barest fraction of an instant Laund crouched, hesitant. Then again came Danny's involuntary cry and the soft thud of his falling body on the grass. Laund hesitated no longer.

The second hawk was mounting in air, carrying its prey toward the safety of the mountain forests; there to be devoured at leisure. But, looking down, it saw its mate stretched senseless on the ground, the crippled child grasping its wing.

Through the courage of devotion or through contempt for so puny an adversary, the hawk dropped its luscious burden and flew at the struggling Danny.

Again Laund hesitated, though this time only in spirit; for his lithely mighty body was in hurricane motion as he sped to Danny's aid. His heart flinched at sight and sound of those swishing great wings, at the rank scent, and at the ferocious menace of beak and claw. Almost ungovernable was his terror at the stark nearness of these only things in all the world that he feared—these flying scourges he feared to the point of insane panic.

Tremendous was the urge of that mortal terror. But tenfold more urgent upon him was the peril to Danny whom he worshipped.

The child lay, still grasping the wing of the hawk he had so luckily stunned. With his other hand he was preparing to strike the hawk's onrushing mate. The infuriated bird was hurling itself full at Danny's defenceless face; heedless of the ridiculously useless barrier of his out-thrust fist. The stunned hawk began to quiver and twist, as consciousness seeped back into its jarred brain.

This was what Laund saw. This was what Laund understood. And the understanding of his little master's hideous danger slew the fear that hitherto had been his most unconquerable impulse.

Straight at the cripple's face flew the hawk. The curved beak and the rending talons were not six inches from Danny's eyes when something big and furry tore past, vaulting the prostrate child and the stunned bird beside him.

With all the speed and skill of his wolf ancestors Laund drove his curved white tusks into the breast of the charging hawk.

Deep clove his eyeteeth, through the armour of feathers, and through the tough breast bone. They ground their way with silent intensity toward a meeting, in the very vitals of the hawk.

The bird bombarded him with its powerful wings, banging him deafeningly and agonizingly about the head and shoulders; hammering his sensitive ears. The curved talons tore at his white chest, ripping deep and viciously. The crooked beak struck for his eyes, again and again, in lightning strokes. Failing to reach them, it slashed the silken top of his head, well nigh severing one of his furry little tulip ears.

Laund was oblivious to the fivefold punishment; the very hint of which had hitherto been enough to send him ki-yi-ing under Danny's bed. He was not fighting now for himself, but for the child who was at once his ward and his deity.

On himself he was taking the torture that otherwise must have been inflicted on Danny. For perhaps the millionth time in the history of mankind and of dog, the Scriptural adage was fulfilled; and perfect love was casting out fear.

Then, of a sudden, the punishment ceased. The hawk quivered all over and collapsed inert between Laund's jaws. One of the mightily grinding eyeteeth had pierced its heart.

Laund dropped the carrion carcass; backing away and blinking, as his head buzzed with the bastinade of wing blows it had sustained and with the pain of the beak stabs.

But there was no time to get his breath and his bearings. The second hawk had come back to consciousness with a startling and raging suddenness. Finding its wing grasped by a human hand, it was turning fiercely upon the child.

Laund flung himself on the hawk from behind. He attacked just soon enough to deflect the beak from its aim at the boy's eyes and the talons from the boy's puny throat.

His snapping jaws aimed for the hawk's neck, to break it. They missed their mark by less than an inch; tearing out a thick tuft of feathers instead. His white forefeet were planted on the hawk's tail as he struck for the neck.

The bird's charge at Danny was baulked, but the hawk itself was not injured. It whirled about on the dog, pecking for the eyes and lambasting his hurt head with its fistlike pinions.

Heedless of the menace, Laund drove in at the furious creature, striking again for the breast. For a few seconds, the pair were one scrambling, flapping, snarling, and tumbling mass.

Away from Danny they rolled and staggered in their mad

scrimmage. Then Laund ceased to thrash about. He braced himself and stood still. He had found the breast-hold he sought.

For another few moments the climax of the earlier battle was re-enacted. To Danny it seemed as if the bird were beating and ripping his dear pal to death.

Beside himself with wild desire to rescue Laund, and ashamed of his own contempt for the dog's supposed cowardice, Danny writhed to his feet and staggered toward the battling pair, his fists aloft in gallant effort to tear the hawk in two.

Then, as before, came that sudden cessation of wing-beating. The bird quivered spasmodically. Laund let the dead hawk drop from his jaws as he had let its mate. Staggering drunkenly up to Danny, he tried to lick the child's tear-spattered face.

From the house and from the barn came the multiple thud of running feet. Mrs. Crae and the men were bearing down upon the scene. They saw a bleeding and reeling dog walking toward them beside a weeping and reeling little boy. From the onlookers went up a wordless and gabbling shout of astonishment.

Danny was walking! Without his crutches he was walking; he who had not taken a step by himself since the day he was stricken with the illness that crippled him; he whose parents had been told by the doctors that he could never hope to walk or even stand up without his crutches!

Yes, he was one of the several hundred children—victims of the same disease and of other nerve-paralysis disorders—who regained the long-lost power over their limbs and muscles; through great shock and supreme effort. But that made the miracle seem none the less a miracle to the Craes and to the former cripple himself.

In the midst of the annual field trials of the National Collie Association, the next month, a gigantic and noisy aeroplane whirred low over the field where the dogs were at work.

If Laund heard or saw it, he gave no heed. He went unerringly and calmly and snappily ahead with his tests—until he won the Grand Prize.

He saw no reason to feel scared or even interested when the airship cast its winked shadow across him. A few weeks earlier he had fought and conquered two of those same flappy things. He had proved to himself, forever, that there was nothing about them to be afraid of.

A Dog Has His Day

HUGH WALPOLE

MR. and Mrs. William Thrush owned a very sweet little house in Benedict Canyon, Los Angeles. That is, the postal address was Los Angeles, but Benedict Canyon is a Hollywood district if there ever was one. The Thrushes liked it for that reason, among others, and it gave William Thrush a very real pleasure when he heard the big motor-trucks between seven and eight in the morning thundering down the canyon on their way to location. This was about as near as he ever got to Pictures. He didn't, in fact, wish to get any nearer, because he had a certain pride; not very much, but enough to make him desire to live in a society where he could be valued. Every morning he read the columns of film-making gossip in his daily paper and always remarked to Isabelle, 'Gosh! If they don't have a time!' Then they both felt happy, and a little superior, too.

Isabelle Thrush had more pride than William. In fact, she

33

C

had a great deal, and she spent most of her time feeding it or inducing other people to do so. Would you say they were a happy pair? If you didn't know all about them, certainly yes. If you did know all about them, you would probably be doubtful, as William often was.

There was something wrong between Isabelle and himself, although they'd been married ten years and very seldom squabbled about anything. They didn't quarrel, because William refused to. Isabelle had undoubtedly a shrill temper, especially when she didn't get what she wanted. Of course, she couldn't get all the things she wanted, because William, who was a clerk in a leading bank in Los Angeles, had but a moderate salary. It happened, however, that a wealthy aunt of his died some three or four years before and left him a pretty little sum. He invested this wisely, so that even through the depression it remained. But Isabelle had all of it and then a little more.

He asked himself sometimes in the privacy of the night whether she were greedy. He couldn't be sure, because he often read in magazines about the tyranny of wives and how they eagerly bled their husbands. Well, Isabelle wasn't as bad as that. Gosh! He'd see to it if she tried anything like that on him. And so, he decided comfortably, she was better than most wives.

Isabelle considered herself a really magnificent creature, filled with all the virtues—courage, wisdom, self-sacrifice, love, and endurance. She thought that William was extremely lucky to be married to her. And this thought produced in her a kindly, motherly air when he was around, as though she were saying, 'Little man, I'll look after you. Don't be afraid.' And then, 'How lucky you really are.'

The Thrushes had no children. That was Isabelle's wish, because she said it was wicked to bring a child into the world when you weren't going to give it everything of the best. William, once when he was feeling peevish because of his indigestion, remarked to her that his aunt's money would look after the child, all right. But Isabelle was indignant, indeed, and said that there was a cruel strain in his nature which he would have to watch.

*   *   *   *

Having no children, Isabelle thought it would be pleasant to have a dog. Many of her lady friends had them. There were, in fact, far more hospitals for dogs in Beverly and Hollywood than for human beings, and everybody said that dog hospitals were so perfectly run that it was worth having a dog just for that reason alone.

Isabelle wanted a dog, but there were problems to be settled. She understood that unless you had it as a puppy it never became really fond of you. On the other hand, puppies had to be trained, and one's beautiful rugs and carpets suffered in the process. Then, what kind of dog should she have? There were darling little cockers, the adorable Scotch terriers, the amusing dachshunds, and the great, big, splendid setters and Airedales. Some very lonely women had Pekinese, and then there were French bulldogs. She couldn't make up her mind, and used to ask William which sort he preferred. And William, while he was trying to guess what she wanted him to say, would look at her with that slow, puzzling stare, which Isabelle always interpreted as a tribute of gratified recognition of her brilliance and beauty. In reality, what he was saying was, 'What is the matter with Isabelle? She has gone somewhere, and I don't know quite where.'

They lived the social life of ladies and gentlemen of moderate means in Hollywood. That is, they went to Previews of celebrated pictures. In the summer they sat in the Bowl and wiped the damp off their fingers as they listened confusedly to symphonies by Brahms and Beethoven. They occasionally, with great daring, went, with a friend or two, to a Burlesque in Los Angeles. They played bridge quite badly, and gave little dinner parties at which the coloured maid was never quite satisfactory. On the whole, it was a happy life.

Then one day William, sitting alone and doing a crossword puzzle in the patio of his little Spanish house, had a visitor. Isabelle was out playing bridge with some friends and he was enjoying the lovely, tranquil sunset, which lay like a golden sheet let down from heaven protectingly over the canyon. In another half-hour the light would be gone, the air would be chill and sharp, and he would go indoors and read his evening newspaper, turn on the heat, and wonder why he wasn't as happy as he ought to be.

Then he saw enter his little garden, through a hole in the hedge, a French bulldog. This dog sniffed around, looked at him from a distance with a very nervous expression, and then slowly advanced towards him, twisting and bending its thick body as though it were made of some elastic substance. William Thrush looked at the dog and disliked it exceedingly.

He'd never had a great passion for dogs, not since, years and years ago his mother, in a real temper, had shaken him and told him he was as silly as a terrier puppy. This meant a great deal at the time, because they had just such a puppy in their house, a puppy that exasperated his mother by its inept habits and aimless amiability. So he'd grown up disliking dogs. And being himself a short, thickset little man, with large glasses and rather bowed legs, short thickset dogs were especially unpleasant to him. In any case, this dog seemed to him the ugliest ever, so very ugly, in fact, that he felt a sort of nausea. He said, 'Shoo! Go-away!'

But the dog was evidently accustomed to being disliked. On looking back over this first meeting, William reflected on the fact that the dog resembled himself, in that, if anyone disliked him, some kind of paralysis seized him and he simply stayed and stayed, although he knew he ought to go away. So did the dog now. It didn't come up to William, but lay at full length on the grass at a short distance and looked at him with bulging, ugly, and, in some unpleasant way, very human eyes.

William went up to it, that he might frighten it out of the garden. But, instead of that, the dog lay over on its back, wriggling its stomach and waving its legs feebly in the air.

'You're horrible!' William said aloud. 'I don't like dogs and never have. For heaven's sake, get out of here!' And then he had a horrible sense of speaking to himself, telling himself to get out of the house and garden and go somewhere.

The dog turned over, and sat up, gave him a beseeching but intimate look, as though it said, 'I know you much better than you think I do. Nothing could destroy our intimacy', and then went quietly out of the garden.

William's wife returned later, vexed because she had lost at bridge. 'Such cards, my dear; you would have thought there was a spell on me. I don't know what to do about it. The cards I've been having lately!'

He told her about the dog, but she wasn't in the very least

interested, and after her absent-minded 'Really? How revolting!' went on with a long story about a shop down town in Los Angeles where you could get a mink coat—or if it wasn't mink it looked very like it—by paying so small a sum weekly that you really didn't know you were paying it.

'No, you wouldn't,' said William, who was most unexpectedly cross, 'because I should be paying it.'

This upset her very much, indeed. She detested mean people, and suddenly, standing there in the garden which the sun had left, so that it was cold and dead, she realized that William *was* mean and that she had been living with a mean man for years and years, and it was quite wonderful of her to endure it. William, on his part, felt, oddly enough, that she had behaved to him just as *he* had behaved to the dog.

'Darn that dog!' he thought to himself. 'I can't get it out of my mind.'

Next morning, however, Isabelle was in excellent temper again, because Helena Peters rang up on the telephone and informed her that she had the most enchanting cocker puppy; in fact, she had two, a male and a female. Which of them would Isabelle prefer? It seems that the breed was perfect and its price in any kind of market would be $50 apiece, but Helena was giving this dog to Isabelle, and it was an act of friendship, because she loved Isabelle so dearly.

'I don't know why she's doing it', Isabelle said to William. 'She wants something or other. Helena never gives anything for nothing—but it sounds a perfect puppy. I'll go around for it myself this morning.'

William very feebly suggested the disadvantages of having puppies—the wear and tear, the unpleasant odours, the certainty that the dog would have distemper and die, and so on. Isabelle waved all these objections aside. She had cherished them herself until William mentioned them. But, as was so often the case, her brain, so superior to William's, insisted that anything he said must be foolish. So she went around and fetched the puppy.

Standing in the doorway at lunchtime, her face rosy with pleasure, the puppy lying in her arms against her dark dress, its large, amber eyes turned up to hers, its tongue suddenly licking her cheek, its soft, brown body, its long, silken ears, there was a picture so lovely that William, with a pang at his heart, wondered why it was that he didn't love her more dearly. 'Oh, how beautiful you are', his soul whispered to hers. But there was no reply, no reply at all. Only, the puppy turned its head slowly towards William and looked at him. Was there in its eyes, even from the very first moment, a certain contempt? Did its gaze wander to the incipient paunch, the bowed legs, and rise again to the round, rather pathetic face, in which the eyes, William's best feature, were hidden behind the thick, gleaming glasses?

As they stood together in the cosy living-room, while the puppy wandered cautiously from table to chair, from chair to sofa, he was sure that Isabelle was above the puppy's social line, and that he—alas!—was below it. The puppy sat down.

'Look out!' William cried. 'He had better be put in the garden.'

Isabelle regarded him scornfully. '*This* puppy is intelligent. Helena tells the most amazing stories about it. It isn't, technically, house-trained, of course, but it is wonderfully mature for a puppy. Helena says it avoids all the really valuable rugs.'

And the puppy did seem to be wonderfully sophisticated. Not that it wasn't a real puppy. It rushed about madly, it bit everything and everybody within sight, it went suddenly to sleep in your arms in the most adorable manner. In fact, it had everything that a puppy ought to have. The trouble was that it knew all about its charm. It was perfectly aware that when it lay on its side and grinned at you over its silken ear, it was entirely bewitching. And when it pretended to be angry, growling, showing its white little teeth and flashing its amber eyes, no one in the world could resist it. It was, in fact, because William did frequently resist it that the puppy showed the contempt which he had noticed on the very first occasion and which now was unmistakably there whenever he approached. Isabelle insisted that it should be called Roosevelt.

'Why?' asked William.

'Well, I think he's the most wonderful man in the world, and the puppy is the sweetest thing in the world.'

'I don't think', said William sulkily, 'that Roosevelt would like anyone to call him the sweetest thing in the world. He isn't at all that kind of man.'

She looked at him reflectively. What had happened to him? Was it, perhaps, that she was only now really beginning to discover him? And if she discovered him a little further, how would it be then? Would she be able to endure it?

There is no doubt that after the arrival of the puppy they bickered a good deal. A happy marriage between two persons depends greatly on mutual charity, unless one of the two is so absolutely a sheep that he doesn't mind what is done to him. Isabelle was a woman who had charity for everyone and everybody, but it never worked unless Isabelle's pride was fed first. William, unfortunately, continued increasingly to look at her with that puzzled bewildered expression which is so justly irritating to wives. And then the puppy confirmed her in her growing sense of injustice. People love dogs because they are so flattering. If you are unjust to your friend and feel a certain shame, your dog quickly restores your self-confidence. It encourages you to be kindly to itself and, when you respond, it loves you.

The puppy, Roosevelt, must have been born a courtier, its tact was perfectly astonishing. For instance, when it arrived in the bedroom in the morning and greeted the twin beds with little yelps of ecstatic pleasure, it almost at once discriminated between Isabelle's bed and William's. It went to William first, so that Isabelle, looking enchanting in her early-morning sleepy bewilderment, was given the opportunity to say, 'Isn't it coming to mummy, then?' And Isabelle's little smile of gratified pleasure when it rushed over to her, as though William never existed, was something enchanting to witness.

When guests were present, as they often were, how Roosevelt was adored. And how, then, he made it appear that it was really because of Isabelle that he seemed so charming. He bit delicately at a lady's dress, or chewed playfully at the corner of a handsome purse, with a side glance at Isabelle, as though he were saying to the ladies, 'It's because I love her so. It's because I'm so wonderfully happy with her that I'm behaving like this.'

William had never greatly cared for Isabelle's lady friends and generally avoided occasions when they would be present. That was one of Isabelle's complaints. But now he simply could not bear to be there. Isabelle's patronage of him was one thing, but Isabelle and Roosevelt together were more than any man could endure. And so they had a quarrel.

'You're behaving ridiculously about that dog.'

'Ridiculously?' That was something Isabelle would never forgive. 'You've hated it', she asserted, 'ever since its arrival. And why? Shall I tell you?'

'Please do', said William stony-faced.

'Because it prefers me to you.'

'Oh, darn the dog!' said William.

Yes. That kind of cruelty and jealousy Isabelle could never forgive. . . .

Meanwhile, the bulldog made frequent appearances, but never when Isabelle was about. Greatly though William disliked it, he began, very reluctantly, to be interested in its personality. It wanted so terribly to be loved, and it was a certainty nobody loved it. Building was in process nearby. And William, after he shaved in the morning, looking out of the window, would watch its approach to the different workmen, wiggling its body and leaping heavily up and down, and all the workmen repulsed it. They were good, kindly men, no doubt, as most workmen are, but they felt about it as William did—that it was too ugly to be born. He christened it "Ugly" and, as soon as he had given it a name, it seemed to have at once a closer relationship with him.

'Get away, Ugly, you beastly dog!' he would say. And the dog would be apparently in an ecstasy of enjoyment at being called anything at all. Once, while William, in a fit of abstraction, sat there wondering why it was that he was so lonely, wondering why everything was going wrong with Isabelle and what it was that she really lacked, Ugly came close to him and, not knowing what he did, he tickled it behind the ear. The dog did not move. Like a lover who, after months of waiting, is at last momentarily caressed, he dared not breathe lest the spell be broken.

As soon as William realized what he had done, he moved away with an irritated murmur. The dog did not follow him, but stayed there, stretched out, looking at him. How unpleasant is this naked sentimentality in this modern, realistic world! And yet William was sentimental, too. Someone loved him and, although he detested the dog, he was not quite so lonely.

*   *   *   *

It happened, of course, that Roosevelt and Ugly had various encounters. Ugly would come across the path into the garden and, finding Roosevelt there, hoped that they might have a game. But Roosevelt, young as he was, played only with his social equals. He did not snarl at Ugly. He did nothing mean nor common. He allowed Ugly supplicatingly to sniff him, to walk around him, even to cavort and prance a little, and then very quietly he strolled indoors. And then Isabelle realized that Ugly existed.

'William, do look at that hideous dog! What's it doing here? Get away, you horrible animal!' And Ugly went.

William found himself, to his own surprise, defending Ugly. 'He isn't so bad', he said. 'Not much to look at, of course, but rather a decent dog.'

'Oh, you would!' said Isabelle. 'It only needs for the most hideous animal I've seen in my life to come your way for you to praise it. Really, William, I don't know what's happening to you.'

William said very gently, 'I don't know what's happened either.'

He made then, almost as though it were under Ugly's instructions, a serious attempt to make Isabelle love him again. He was very patient, thoughtful, generous. A few people in the world knew that William Thrush had an extraordinary amount of charm, even a kind of penetrating wit when he tried to summon it. And now, the more he tried, the more irritating to her he became. She was quite fair in her judgement of him. No really strong-minded person likes those who crawl. Nor do they like a defiant independence, either. The breach grew wider, and Isabelle confessed to her closer friends that she didn't know whether she could stand it much longer

Then, as nothing ever stays where it is, but always advances to its appointed climax, the catastrophe occurred.

One of the troubles between William and Isabelle had always been that William liked to read and Isabelle did not. William liked long, long novels, preferably about family life; novels that went on and on forever and ever, in which you could be completely lost. Isabelle, on the other hand, could not bear to read. She looked at the social column of the daily paper and sometimes a film magazine or a fashion monthly, but for the most part, as she said, she 'adored to read but just didn't have the time to open a book.'

On this particular day William was deep in a novel by one of those novelists who have so many characters in their family that they have to have a genealogical table at the end of the book. To this same table he would often refer, with a pleasing sense that he was staying in the most delightful house with an enormous family of cousins.

The door leading to the porch was open and the afternoon sun poured bountifully in. He was aware then that something had occurred. There had been no sound, no movement, but, looking up, he beheld a very horrible sight. Ugly was advancing towards him and one of his eyes, a blood-red ball, was nearly torn from his head. The dog made no sound whatever. He simply came towards William, only once and again lifting a paw feebly as though he were absurdly puzzled as to what had happened to him. When he got near to William he crouched down and, still without a sound, looked up into his face.

William's first feeling was of nausea. He hated the sight of blood. Then almost at once he was overwhelmed with pity. He'd never in his life before been so sorry for anything. Something in the distressed, trusting patience of the dog won his heart completely and forever. That the animal should be so silent, making no complaint, seemed to him, himself, as he ought to be. That was how he'd wish to behave had such a horrible thing happened to him; how, he was sure, he would *not* behave.

He said nothing, but arose from his chair and was about to take the dog in his arms and hasten at once with it to the nearest dog hospital, when Isabelle entered and Roosevelt scampered out from a room near by. She was smiling and happy. She greeted the cocker puppy with little cries of babe joy: 'Oh, the darling! The ickle ickle darling! Wasn't he an angel to come and see his mummy?' And then she saw the other dog. Ugly had turned his head and was looking at her. She screamed. She put her hands in front of her face.

'Oh, William, how horrible! How frightful! It must be killed at once!'

William got up, took the heavy, bleeding dog in his arms, and, without a word, passed her and went out. The dog lay in his arms, made no movement, and uttered no sound. William was exceedingly tender with it. He went into the garage, laid the dog on the old rug, got out his car, picked up the dog again, got into the car with him, and drove off to the dog hospital.

Here he talked to a very kindly, plump little man and discussed whether Ugly should be destroyed or not. When the little man took Ugly in his arms to examine him, the dog very slowly turned its head and with its one eye looked at William, as much as to say, 'If you think this it the right thing for me to do, I'll suffer it.' William even nodded his head to the dog, and a silent understanding seemed to pass between them.

'It seems to have no damage anywhere else', the doctor said. 'It was done, of course, by another dog. They do that. They just take hold of one place and don't let go again. Poor old fellow!' The dog doctor caressed him. 'Not very handsome, anyway, is he?'

'Oh, I don't know', said William. 'He's got a kind of character about him, I think.'

'Is he your dog?' asked the doctor.

'No. I don't think he belongs to anybody, but he comes to our garden sometimes. I've grown interested in him.'

'Well, I can tell you this', the doctor said. 'I guess he'll be all right. We can sew it up so you'll hardly notice it. He won't exactly be a beauty, you know.'

'Yes, I know', said William, who wasn't a beauty, either. He went home.

For some reason or another Isabelle had been greatly excited by the incident. She sat there and gave William a terrific lecture, the total of which was that for ever so long now he'd been letting himself go. He was becoming soppy, almost a sissy, in fact.

'A sissy?' said William indignantly.

'Oh, well, you know what I mean. You're getting dreadfully sentimental. You always had a tendency that way, but lately it's been terrible. All my friends notice it.'

I don't know why it is, but there is almost nothing so irritating in the world as to be told by someone that one's friends have been silently, mysteriously observing one, to one's disadvantage. William, for the first time in their married life, lost all control of himself. He stood up and raved. He said that it didn't matter whether he was getting sentimental or not, but anyway, perhaps sentiment wasn't a bad thing. What really mattered was that Isabelle was selfish, cold, and unkind, that she hadn't any idea of the horrible woman she was becoming.

Isabelle suitably replied. In fact they both thoroughly lost their tempers. And while this was going on Roosevelt sat in Isabelle's lap making little playful bites at Isabelle's dress and beautiful fingers. While he sat there he looked at William with a really terrible sarcasm in his soft, amber eyes, sarcasm and scorn.

'I tell you what,' William cried in a last frenzy, 'I hate that dog! Puppies ought to be nice, gentle, loving creatures. Look at him! He's as hard as iron and the most horrid snob.'

So then Isabelle burst into tears, went to her room, and locked her door. There followed days of constrained silence, and after that William went down to the dog hospital, saw Ugly with a bandage over one eye, reminding him of an old coloured woman they'd once had who was beaten so often by her husband at night that the morning when she didn't arrive with a bandage over her eye was a lucky one for them all.

'He's a patient dog, I must say', the doctor remarked. 'Never a whine. Seems fond of you, too.'

William was surprised at the pleasure that he felt at the tribute. The day came when Ugly's eye was gone, the empty space sewed up, and his whole air rather that of a drunken soldier who had been in the wars. What was to be done with him? William, realizing that the crisis of his life was upon him, decided that Isabelle had her Roosevelt, he should have his Ugly. He went home and told her so.

This was at breakfast. She said no word, and he left for his work in the city. When he returned in the late afternoon there was a strange silence about the house. He had been thinking, and had decided that in some way or another this awful trouble with Isabelle must be stopped. After all, surely he loved her. Or, if he didn't, they were at least man and wife. How miserable he would be without her.

Would he? At that appalling wonder, his whole soul shook. So he returned home with every intention of making everything all right again, although how he was to do that he didn't in the least know.

Ugly greeted him, coming in from the garden, rolling his

body about, baring his teeth, showing an ecstasy of pleasure. But Isabelle was not there, nor Roosevelt.

On his writing table lay the note so essential to all dramatists and novelists who have learnt their job. What it said was that Isabelle had gone to her mother in Santa Barbara and would remain there. She wished that William would give her a divorce. She had been seeing for a long time now how impossible things were. She had taken Roosevelt with her.

William read the note and felt a dreadful shame and despair. His impulse was to depart at once for Santa Barbara. And so he would have done if it had not been for Ugly. He could not leave him just then. The dog was new to the house, and the maid had no especial affection for him. In a day or two he would go.

But he did not. The days passed, and he did not. A quite terrible thing had happened to him. He found that he adored his freedom. Having liberty of action and thought showed him what all these years he'd been missing. He discovered a number of other things. He took long walks up the canyon with Ugly. He talked to the dog, and it seemed to him that the dog answered him. Strangest of all, he was less lonely than he had been when Isabelle was there. He felt that he was on the verge of making a tremendous discovery. He was about, in thought, to discover the answer to what had been lacking in Isabelle for him. He was about to find out for himself what was the real meaning of life. It was as though for years there had been a padlock on his mind. Someone, something, had all this time inhibited his thought.

A letter came from Isabelle, and he made his discovery. In her letter she said she was now ready to return. Santa Barbara wasn't half the place it had once been, and her mother was in many ways unsympathetic. And that she missed her dear old William. As he wrote his reply to her letter, he solved his problem. He wrote:

Dear Isabelle:

I don't want you to come back. This sounds very unkind and rude on my part, but I've done a lot of thinking in the last few weeks, and I know that I must be honest.

For a long while I've been wondering what it was that was wrong between us. I admire you so much. You are far finer than

I. You had been so good and so kind for so long, that it seems absurd to say that you are lacking in anything.

But you are. You have no heart. That sounds like a thing you read in a novel, but I mean it just like that. I don't think you're any the worse for not having one—it is only that I have suddenly discovered that that is one real difference between human beings. Either you have a heart or you haven't one. What I mean is either the heart is part of the body that functions more than any other or not.

This is the one insuperable difference between people. Not whether you're a Fascist or Communist, American or French, teetotaller or drunkard, clever or stupid. All those things can be got over quite easily. I'm not saying, either, that the people with hearts are preferable to those without. I think it is possibly just the opposite. The people with hearts are nearly always too sentimental, too emotional, prevent the work of the world being done, get in the way of real thinkers.

The people without hearts are, as the world is now going, the ones we really want. But the difference is there. I can't help feeling emotionally about things. You can't help the opposite. But we mustn't live together any more. This is a difference that nothing can get over.

Yours sincerely,
WILLIAM THRUSH

PS. There is the same difference between Roosevelt and Ugly.

When he had posted the letter and was walking in a last cool flash of sunshine up the canyon, Ugly ambling along beside him, he thought that possibly no one had ever written so silly a letter. And yet he had the sense that he had made this marvellous discovery. He had, of course, only found out through personal experience one of the tritest of the little platitudes, but it seemed to him to change everything. He looked at all his friends, male and female, and saw the dividing line with absolute clearness.

Ugly, whose vision, of course, was now sadly dimmed, saw a golden leaf, one of the first signs of autumn, twirling through the air. He leaped rather foolishly, ran a little way, and looked back at William. William smiled encouragement. Then he turned back home, Ugly delightedly following.

Fritzi

CAROLIN LORENTZ

FRITZI the dachshund is dozing on the terrace of the little mountain hotel and sunning his sleek brown pelt. He finds it pleasant to be caressingly warmed by the rays of the autumn sun, his narrow head with the long hanging ears tilted slightly to one side, his fat, wrinkly forepaws planted in the smooth, warm sand.

Tables had been standing here only three weeks ago, tables with multicoloured sun-umbrellas. On sunny days the guests of the hotel used to take their meals on the terrace, and then Fritzi could admire shapely, tanned legs or growl at heavy mountain boots lurking like pre-historic monsters in the shadows under the tables. Sometimes he would trot from table to table and permit ladies to stroke his smooth fur and throw him titbits.

Now, however, things are dead. Soon the last of the guests will depart and the general cleaning-up will begin. Windows and doors will be thrown wide open, inviting hateful draughts; the plush furniture in the salon will be hidden under horrible, hard linen covers; and then there won't be a comfortable spot anywhere for a poor dachshund.

Uneasily Fritzi shakes his soft drooping ears. Terrible—such a dead season as now looms for the dog of an hotel owner. Not even the skiing guests who will eventually arrive are worth

47

much. What good is it if pretty young ladies want to take you along to the practice descent? On your short, crooked legs you simply sink into the snow and make yourself ridiculous.

Golden, though, the autumn sun is still shining. Fritzi lifts his somnolent head toward it as if to store up enough to last through the dull wintry days to come. His fine snout, black as India ink, sniffs the bracing air in which yet lingers the softness of the waning summer. The air carries to his nostrils news of the surrounding woods. Three thoughtful furrows appear on Fritzi's forehead; one of his ears is cocked back. For there in the forest the season has just begun.

Women gathering mushrooms grow frightened and drop their baskets if you bark at them. Children, picking berries, run away with loud shrieks if you snap at their naked brown legs. Squirrels scurry through the tree tops, and all you can do is bark at them. And then, oh joy, there is game!

Game, drunk with the rich autumnal ripeness all around; hares which you rout out of their hideaways and chase, with your tongue hanging from your mouth, until you yourself break down from sheer exhaustion; majestic stags which you can approach close, quite close, half insane with the lust of the chase; partridges that flutter up with anxious little cries as soon as they notice you; moles and mice into whose field-holes you stick your snout so deep that you can actually hear the secret noises of the earth and breathe its strange smells. Over there in the birch wood, where you stroll lazily along on the soft mossy bed, is even a fox, they say.

Yes, that's the forest.

Fritzi yawns, stretches his four legs, and shakes himself a bit. Too bad that this forest is a forbidden paradise! Too stupid for words, he reflects, that business of the doe. A few weeks ago he was out hunting with Susi, the brown female dachshund. True, it was still the closed season for hunting, and the doe that hopped through the forest on its high, fragile legs was really pitifully young. But what dachshund wouldn't have taken up the scent and hounded it a bit, just for fun? Trouble was, gamekeepers don't know what fun is; so when Susi, that silly creature, barked especially loud—well, she got some birdshot in her forepaw. She is still lame, and now will not hear any talk of hunting.

*   *   *   *   *

Now it isn't half so much fun to go alone, and anyway the gamekeeper has sworn to take revenge on you for bringing misery to a few hares and a stag family. . . .

Slowly and with displeasure Fritzi trots over to the kitchen and wheedles a bone out of the cook. But he soon lets it drop, for here is a chance to tease fat old Minka, who is forever having kittens, by gobbling up her food. Then he brings unrest to the bird house—just a few sharp barks, enough to make sparrows and robins abandon their dinner trays. But none of this can replace the thrills of the woods, a chase after a hare or a doe or a partridge, especially in good company.

A sudden gust of wind wafts to Fritzi's nostrils the breath of the forest, the smell of ripe earth; and he even seems to hear the rustling of the light-hoofed doe making its way through the underbrush.

Fritzi begins to tremble. Enough of these silly games, enough of cat-teasing and bird-scaring, enough of this boresome house-dog existence! He wants to run madly through the forest. He wants to hunt. He wants to stir up game, to bark and pursue, to worry the neck of the pursued. But Susi refuses to come along. She is afraid of the gamekeeper. And without another hunt-mad dog along whom you can boss around in shrill, excited dog-language, toward whom you can force the game, why be bothered going?

Woolly, the little griffon belonging to an elegant old lady guest, comes tripping along. Woolly loves Fritzi; that cannot be gainsaid. She does not even try to hide the fact, but jumps up toward him in little jerky bounds whenever she espies him. Also, she always waits until he has taken the most desirable morsels from her plate; and with her tiny pink tongue, delicate as a rose petal, she kisses him on his black snout. Yet Fritzi is not very fond of Woolly. This hazel-brown ball of wool, always shivering in spite of the warm autumn sun, who can scarce breathe through its tiny nose, is no fit companion for him. Even to-day Fritzi would protest her caresses, growling, if he hadn't been so full of hunt-fever and of the longing for somebody to share it with.

An appraising glance from his almond-shaped eyes passes over Woolly. After all, to take this trembling, puny thing into the great forest might be fun. And so, as Woolly hops up beside

D

him, he whispers into her tiny, fuzzy ear. Two minutes later they lope through the garden gate into the woods.

Woolly hasn't seen much of the world. Her mistress is kind-hearted but ailing; she labours along on her walking stick or is carted about in a carriage. And Woolly has passed her days quietly, sheltered either in her basket or on her mistress's lap. She does not know the woods. And to-day she is to see it, this mysterious, dark forest, accompanied and protected by the dachshund she adores. She is beside herself with joy, yipping in her shrill, piping voice and rolling along like a little ball over the mossy ground.

Only with difficulty does the sun make its way through the tree tops. Woolly's weak eyes are blinded, she does not see much of the marvels all around; but Fritzi has already picked up a scent and is pressing on. There is a deal of underbrush, and many a sharp little twig gets stuck in Woolly's fur. She would like to stop for a moment and catch her breath, but Fritzi is setting a brisk pace. He runs with his nose close to the soil, a lecherous expression on his face. His lips are moist and covered with foam. You can see his pointed white teeth.

To Woolly his excitement is hard to understand; she can smell very little with her tiny, stunted nose. She does not understand the reason for this wild chase. Aren't the woods attractive in themselves? You might play with the acorns, or with the big pine cones. Or you might sniff at the red mush-rooms sprouting everywhere.

By now Fritzi is way ahead of Woolly, who is panting hard. But Fritzi runs on, ever faster, his tongue dangling from his mouth and his ears flying. No longer does Woolly call gaily; all she can produce are tiny frightened yelps and her little heart is about to burst. But if she should stop now she would never catch up with Fritzi, and then she would be alone, all alone in the great forbidding forest!

Woolly's stubby hair becomes matted to her moist body, she feels a stinging pain in her chest. If only Fritzi would stop chasing along so senselessly . . . but Fritzi is close upon game; any minute now a frightened doe will break from the thicket and the wild, marvellous hunt can begin in earnest.

A sharp stone has hurt Woolly's paw, has made it burn like fire. The trees begin to run into one another, the soil is disappearing from under her feet. Sky, forest, and earth are going around and around. A small clearing appears before her, a grassy plot covered with wild flowers. Here all is peaceful, here you can rest. Woolly drags herself under a fir tree and with her dry, hot tongue sets to licking her wounded paw.

Fritzi, well across the grassy plot, chases on like mad; there, over there behind the thicket of young oaks, is hidden the wonder, the miracle, the sensation! He smells it, senses it with every nerve in his body. And sure enough, a young doe bounds up. But Fritzi, seeing it, yowls a lament—as if he, not the doe, were in danger.

Woolly, under her fir tree, has been about to make her peace with the forest. Gay butterflies flutter over the flowers. Ants crawl restlessly over immense obstacles. Shiny bugs hold each other in close embrace, in love or in hate. Then the tranquillity is shattered by Fritzi's strange cry.

Now Woolly, well-bred but city-bred, knows nothing about the ways of a hunting dog. She knows better than to bark at her lady's cane. She knows that in the dining-room you must not beg for morsels. If she were ever to yowl as Fritzi has just done, her lady would carefully lift her on her lap, stroke her fur, and console her.

And so, naturally enough, Woolly mistakes Fritzi's hunting cry for a yelp of pain. Fritzi needs her! She scrambles to her feet. Her paw hurts as she runs across the grass, leaving bloody spots at every step. She looks back once, sadly, at the shady retreat; then Fritzi cries again—he must be badly hurt! Woolly plunges into the high grass, where she almost disappears.

Step by step she struggles on, her head appearing like a strange hazel-coloured chrysanthemum growing amid the bluebells.

Woolly feels weak; once she tries to leap high to see what has happened to Fritzi. Suddenly a shot sounds, and Woolly feels something hit her head. Her thin legs refuse to obey her any longer; yet over there, across the grass, must be Fritzi, helpless and in agony! The mysterious rustling of the forest turns to thunder, and Woolly, who has never hurt a fly, sinks dying into the fragrant lush grass. . . .

At night Fritzi returns home, alone. He is dead tired, his paws are swollen from the long chase, and he has a fresh scar on his velvety ear. But he is very proud. His hunt has been marvellous—two does, one hare, and a dozen partridges—and he fooled the gamekeeper completely. He made a detour around the grassy plot where Woolly met her death. There something terrible happened, he knows that well enough, but that doesn't dampen his gay humour. After all, the woods are not for lap dogs. . . .

Since then, however, Fritzi has been shunned by all the animals thereabouts. Even the domestic animals with whom he used to romp won't have anything to do with him. For in the animal world evil tidings quickly make the round. They cannot forget that Woolly died for him, Woolly who was so innocent of the dangers of the hunt and who had only been looking for some simple play.

No, they cannot forget, and they will not forgive.

The Comet

SAMUEL A. DERIEUX

NO puppy ever came into the world under more favourable conditions than Comet. He was descended from a famous family of pointers. Both his mother and father were champions. Before he opened his eyes, while he was still crawling about over his brothers and sisters, blind as puppies are at birth, Jim Thompson, Mr. Devant's kennel master, picked him out:

'That's the best un in the bunch.'

When he was only three weeks old, he pointed a butterfly that lit in the yard in front of his nose.

'Come here, Molly', yelled Jim to his wife. 'Pointed—the little cuss!'

When Thompson started taking the growing pups out of the yard, into the fields to the side of the Devant's great Southern winter home, Oak Knob, it was Comet who strayed farthest from the man's protecting care. And when Jim taught them all to follow when he said 'Heel', to drop when he said 'Drop', and to stand stock-still when he said 'Ho', he learned far more quickly than the others.

At six months he set his first covey of quail, and remained

53

perfectly staunch. 'He's goin' to make a great dog', said Thompson. Everything—size, muscle, nose, intelligence, earnestness, pointed to the same conclusion. Comet was one of the favoured of the gods.

One day, after the leaves had turned red and brown and the mornings grown chilly, a crowd of people, strangers to him, arrived at Oak Knob. Then out of the house with Thompson came a big man in tweed clothes, and the two walked straight to the curious young dogs, who were watching them with shining eyes and wagging tails.

'Well, Thompson', said the big man. 'Which is the future champion you've been writing me about?'

'Pick him out for yourself, sir', said Thompson confidently.

After that they talked a long time planning for the future of Comet. His yard training was now over (Thompson was only yard trainer), and he must be sent to a man experienced in training and handling for field trials.

'Larsen's the man to bring him out', said the big man in tweeds, who was George Devant himself. 'I saw his dogs work in the Canadian Derby.'

Thompson spoke hesitatingly, apologetically, as if he hated to bring the matter up. 'Mr. Devant, . . . you remember, sir, a long time ago Larsen sued us for old Ben.'

'Yes, Thompson; I remember, now that you speak of it.'

'Well, you remember the court decided against him, which was the only thing it could do, for Larsen didn't have any more right to that dog than the Sultan of Turkey. But, Mr. Devant, I was there, and I saw Larsen's face when the case went against him.'

Devant looked keenly at Thompson.

'Another thing, Mr. Devant,' Thompson went on, still hesitatingly; 'Larsen had a chance to get hold of this breed of pointers and lost out, because he dickered too long, and acted cheesy. Now they've turned out to be famous. Some men never forget a thing like that. Larsen's been talkin' these pointers down ever since, sir.'

'Go on', said Devant.

'I know Larsen's a good trainer. But it'll mean a long trip for the young dog to where he lives. Now, there's an old trainer lives near here, Wade Swygert. There never was a straighter man than him. He used to train dogs in England.'

Devant smiled. 'Thompson, I admire your loyalty to your friends; but I don't think much of your business sense. We'll turn over some of the others so Swygert, if he wants 'em. Comet must have the best. I'll write Larsen tonight, Thompson. Tomorrow, crate Comet and send him off.'

Just as no dog ever came into the world under more favourable auspices, so no dog ever had a bigger 'send off' than Comet. Even the ladies of the house came out to exclaim over him, and Marian Devant, pretty, eighteen, and a sportswoman, stooped down, caught his head between her hands, looked into his fine eyes and wished him 'Good luck, old man.' In the living-room the men laughingly drank toasts to his future, and from the high-columned portico Marian Devant waved him good-bye, as in his clean padded crate, he was driven off, a bewildered youngster, to the station.

Two days and two nights he travelled, and at noon of the third day, at a lonely railroad station in a prairie country that rolled like a heavy sea, he was lifted, crate and all, off the train. A lean, pale-eyed, sanctimonious-looking man came toward him.

'Some beauty that, Mr. Larsen', said the agent as he helped Larsen's man lift the crate on to a small truck.

'Yes,' drawled Larsen in a meditative voice, 'pretty enough to look at—but he looks scared—er—timid.'

'Of course he's scared', said the agent; 'so would you be if they was to put you in some kind of a whale of a balloon an' ship you in a crate to Mars.'

The station agent poked his hands through the slats and patted the head. Comet was grateful for that, because everything was strange. He had not whined nor complained on the trip, but his heart had pounded fast, and he had been homesick.

And everything continued to be strange: the treeless country through which he was driven, the bald house, and huge barns where he was lifted out, the dogs that crowded about him when he was turned into the kennel yard. These eyed him with enmity and walked round and round him. But he stood his ground staunchly for a youngster, returning fierce look for fierce look, growl for growl, until the man called him away and chained him to a kennel.

For days Comet remained chained, a stranger in a strange land. Each time at the click of the gate announcing Larsen's entrance, he sprang to his feet from force of habit, and stared hungrily at the man for the light he was accustomed to see in human eyes. But with just a glance at him, the man would turn one or more of the other dogs loose and ride off to train them.

But he was not without friends of his own kind. Now and then another young dog (he alone was chained up) would stroll his way with wagging tail, or lie down near by, in that strange bond of sympathy that is not confined to man. Then Comet would feel better and would want to play, for he was still half puppy. Sometimes he would pick up a stick and shake it, and his partner would catch the other end. They would tug and growl with mock ferocity, and then lie down and look at each other curiously.

If any attention had been paid to him by Larsen, Comet would have quickly overcome his feelings of strangeness. He was no milksop. He was like an overgrown boy, off at college, or in some foreign city. He was sensitive, and not sure of himself. Had Larsen gained his confidence, it would all have been different. And as for Larsen—he knew that perfectly well.

One fine sunny afternoon, Larsen entered the yard, came straight to him, and turned him loose. In the exuberance of his spirits he ran round and round the yard, barking in the faces of his friends. Larsen let him out, mounted a horse and commanded him to heel. He obeyed with wagging tail.

A mile or more down the road, Larsen turned off into the fields. Across his saddle was something the young pointer had had no experience with—a gun. That part of his education Thompson had neglected, at least put off, for he had not expected that Comet would be sent away so soon. That was where Thompson had made a mistake.

At the command 'Hi on' the young pointer ran eagerly around the horse, and looked up into the man's face to be sure he had heard aright. At something he saw there, the tail and ears drooped momentarily, and there came over him again a feeling of strangeness, almost dismay. Larsen's eyes were mere slits of blue glass, and his mouth was set in a thin line.

At a second command, though, he galloped off swiftly, boldly. Round and round an extensive field of straw he circled, forgetting any feeling of strangeness now, every fibre of his being intent on the hunt, while Larsen, sitting on his horse, watched him with appraising eyes.

Suddenly there came to Comet's nose the smell of game birds, strong, pungent, compelling. He stiffened into an earnest, beautiful point. Heretofore in the little training he had had, Thompson had come up behind him, flushed the birds, and made him drop. And now Larsen, having quickly dismounted and tied his horse, came up behind him, just as Thompson had done, except that in Larsen's hand was the gun.

The old-fashioned black powder of a generation ago makes a loud explosion. It sounds like a cannon, compared with the modern smokeless powder, now used by all hunters. Perhaps it was only an accident that had caused Larsen before he left the house to load his pump gun with black powder shells.

As for Comet he only knew that the birds rose; then above his head burst an awful roar, almost splitting his tender ear drums, shocking every sensitive nerve, filling him with terror such as he had never felt before. Even then, in the confusion and horror of the surprise, he turned to the man, head ringing, eyes dilated. A single reassuring word, and he would have steadied. As for Larsen, though, he declared afterward (to others and to himself even) that he noticed no nervousness in the dog; that he was only intent on getting several birds for breakfast.

Twice, three times, four times, the pump gun bellowed in its cannon-like roar, piercing the ear drums, shattering the nerves. Comet turned; one more glance backward at a face, strange, exultant—and then the puppy in him conquered. Tail tucked, he ran away from that shattering noise.

Miles he ran. Now and then, stumbling over briars, he yelped. Not once did he look back. His tail was tucked, his eyes crazy with fear. Seeing a house, he made for that. It was the noon hour and a group of farm hands was gathered in the yard. One of them, with a cry 'Mad dog', ran into the house after a gun. When he came out, they told him the dog was under the porch. And so he was. Pressed against the wall, in the darkness, the magnificent young pointer with the quiver-

ing soul waited, panting, eyes gleaming, the horror still ringing
in his ears.

Here Larsen found him that afternoon. A boy crawled underneath the porch and dragged him out. He, who had started life
favoured of the gods, who that morning even had been full of
high spirits, who had circled a field like a champion, was now
a cringing, shaking creature, like a homeless cur.

And thus it happened that Comet came home, in disgrace—
a gun-shy dog, a coward, expelled from college, not for some
youthful prank, but because he was—yellow. And he knew he
was disgraced. He saw it in the face of the big man. Devant,
who looked at him in the yard where he had spent his happy
puppyhood, then turned away. He knew it because of what he
saw in the face of Jim Thompson.

In the house was a long and plausible letter, explaining how
it had happened:

> I did everything I could. I never was as surprised in my life.
> The dog's hopeless.

As for the other inhabitants of the big house, their minds
were full of the events of the season: de luxe hunting parties,
more society events than hunts; lunches in the woods served by
uniformed butlers; launch rides up the river; arriving and departing guests. Only one of them, except Devant himself, gave
the gun-shy dog a thought. Marian Devant came out to visit
him in his disgrace. She stooped before him as she had done on
that other and happier day, and again caught his head between
her hands. But his eyes did not meet hers, for in his dim way
he knew he was not now what he had been.

'I don't believe he's yellow—inside!' she declared, looking
up at Thompson, her cheeks flushed.

Thompson shook his head.

'I tried him with a gun, Miss Marian', he declared. 'I just
showed it to him, and he ran into his kennel.'

'I'll go get mine. He won't run from me.'

But at sight of her small gun it all came back. Again he
seemed to hear the explosion that had shattered his nerves. The
Terror had entered his very soul. In spite of her pleading, he
made for his kennel. Even the girl turned away from him now.

And as he lay panting in the shelter of his kennel he knew that never again would men look at him as they had looked, or life be sweet to him as it had been.

Then there came to Oak Knob an old man, to see Thompson. He had been on many seas, he had fought in a dozen wars, and had settled at last on a little truck farm near by. Somewhere, in his life full of adventure and odd jobs, he had trained dogs and horses. His face was lined and seamed, his hair was white, his eyes piercing, blue and kind. Wade Swygert was his name.

'There's been dirty work', he said, when he looked at the dog. 'I'll take him if you're goin' to give him away.'

Give him away—who had been Championship hope!

Marian Devant came out and looked into the face of the old man, shrewdly, understandingly.

'Can you cure him?' she demanded.

'I doubt it, miss', was the sturdy answer.

'You will try?'

The blue eyes lighted up. 'Yes, I'll try.'

'Then you can have him. And—if there's any expense—'

'Come, Comet', said the old man.

That night, in a neat, humble house, Comet ate supper placed before him by a stout old woman, who had followed this old man to the ends of the world. That night he slept before their fire. Next day he followed the old man all about the place. Several days and nights passed this way, then, while he lay before the fire, old Swygert came in with a gun. At sight of it, Comet sprang to his feet. He tried to rush out of the room, but the doors were closed. Finally, he crawled under the bed.

Every night after that Swygert got out the gun, until he crawled under the bed no more. Finally, one day the man fastened the dog to a tree in the yard, then came out with a gun. A sparrow lit in a tree, and he shot it. Comet tried to break the rope. All his panic had returned; but the report had not shattered him as that other did, for the gun was loaded light.

After that, frequently the old man shot a bird in his sight, loading the gun more and more heavily, and each time after the shot, coming to him, showing him the bird, and speaking to him kindly, gently. But for all that the terror remained in his heart.

One afternoon the girl, accompanied by a young man, rode

over on horseback, dismounted and came in. She always
stopped when she was riding by.

'It's a mighty slow business', old Swygert reported; 'I don't
know whether I'm makin' any headway or not.'

That night old Mrs. Swygert told him she thought he had
better give it up. It wasn't worth the time and worry. The dog
was just yellow.

Swygert pondered a long time. 'When I was a kid,' he said
at last, 'there came up a terrible thunderstorm. It was in South
America. I was water boy for a railroad gang, and the storm
drove us in a shack. While lightnin' was hittin' all around,
one of the grown men told me it always picked out boys with
red hair. My hair was red, an' I was little and ignorant. For
years I was skeered of lightnin'. I never have quite got over it.
But no man ever said I was yellow.'

Again he was silent for a while. Then he went on: 'I don't
seem to be making much headway, I admit that. I'm lettin'
him run away as far as he can. Now I've got to shoot an' make
him come toward the gun himself, right while I'm shootin' it.'

Next day Comet was tied up and fasted, and next, until he
was gaunt and famished. Then, on the afternoon of the third
day, Mrs. Swygert, at her husband's direction, placed before
him, within reach of his chain, some raw beefsteak. As he
started for it, Swygert shot. He drew back, panting, then,
hunger getting the better of him, started again. Again Swygert
shot.

After that for days Comet 'Ate to music', as Swygert expressed
it. 'Now,' he said, 'he's got to come toward the gun when he's
not even tied up.'

Not far from Swygert's house is a small pond, and on one
side the banks are perpendicular. Toward this pond the old
man, with the gun under his arm and the dog following, went.
Here in the silence of the woods, with just the two of them
together, was to be a final test.

On the shelving bank Swygert picked up a stick and tossed
it into the middle of the pond with the command to 'fetch'.
Comet sprang eagerly in and retrieved it. Twice this was
repeated. But the third time, as the dog approached the shore,
Swygert picked up the gun and fired.

Quickly the dog dropped the stick, then turned and swam
toward the other shore. Here, so precipitous were the banks,

he could not get a foothold. He turned once more and struck out diagonally across the pond. Swygert met him and fired.

Over and over it happened. Each time, after he fired, the old man stooped down with extended hand and begged him to come on. His face was grim now, and though the day was cool sweat stood out on his brow. 'You'll face the music,' he said, 'or you'll drown. Better be dead than called yellow.'

The dog was growing weary now. His head was barely above water. His efforts to clamber up the opposite bank were feeble, frantic. Yet, each time as he drew near the shore Swygert fired.

He was not using light loads now. He was using the regular load of the bird hunter. Time had passed for temporizing. The sweat was standing out all over his face. The sternness in his eyes was terrible to see, for it was the sternness of a man who is suffering.

A dog can swim a long time. The sun dropped over the trees. Still the firing went on regularly, like a minute gun.

Just before the sun set an exhausted dog staggered toward an old man, almost as exhausted as he. The dog had been too near death and was too faint to care now for the gun that was being fired over his head. On and on he came, toward the man, disregarding the noise of the gun. It would not hurt him, that he knew at last. He might have many enemies, but the gun, in the hands of this man, was not one of them. Suddenly old Swygert sank down and took the dripping dog in his arms.

'Old boy,' he said, 'old boy'.

That night Comet lay before the fire and looked straight into the eyes of a man, as he used to look in the old days.

Next season, Larsen, glancing over his sporting papers, was astonished to see that among promising Derbys the fall trials had called forth was a pointer named Comet. He would have thought it some other dog than the one who had disappointed him so by turning out gun-shy, in spite of all his efforts to prevent, had it not been for the fact that the entry was booked as Comet; owner, Miss Marian Devant; handler, Wade Swygert.

Next year he was still more astonished to see in the same paper that Comet, handled by Swygert, had won first place in a Western trial, and was prominently spoken of as a National Championship possibility. As for him, he had no young entries to offer, but was staking everything on the National Championship, where he was to enter Larsen's Peerless II.

It was strange how things fell out—but things have a habit of turning out strangely in field trials, as well as elsewhere. When Larsen reached the town where the National Championship was to be run, there on the street, straining at the leash held by old Swygert, whom he used to know, was a seasoned young pointer, with a white body, a brown head and a brown saddle spot—the same pointer he had seen two years before turn tail and run in that terror a dog never quite overcomes.

But the strangest thing of all happened that night at the drawing, when, according to the slips taken at random from a hat, it was declared that on the following Wednesday, Comet, the pointer was to run with Peerless II.

It gave Larsen a strange thrill, this announcement. He left the meeting and went straightaway to his room. There for a long time he sat pondering. Next day at a hardware store he bought some black powder, and some shells.

The race was to be run next day, and that night in his room he loaded half a dozen shells. It would have been a study in faces to watch him as he bent over his work, on his lips a smile. Into the shells he packed all the powder they could stand, all the powder his trusted gun could stand, without bursting. It was a load big enough to kill a bear, to bring down a buffalo. It was a load that would echo and re-echo in the hills.

On the morning that Larsen walked out in front of the judges and the field, Peerless II at the leash, Old Swygert with Comet at his side, he glanced around at the 'field', or spectators. Among them was a handsome young woman, and with her, to his amazement, George Devant. He could not help chuckling inside himself as he thought of what would happen that day, for once a gun-shy dog, always a gun-shy dog—that was *his* experience.

As for Comet, he faced the straw fields eagerly, confidently, already a veteran. Long ago fear of the gun had left him, for the most part. There were times, when at a report above his head, he still trembled, and the shocked nerves in his ear gave a twinge like that of a bad tooth. But always at the quiet voice of the old man, his god, he grew steady, and remained staunch. Some disturbing memory did start within him to-day as he glanced at the man with the other dog. It seemed to him as if in another and an evil world he had seen that face. His heart began to pound fast, and his tail drooped for a moment. Within an hour it was all to come back to him—the terror, the panic, the agony of that far-away time.

He looked up at old Swygert, who was his god, and to whom his soul belonged, though he was booked as the property of Miss Marian Devant. Of the arrangements he could know nothing, being a dog. Old Swygert, having cured him, could not meet the expenses of taking him to field trials. The girl had come to the old man's assistance, an assistance which he had accepted only under condition that the dog should be entered as hers, with himself as handler.

'Are you ready, gentlemen?' the judges asked.

'Ready', said Larsen and old Swygert.

And Comet and Peerless II were speeding away across that field, and behind them came handlers, and judges and spectators, all mounted.

It was a race people still talk about, and for a reason, for strange things happened that day. At first there was nothing unusual. It was like any other field trial. Comet found birds, and Swygert, his handler, flushed them and shot. Comet remained steady. Then Peerless II found a covey, and Larsen flushed them and shot. And so for an hour it went.

Then Comet disappeared, and old Swygert, riding hard and looking for him, went out of sight over a hill. But Comet had not gone far. As a matter of fact he was near by, hidden in some high straw, pointing a covey of birds. One of the spectators spied him, and called the judges' attention to him. Everybody, including Larsen, rode up to him, but still Swygert had not come back.

They called him, but the old man was a little deaf. Some of the men rode to the top of the hill, but could not see him. In his zeal, he had got a considerable distance away. Meanwhile, here was his dog, pointed.

If anyone had looked at Larsen's face he would have seen the exultation there, for now his chance had come—the very chance he had been looking for. It's a courtesy one handler sometimes extends another who is absent from the spot, to go in and flush his dog's birds.

'I'll handle this covey for Mr. Swygert', said Larsen to the judges, his voice smooth and plausible, on his face a smile.

And thus it happened that Comet faced his supreme ordeal without the steadying voice of his god.

He only knew that ahead of him were birds, and that behind him a man was coming through the straw, and that behind the man a crowd of people on horseback were watching him. He had become used to that, but when, out of the corner of his eye, he saw the face of the advancing man, his soul began to tremble.

'Call your dog in, Mr. Larsen', directed the judge. 'Make him backstand.'

Only a moment was lost, while Peerless, a young dog himself, came running in and at a command from Larsen stopped in his tracks behind Comet, and pointed. Larsen's dogs always obeyed, quickly, mechanically. Without ever gaining their confidence, Larsen had a way of training them into finished field-trial dogs. They obeyed, because they were afraid not to.

According to the rules the man handling the dog has to shoot as the birds rise. This is done in order to test the dog's steadiness when a gun is fired over him. No specification is made as to the size of the shotgun to be used. Usually, however, small-gauge guns are carried. The one in Larsen's hands was a twelve gauge, and consequently large.

All morning he had been using it over his own dog. Nobody had paid any attention to it, because he shot smokeless powder. But now, as he advanced, he reached into the left-hand pocket of his hunting coat, where six shells rattled as he hurried along. Two of these he took out and rammed into the barrels.

As for Comet, still standing rigid, statuesque, he heard, as has been said, the brush of steps through the straw, glimpsed a face, and trembled. But only for a moment. Then he steadied, head high, tail straight out. The birds rose with a whirr—and then was repeated that horror of his youth. Above his ears, ears that would always be tender, broke a great roar. Either because of his excitement, or because of a sudden wave of revenge, or of a determination to make sure of the dog's flight, Larsen had pulled both triggers at once. The combined report shattered through the dog's ear drums, it shivered through his nerves, he sank in agony into the straw.

Then the old impulse to flee was upon him and he sprang to

his feet and looked about wildly. But from somewhere in that
crowd behind him came to his tingling ears a voice—clear,
ringing, deep, the voice of a woman—a woman he knew—
pleading as his master used to plead, calling on him not to run,
but to stand.

'Steady', it said. 'Steady, Comet!'

It called him to himself, it soothed him, it calmed him, and
he turned and looked toward the crowd. With roar of the shotgun the usual order observed in field trials was broken up. All
rules seemed to have been suspended. Ordinarily no one
belonging to 'the field' is allowed to speak to a dog. Yet the
girl had spoken to him. Ordinarily, the spectators must remain
in the rear of the judges. Yet one of the judges had himself
wheeled his horse about and was galloping off, and Marian
Devant had pushed through the crowd and was riding toward
the bewildered dog.

He stood staunch where he was, though in his ears was still a
throbbing pain, and though all about him was this growing
confusion he could not understand. The man he feared was
running across the field yonder, in the direction taken by the
judge. He was blowing his whistle as he ran. Through the
crowd, his face terrible to see, his own master was coming. Both
the old man and the girl had dismounted now, and were running toward him.

'I heard', old Swygert was saying to her. 'I heard it! I might
'a' known! I might 'a' known!'

'He stood,' she panted, 'like a rock—oh, the brave, beautiful
thing!'

'Where is that—' Swygert suddenly checked himself and
looked around.

A man in the crowd (they had all gathered about now),
laughed.

'He's gone after his dog', he said. 'Peerless has run away!'

E

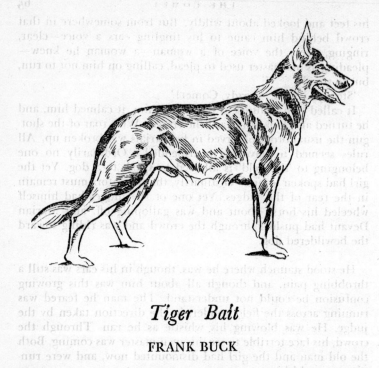

Tiger Bait

FRANK BUCK

JOHNSON'S eyes were serious, a bit wistful, as they followed a little yellow dog running past. 'Frank,' he said, 'want to come up on my plantation and get a tiger?'

We were on the terrace of the Keppel Harbour Golf Club, and a sheep-laden Australian mail boat was coming into Singapore, just behind it.

'Don't tell me that pup reminded you of a tiger!' I exclaimed.

'Yes, it did. And if you really want a live tiger—' He took out cigars and handed me one.

'You know Dick Scott?' he asked. 'Well, Dick's got two kids, and he had the idea of getting them a dog. Last time he was on vacation he got one—an Alsatian, strong, grey, and lean as a wolf. They named him Binji, he turned out a marvellous dog; gentle, and a grand watchdog; a wonderful playmate for the children.'

'You're putting all this in the past tense', I said.

Johnson's eyes moved across to the ship. 'Yes,' he said, 'and boats like that are the reason. They fatten up those sheep, after their voyage, on the grazing land near where Dick lives. One night the flock stampeded, and in the morning they had six dead sheep with torn throats.'

'Binji?'

'Yes, it was Binji. No doubt of it. He had shreds of wool and blood on his muzzle, and his chain was broken. After that they kept the dog at nights on a chain strong enough to hold a leopard.

'But Binji was strong, Frank—and he'd tasted sheep's blood. One night he broke loose again, and that time a cool dozen sheep were slaughtered. Of course this was the last straw. Dick didn't want a killer-dog. So that afternoon he took Binji down to the hotel. This is where I come in.

'I'd never seen Binji until I walked into the hotel bar. Dick was there, and the dog, curled up at his feet, was a beautiful animal. I admired him. "You can have him if you want him", Dick said. "He's a killer. I've paid for eighteen sheep and I don't intend to pay for any more."

'Well, I didn't want a "killer" either. But then all at once I remembered something a dog *would* be good for. "All right", I said. "I'll take him."

'Dick handed me the chain without a word. The dog looked first at Dick and then at me. His eyes weren't reproachful— just questioning. He went off with me easily—seemed rather pleased.'

Johnson paused; then, without looking at me: 'You know what I wanted that dog for, Frank? Tiger bait.

'I told you there's a tiger on my plantation. You know all the red tape about getting permission to shoot one; but there's no law against trapping one alive, so I had had a log trap built. But I had to have good bait—something that would howl and make a racket at night. So I decided to use this sheep-killer.

'You've got to understand, Frank, that I'd never seen this dog before. I thought he'd be savage. And now it seemed to me impossible that this gentle, loving dog was really a sheep-killer. You know my plantation's eight miles across and up the river. Well, I didn't have to coax Binji into the launch; he came as if he trusted me—as if he'd been hoping all his life for this ride. He barked at the waves, and caught bits of foam in his teeth. Then he'd slip his muzzle under my hand and look up at me as if to say: "We're having a swell time, aren't we?"

'I had my supper. Binji lay on the floor looking up at me. He didn't beg for food—he just sort of *hoped*. I'm afraid I threw him a few scraps, something I never do with dogs at table. It was—well, he was going to die, you see; but even condemned criminals have a last meal. And it was nice to see the grateful look in his eyes when he caught a scrap. On the porch afterwards I lit my pipe and sat watching the stars. Presently Binji's head was on my knee. He didn't ask to be petted; he just put his big head there for companionship. I got hastily to my feet and called my houseboy, "Come on", I said. "We're going to bait that trap."

'Binji came gladly. He delighted in this unlooked-for walk up the jungle trail. I could see the white-grey of his tail waving as his nose explored the underbrush. I think a dog loves that more than anything—to be loose, free, but with a man behind to call his name in the dark. We got to the trap finally. You know the kind: heavy, log-type, with a sliding door that works when a trigger is pulled. It was only after the boy had left him tied in the cage that Binji realized there was something queer in this business. He started to whine.

'Binji was a killer—a bad dog. Dick had been going to shoot him anyway. I told myself this as I walked back. Behind I could hear Binji howling now, loudly. "Dog make very fine tiger bait", my boy said. "He howl loud. Tiger come sure." Somehow that didn't much comfort me. That beautiful Alsatian, alone in the dark, and somewhere near, a tiger that could silence him with one blow!

'I went to bed, but I couldn't sleep. I thought of all sorts of queer things and through them all I saw that dog: great, brown eyes, wrinkled nose, big paws warm and friendly against my leg. I began to reason. I hadn't a dog on the place. Binji might be a sheep-killer, but here there were *no sheep* to kill! Why shouldn't I *keep him*?

'It's strange how quickly a man can change his ideas. Until now I had wanted to trap that tiger. Now I hoped I *hadn't* trapped him! Call it sentiment; call it Binji's wet muzzle on my knee in the car, his eagerness in the boat, the look in his eyes as he lay at my feet—or call it plain dog-consciousness. I routed out my boy: "Come on! We're going to get the dog out of that trap!" We covered that half mile on a dead run. You'll understand if you've ever had a dog.

'As we neared the trap there was no sound; to me that meant the tiger had got him. Then I heard a low whine—the whine I imagine babies make when left alone. Then ahead I saw Binji, his black nose through the bars of the cage, his eyes shining straight into the torch's beam, and that grey-white tail wagging friendship and confidence, as if to say: "Well, we've played *this* game long enough—let's try another!" Untied, he came bounding out. He didn't jump on me. He just came running up, eager, his tail swishing and his red tongue hanging out. "Come on," I said, "we're going home, Binji!" He ran down the trail just as he had come up it, frisking, investigating, now far ahead, now close up, just under my feet, sniffing and pure dog.

'Suddenly something happened—so quickly and so close that I couldn't even get the torch up—a dusky, rushing movement in the dark. I saw two spears of ivory gleaming, coming straight towards me—cruel, sharp as needles! I had stumbled on a wild boar protecting a sow with a litter. Two hundred pounds of fierce animal dynamite about to gore me! There was no getting my rifle up. It was all so quick—so sudden. And then a grey streak sprang from the black. I heard the boar grunt with the impact. I saw two gleaming tusks disappear in the dark. And then I heard Binji's cry of pain, followed by his low, savage growl—his sheep-growl!

'I shot the boar', said Johnson slowly. 'And I found Binji— both those tusks through his breast, but with his great, white teeth firm and fast in the boar's throat.'

The Dog of Montargis

JOSEPH E. HARRY

I

IT was in the month of July; the sun was shining in a cloudless sky and seemed to be placing a crown of fire on the high turrets of the manor of Villemonble. In one of the shady avenues of the park a young man and a young lady, Isabelle, were strolling together. In the front of them ran a magnificent greyhound, who would stop from time to time and leap up to them joyously. In the copse the blackbirds were singing and amid the boughs of the large beeches the goldfinches and the tomtits were chattering.

The young man was Aubry de Montdidier and wore the uniform of the royal archers; his companion was the châtelaine of Villemonble. An orphan, beautiful and rich, Mlle Isabelle's hand was sought by all the young nobles of the court of Charles V. One refusal after another had removed most of the suitors;

70

others had prudently retired, leaving an open field to Aubry de Montdidier, who, thanks to a very marked preference on the part of Mlle Isabelle, seemed to be destined to carry off the prize. Among these was one whom nothing could discourage: he cherished the foolish hope of becoming the husband of the charming châtelaine, in spite of the disdain she showed for him.

This courageous pretender was also a royal archer, and was called Chevalier Macaire. Needless to say, the Chevalier detested Aubry. Although he endeavoured to conceal the hate that filled his heart, more than once, while speaking of his rival, he had uttered words that betrayed his secret.

'Be on your guard against Macaire', Aubry was warned by his friends. And the young man had replied: 'I am not afraid.'

Hence, as he was walking in the park with his beautiful fiancée, he thought only of her and not at all of his enemy. The young lady had put her hand in his and, engrossed in the happiness of the moment, they talked of their future. When they came to the end of the avenue, they sat down on a turf-bench. The greyhound came and lay down at their feet.

'So, Messire,' said the young lady, continuing the conversation, 'you will speak this very evening to the king, our lord?'

'Yes, my dear Isabelle, and as I am certain in advance that he will approve, you will be my dearly beloved companion.'

'How long this week will seem to me!' she replied; 'but you will come every day to the château, will you not? You promise me?'

'Oh, yes; you know that the hours I spend by your side are the happiest of all!'

The maiden smiled at him deliciously; but immediately a cloud passed over her brow, and she leaned her head on the young man's shoulder.

The latter noted that sudden sadness.

'What ails you, dear Isabelle?' he asked; 'your sweet smile has vanished, I see tears in your eyes; have I unwittingly caused you pain?'

'Pain from you, Aubry, whom I love! Never—'

'Whence then your sadness?'

'Because you are going to leave me to return to Paris; I wish I could follow you there, never live separated from you—Oh! I deserve to be scolded, Aubry; I do not know what is going on inside of me, but foolish fears assail me; just now it seemed to me that we were going to say good-bye to each other and that I would never see you again.'

'Those are foolish fears, indeed.'

'Aubry, my dear Aubry, the Chevalier Macaire is a bad man; he hates you; be on your guard.'

'If Macaire hates me, it is because he loves you; but don't be uneasy, dear Isabelle, the chevalier is not formidable, and I question whether he would dare try his strength against me.'

'No matter, Aubry, be prudent, and avoid every occasion of meeting the man.'

'I shall do as you command, Isabelle. But the time to say good-bye has come', said he rising; 'I must be in Paris before nightfall.'

The young lady accompanied him as far as the little gate of the park, near which his horse, held by a servant of the château, was waiting for him.

Aubry de Montdidier threw himself into the saddle and with his hand and his heart sent a last adieu to his fiancée.

Before he left, the greyhound came to lick her hand. She returned his caresses, saying:

'Watch well over your master, and if anyone tries to harm him, defend him.' Half an hour later Aubry de Montdidier was galloping gaily through the forest of Bondy. As the weather was excessively warm, he had taken off his helmet and was carrying it in one hand, while with the other he amused himself by making signs to his dog. The greyhound ran hither and thither, barking joyously. Suddenly he stopped and stood still; as if he had just perceived a roebuck or a deer in the thicket. Aubry stopped his horse and looked, expecting to see the animal dart out at any moment. Suddenly the greyhound ran at full speed toward his master, who observed all his movements with surprise. At the same instant a man darted out from behind a tree and before he could be perceived by the man on horseback, thrust a dagger in his side.

Aubry, feeling that he was wounded, turned round and attempted to seize a weapon to defend himself; but before he had time to do so, his assailant stabbed him a second time, this time in the breast, and the blade penetrated his heart. The unhappy man first fell back upon his horse, then rolled off to the ground.

He was dead.

On seeing his master stretched out on the ground motionless, the dog flew into a terrible rage and hurled himself upon the assassin. A desperate struggle ensued; but the man finally got the upper hand. Believing that he had beaten the greyhound to death, he dragged him away and rolled him into the ditch that bordered the highway. Then wishing to remove all trace of his crime, he dug a hole at the foot of a tree and buried the body of his victim. Meanwhile the horse had run away and had disappeared in the depths of the forest.

But the hound had only been stunned by the blow he had received; he soon recovered consciousness; he leaped out of the ditch and returned to the place where the attack had been made. The murderer had disappeared. Not finding the body of his master, the faithful animal began to utter plaintive wails; but soon his instinct guided him to the foot of the tree where the body had been buried. He lay down upon the grave and for two days the forest resounded incessantly with his howls. Finally, oppressed by hunger and thirst, he decided to leave the grave, and he ran without stopping to Paris and went to the house of a friend of his master. There his sad howls seemed to announce the loss he had suffered. But his language was not understood. They gave him food and he appeased his hunger, but began again at once to utter his piteous cries. Vain efforts! He ran to the door, turned and looked to see if they were following him, came back, returned again, pulled at the clothes of those who had given him bread and finally, seeing the futility of his efforts, he ran off howling. He went back again and lay down on the grave of his master, remained there one day, and then returned to the château of Villemonble.

II

For three days the young châtelaine had been a prey to the greatest fears; she had passed through all kinds of anxiety. Locked in her room and a prey to the darkest thoughts, she prayed and cried: nevertheless, in spite of the cruel admonitions of her heart, she tried to summon up smiling illusions; she forced back with all her might the possibility of a misfortune and hoped to see her fiancé arrive at any moment.

At last, when she could no longer find consolation amid her

doubts and uncertainties, she thought of sending to Paris one of her faithful servants.

'Jehan,' she said to him, 'take the best horse from the stable and go to Paris.'

Jehan bowed.

'In Paris call at the house of Messire Aubry de Montdidier. If he is not in, wait until he returns. I command you not to return here without having seen him and without bringing me a note written by his hand.'

'Your orders shall be executed', replied Jehan.

And he went to get ready to leave.

As he was mounting his horse and they were lowering the drawbridge, the greyhound darted into the court of the château howling with all his might.

Isabelle ran out on hearing his cries. The dog rushed toward her, lay down at her feet, looked at her sorrowfully, got up again and began to howl once more.

'It is the messenger of death', cried the young lady.

And she fell unconscious in the arms of her attendants. While the women crowded around her and gave her attention, the servants gathered and, obeying the voice of the dog which seemed to be calling them, they followed him closely until they reached the edge of the forest.

All at once the greyhound left the highway and stopped at a place where the earth seemed to have been recently turned up. The dog was seen to be agitated, seized by a sort of convulsive trembling; then scratching the soil with his paws, he gave a long wail.

They began to dig the earth immediately, and soon they discovered the body, which was easily recognized as that of Aubry de Montdidier. The two wounds which he had received left no doubt as to the manner in which he had met his end. A crime had been committed; of that there was not the shadow of a doubt. But who was guilty of that crime?

The body was carried to the château and buried the following day in the chapel. The same day Isabelle announced to the servants that she was leaving the château to go and live in Paris. Before departing from the place where the body of her fiancé reposed, she went and knelt upon his tomb. 'Adieu, noble friend,' said she, 'adieu, but only for a time; I shall come back, and as soon as thou hast been avenged; then, I hope, death, which separates us now, will reunite us under this stone. No one, except me, knows the name of thy murderer. I go to deliver him up to his punishment. Forgive me, if I leave thee, my dearly beloved; my heart remains with thee, I take with me only my grief and my regrets.'

The châtelaine of Villemonble departed, followed by the faithful greyhound of Aubry.

III

*But there is come
A witness dumb not heard upon thy trial.*

Isabelle had been in Paris for a month and she had not yet been able to put into execution her plans of vengeance; she was even on the point of giving them up, so difficult did the project seem to be when closely examined; for, after all, to make an accusation one must have proofs; and she was unable to furnish a single one.

She saw herself forced to consign to God the case for her vengeance; to God, whose inflexible justice, soon or late, knows how to punish the guilty.

One day as she was crossing the square accompanied by the greyhound, who never left her side, the latter, barking furiously, darted into the midst of a group of archers and leaped to the throat of one of them. By dint of blows they succeeded in driving him off, but he came back to the charge each time more furious than the last, and, three different times, he hurled himself on the same archer. The latter, to escape the fury of the dog, was obliged to flee. Then the animal, which they prevented from approaching, became restless and uneasy and barked at a distance, addressing his threats in that direction in which the individual had escaped.

The archer against whom the greyhound had just declared war, was the Chevalier Macaire.

'God be praised!' said Isabelle to herself, 'I have my vengeance; that man will not escape me now. The dog of his victim will testify against him.'

From that day she showed herself constantly on the promenades and in the places frequented by the archers of the king. Henceforth it was war with a vengeance between the greyhound and Macaire, a war without truce or quarter. Every time the animal met his enemy he attacked him and pursued him with unprecedented tenacity and blind courage. These multiplied assaults, this strange fury of an animal that was gentle and kind, began to arouse suspicion. People began to remark:

'The Chevalier Macaire detested Aubry de Montdidier. When Aubry disappeared, Macaire himself was absent. On his return he looked troubled; his clothes were torn and in disorder. Did Macaire, driven by jealousy, murder Aubry?'

This gossip reached the ears of the king, who had already heard about the persistence of the dog in pursuing Macaire. He desired to witness the movements of that noble animal and so gave orders to have the dog brought into his presence.

Isabelle presented herself before Charles V, accompanied by her dog. Weeping she told him her sad story and ended by accusing the Chevalier Macaire of having murdered her fiancé.

'We shall compel the Chevalier, if he is guilty, to confess his crime,' said the king, 'and justice shall be done.'

He sent for the archer at once and ordered him to conceal himself in a large group of courtiers. The dog was then brought in from an adjoining room which Isabelle had entered with him. No sooner had the dog come in than he rushed upon the murderer with his accustomed fury; he went straight to him without the least hesitation and picked him out from among all the noblemen. By his barks and his piercing cries he seemed to be demanding justice of the king.

'Take the dog out', commanded the monarch; 'what I have just seen is strange and marvellous, Chevalier Macaire. Answer. You are accused of having treacherously slain one of your comrades to whom this dog belonged.'

'It is an infamous calumny!' exclaimed Macaire.

'Why then was the dog so enraged at you?'

'This is probably the reason. One day I had a quarrel with his owner; he rushed upon me, and I struck him; since that time he has been pursuing me with his anger every time he encounters me.'

'Where were you the day Aubry was assassinated? On your return why were you confused and perturbed? Why were your clothes torn?'

'Sire, I recall none of those circumstances; but as God is my judge, I protest my innocence.'

'Appearances accuse you, Chevalier Macaire. You call God to witness for your innocence. So be it. God will decide between you who deny your guilt and the dog who seems to accuse you. I command that a single combat take place between you. That will be the verdict of God!'

IV

In olden times there existed a barbarous law in France. That law declared that if anyone was suspected of a crime, he should prove his innocence by fighting his adversary in the lists. In that period of ardent faith this custom had its origin in the belief that Heaven could not permit crime to go unpunished, as if God did not have his own methods of punishment for the guilty man who escaped the justice of men. These combats were prescribed by authority of justice and were preceded by lugubrious ceremonies. The vanquished was forewarned of his fate. He was to be dragged by the feet outside the lists and attached to the gibbet. This sentence was executed in the case of the dead as well as of the living, for it might happen that the vanquished would be only wounded. These duels were called 'Judgements of God'.

Now, the day came when the Chevalier Macaire was to fight the greyhound and prove by a victorious contest that he had been falsely accused. It was the eighth of October, 1381, and the combat took place with as much solemnity as if it had been between two knights.

At an early hour an immense crowd assembled around the lists which had been set up in the Isle of St. Louis (now Notre Dame), at that time uninhabited.

A few minutes before the entrance of the two champions in the arena the king and all his court took their places in the reserved seats in the grandstand. The field judges then came and sat down on their benches under the royal box. A moment later the two antagonists were led in.

Macaire was armed with a large club having the form of a bludgeon, the dog with his claws and teeth.

The trumpets sound. It is the signal. The dog is released. He does not wait for his enemy to come to him; he runs, leaps, darts, rushes upon his assailant, retreats, gets out of the way, turns, comes back, dodges the blows that threaten him; now on one side, now on the other, he does not cease attacking Macaire a single instant. A blow which he receives sideways removes the skin from one of his legs.

The animal howls with pain; Macaire marches upon him with club raised high, ready to break it over the brute's head; the dog recoils; he is about to take refuge in flight—and victory belongs to the murderer of his master.

The crowd, silent and palpitating with excitement, looks and waits.

Suddenly, a woman dressed in black rises against the palisade opposite the greyhound. Her face is white as snow; her long black hair falls dishevelled over her shoulders.

With eyes fixed on the dog and her hand pointing to the Chevalier Macaire, she cries:

'Avenge your master!'

That well-known voice restores to the dog his strength, his courage, and redoubles his fury. Just when the spectators believe him to be already conquered, he rushes afresh upon his enemy; by a movement prompt and skilful he avoids the blow that threatens his head, glides stealthily and swiftly under the arm suspended in the air, seizes Macaire by the throat and fastens himself so firmly to it that he upsets him on the field of battle and forces him to cry for mercy.

Then the king gives orders for the man to be released from the grip of the dog; at a fresh order, the judges approach.

Chevalier Macaire, brought before them, confessed that he had assassinated his comrade Aubry de Montdidier, without anybody's being able to see him except the greyhound by whom he acknowledged his defeat.

The sentence was immediately executed; the murderer was dragged outside of the lists, conducted to the gibbet, and hanged.

Six months later the châtelaine of Villemonble died: her body was placed in the tomb which she had had constructed for her fiancé, under the cupola of the chapel of the château.

After the funeral ceremony the doors of the chapel were locked and the château itself remained unoccupied for several years. Finally a nobleman acquired it and came to install himself with his family. The day when the new lord of the manor of Villemonble had the doors of the chapel opened again, they found the skeleton of a dog on the tomb of Isabelle and Aubry de Montdidier.

Enter Bingo

A. A. MILNE

BEFORE I introduce Bingo I must say a word for Humphrey, his sparring partner.

Humphrey found himself on the top of my stocking last December—put there, I fancy, by Celia, though she says it was Father Christmas. He is a small yellow dog, with glass optics, and the label round his neck said, "His eyes move". When I had finished the oranges and sweets and nuts, when Celia and I had pulled the crackers, Humphrey remained over to sit on the music-stool with the air of one playing the pianola. In this position he found his uses. There are times when a husband may legitimately be annoyed; at these times it was pleasant to kick Humphrey off his stool on to the divan, to stand on the divan and kick him on to the sofa, to stand on the sofa and kick him on to the bookcase; and then, feeling another man, to replace him on the music-stool and apologize to Celia. It was thus that he lost his tail.

When the war broke out we wrote to the War Office, offering to mobilize Humphrey. Already he could do "Eyes *right*, eyes *front*". But the loss of his tail was against him. Rejected by the medical authorities as unfit, he returned to the music-

79

stool and waited for a job. It was at this moment that Bingo joined the establishment.

Here we say good-bye to Humphrey for the present; Bingo claims our attention. Bingo arrived as an absurd little black tub of puppiness, warranted (by a pedigree as long as your arm) to grow into a Pekinese. It was Celia's idea to call him Bingo; because (a ridiculous reason) as a child she had had a poodle called Bingo. The less said about poodles the better; why rake up the past?

'If there is the slightest chance of Bingo—of this animal growing up into a poodle,' I said 'he leaves my house at once.'

'*My* poodle', said Celia, 'was a lovely dog.'

(Of course she was only a child then. She wouldn't know.)

'The point is this,' I said firmly, 'our puppy is meant for a Pekinese—the pedigree says so. From the look of him it will be touch and go whether he pulls it off. To call him by the name of a late poodle may just be the deciding factor. Now I hate poodles; I hate pet dogs. A Pekinese is not a pet dog; he is an undersized lion. Our puppy may grow into a small lion, or a mastiff, or anything like that; but I will *not* have him a poodle. If we call him Bingo, will you promise never to mention in his presence that you once had a—a—you know what I mean— called Bingo?"

She promised. I have forgiven her for having once loved a poodle. I beg you to forget it. There is now only one Bingo, and he is a Pekinese puppy.

However, after we had decided to call him Bingo, a difficulty arose. Bingo's pedigree is full of names like Li Hung Chang and Sun Yat Sen; had we chosen a sufficiently Chinese name for him? Apart from what was due to his ancestors, were we encouraging him enough to grow into a Pekinese? What was there Oriental about "Bingo"?

In itself, apparently little. And Bingo himself must have felt this; for his tail continued to be nothing but a rat's tail, and his body to be nothing but a fat tub, and his head to be almost the head of any little puppy in the world. He felt it deeply. When I chaffed him about it he tried to eat my ankles. I had only to go into the room in which he was, and murmur, 'Rat's tail', to myself, or (more offensive still) 'Chewed string', for him to rush at me. 'Where, O Bingo, is that delicate feather curling gracefully over the back, which is the pride and glory of thy great-grandfather? Is the caudal affix of the rodent thy apology for it?' And Bingo would whimper with shame.

Then we began to look him up in the map.

I found a Chinese town called 'Ning-po', which strikes me as very much like 'Bing-go', and Celia found another one called 'Yung-ping', which might just as well be 'Yung Bing', the obvious name of Bingo's heir when he has one. These facts being communicated to Bingo, his nose immediately began to go back a little and his tub to develop something of a waist. But what finally decided him was a discovery of mine made only yesterday. *There is a Japanese Province called Bingo.* Japanese, not Chinese, it is true; but at least it is Oriental. In any case conceive one's pride in realizing suddenly that one has been called after a province and not a poodle. It has determined Bingo unalterably to grow up in the right way.

You have Bingo now definitely a Pekinese. That being so, I may refer to his ancestors, always an object of veneration among these Easterns. I speak of (hats off, please!) Ch. Goodwood Lo.

Of course you know (I didn't myself till last week) that 'Ch.' stands for 'Champion'. On the male side Champion Goodwood Lo is Bingo's great-great-grandfather. On the female side the same animal is Bingo's great-grandfather. One couldn't be a poodle after that. A fortnight after Bingo came to us we found in a Pekinese book a photograph of Goodwood Lo. How proud we all were! Then we saw above it 'Celebrities of the Past. The Late—'

Champion Goodwood Lo was no more! In one moment Bingo had lost both his great-grandfather and his great-great-grandfather!

We broke it to him as gently as possible, but the double shock was too much, and he passed the evening in acute depression. Annoyed with my tactlessness in letting him know anything about it, I kicked Humphrey off his stool. Humphrey, I forgot to say, has a squeak if kicked in the right place. He squeaked.

Bingo, at that time still uncertain of his destiny, had at least the courage of the lion. Just for a moment he hesitated. Then with a pounce he was upon Humphrey.

Till then I had regarded Humphrey—save for his power of rolling the eyes and his habit of taking long jumps from the

F

music-stool to the bookcase—as rather a sedentary character. But in the fight which followed he put up an amazingly good resistance. At one time he was underneath Bingo; the next moment he had Bingo down; first one, then the other, seemed to gain the advantage. But blood will tell. Humphrey's ancestry is unknown; I blush to say that it may possibly be German. Bingo had Goodwood Lo to support him—in two places. Gradually he got the upper hand; and at last, taking the reluctant Humphrey by the ear, he dragged him laboriously beneath the sofa. He emerged alone, with tail wagging, and was taken on to his mistress's lap. There he slept, his grief forgotten.

So Humphrey has found a job. Whenever Bingo wants exercise, Humphrey plants himself in the middle of the room, his eyes cast upwards in an affectation of innocence. 'I'm just sitting here', says Humphrey; 'I believe there's a fly on the ceiling.' It is a challenge which no great-grandson of Goodwood Lo could resist. With a rush Bingo is at him. 'I'll learn you to stand in my way', he splutters. And the great dust-up begins. . . .

Brave little Bingo! I don't wonder that so warlike a race as the Japanese has called a province after him.

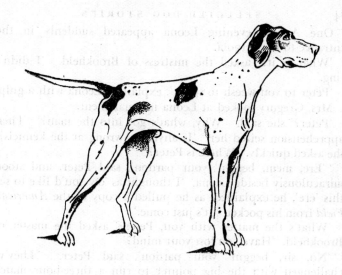

Dumb-Bell's Cheque

JOHN TAINTOR FOOTE

I

DURING the summer months early dinner was the custom at
Brookfield. It was served out of doors, weather permitting,
either on the terrace or beneath the canopy of vines which
crept with artful abandon from end to end of the pergola.

In the latter case it meant that the master and mistress of
Brookfield were alone and it would be a 'cosy' dinner, as they
called it, hidden from the many staring windows of the big
house by the dumb and eyeless vine.

At such times those who served them did so swiftly, and with-
drew. Then they helped themselves and stole choice morsels
from each other's plates, and giggled, and 'scrapped', as in
days gone by, and sometimes upset things, which was dreadful.
But no one would come except at the voice of the silver bell
with the carved ivory handle, and they were careful not to
touch it lest its fatal clamour occur.

❀　　❀　　❀　　❀

One August evening Leona appeared suddenly in the entrance to the pergola.

'What is it?' asked the mistress of Brookfield. 'I didn't ring.'

'Peter to you weesh to speak', explained Leona with a gulp.

Mrs. Gregory looked at Leona in amazement.

'Peter?' she said. 'Why, what's got into the man?' Then apprehension seized her. 'Is anything wrong at the kennels?' she asked quickly. 'Where is Peter?'

' 'Ere, mem, beggin' your pardon', said Peter, and stood miraculously beside Leona. 'I thought as 'ow you'd like to see this 'ere', he explained, as he pulled a copy of the *American Field* from his pocket. 'It's just come.'

'What's the matter with you, Peter?' asked the master of Brookfield. 'Have you lost your mind?'

'No, sir, beggin' your pardon', said Peter. 'They've challenged with the big pointer to run a three-hour match against Dumb-Bell for a thousand dollars. It's all in 'ere', he added, flourishing the paper. 'You can see for yourself.'

The master of Brookfield scowled at Peter.

'What of it?' he said. 'Why do you come here with it *now*?'

'Well, you see,' said Peter, a shade uncertainly, 'the quicker you knew about it, the quicker you could take 'em up. You can wire yet tonight, sir.'

Mrs. Gregory watched the master of Brookfield with dancing eyes. But the master of Brookfield did not smile. 'Why should I "take 'em up"?' he asked.

Peter's jaw dropped.

'Why, now—er—' he began, and became speechless as his world fell about him. At last he looked up, dull-eyed. 'I never thought,' he said, 'as 'ow you'd let 'em say we was afraid to race the big 'ound. . . . I ax your pardon for disturbin' of you.' He folded the paper, stuffed it into his pocket, and turned slowly away. 'Good night, mem', he threw over his shoulder, and was gone.

'Oh, Jim!' said Mrs. Gregory. 'He's heart-broken—he thinks you mean it! Peter!' she called, 'Peter!' But Peter was out of ear-shot, and she rang the bell.

While someone went to summon Peter, the master of Brookfield wrote a telegram. As he finished, Peter again appeared.

'They said as 'ow you wanted me', he muttered, looking straight before him.

'Why, yes', said the master of Brookfield. 'You left in such a hurry you forgot to take this with you. . . . I want it sent tonight.'

Peter took the telegram and read it carefully. He looked up with blazing eyes.

'That's tellin' 'em!' he said. 'I'll start workin' the little dog tomorrow. We'll need all of two months to get 'im ready,—e'll 'ave to go to Ramsey for a month on chicken.'

II

There are two championships in which field trial dogs compete. The winning of either of them means everlasting glory. One, the 'National', is run in Tennessee on quail. The other, the 'All America', is run in the Far West on prairie chicken.

The winner of the 'National' or the 'All America' has *Champion* written before his name from that day on, and never again may he compete in open trials. He is crowned king, whose sons and daughters are of the blood royal. He may not stoop to struggle with more common clay.

But a champion may run a match race against any dog with the temerity to meet him. And now Champion Brookfield Dumb-Bell, winner of the 'National', has been defied in public print by the owner of Champion Windem Bang, winner of the 'All America', and Peter was in a fever. The telegram he sent that night read:

MEET YOU ANY TIME, AFTER OCTOBER FIRST, AT ANY PLACE, FOR ANY SUM.

And it meant that 'the little white ghost' must leave his leather chair in the living-room and take to the open for the honour of Brookfield.

So, early next morning, Peter, a kennel boy, and the small champion went over the hill to the broad meadows across which the brook lay like a silver serpent.

Peter rode a good horse. Dumb-Bell had not been hunted for pleasure as yet, and no man on foot could keep within sight of the ghost at his work.

'Turn 'im loose!' said Peter to the kennel boy. 'An' meet me by them there willows in thirty minutes.'

'O-o-o-o!' said the kennel boy a moment later, his eyes on something white fading, fading in the distance.

' 'E's 'ell! ain't 'e?' said Peter, gathering up his reins. 'Come on, 'oss! you wouldn't let a little thing like that get away from you, would you?'

Morning after morning from then on they went forth, and little by little the thirty minutes were increased until at the last Dumb-Bell could do the full three hours at top speed, wolf down his meal that night, and ask for more.

According to science, fatigue produces a toxin. When an animal is overworked he cannot throw this off. The poison dulls the nerves of his stomach and plays havoc with his appetite. Peter knew nothing of science, but he scanned a tin plate anxiously every evening. When, after the full three hours, it was licked to mirror brightness—

' 'E's ready', said Peter, 'to beat anybody's dog!'

Meanwhile the field trial world divided over this meeting of champions. Pointer men prayed, in private, for big slashing, smashing Windem Bang. In public they admitted that perhaps the Brookfield setter had a shade in nose and bird sense, but for courage and headlong brilliancy there was 'nothing to it' but the pointer. Furthermore, since Gregory had allowed his adversary to name the place for the meeting, the owner of the pointer had of course chosen North Dakota, the home of the prairie chicken. The country and the birds were an old story to the pointer, whereas the Brookfield dog was more familiar with the haunts of quail.

Setter men thought of the white ghost with his uncanny nose, and smiled. *Their* champion was to have a month's work on the prairies before the battle.

'And', said Scott Benson, 'if they just let him go, in a month he'll be an old friend to every chicken from the Gulf to Canada.'

On one subject, however, everyone was in accord. Dog men all over the land had learned to hate the owner of the pointer. For years he had bred dogs—good dogs, they regretfully admitted—and at last fate had breathed the spirit of a champion into one of them. Furthermore, he was a great champion. This they admitted, also, but with more than regrets. That Emmett

Fry should own such a dog was beyond mere regretting—it was a calamity.

Chuck Sellers relieved himself on the subject with a few well-chosen words.

'There's more class in the tip of that pointer's tail', he said, 'than Emmett's got in his whole carcass.'

Since the tail of Champion Windem Bang was needle-pointed, this was repeated by broadcast and found much favour.

All this was man's talk, and not for women's ears. So the mistress of Brookfield heard no word of it, but she felt cold steel in the air when Emmett Fry was mentioned, and it puzzled her.

'You don't like this man Fry, do you?' she said to Gregory one morning, and felt his arm stiffen within her own.

'I don't know him', said the master of Brookfield, shortly. 'Are you sure you want to go out to this match, Chief? It's a hard trip.'

'I'm going', she stated. 'I've never seen Dumb-Bell run, you know, and this may be my last chance. . . . Why don't you like him?' she asked, returning to the charge.

'I don't know him', he repeated. 'How can I like him or dislike him?'

She knew this to be an evasion, but let it pass, and questioned Peter the next day.

'What sort of a man is Mr. Fry?' she asked him.

Peter was dusting a puppy with flea powder. He straightened up and spoke with difficulty, for flea powder is as certain in its action as snuff.

'A-choo-o!' he said. 'Just plain skunk . . . a-choo-o! . . . beggin' your pardon!'

'What has he done, what does he do, that makes you say that, Peter?' she questioned.

'Well,' said Peter, 'I'll tell you one thing he done. Six years ago, come November, Emmett Fry starts a pointer derby, by Damascus out of Old Rose, in the Continental. 'e was a nice-goin' pup but a leetle gun-shy—just flinchy-like. 'e run a good 'eat an' it was between 'im an' a young bitch by Gladstone in the finals. The judges were 'ard put to it for a decision, but they noticed that Emmett don't stand close to 'is pup when 'e fires.

' "At his next point, Mr. Fry, shoot directly over your dog",
they tells Emmett, an' he done so. At the crack of the gun the
pup breaks for the woods, 'is tail between 'is legs—an' that lets
'im out.

'Well, Emmett goes into the woods after 'is pup, an' next we
'ear 'is gun—both barrels. When 'e comes out of the woods, . . .
'e's alone. "An' ", says Emmett, " 'e'll not run away from a gun
no more." '

Peter caught up the can of flea powder, and bent abruptly to
his work.

'Oh!' said Mrs. Gregory. 'The beast . . . the beast!'

And presently the master of Brookfield looked up from his
desk into a white and quivering face.

'Good lord, Chief!' he said, 'what's happened?'

'You knew about it all along!' she accused. 'And let Dumb-
Bell meet his dog . . . a man like that! How could you do
such a thing! . . . How could you!'

'I've never met this man', the master of Brookfield said
slowly. 'When he did . . . what he did, I used what influence
I had to have his entries refused by all field trial clubs in
America. Since then I have made it a point never to enter a
dog where he was a competitor. But now—it is a question of
setter against pointer; and because I believe in the setter as the
greatest of all bird dogs, and many men agree with me and look
to my dog to prove it, we owe it to them to beat this pointer—
if we can . . . Don't you think so?'

There was a moment's silence.

'What about the thousand dollars you may win from him?'

The master of Brookfield regarded her gravely. Then the
corners of his mouth twitched ever so little.

'Why,' he said, with a bow, '*you* may have that, Chief.'

She had him by the coat lapels in an instant, and did her
futile best to shake him.

'I'll tear it up!' she said, between her teeth.

'Indeed?' said Gregory. 'And what about that family on
Rock Ridge who haven't a shoe to their back, and the lame
man who needs a wooden leg or an aeroplane or something,
and the woman who has delirium trem— Excuse me, it's her
husband—isn't it? And that girl who should have her voice
cultivated, and—er—all the rest of 'em?'

The mistress of Brookfield knitted her brows in thought.

'They won't get a cent of it!' she announced at last. 'If Dumb-Bell wins it, *he* will send it to the S.P.C.A.!'

The hotel at Belmont, North Dakota, was packed to bursting. Its occupants lifted up their voices and discussed bird dogs, past, present, and to come. The noise was bewildering. From a little distance it sounded like the roar of falling waters, and seemed as endless.

Back in the kennels it was comparatively quiet. "Derbys" might bay a neighbour, old veterans might rustle the straw as they dreamed of whirring birds; but though the match between Brookfield Dumb-Bell and Windem Bang was to be run as a final to the Great Western Trials, and a hundred dogs were all about them, Peter spoke almost in a whisper to Bill Ramsey as they examined the white ghost by lantern light.

'I don't like it!' said Peter. ''e never ate a bite. . . . 'is eyes don't look good to me, neither.'

'Pshaw, Pete!' said Ramsey. 'There's nothin' wrong with him. He knows why he's here as well as you an' me. He's excited, that's all. Why, look how you passed up them ham an' eggs yourself tonight! Let him alone—let him get his rest!'

'Feel 'is nose!' said Peter. 'An' why don't 'e lie down like 'e ought?'

Ramsey took Peter by the arm.

'Come on out of here!' he urged. 'If a big mutt was to keep a-rubbin' at your nose you wouldn't go to sleep, neither. He'll run his race if you let him alone. If you mess with him all night Emmett'll beat me tomorrow. *I've* got charge of this dog, . . . now, come on out of here!'

So Peter, with a last troubled look at the suspiciously bright eyes of the Brookfield champion, followed the handler from the kennels; and Dumb-Bell dropped his head on his paws to pass the night in a twitching and uneasy slumber.

A pale blue sky appeared next morning and hung above an endless rolling stubble. Two months before, this stubble had been wheat a golden guarantee that North Dakota could put bread into the mouths of half a continent. But the gold had been garnered, and now in its place was a lesser metal, for the stubble was heavy with frost and the rising sun had turned it to a plain of glistening silver.

Calm to majesty was this plain of silver, unruffled by the fact that it would soon become a battlefield. The last day of the Great Western Trials had arrived; two champions would meet that morning, and over the stubble would prove the mettle of their sires.

When the sun was an hour high, black dots appeared at the far edge of the plain. Presently they became horsemen—hundreds of horsemen—with a sprinkling of buggies, buckboards, and even an automobile or so, strung about a wagon, from which came, now and then, a beseeching whine.

This whine was the voice of Champion Windem Bang, who gazed out through the slats that penned him in and longed to be away.

His small rival was quieter. The white ghost knew what all these horsemen meant; he knew what was expected of him that day; but he knew that his body ached, that his throat was dry, and that the rolling stubble called but faintly to him. The day before he had eaten a piece of tainted meat no bigger than a lump of sugar, and now it was better to lie quietly in the soft straw than to pit one's speed and nose against another over those long, long miles.

So the gulf which never can be crossed, between the human animal and his passionately devoted friend, was between the little setter and fair play. One word would have told these humans, one word—and yet it was denied him. He would be judged by what he did that day, without it. . . . And so he lay in the wagon and grinned a hopeless grin when the big pointer yelped reproaches at those about him, or scratched and bit at the slats.

An iron-grey man on a big roan horse drew rein at last.

'I think we might put them down here, Frank', he said. 'What time is it?'

A man riding beside him nodded and took out his watch.

'All right, Mr. Fry! All right, Mr. Ramsey!' he called. 'We'll let them go at eight sharp—that gives you five minutes.'

It was only after a struggle that his handler snapped the leash on Windem Bang. When this was done, the pointer soared out of the wagon with a yelp, and bounded like a rubber ball to the end of his tether. Emmett Fry threw his weight against the leash and smiled.

Chuck Sellers saw the smile and leaned down confidentially from the saddle.

'Better save some of that, Emmett!' he advised. 'You'll need it.'

The handler looked up with a sneer.

'A hundred even on him!' he said.

'Got you!' said Chuck cheerfully. 'Come again!'

'Make it two!' said Fry.

'Got you!' Chuck repeated. 'Are you through?' But the pointer had dragged his handler out of earshot, and Chuck turned to Ramsey. 'You heard that, Bill?' he asked.

Ramsey nodded as he snapped the leash on the white ghost.

'We'll give you a run for your money', he promised and led his dog to the starting point.

With the feel of the stubble underfoot, with the big pointer straining at his leash beside him, Dumb-Bell's spirits revived a little. He was better, there was no doubt of that. The water that Ramsey had given him a moment before had cooled his throat. His legs felt stronger, too. He even wanted to run. He *would* run, that was sure! Fast enough, perhaps, to beat an ordinary dog. But Windem Bang, big, splendid Windem Bang, was not an ordinary dog. And in addition to the running the white ghost must read the crisp wind that sang across a thousand miles of prairie, and miss no word of its message!

The little setter lifted his head. His nostrils quivered as they explored the wind. Then he knew that his nose would betray him. It was no longer the nose of a champion, but a dull, uncertain thing—the kind with which ordinary shooting dogs go slowly and make mistakes. As he heard the 'Get away!' of his handler, which is the field trial call to battle, he grinned his hopeless grin.

When his leash is slipped, a field trial dog races straight away. He is driven to this first exultant rush by an overwhelming energy. A pair of high-class dogs make this preliminary flight a trial of pure speed. It was the custom of the white ghost to give his rival fifty feet or so and then sweep by him.

That Windem Bang could go like a comet made no difference to him. Had Dumb-Bell been himself, he would have matched the pointer stride for stride, with joy in his heart. But now his heels had failed him and he called on the big brain of Roderigo that was in his little head. He let Windem Bang go on alone into the far distance, while he shot away to the left.

He saw a patch of green alfalfa as he ran, and he headed for it. It was a likely place for chicken; there was a good half mile of it and he went down the lower edge, his head well up, as fast as he could go.

But Windem Bang did not run blindly long. He too, had brains, a champion always has. When he found himself alone, he looked about him. Then he caught the green of the alfalfa, and he swung in a magnificent curve to strike the lower edge, down wind. He was moving like a race horse, directly behind the ghost. At each terrific bound he made, he cut down the distance between them.

Dumb-Bell heard him coming. He must get wind of the covey somewhere in the green alfalfa before the pointer passed him! He put every ounce of strength he had into his running. He no longer heard the pointer. Good! He could still run, it seemed. Then he heard, far away, another sound. It was the spectators shouting. He turned his head, and there was Windem Bang, on the very spot where he himself had passed ten seconds before, tense as steel, as moveless as a stone.

There could be no mistaking what the panther crouch of the big pointer meant. From his eager muzzle, to his stiff and lancelike tail, every line of him said: 'Birds!'

Dumb-Bell's heart was bitter within him as he whirled and acknowledged his rival's find with an 'honour' point.

'Missed 'em!' burst out a pointer man. 'Missed 'em clean! *There's* your setter champion for you! Oh mama! Did you see that Bang dog nail 'em?'

'He—he didn't d-do very well that time, did he, Jim?' said the mistress of Brookfield, as their buckboard swayed and bounded toward the pointing dogs.

'No', said Gregory. 'I don't understand it. It may be a false point.'

But it wasn't a false point. Emmett Fry flushed a mighty bevy of prairie chickens thirty feet ahead of Windem Bang. They rose like one bird, and sailed off in stately flight to scatter in the stubble nearly a mile away.

The man on the roan horse kept his eyes on the two champions. Neither moved.

'Send them on, gentlemen!' he called to the handlers. 'We'll follow this covey up. We'll let them work on singles for a while.'

Then followed a terrible half hour for Dumb-Bell. In the race to the scattered covey he was beaten, and he saw the pointer make a smashing find two hundred feet ahead of him. Once more he came to an honour point. Once more a yell of delight went up from those who favoured Windem Bang. Once more the setter men looked at each other and were silent.

And now it was a race among a scattered covey at top speed, for champions must catch the faint scent of a lone bird while going like a rocket; and this takes nose, and nose, fine as a hair and certain as a compass, . . . Dumb-Bell's was hot with fever.

So he drove his aching body along, while Emmett Fry called 'Point, Judge!' again and again, as his dog cut down the singles with swift precision.

For Dumb-Bell the wind was a blank. Had he slowed down he might have read it, but he was a champion, and he must make his points high-headed and like a flash of lightning, or not at all. He worked in a frenzy, his sides heaving, his eyes shot with blood, only to honour Windem Bang, who was going faster than he, and with a razor nose.

'Why, Pete!' said Chuck Sellers at last in wide amazement, 'they're goin' to beat us!'

Peter turned to him with a set and stony face.

'Beat us!' he said. 'An' why wouldn't they beat us? 'e 'asn't no more nose than I 'ave! I knowed it last night, an' I let Bill talk me out of it! 'e's a sick dog! An' we're tryin' to beat the best pointer that ever lived, with 'im. I ain't a trainer, I'm a bum! An' *Bill*! . . . they'd ought to shoot '*im*! 'e's sick, I tell you, . . . 'e's sick this minute!' He turned his horse and galloped back to the master of Brookfield.

' 'ave him took up, sir!' he said. ' 'e's off—away off—'e ain't got nothin'. 'ave him took up!'

The master of Brookfield hesitated.

'It won't do, Peter', he said finally. 'We should have known that before they started.'

'*I* knowed it', said Peter. 'I knowed it last night. I'm a big slob,—beggin' your pardon,—I ain't fit to 'andle 'untin' dogs, let alone '*im*! You can fire me tomorrow, sir; but take the little dog up! 'e's sick—we may be 'armin' of 'im!'

They had come to a halt while a chicken was flushed to the credit of Windem Bang. Peter's voice had risen to a wail, and many heard what he had said.

'That's right, Gregory!' called a pointer man. 'Take him up! He's got no business with *that* kind of a dog. *He's* sick, all right, and gettin' sicker! . . . Take him up!'

The master of Brookfield felt a slender hand creep into his own. He squeezed it slightly, and smiled a grim smile.

'He'll have to take a beating, Peter', he said quietly. 'Go on, driver!'

So, Dumb-Bell took his beating for half of the three hours that he must run, and a fearful beating it was. For an hour and thirty minutes he ran, gasping for air, slobbering at the mouth, while his nose told him nothing.

Then as he passed a patch of ragweed he caught a faint trace on the wind. He turned like a flash and froze into a statue. He had taken a desperate chance of making a false point. He had acted with the certainty of a good nose, when he was far from certain. He grinned with anxiety as he waited for his handler, while faint, very faint, came that trace on the wind.

'Steady, boy!' said Ramsey. An instant later twenty feathered bombs shot up from the stubble and sailed away.

'Some find!' said Chuck Sellers, brightening. 'How does that suit you, Peter?'

But Peter did not reply. He was watching a white streak flash along the stubble, neck and neck with Windem Bang.

This was the turning of the tide. The violent effort he had made on courage alone was the little setter's salvation. His pounding heart had at last cleared his blood of the ptomaine that had drugged him.

As he raced for the scattered covey he felt a new vitality surge within him. . . . Ten minutes more and Dumb-Bell was himself again—a white ghost with a magic nose.

But Windem Bang was a great dog, backed by a tremendous lead. Only a miracle could save the day for Brookfield. The white ghost knew this as well as those who watched, and from that moment he became a miracle in nose and range and speed. Windem Bang was still going like the wind—few dogs could have held him even. But now ahead of him, always ahead of

him, was a white and fleeting thing that skimmed the stubble
with no apparent effort, and found birds in all directions.

The big pointer was puzzled. For the first time in his life
he was being outpaced, and he couldn't understand it. He had
run rings around this little setter until now! He would do it
again, he told himself—then every sinew in his body drank
deep of his vitality while he ran as he had never run before.

An hour went by, and Windem Bang began to wonder. A
shadow came and dimmed the eager light in his eyes. The
shadow was fatigue, and it frightened him. He fled from it in a
tremendous burst of speed, found a bevy, and went on. But the
shadow grew deeper. It was blotting out all the fire, all the
brilliancy of his efforts. In nose and heels and heart he felt it
now, and he looked anxiously ahead. Despair seized him as he
looked; for Brookfield Dumb-Bell was going like a driven
spirit, immune from the weakness of flesh.

'Call in your dogs, gentlemen!' said the man on the roan
horse. 'They have been down three hours.'

In another moment he was the centre of a crowding mass of
horsemen that grew larger every instant.

'Who wins?' they howled. 'Who wins?' And many answered
the question themselves.

The man on the roan horse held up his hand for silence, and
obtained it.

'Gentlemen,' he began, 'the judges have decided that this
match, so far, is a draw. We—' He got no further.

'Draw! Hell! The setter couldn't smell nothin' for two
hours!' . . . 'Two hours! Forget it! Look what he done all
the last end! The setter wins!' . . . 'You're a liar!' . . . 'Get
down off that hoss an' say it again!'

At last quiet was restored.

'As I said before, gentlemen, this match, as it now stands, is
a *draw*. It becomes a matter of stamina. The judges ask that
the dogs go on until we can render a decision!'

'Why, certainly', said the master of Brookfield when Peter
brought him the word.

But Emmett Fry faced the judges with the panting Windem
Bang on leash beside him.

'Do you think these are huntin' dogs?' he inquired. 'Do you
want 'em to go all day? This was a three-hour match. I've run

it *and* won it, and I want a decision *now*! I won't turn this dog loose again for nobody!"

The man on the roan horse looked at Emmett coldly.

'Very well, Mr. Fry', he said. 'If you refuse to go on, we shall decide now—in favour of the setter.'

The handler's face became grey with rage. He took a step forward, opened his lips, closed them again, and turned abruptly to Bill Ramsey.

'I'm ready whenever you are', he said hoarsely.

Ramsey stooped and cast off his dog.

'Get away!' he said with a wave of his hand—and the white ghost was gone.

An instant later Windem Bang flung himself across the stubble at the top of his clip, and the battle was on again.

The short rest had helped the big pointer. He went away with a rush. For twenty minutes more he went, a splendid thing to see. Then suddenly a red darkness fell about him. It was hot and suffocating, it filled his nostrils so that his breath came in struggling gasps.

It was hard to go on in this darkness. But champions must go on and on until they hear a whistle. He went on until a weight, an immense weight, seemed to fall across his loins. It was not fair to make him carry such a weight, he thought, and faltered in his stride. . . . The voice of his handler came like the lash of a whip:

'You Bang!—go on!' it said.

Yes, he must go on. He had forgotten for a moment. He saw a swale ahead and to the right. Its edge was dark with rag-weed, and he plunged toward it. The swale was half a mile away, and he called on the last of his strength to reach it. He was nearly there when a white flash shot from the left, cut in ahead of him, and stiffened into marble. Windem Bang lurched to a point in acknowledgement, swaying where he stood.

This was the end. As the birds were flushed, the pointer staggered on—he didn't know where. The voice of his handler had lost its meaning. He must go on, he knew that. So he went —in an aimless circle.

The man on the roan horse rode forward to the pointer's handler. His eyes were full of pity.

'You have a great dog, Mr. Fry,' he said, 'but—call him in, please.'

'Damn his heart . . . damn his yellow heart!' said Emmett Fry, and blew his whistle.

Windem Bang swung toward the sound of it, and came in. He was too far gone to dodge the loaded butt of the heavy dog whip, and he went down without a sound when it descended across his back. Nor did he make much of an outcry as it descended again and again. Only a moan came from him. He was too exhausted to do more. . . .

The mistress of Brookfield gave a choking cry, flung herself from the buckboard, and rushed forward like a fury. Emmett Fry heard her coming, and looked up blindly.

'The dirty hound quit!' he said. 'He had it won . . . the dirty hound . . . but he quit!'

'You vile beast!' flamed the mistress of Brookfield. 'Don't you dare touch him again!' She dropped in the stubble beside Windem Bang, throwing her coat over him as she did so.

The master of Brookfield lifted her up.

'This won't do, Chief', he said, and all but carried her to the buckboard.

'Oh, Jim!' she pleaded, 'he tried so hard!'

Then a thumping sound, followed by a moaning whimper, came to her. She covered her ears and sank in a heap to the floor of the buckboard.

'If Dumb-Bell had only lost!' she sobbed. 'If Dumb-Bell had only lost. . . .'

'Never mind, little Chief!' said the master of Brookfield. 'I'll take care of that!'

He strode back until he faced the owner of Windem Bang.

'I have taken—a fancy—to your dog . . . ' he managed to say, but could get no farther. Suddenly he tore a cheque book from his pocket and wrote with a shaking hand. He held out a signed cheque for the other to see. 'Fill it in—quick—for God's sake!' he said.

III

No one will ever know what Champion Windem Bang cost the master of Brookfield. He said no word to any man as he led the first pointer he had ever owned to the buckboard. But

G

as he drove away a pair of dog eyes, trusting, faithful, looked up into his face, and a slim arm went about his neck. So perhaps, everything considered, he did not pay too much.

A few days later the secretary of a certain benevolent society received the following letter:

Being heartily in sympathy with the work you do, it gives me great pleasure to enclose my cheque for one thousand dollars.

Faithfully yours,

Champion BROOKFIELD DUMB-BELL.

Jo

ILYA EHRENBURG

I KNEW Jo before the war. He was a young dog who loved to
run, his tongue out, through the narrow streets of a quarter in
Moscow. His ancestors had not been of the high nobility. He
had short crooked legs, and an enormous shaggy head. Everybody asked his owner, Maltsev, with some malice: 'Wherever
did you unearth such a beauty?' Even Tamara herself said, 'I
understand that one might love a shepherd dog, but that
thing. . . .' She was fond of the theatre and of art, while
Maltsev was a taciturn scholar with a rounded back. He had a
passion for big tedious tomes.

Jo knew that he must not bother Maltsev when he was
seated at his work table. Sometimes this was difficult, for
example, when the bell rang and he longed to hurl himself into
the hall with joyous barking, or again when he heard coming
from the kitchen certain suspiciously interesting sounds, Lena
clattering the pans. But Jo did not dare open the door; instead
he sniffed, his spirit on the alert. But when Maltsev got up, Jo
ran delightedly around the room.

This dog had an inexhaustible fantasy and he spent his life inventing games full of puckish fun. He would hide a stone in the snow, then he would dig it out and, overjoyed by this farce, he would run to his master to show him his find. Maltsev had taught him to carry the newspaper to old Gnedin who lived in a neighbouring alley. The old man would laugh loudly; 'In America, they have special delivery, but you, if I dare say it, have a canine mail service.' Maltsev said nothing. He knew that no one would understand his attachment for his hairy and lame dog of the streets.

Came the war. Jo and his master found themselves in the forests of Smolensk. Major Sokolovsky joked, 'You didn't by any chance come from a circus? Or perhaps you hoped to frighten the Germans with that dog?'

Maltsev gave a short reply, shrugging his shoulders, 'Jo is no imbecile.' In relating this conversation, the major guffawed, 'Lieutenant Maltsev has placed all his hopes in the strategic capacities of his mongrel, so help me!'

Meanwhile Jo frolicked among the trees and chewed the dead leaves. He didn't yet understand what war was.

Suddenly a terrible quake made the earth tremble. A cloud of earth was hurtled toward the sky. Maltsev was stretched in the mud, and Jo was frightened. He knew instinctively that some horrible thing had happened. The men scanned the heavens. Jo raised his head too; unable to hold himself in any longer, he emitted a groan of lamentation. Maltsev burst out laughing, 'Well, my old man, are you scared?'

At the sight of his master's laughing face Jo calmed himself, and even began to beat the earth with his tail, at once happy and ashamed. But the thunder burst again. One of Maltsev's friends held his head in his hands, and fear again invaded Jo. He wanted to run away. But instead of that he remained lying down, his head against the earth, without for an instant taking his eyes off his master. Maltsev was there, he helped to dress a man's wounds. . . . Run away? Oh no, Jo was no coward. He wouldn't even bark after Maltsev cried 'Shut up!' He just barely mumbled a bit. He understood that life had been transformed, that never again would he have a little rug on which to sleep, nor a cook, nor those delicious hours when Maltsev rustled the pages of his books and when Jo had strange dreams, as that one about the sausages that fell from an old woman's basket or that one where he was chasing a cat.

Thus Jo vanquished his fear. The bombing planes made their raids. The shells burst. The machine guns went off with a disagreeable noise, as if someone was banging on the door with impatience. Passing over a mine, a truck exploded. Jo knew that death lurked everywhere, on the earth and in the sky. But if Maltsev had no fear it was useless to be terrified. Evidently the master was not having an easy life, doubtless he would have preferred to read or to stroll along the quays with Tamara. At Moscow, Jo sometimes forgot his master, while he chased the birds or fought with the conceited bulldog that lived in the same street. Here, Jo never took his eyes off Maltsev. He loved him with a love simple, absolute, with that love which men called condescendingly 'the love of a faithful dog'.

Maltsev did not get accustomed all at once to life at the front. He had no fear of death; he had fear only of not being up to it on the firing line; he dreaded not being able to find the word he would need to encourage his men. He was a man used to books, not talkative. Tamara rarely wrote and her letters were cold. Maltsev knew that after a month or two she would stop writing him entirely because she had never loved him. She had barely consented to his loving her.

Things weren't going well at the front; a retreat was necessary. The men were asking, 'When are we going to stop?' Maltsev made war with gritted teeth. Jo reminded him of his happy former life, his books, his dreams, his youth.

Jo had changed. He always seemed anxious. For a long time now he had been accustomed to the artillery fire, to crawl across open spaces, and to hide himself in shell holes. One day, a yellow dog hurled itself upon him barking, in one of the streets of the village. Formerly Jo would not have turned down a scrap for he was lively of temperament. This particular day he went on his way without even turning around, for he knew that there were much more important things to do.

As night fell under the tent, Jo awoke at the caress of his master. Maltsev had the blues. The evening before, a soldier had said to him, 'Do you think we can ever stop them?' Maltsev knew that they could be stopped, but these defeatist words laid hold of him. Their bitter taste prevented him from sleeping. Jo understood the meaning of this awkward caress, and he rubbed his shaggy nose against Maltsev's palm.

Winter arrived early this year, and the cold was sharp. When Maltsev reported to headquarters, Jo followed him, trotting along on feet that were stiff with cold. For a week they had been stationed on a hill near a little frozen river. Jo ran from one machine gun post to another. The soldiers were used to him. The dog had such a quiet manner that he created a sense of peace around them and reminded them of happy yesterdays.

On this particular day, Jo was cold and sad. He did not understand why they hadn't gone to the headquarters in the village. There, there was a fat major who played with him every day. But Jo did not know that the Germans had cut the road to the village and that the soldiers had received orders to hold to the death. Jo only saw one thing, that Maltsev was distracted. As if he felt guilty, the dog tried to make himself small, and his ears lay flat on his head. In appearance, Maltsev was calm, but within him passed a torrent of emotions. The munitions were almost exhausted: it would have been necessary to open fire of the cannon on the route leading to Kruglovo; the radio wasn't working, the telephone lines had been cut. Twice, he had tried to send a soldier to the village; the first one had been killed, the second had returned wounded. If the munitions didn't arrive, it would be child's play for the Germans to capture the garrison tonight.

Maltsev was thinking neither of himself nor his comrades. He had but one preoccupation: to stop the Germans. To open fire on the road was for him to-day the whole meaning of a life which formerly had seemed to him so complex and incomprehensible. Suddenly Maltsev understood; he must send Jo. He covered the dog with a white chemise to camouflage his body against the snowy surface, and to his collar he attached a message: 'Munitions exhausted. Fire on the road to Kruglovo on the left of the woods.' Then he said to Jo, 'Run, run to the major.'

But Jo didn't understand. He saw that his master needed his help, but he didn't know what he ought to do. He gazed anxiously at Maltsev with eyes which were faithful and sad. Then Maltsev gave him an old newspaper carefully preserved to serve as paper for cigarettes. Jo took the paper between his teeth and reflected. He had understood that he must go to the village where each day he went with his master. Maltsev pointed with his finger and exclaimed, 'Run!' Jo started out.

The village was three kilometres away. Jo crawled, stopped, buried himself in the snow and got up again. He was afraid of losing the newspaper and it was difficult for him to breathe. First he crossed a valley, then came a climb. Jo remembered the way. Everything around him was calm. He reached the summit and emerged on a line of fire. He turned to the right and started to crawl in a zig-zag. This was the way he always walked with Maltsev. Suddenly he felt a violent pain and stopped short. An exploding mine had crushed his hind paws.

He fell unconscious in the snow. Presently he came to himself, groaned and remembered his mission. He must carry the newspaper. With difficulty he started again to crawl or rather to swim, for his front legs were pushing away the snow.

He arrived just in time. The commander of the post was getting ready to leave the region. The major read the note and cried, 'It's Maltsev.' He gave the order to notify the battery and to send help. Impatient, nervous, the major jostled his adjutant. A car stood before the door. Nobody paid any attention to the dog. But Jo saw that the newspaper which was the cause of his trip had fallen on the ground. He barked to say, 'Pick up the newspaper.' But the men had other cares on their minds. The major and three other men left the house. Jo remained alone. With pain, he began to crawl, he wanted to go back near his master but couldn't open the door. He remained lying down all night, all day, and then another day. He was tortured by thirst; he passed his dry tongue over his broken paws. With sadness he thought, 'Where is Maltsev?'

The shadows fell, and the dog felt the whole weight of his solitude. He wanted to bark but had no strength. He lost consciousness and dreamed that he was very little. He had nightmares and cried, 'Where is Maltsev?'

Well, Maltsev was very happy. When the cannon opened fire on the road to Kruglovo, he understood that Jo had accomplished his mission. At four in the afternoon, it was already dark, and the reinforcements arrived in time. Maltsev asked where his dog was. No one knew. At dawn, the Germans tried to attack but they were repulsed. Later, Maltsev and Redko, the chief of the reinforcement detachment, counter-attacked and were able to push the Germans along the road. At nightfall Maltsev left for the village. In the empty shack where the major had formerly stayed, he found Jo. The dog came to him but couldn't even lift his head. His tail wagged imperceptibly, and all that his poor dog's spirit felt passed into his eyes as he looked on Maltsev.

The man turned, bent over, and caressed Jo, remaining for a moment silent, then caressing him again. Quickly taking his revolver, he fired, then left the room without turning. He had to get to headquarters.

To-day, Maltsev is a colonel. On his breast are ribbons of his decorations given for his wounds. Who would recognize in this experienced military officer the timid scholar? He has found the way to the hearts of other men, he has found worthwhile friendships and the regiment is his family. He has seen much; the red smoke of Stalingrad and a well filled with the bodies of children. His eyes wear the heavy look of men who have seen more than any human being ought to see.

I met him recently. We passed a whole evening in a damp foxhole speaking of faithfulness and of human frivolity, and how difficult it is to uncover the nobility of the human heart.

We talked of Moscow before the war, the quiet street where Maltsev lived. Suddenly, he said to me, 'You'll be astonished, but I cannot forget the eyes of Jo when he saw the revolver in my hand.'

Cinders

JOHN A. MOROSO

I

HE was the son of Smoke and the great-grandson of Blaze. That's enough to identify Cinders in the fire department of the City of New York, except that there was never a mascot loved his driver and the pole horse of his team as he did Donohue and old King. Lots of dogs get so sentimental at times that they go plumb fool and Cinders was one of them, although it didn't hurt his capacity as a mascot, for he had the lungs and legs of a deer and could clear the way for our company over the longest run ever made by a big steamer.

When Donohue was laid up for a week while the doctors uncaked the smoke that had settled in his chest during the warehouse blaze, Cinders was a lost dog, until he got the scent of the hospital. He wouldn't eat or run to a fire, or even wag his tail when the captain's little girl would come around to the house of a pleasant afternoon. He just sat in a corner with his nose touching the ground, and we were all thinking that he was going to make a croak of it, when the captain came in one day with the scent of Donohue on his hands and clothes after visiting him at the hospital. Then Cinders knew that his boss wasn't dead, and he went over to the captain and wagged himself so hard that I thought he would break in half. Having expressed his thanks for the important information, he walked out of the engine house and followed the captain's trail back until he reached the Hudson Street hospital, not many blocks away.

Sure there was trouble at the hospital! Cinders got in between the legs of an ambulance surgeon, but lost the captain's scent on the first floor. The attendants tried to rush him out, but Cinders showed his fine teeth and his hair stood up on his spine when they came so close to him that they bothered him in his investigation. He took a peek into every corner of the first floor and then trotted up the stairs to the second.

The superintendent got sore and he sicked a dozen men and boys after the brute with broomsticks and floor mops. Some of the nurses thought the dog was mad, and made a rush for safety, screaming like so many fire engines in need of more coal at a big fire. A couple of souse patients thought they had 'em again and howled for the needle. Cinders was getting warm on the trail, however, and was so busy that he didn't bother about the excitement and failed to see an old party hobbling down the hall on a pair of crutches. He knocked one of the pins from under him and the old party went down like a scaffold in a March storm.

The only time in all its history when the hospital was as noisy in one afternoon was when Garry McLaughlin had two broken legs set after refusing to take ether for fear that some young doctor might get interested and cut 'em off.

Cinders ducked a cuspidor and a dozen wild pitches with brooms, floor mops, books, and chairs and trotted up to the third floor. He no sooner hit the top of the flight of stairs than he got Donohue's scent good and strong, and he announced it with his familiar voice.

'Whut you doing here, ye hound of heaven!' yelled Donohue from the sheets. 'Hi! Hi! Over here, ye hellion!' He was as glad as the dog was. Cinders was snouting out the terrified patients in the ward when he got sight of the face of his boss. Then he cleared two cots with one spring and hopped in bed with him.

The rest of the time Donohue was in the hospital Cinders gave the engine house only four hours a day and four hours a night. When he would fail to make a successful sneak into the hospital he would get under his driver's window and serenade him with a voice that had John McCormick, the great Irish tenor, sounding like a whistle on a peanut stand. When he came to the engine house he spent his time in smelling around old King's stall, just to make sure that his other special friend was all right. King would nose the dog all over and nibble at him as if he were a fine piece of chocolate. No man in our company ever saw a man, a dog, and a horse stick together so close as Donohue, Cinders, and King.

We always had trouble when Donohue was away from the job, especially from King. The big white pole horse had the blood of an Arab stallion in him, the contractor who sold him to the city having picked him up at a sale of circus horses. He looked his name more and more as he grew older and heavier. He was white as a bank of snow in the country, with a proud arch to his neck and his long tail stood out clear from his buttocks, falling like a cascade of silver.

Donohue didn't care for dominoes and the other games the men played in the engine house, and so he had plenty of time in which to groom the favourite of his three horses. King had the nerves that a steed of the desert is supposed to have, and he had fidelity to only one friend, and that one friend was Donohue. Cinders was more than a friend of King's. He was like a blood relation. With the love and devotion of his two dumb friends and his own love for his job, Donohue was about as happy a driver as ever leaned over a seat with the reins playing between his fingers.

'Whut is ther in mankind,' he said one day after all the smoke had been cleared out of his deep chest, 'whut is ther in mankind that approaches the fidelity of his dumb friend the dog and the dog's friend, the horse? If I was to croak tonight Cinders would starve himself to death, and ye'd have to shoot King in a week, for he would have none of ye trying to drive him and groom him. He would give somebody one bite or one kick that would end somebody's 'arthly career. He understands me every word and mood. Don't ye, ye big wall-eyed ton of

sausage? Shake hands wid me.' King held up his right hoof.
'And wid the other fut, ye divil', and the brute did as he was
ordered. 'And if there's a lump of sugar in me coat pocket,
ye're welcome to it, ye big slob.' King nosed into Donohue's
pockets for the sugar. It was uncanny, for the devil of a brute
had inherited all the circus stunts of his father, and Donohue,
who went to his duties on the first Friday of every month, being
a member of the Sodality of the Sacred Heart, never let the
beast roll over on his bedding at night without making him
kneel down and say his prayers.

'It's sacrilegious to make a horse pray every night', the
captain objected one evening. 'If he was in vaudeville and
doing it for a salary it would be all right,' says he, 'but you're
treating him too much like a human being, Donohue.'

'Begging your pardon, Captain,' speaks up Donohue, 'but
if a good dumb beast can be grateful to a human being there's
no reason why he can't be grateful to the God that made him
and all the rest of us.'

'You're bugs', says the captain. 'I heard once that the bug
doctors call it "zoophil-psychosis".'

Donohue laughed, but he had his reply ready. 'I may be
bugs, Captain,' says he, 'but if Cinders and King and myself
didn't all work together and do it gladly many's the time the
big steamer would have gone to pieces against an elevated
pillar or trolley with all of us having our heads cracked. It's
the team work we have that puts us on the street in six seconds
after the bell taps and puts us answering every call in faster
time than any company can boast, and we have the company
medal in the house to prove it. Am I right?'

'You're right', the captain admitted.

'I been a long time in the department,' continues Donohue,
as he was combing King's forelock again, 'and I'm getting
ready to back up to the pension list and live in a little Staten
Island cottage I'm after buying for the old woman and the two
gran'-children. There's only one thing I'm worrying about, and
it's that something might happen to take either of me good
dumb friends away from me.'

II

Our engine house is south of Division Street and just east of
Park Row, where the streets are chopped up like confetti

because some cow in the days of the Dutch wandered around the island south of Canal and made a path that later turned out to be Pearl Street. There are all kinds of gore strips on which are little tobacco stores and 'fences', showing noses as sharp as razors, for every inch of the land is covered. Down in our section, every now and then, when you think you are on Rose Street you'll find yourself standing where four streets butt into each other, New Chambers popping up where Chambers got lost, Duane Street somewhere in the discard and Oak or Roosevelt shaving the corners to a point suddenly. It's a regular spider's web and with the heaviest kind of traffic, for the great trucks loaded with print paper for the *Journal* and the *World* and the unpopular down-town papers crowd the street day and night.

It takes a *dog* to clear a way for a fire company in that section. Just an ordinary animal with four legs and a bark couldn't get away with it at all. And it takes a pole horse who knows and loves his master and is close pals with the dog ahead to get a big engine safely through that traffic without killing anybody. Cinder's father, Smoke, was famous for knocking kids out of the road, and one time I saw him—but that's an old story. I just mention it because there are some people who don't believe that blood tells.

It was in the spring of 1911 that we were notified that the old engine house we had been in for more than twenty years was to be pulled down and a real engine house built for us on the same site. There was only one way to shelter us while the new building was under construction. We stayed in the old place until the workmen were ripping out the ceiling of the ground floor and we just had to move for the horses were getting restless. A board shack had been put up for us in the space west of the Newsboys' Home where Duane and New Chambers streets bump into each other. It would do for a summer home. The contractors promised to have the new engine house ready for us before winter, and to the surprise of every man in the company and the aldermanic committee overlooking the job the contractors delivered the goods.

There weren't any ceremonies about opening our new home. The doors swung open, the chain dropped, and we rolled in backwards with Donohue guiding the team just as if we'd come back from a one-alarm. It was November and the chill was in the air, and so you can make an easy guess that we were all pretty well pleased when we found the new engine house steam-heated, snug, cosy, clean, and with all the modern conveniences you read about in the advertisements on the real estate page. We had shower-baths, big lockers, a loafing room with plenty of tables and chairs, and there were electric reading lights for those of us who couldn't read fast enough to finish the report of the ball game before night fell. And there was a new brass pole so slick and firm that all you had to do was to weave your arms around it and find yourself on a soft cushion of rubber at the bottom. There were never such luxuries provided for man or beast. Even Cinders wasn't forgotten. There was a box for him, raised from the floor on struts so he wouldn't get the draught and catch a cold—only it happened that Cinders always slept with King, cuddled up against the big horse's white belly, and no beating or other argument could get him to sleep in any other place.

'Now, whut in heaven's name is this?' I heard Donohue shout suddenly while we were looking over the modern improvements. He roared out the question as if he had been insulted, and his square, clean-shaven face showed a look of puzzlement. In his eyes there was a flash of anger, too. He pointed with a big, powerful, bony hand at the side of King's new stall.

I took a second look at the stall and noticed that the side was screwed to the floor and that it seemed to be a temporary arrangement. There was no solid work about it. A carpenter could clear the house of that stall and all the other stalls in a half hour, using only a screwdriver.

King was nibbling on Donohue's big red neck with little love bites, for the big Arabian loved the ground his driver walked on.

'Suppose I'm sick or dead or retired,' snorts Donohue, 'and the beast gets sore because I'm not around. Why, he'd kick that thing into the tinder heap with one small shake of his left hind leg.'

The captain who was wise to the inside doings of the department shrugged his shoulders and turned away. As he started upstairs to look over his new room he said, 'Don't be borrowing trouble, Mike Donohue. We're living in a different and a faster age, old boy. What was good eighteen years ago when you come in here on probation, thinkin' ye'd set the world afire while puttin' out fires, a lot of people don't think good enough for to-day.'

Donohue scowled until his face was as black as a County Sligo man paying his ground rent to a Sassenach.

'G'long wid their new fandangles of gasoline', he muttered. 'Whut was good eighteen years ago is good to-day.' Then he laughed and patted King on the nose and rubbed his heavy jowl on his neck. Cinders came over and tucked between the front hoofs of the big Arabian, looking up at his boss.

'I guess we've showed 'em for eighteen years whut we can do', says Donohue to his pole horse and his dog. But the dog whimpered, for it was a different kind of stall from the one he was used to and he knew that something was wrong.

III

It began to snow about the end of December. Then it snowed harder when January came in, and about the middle of January it *snowed*. It was like the Lord had said: 'I'll show you people how it *can* snow, and when you get it good and deep you'll have to give jobs to the two hundred thousand people of Mine in your town you call bums!'

It was a bad winter, even for those who had jobs, but it was a worse winter for those who didn't have jobs. In February the snow froze, and many is the time I saw old men picking at heaps of it, desperate-like, but not getting results. The Municipal Lodging House was taking care of twelve hundred of the homeless, and the Morgue was opened so that those who were perishing from cold might die handy to the nice marble lockers where they stick the stiffs at the end of Misery Lane.

Big Bill Edwards was on the job, giving out interviews to the papers and cleaning the sidewalks of Fifth Avenue and Wall Street. The newspapers were proud of Bill, for he cleared the streets for their delivery wagons and all went merry as a false alarm. The mayor's sidewalk was clear, the poets were throwing the bull about 'the beautiful', and east of Park Row and the Bowery there were garbage cans stuck twenty feet in the air on snow piles that the Tammany snow removal contractors were leaving for a warm spell. Any hardy explorer like Doctor Cook, used to swigging whale oil and eating fried blubber, could have stood it, but plain ordinary East Side folks who never get farther north than Twenty-third Street began wishing they were back in Italy, Russia, Greece, Poland, Scandinavia and other countries where New Yorkers first see the light of day.

There was a high record for fires during February, for the going was terrible and business was bad for a lot of merchants and manufacturers. We kept the rough shoes on the horses, of course, but ploughing through frozen snow made them as smooth as glass after a very few minutes. Everything depended on the driver and the sense of the pole horse, while an intelligent mascot's guidance meant a lot.

I was the engineer of the company that winter and, as the regulations required, the captain always swung alongside of me on the ash pan. On many of these terrible February runs he'd lean far over on his side, looking ahead, and I would on my side.

We could see the team working away like Trojans through the black smoke that swept down across our faces, and we could hear Donohue talking to King just as if the big Arabian at the pole were a living, human being. Sometimes the wind would whip back flakes of foam from the mouthing jaws of the horses as they tore at the bits as if they were trying to get a hold with their teeth as well as with their hoofs. It would slap us in the eyes, and I know the captain felt as I did—that a good fire-horse does more work and braver work than a good fireman.

Off in the distance ahead we always heard the yelp of Cinders, clearing the crossings for us and warning the kids of the poor with their soap box sleds. It was a lesson for any human being the way those brutes plugged through the frozen mire day after day, and there wasn't a time when we'd come in from a run that a dozen men didn't volunteer to help Donohue rub down the team and give them the chin and the petting that dumb brutes like. He attended to King himself—none of us wanted to, knowing the nature of the beast—and Cinders always looked out for himself, snuggling to the radiator and posing as a stove hound.

Springtime came again and the Tammany contractors gathered in their large graft. A lot of firebugs were on trial and crooked insurance adjusters were committing suicide or turning state's evidence. The number of fires decreased and we had a long spell of laziness. Donohue, however, never let his team get lazy. At stated intervals, prescribed in the regulations, he would take the horses out for a jog, riding King and leading his team mates on either side. He not only kept the team in fine condition but his harness as well, and he didn't neglect himself either, for as old as he was he would spend an hour a day wrestling with the toughest and youngest of our company who yearned for excitement on the mat.

He was one grand fireman and solid citizen, was Donohue. He had no care for the booze, or the other sports that those who draw city money have a leaning for. He had only one child, a daughter, married and with two little ones. Her husband was a cop, and he was killed in the performance of his duty before the second baby was born. His name in bronze is on one of the tablets in the rotunda of the new police headquarters building. Donohue loved his memory and cared for his kids. Some of these people who write stories about firemen could have put him in a book—he was that fine. But Donohue was old and grey in his hair. Younger people said he was behind the times. He was. I'll tell you about that.

The first real warm day of summer came and the breeze from the East River was welcome as it came with whirling clouds of dust up the street. I remember that it was late on a Friday afternoon, for the orthodox families of Baxter Street were all trooping to synagogue, the old whiskered merchants and pedlars in their shiny frock coats and second-hand beaver hats; their wives lumbering beside them with their glossy hair and fat faces framed in dark shawls and the little Abies and Rachels running at their heels. The captain and I were watching them pass when Donohue came up.

'Captain,' he said, 'I guess there won't be any kick on our record for last winter.'

'How's that?' asked the captain.

Donohue fished a little book from a hind pocket, squinched his eyes and cleared his throat.

'The reports of the battalion chief will show', he said, and

H

his voice was a little shaky, 'that this company trimmed the new motorized company in this same battalion for eighteen out of twenty fires during January, February, and March.'

'Is that so?' says the captain. 'But did ye allow for the big bunch of fires we had this side of Park Row?'

'I did that', says Donohue. 'I even measured off the stretches and give them elapsed time for busy crossings. Our horses just killed them dead when it came to getting through the snow.'

'I know how they worked', the captain told Donohue, putting an arm over the old driver's shoulders. 'They're wonders, and old King seemed stronger than he was twelve years ago when he first got in the business.'

'Didn't the old fellow work, Captain?' cried Donohue. 'But *didn't* he show the stuff in him! Did yuh ever hear of a fire-horse that could stand up the way he did last winter wid the streets like they was?' Some of the dust from outside got in his eyes, for they got leaky. Cinders, always snouting at his heels, coiled up with a whine, with one paw over his master's shoe.

'He is a *horse*, Donohue', said the captain.

Then Donohue reeled off his figures, showing how his team had trimmed the big auto-engine and auto-truck on the other side of Park Row.

'It's a fine showing for all of us, Donohue', said the captain; 'but we don't have much snow any more in New York and ten out of twelve months the gasoline will beat out the hay."

The captain was trying to break it to him easy. I saw Donohue turn away from him without another word, as if the handwriting had been flashed on the wall. He went over to King's stall, pretended to be fixing something about his bit, and then he and Cinders walked up the stairs slowly. The dog's tail was tucked low and his ears hung over his nose.

One month afterward a department carpenter came and un-screwed the new-fangled stalls and carted them out. The feed bags, the blankets, the whips, the extra harness, extra horse-shoes, the curry-combs, water pails and brushes were all carried off to the lumber room. Donohue placed King at the pole and his white mates on either side; snapped on the harness; crawled up to his seat and drove out with Cinders barking ahead and, as they cleared the entrance, the new big motor engine and the motor hose wagon backed in.

IV

It was well into August before we could get used to the change. The men complained that they couldn't sleep on account of the smell of gasoline, and all of us missed the sounds of the horses in their stalls and the pleasant smell of hay and oats and straw. Donohue had put in his application to be retired on pension, for his time had passed and he was out of the running for ever. Just what happened in other motorized companies happened in ours—the mascot refused to run ahead of the apparatus. For quite a while Cinders would bounce to his feet and dart through the door at the tap of the bell, but there was no clatter of hoofs or whinnying of eagerness from his old friends. There was a roar from the exhaust, the bitter stench of burnt gasoline and then a sudden realization on the part of Cinders that his time, too, had gone, and that *he* also was out of the running. He would stop suddenly in the middle of a whirling jump and slink back into the house.

But Donohue was faithful to the end. It was a bitter dose for a charioteer like him to turn chauffeur in his old age, but he had taken the necessary instructions and was at the wheel, his eyes and hands steady but his mouth shut tight, for there's nothing in a gasoline engine to gain the heart-interest of a man. He couldn't talk to it like he used to talk to his big, snow-white friend who said his prayers in his stall every night.

Our old apparatus had been taken to a company far down near the East River in the Corlears Hook section and the horses had been turned over to the city to be sold to the highest bidder. One of the men at the Hook came over on his day off soon afterward and told us that the big Arabian looked sick when Donohue said good-bye to him and that poor Cinders had howled his head off as if calling to him to follow when he went away at the heels of his boss. It must have been awful tough for the old man. There were stories floating around that he had tried to buy King, but the price went too high for him and he couldn't get the money together because he had just paid an instalment on his little Staten Island farm.

It was during August that Cinders began to cut us out. He would disappear for hours and frequently stay away all night, and all the beatings that Donohue would give him didn't change him a bit. He was turning bum, not a hard thing for a fire mascot who knows all the streets and corners of the city to accomplish. Sometimes we'd get telephone calls from points two miles away saying that someone had picked him up and was holding him for us. We always sent for him, of course, for we felt sorry for him, as we did for Donohue, and for ourselves for that matter. None of us were crazy about gasoline.

One day Cinders came in after a long stretch of bumming the streets and began to jump on Donohue, barking his head off. The old driver couldn't make him go to his corner. The brute was frantic, and kept bouncing up in the air and yelping until the water poured from his jaws and his tongue hung down on his throat. That very day Donohue had received his notice of retirement and he was to leave the house and the service of the department at midnight. His few things were packed and the boys had taken up a collection amounting to fifty dollars to present him as a testimonial of affection. The plan was for the whole company to come down the pole at the stroke of midnight, crowd around Donohue, give him three cheers, surprise him with the money, and then three cheers more as he went out of the door for the last time.

We were all wondering whether Cinders had gone crazy with the heat when Donohue ripped out an oath and picked up the dog and held him to his shoulder.

'Captain! Jim! Mike! Barney! Johnny!' he cried. 'Cinders has found King, as sure as I have me pension papers in me pocket! He's found at last, glory be! He never come back from one of these tramps like this before, and *he's found King!* I'd stake my life on it.'

Then things began to happen. It was about five o'clock in the afternoon and toward bridges, ferries, subway and elevated stations the hundreds of thousands of men and women packed in the great down-town skyscrapers began to move in the rush hour lockstep.

Zing!

It was our call, and it came from the old Beekman Swamp section filled with old ramshackle buildings stored with hides, tallow, paint, printers' ink, and drugs and chemicals.

Every man bounced for his place on the apparatus and we

were out in three seconds, just half the time we used to take with the horses. Cinders ran ahead of us this time and performed his duty as a real mascot born in the business and descended from mascots should perfom it. We headed south with the siren shrieking all the time and the bell going, the cops waving back vehicles and streams of people and Cinders lengthening his lead as we crossed New Chambers and headed down William Street.

Some distance ahead of us I saw a big truck piled high with tons of print paper in great rolls for the *World's* pressroom being drawn over to one side. Two of the big horses were chestnut, but the centre horse was pure white and he was restless. Cinders cut over in front of him and began his jumping and barking before the team. I felt the engine slow a bit as Donohue took in the situation, and saw the peril of it.

The big white brute tore himself free of the driver, gave a lunge that carried his two frightened mates along with him, and off went that towering, tottering truckload of paper in a wild runaway, the wildest and most dangerous that ever coursed through the streets of New York. No one man or two men or ten men could have stopped it, but Cinders was on the job, clearing the way, and Donohue put on more speed and moved up close, running a terrible chance of being wrecked, for if one of the great white rolls fell in our course we would sure turn turtle. The shriek of our siren so close behind them made the truck team work all the harder, but it was necessary for us to stick close so as to warn the crowds ahead. Cinders might have been wild with joy at being in the running once more, but at the same time he did his work as neatly as any fire dog that ever coursed a street during the rush hour.

I was expecting the worst to happen at any moment, and was ready for a flying jump when the crash came. A mounted cop joined in the race at Beekman Street, putting the spurs into his mount and helping Cinders get people out of the reach of trouble. One thing all of us, except Donohue, perhaps, had overlooked, and that was the long years of training that King—the pole horse of the runaways—had in our favour. The great Arabian could use his brain as well as his great muscles. After five blocks of flirting with death there loomed ahead of us a cop in the middle of the street waving his club while from the windows of a four-story building there poured clouds of black smoke. Cinders slowed up until the runaway team was almost on him. Then King began pulling back. Fortunately we were then on a slight upgrade, and the fine old fire horse's fight to bring his crazy team mates to a stop at the first hydrant near the fire was won. The mounted cop was on the job in a minute and a bunch of truck drivers helped him. The three big brutes were held, trembling and exhausted in their tracks, with the heavy load of paper still safe in the truck.

The fire was an easy one to squelch and we squelched it in less than fifteen minutes. When I got back to the street and company roll call I found Donohue standing by King with Cinders at his heels. The three of them had wound up their services to the City of New York in grand fashion, and Donohue was grinning from ear to ear as a big citizen with a diamond the size of a chestnut in his bosom was lifting up his voice and swearing and raging in broken Italian.

'What's the trouble?' says I to the big galoot, not knowing whether he needed to be tapped on the coco' or just turned over to a cop.

'Deesa dam' horse—da bigga fel'', he shouted. 'I buy-a heem from-a da cit'—me, Caselli, da truckman. I pay one hundred dol' and he bite-a two fel' in da stable, kick da whole-dam' place in small piece, kick ma brotha Giovanni Caselli out da window and now he run away with two good-a horse and da pape'.'

King, who didn't seem to like Mr. Caselli, straightened out his neck and nipped at him, ripping his coat sleeve wide open.

Caselli let out a yell of terror as he jumped back, and began to cry like a baby.

'Meesta fireman, signor,' he begged, 'take heem back. I sell-a heem for fifty dol' right now. You pay me one dol' a week. I trust you, signor.'

Donohue stroked King's big white, sweaty neck and the brute nibbled at one of his freckled ears, to the horror of the truckman.

It was night before all the excitement was over and the police had secured evidence for a complaint against Caselli for using a dangerous horse in the streets. The captain left his lieutenant in charge of the company while he conferred with various persons, among them Caselli.

There were no calls during the first part of the night and the men were all up in the dormitory pretending to be asleep after each had said good-bye to old Donohue. At midnight the bell sounded and down came the whole crew all ready for a run but all grinning and muttering to each other. The door flew open and the new chauffeur was at the wheel of the big auto-engine, but we did not roll. Instead, in walked the captain with King following in halter and Cinders whooping it up and waking the neighbours. The electric lights were switched on and showed Donohue standing with his clothes packed in a bundle and on his shoulder. In his left hand was the exercise bridle he had used on King for so many years and which he had kept as a souvenir.

'Whut's all this?' he demanded, wondering why the company did not roll in answer to the alarm which we had arranged with headquarters to fake.

Then King's big hoofs hit the cement floor and Donohue turned and saw his two dumb friends waiting for him.

'Donohue,' said the captain, 'the boys asked me to give you this testimonial.' He handed the halter strap to him. 'There'll be lots of fun for the two of ye on the little farm, and if the dog should happen to follow you, why there ain't any of us can stop him.'

Donohue was a man of few words. He did his best to get two or three of them together in a way that might sound like something but he couldn't manage it, so he shook hands all around. Then he gave a sign to King and the big son of a circus stallion dropped on his knees and bowed his head until his forelock swept the floor.

'Git up', said Donohue, and he swung over the sleek white back, grabbing his pack as the captain slung it to him.

'Good-bye, fellers, and God bless you', he called, and we gave him the three cheers as Cinders darted out ahead of him. Then we all got out on the sidewalk and gave him three more and the tiger as King became just a patch of white far down the starlit street on the way to Staten Island ferry.

We could hear the yelp of the son of Smoke getting fainter and fainter in the distance long after we could see the patch of white that represented King. When the voice of the dog died off into the distant hum of the ferryboats and only the city's sounds were left to our weatherbeaten and fire-frazzled ears we drifted back into the engine house with a good part of the fun of fire-fighting gone from us for ever.

'I'm glad it happened', said the captain. His eyes were hazy. 'I'm glad it happened', says he. 'Donohue has got the best of us all; he's got his old friends and his true friends. Get up to bed, ye tarriers.'

Old Duke

ARTHUR TRAIN

THE trouble involving Old Duke began the afternoon that young René d'Auriac knocked Samuel Bullock, the younger, off the sand bunker and head foremost into the water hazard on the Valley Fair golf course. This incident, which fifty years before would inevitably have resulted in a meeting between the participants at sunrise next morning on the old duelling-ground among the cotton-woods by the river bank, excited an ill-concealed satisfaction, not only among the club members, but the townsfolk generally, despite the fact that Samuel Bullock, senior, had been largely interested in laying out the links which were the scene of the tragedy. As, however, an attractive young lady was involved, the matter was hushed up, especially since everybody knew that René was courting Helen Peyton, although their respective fathers did not speak.

The feud between Major d'Auriac and County Judge Peyton was one of the traditions of the 'Blue Grass', entwined in the post-bellum history of the State and with the romantic memory

121

of a certain celebrated beauty who in their boyhoods had encouraged both gallants to love her and had ended by marrying neither. Of course it was at bottom the Major's fault, but the Judge's pride was also partly to blame. Each in his own way, these old men were the two leading citizens of Valley Fair, and as each had his followers—Montagues and Capulets of affection —it was felt that their aloofness added a certain distinction to local society. At any rate it gave people something to talk about, particularly when it became common knowledge that René d'Auriac had fallen under the spell of Helen Peyton's languid charm.

The secret might have been kept for a long time had it not been for Old Duke. For Old Duke, perhaps because he was a d'Auriac and therefore an aristocrat, had made it evident that he thought very little of the Bullocks, even if they had donated the golf course.

Of course Old Duke should not have followed René on to the Valley Fair golf course and nozzled the junior Bullock's ball on the putting-green, but the links were built on land purchased from the d'Auriacs and Old Duke had careered over it from puppyhood and knew every bush and pile of stones upon it. The Bullock family were playing a somewhat leisurely and arrogant twosome when Helen and René overtook them at the eleventh and sat down on the adjacent bunker to wait for them to hole-in, while Old Duke stood wagging his tail and snapping at grasshoppers at the edge of the green. The elder Samuel putted and missed; the younger Samuel putted and missed, and his ball rolled confidingly between the hound's paws. What more natural than that any well-mannered dog should acknowledge the little stranger's presence by first smelling of it and then giving it a gentle push with his nose?

The younger Bullock, who had made a flagrant bad shot, glanced with a scowl to where René sat.

'I'll thank you to keep your damn dog off the green!' he remarked insolently.

René sprang to his feet.

'I'll thank you to keep a civil tongue in your head!' he retorted.

The youth reddened and turned savagely to where Old Duke was toying with a beetle on the side of the bunker.

'Get out of my way! Get off the course, damn you!' he cried, kicking the dog violently in the ribs.

Old Duke uttered a whine of pain. Next instant René had seized Bullock junior by the collar of his tweed golf-jacket, yanked him to the top of the bunker and hurled him into the water hazard. Bullock senior leaped toward René, brandishing his mashie, but stopped short at sight of Old Duke crouching between, every hair on end and fangs exposed.

'I'll get you for this!' roared the father. 'You and your infernal dog!'

'Quiet, Duke!' cautioned René, his jaw quivering. 'Leave him alone! Come here, boy!'

From the piazza of the golf club, two hundred yards away, the élite of Valley Fair watched the bedraggled scion of the house of Bullock scrambling on hands and knees to safety. A faint cheer echoed across the links.

The elder heard it and shook his fist in the direction of the club-house.

'I'll get 'em!' he muttered. 'That stuck-up young popinjay and the old popinjay, his father, and that cursed dog—the entire outfit! Just let 'em wait.'

The town of Valley Fair lies in the southerly part of Bourbon County on the edge of the Blue Grass, famous from time immemorial for its thoroughbreds, human and equine. In late March and early April the low ground oozes like a green sponge and even the uplands yield their latent moisture to the warmth so that the moon rises upon a white sea of mist through which grope the feathery branches of budding trees and the lights of the farms gleam as if across fields of midnight snow.

It was on such an evening that Judge Peyton sat waiting on his piazza for his daughter to come home. He was a pink old man, running to fat, with thin streaks of silvery hair radiating like a fringe from a central point on the top of his head, and he wore an alpaca jacket and wrinkled, white cotton socks.

'Drat the girl!' thought the Judge, knocking the ashes from his corncob into the crack of the steps. 'Where the devil can she be?'

Then he removed his feet from the railing, assisted himself to rise by a peculiar shifting forward of his centre of gravity, and descended into the 'garden'. It was still excessively hot in spite of the fact that it was evening, and the Judge was pondering upon the advisability of a second julep when there was a brisk tapping of a cane upon the sidewalk and the figure of Major d'Auriac came into view beyond a buttonwood.

Each step, each click of the cane, brought his enemy nearer. Should he turn and flee, ignominiously? Not much! He would look the Major squarely in the eye! In fact, he took a step forward which brought him flush with the iron fence, and waited. Another moment and the Major was almost beside him. For a second they regarded each other, the Judge flushing slightly, the Major's chin stiffening. The next instant the latter had passed on. But in that fleeting second the Judge had experienced a pang. He had not imagined Louis would look so old. Did he look old like that himself? He had a momentary impulse—indeed his lips moved—to call the Major back. Then, with the barest of sighs, he restrained himself. No, it was up to Louis to make the first move; he was the offender.

And then for the time being he forgot all about the Major, for he caught sight of Helen coming up the street swinging her golf-sticks lightly from her left shoulder, and the emotions started by the unexpected appearance of his boyhood friend, now a stranger to him, were transmuted into a glow of affection for the child of his old age.

'Hello, dad!' she called in a voice that matched the silver of the dusk. 'Sorry to be late.'

'What kept you, honey?' he asked, slipping his arm about her. 'I nearly sent the sheriff after you.'

Meanwhile the Major continued stiffly upon his way—with a dignity befitting one of his distinguished lineage. He was a slender figure of an old gentleman, rigidly erect, with a white goatee and sloping shoulders, not five feet and a half in height —a little pepper-pot, known in his salad days for a trouble-maker all the way from the Mississippi to the Cumberland on both sides of the border. Some of this violence—like many other things about the Major—was exaggerated, for the old gentleman was a victim to the delusion that he must live up to his reputation. The d'Auriacs had all been fire-eaters—hard-drinking, hard-riding, hard-cursing; staunch friends and bitter enemies. He had no intention of having the race become emasculated; indeed, he rather deprecated his son's comparative mildness of character.

In one respect, however, René fully lived up to his father's ideal of what a d'Auriac should be—he rode like a demon, and there was no fox-chase within twenty miles that he did not attend, mounted on his father's old chestnut hunter 'Beauregard'. The Major had had to give it up ten years or more ago after dislocating his hip while attempting to take a four-bar gate. But he still kept a small pack of hounds of which Old Duke was the leader, the favourite not only of his master, but of the countryside.

Everybody in Valley Fair from Ruf' Jackson, who drove the ramshackly hack from the depot to the Culpeper House, up to Jack Tolman, the sheriff, was fond of Old Duke. He was a public character, like his master, and held in fully as much esteem. Very likely it was because of his combination of gentleness and strength, for he was a big dog, deep of chest, massive in head, with legs of iron and eyes that regarded you with such perfect trust that, as the Major said, 'No one could help being a gentleman, sir, with Old Duke around!' His marking was peculiar and made him readily distinguishable among other dogs, for a broad white band ran around the slats of his barrel and he carried a white star over his right eye. He had never harmed a human being or a domestic animal—except possibly a cat or two—and he had but three interests in life: his master, his master's son, and the pursuit of his natural enemy, the fox. Local opinion was divided whether René or Old Duke came first in the Major's heart.

Now it is alleged that no man can be really bad if he loves a dog; and it is certain that the Major was not half as choleric as he pretended to be. The fact is that when he had come upon his old friend the Judge so unexpectedly standing on the edge of his front lawn, he too had felt an almost irresistible impulse to stop and speak to him. Then pride had reasserted itself and, ashamed of his momentary weakness, he had tilted his chin in the air, looked the Judge coldly in the eye, and tried to face him down.

By the time Major d'Auriac had reached 'Malmaison' his encounter with Judge Peyton had resulted in that state of fury habitually caused by the secret realization that he had alienated his best friend, that he had nobody to blame for it but himself, and that unless he was prepared to eat humble pie and acknowledge himself to be in the wrong there was nothing to be done about it. Therefore he boiled over, rumbling all through dinner and wagging his little white goatee while he anathematized the Randolphs and the Peytons, and all their ancestors to the third and fourth generation as upstarts, vulgarians, half-breeds.

The Major having thus relieved his feelings and lighted his pipe, arose stiffly, filled a tin plate with remnants from the meal, and carried it out upon the veranda, followed by Old Duke. René remained moodily at the table, watching the candle light through the smoke of his cigarette. For the hundredth time he had almost made up his mind to disclose his secret to his father and for the hundredth time he had lost courage. After all, they were young and could wait a while.

They played a few games of piquet silently, until the elder d'Auriac, the little Louis XVI clock having struck ten, declared that it was time for bed—at any rate for him. René kissed the old man good night upon his forehead and waited for the light to be extinguished in his bedroom. Then calling to Old Duke under his breath, he stepped out into the night. Over the golf course a white pall of mist had spread itself out like a shallow silvery lake, and right above, within arm's reach as it were, hung an immense golden moon, only there was no moon path. It reminded him of the mists he had watched rising in the Argonne under that same old moon. It seemed like centuries ago.

Suddenly from out of the mist came the thud of hundreds of scampering hoofs. Old Duke had stiffened, his ears lifted, his muscles trembling. Before René could grasp his collar the hound had darted forward, cleared the hedge, and was careering toward the golf course.

Major d'Auriac had just finished his luncheon the next afternoon and was on the point of taking a short siesta when Jack Tolman drove into the yard. Old Duke, who had been lying beside one of the pillars of the veranda, lumbered to his feet and capered sideways over to the democrat wagon in which the sheriff sat, for they were old friends and had hunted many a fox together.

'Good evening, sheriff', said the Major with his customary courtesy. 'Won't you hitch your horse, sir, and come in and have something?'

'No thanks', the sheriff replied. 'I reckon I won't get out.
I'm sorry to say this is a business trip.'

Old Duke was standing on his hind legs between the wheels,
his big nozzle resting on Tolman's leg. The man laid his hand
on the dog's head.

'Poor Old Duke!' he murmured.

'What are you "poor Old Duking" about?' demanded the
Major suspiciously. 'Is some nigrah claimin' chicken damage?'

'No *nigrah*!' responded Tolman significantly. It's a heap
worse'n that. Fact is—' he paused. 'Fact is, Sam Bullock has
sworn out a summons for Old Duke. He lost a sheep last
night.'

'A sheep!' cried the Major. 'The infernal liar! That
miserable white trash! Who ever heard of Old Duke lookin' at
a sheep? I'll law him clean to hell for libel, by—'

The sheriff rubbed his chin apologetically.

'It don't hardly seem possible!' he agreed. 'However, Bill
Evans says he caught him with the carcass last night and he's
sworn to it.'

'Last night! Last night!' roared Major d'Auriac in a frenzy.
'My dog was locked up in the house all last night. This is a
conspiracy, sir! A conspiracy!'

'I'm sorry, Major!' said Tolman. 'I sure am! But law is
law, and here's the summons.'

He fumbled in his pocket and, leaning over, handed the
Major a square piece of soiled paper.

For a moment Major d'Auriac studied the paper in bewilderment. Then he dropped it upon the veranda as if it were infected with some deadly plague.

'Randolph Peyton!' he choked. 'So! What a dastardly
revenge!'

He leaned against the nearest pillar, his goatee trembling.

'You tell Judge Peyton—' his voice shook.

'Now, Major,' protested the sheriff, 'you know the Judge
ain't to blame for this.'

'I see the whole thing!' the Major declared fiercely. 'That
Yankee owns Peyton, body, boots and breeches. You say, "law
is law". Well, I say "justice is justice". I'll show this upstart
that he can't come down here and run God's country.
No, sir!'

Old Duke had stalked over to the Major and was looking up

into his face, slowly swinging his long tail. The old man bent over him and put his arms around the hound's neck.

'So they want to kill you, do they?' he said. 'Well, we'll show 'em!'

He gently separated the dog's soft lips with his fingers until he had exposed the glistening fangs and half the red gums. Old Duke looked mildly surprised.

'You can see for yourself there's no wool between his teeth.'

The sheriff smiled apologetically.

'Perhaps he's got rid of it somehow', he replied. Then he looked awkwardly away.

'By right,' he hazarded as if to himself, 'I ought to take the animal into custody, but I'll be damned if I will!'

Just then René came through the hedge. At sight of the sheriff he turned colour.

'René, my boy,' called out his father, 'this is the last straw! Judge Peyton has issued a summons against Old Duke for sheep-killing!'

René did not reply. His handsome face was pale.

'It's a damnable piece of perjury!' ejaculated the Major. 'René, you know Old Duke was in the house all last night.'

For several seconds there was no sound save the muttered endearments of the Major as he pressed the hound's head to his bosom. The René answered slowly:

'I can swear that when I locked up the house last night Old Duke was in the library; and this morning he was still there.'

Valley Fair rapidly filled for the great legal sporting event of the decade. The Culpeper House overflowed and there was no residence in the town which did not have its quota of guests. On the morning of the trial Main Street was a solid line of flivvers and the railroad ran a 'special' up from Winchester.

The Valley Fair courthouse had never been intended for a colosseum. It is a small, red-brick affair of the early seventies, with huge windows and a seating capacity of only two hundred people. By nine o'clock in the morning the square was impossible for vehicular traffic and the drug-store had already run out of ice cream and soda. It was no use for the sheriff to order the boys off the portico, for the minute he went around to the other side they were up again. Only such as had arrived before daylight had a chance to get inside, but the throng was good-natured and by stretching could catch glimpses of the courtroom through the wide-open windows.

When Judge Randolph Peyton ascended the bench every seat was occupied, and even the wall-spaces and aisles were crowded with friends of the defendant from the town itself and all parts of the countryside. But the chief character in the play was not a man. On a slightly elevated railed platform, or dock, sat a grand old fox-hound, his black coat combed and rubbed until it glistened with every move of the muscles beneath, his broad belt and the star over his eye white as snow, his freshly polished collar shining, an aristocrat of aristocrats, a true dog of the d'Auriacs—Old Duke, the defendant, on trial for his life. There was a somewhat puzzled look in his brown eyes and the confusion, although subdued, obviously had excited him, but he sat there obediently turning his head now and again to look at the Major and occasionally, as he recognized some one, thumping the platform with his tail.

'We will proceed, gentlemen', announced the Judge as the clerk handed him the complaint, and instantly the packed room became silent. 'The defendant, Old Duke, is on trial before me for the offence of sheep-killing under section sixty-seven of the Kentucky statutes, which provides that a justice of the peace, on proof that any dog is mad, or has been bitten by a mad dog, or has killed or wounded any sheep, shall order such a dog to be killed.

'The affiant in the moving papers upon which I have issued the summons, to wit, Samuel Bullock, senior, a citizen of this town, has sworn that Old Duke, owned by Major Louis d'Auriac, killed a sheep belonging to said Bullock during the night of May fourteenth.

'How says the defendant? Does he plead guilty or not guilty?'

Before his counsel could respond, Major d'Auriac, who had been nervously twirling his moustache, bobbed to his feet.

'I protest', he cried in a shaking voice amid a profound silence, 'against Judge Peyton presiding in this case! He has publicly expressed sentiments toward myself that make it improper for him to act where my interests are involved. I appeal to his sense of honour—if he has any.'

'Father!' whispered René in horror, grasping the Major by the arm.

*　　　*　　　*　　　*

I

An angry red slowly rose over Judge Peyton's rubicund face. The spectators, thrilled, craned their heads delightedly. The Major and the Judge were bristling at one another like a little game cock and mastiff.

'I protest', continued the Major. 'I—'

The Judge banged angrily with his gavel.

'Father!' groaned René. 'Please!' And he pulled the feebly resisting old gentleman back into his chair.

'Call the jury', directed Judge Peyton, whose face had once more resumed its normal colour.

The box was quickly filled, neither side challenged, the jury was sworn and the district attorney stated his case. He confessed to the jury that his task was an unpleasant one, that he knew Old Duke well and had always believed him to be a quiet and well-behaved dog. At the mention of his name the hound half rose and looked up into his face. The jury nodded. They too knew Old Duke, well. But, continued the prosecutor, the evidence was convincing and the law was clear. If the dog was a sheep-worrier, he must die. It would be the jury's duty to find the defendant guilty and leave the sentence to the wisdom and mercy of Judge Peyton. He bowed and called William Evans to the chair.

There was no question as to the witness's sincerity. He was, he said, employed by Mr. Samuel Bullock as farmer and shepherd. On the night of May fourteenth he was just going to bed when he heard a wild bleating and stampede of sheep. It was a fine, clear night with the moon nearly at the full and a low mist hanging over the meadow. He hurried out of the yard just as the frightened sheep came pouring in through the gate out of the mist. In the rear of the flock he could see a dog running in and out and jumping at their throats. At sight of him the dog abandoned his quarry and darted off into the mist again. He counted the sheep and found that one was missing, fastened the flock into the enclosure and started across the pasture to see what he could find. The sheepfold was in a depression and as he came up the rise he left the mist behind and below him and emerged into the clear moonlight. Instantly he saw the dead sheep lying white on a small hillock not fifty yards away. Standing beside it was a dog, a dog with a white belt and a white patch over one eye. He positively identified Old Duke as that dog. He had known him for years; could not be mistaken. The prosecutor shrugged his shoulders and sat down. That was the case; and it was enough. The crowd held its breath and the jury glanced at one another uneasily. The evidence was more positive than they had anticipated. But Mr. Townsend, the old lawyer retained by the d'Auriacs, was getting up. He asked the shepherd if he heard him aright to say that he had known Old Duke for years. The man answered that he had. Had he ever known him to kill or attack a sheep? No. What was Old Duke's reputation for peace and gentleness —wasn't it of the best? The witness readily admitted that it was. Then Mr. Townsend paused for a moment while he caressed his long, lantern jaw.

'Why didn't you kill Old Duke then and there when you found he had murdered the sheep?' he asked gently.

Even Judge Peyton seemed to await the answer with interest.

'Because I didn't want to!' finally answered the witness.

'You were satisfied he had killed the sheep?'

'Yes.'

'Did you refrain from killing him because you doubted your legal right to do so?'

'No.'

'Then why didn't you kill him?'

There was a long silence, broken only by the thump of the hound's tail. He knew all these friends of his were talking about him.

'Well,' answered Evans at length, 'I had about made up my mind to do it—but somehow I couldn't bring myself to. You see, he didn't run away or anything. Just stood there sniffing at the sheep, and when I called to him he came right over to me. If he had run, I'd have shot. But he didn't seem to have nuthin' on his conscience and—'

'And you didn't want to have anything on yours?' concluded the lawyer softly.

'I dunno!' he muttered a little shamefacedly. 'I just couldn't do it, that's all.'

'Your sympathy does you credit!' declared Mr. Townsend. 'Now let us inquire a moment into your legal right to kill the dog had you seen fit to do so. Where was it you found the sheep lying?'

'On the upper pasture.'

'Whose pasture?'

'The one they laid out for the new golf course.'

'Who owns it?'

'Why—' he hesitated. 'It's the land Major d'Auriac soid to Mr. Bullock.'

'Didn't Mr. Bullock deed it to the "Valley Fair Golf Club?" '

A buzz went through the room and through the windows. The old fox!

'I guess so', agreed the witness.

'How did Mr. Bullock's sheep happen to be on land belonging to the club?'

'Mr. Bullock told me to run 'em in there that afternoon.'

The old lawyer raised his lean face triumphantly to the Judge.

'So both the sheep and you were trespassing on the property of another? I submit it is clear the witness had no legal right whatever to kill this dog.'

There was an outburst of approval from the crowd. The lank old lawyer had scored—not heavily, but still a hit. Even the Major nodded—grimly; but almost immediately his face hardened again when Judge Peyton replied:

'The charge before me is not dog-killing, Mr. Townsend, but sheep-killing. If a dog is shown to have attacked a sheep, a justice of the peace or any judge of greater jurisdiction can, on proper proof, direct that he be killed. This is the proceeding being taken here.'

Mr. Townsend bowed gravely.

'I see your honour's point. I will discuss it at the conclusion of the evidence. Meantime, I desire to ask one or two more questions of the witness.'

'Mr. Evans, what reason, if any, did Mr. Bullock give you for wishing the flock turned on to the golf-links?'

At this question the elder Bullock gave marked evidence of discomfort, even going so far as to lean forward and make vague signs at the witness-chair. Evans hesitated.

'I object', interposed the prosecutor perfunctorily.

'Overruled!' retorted Judge Peyton.

'I press the question!' averred Mr. Townsend.

'Well,' remarked the witness gazing toward the ceiling, as if seeking guidance there, 'Mr. Bullock said—you'll pardon me, judge, to use his exact words?—he said, "He'd teach those —

— — d'Auriacs a lesson." Shall I go on, judge?—"I'm sick of that little billy-goat bearded whippersnapper of a major," said he, "and of that spider-legged stuck-up son of his. You'd think the way they act," he said, "that after God Almighty made the world he'd turned it over fer them to run fer him!"'

Major d'Auriac uttered a snort of indignation and faced toward the two Bullocks, brandishing his cane. An awed silence at such *lèse-majesté* fell upon the room. Judge Peyton tapped the bench with his gavel.

'I think you have gone far enough along this line, Mr. Townsend', he remarked hastily. 'Have you anything further?'

'One more question', answered the old lawyer. Addressing the witness, he asked, 'Have you lost any other sheep recently?'

'I lost a ram a couple of weeks ago,' he admitted, 'but I don't charge it against Old Duke.'

Again at the sound of his name the big foxhound knocked on the platform with his tail; then giving a deep sigh, he dropped his head comfortably upon his paws. Through the open windows came the murmur of the throng outside as the shepherd's testimony was passed from lip to lip.

'That is all', remarked Mr. Townsend. 'I move that the charge be dismissed on the ground that the owner of the sheep had deliberately turned them loose upon land belonging to others for the admitted purpose of satisfying a private grudge.'

Distress and embarrassment were both visible upon the Judge's face. There was no doubt whatever but that the sympathies of the crowd were entirely against the Bullocks and with Old Duke; and should he rule against Mr. Townsend it might be constructed as indicating that he shared Mr. Bullock's opinion with respect to the Major's personal character. It was an awkward moment and the Judge's round, rather flabby face glistened with a slight dew of perspiration born of his mental struggle. Then he pressed his lips together and shook his head.

'The circumstances, if true are immaterial', he remarked shortly. 'I rule the evidence here to be sufficient to justify a verdict of guilty and I shall give the case to the jury.'

'Poltroon! Scallawag!' muttered the Major, his goatee vibrating with fury. That he should be placed in such a humiliating and defenceless position before his enemy was too much for his pride to bear.

'Does your honour rule that the defence must proceed?' inquired Mr. Townsend.

'I do', returned the Judge solemnly. 'Mr. Bullock's remarks to the witness or the fact that his sheep were trespassing upon the golf course have no bearing upon the question of whether Old Duke killed one of them. So far the evidence is clear and uncontradicted and will amply support a verdict of guilty. Indeed I should be constrained in a civil case to direct such a verdict.'

There was an outburst of protest from the rear benches and the sheriff knocked for order upon the railing with his toad-stabber.

Mr. Townsend rose again.

'If the court please,' he said gently, 'I had hoped to be spared the necessity of calling my only witness, but your honour's ruling makes it necessary. Miss Helen Peyton, please take the stand.'

Throughout the room arose a scuffling of feet and creaking of benches as the occupants turned with one accord to where Helen Peyton had been sitting unobserved near the door leading to the sheriff's office. A flush stole up from the Judge's ample collar until it covered his entire scalp. What in the name of 'Lord Eldon' had his daughter to do with this dog case? Why should she be mixed up in this affair? Was it some trick of the d'Auriacs? No, the Major seemed equally surprised, for he sat scowling and pulling his moustache in obvious bewilderment that Mr. Townsend should be seeking reinforcements from the enemy. If Peyton wanted to find Old Duke guilty, why call Peyton's daughter as a witness? The Major mopped his forehead. Things were getting beyond him. Perhaps it was the heat. That *was* Peyton's daughter wasn't it? He caught his breath. Lord, how much she resembled her mother. That low forehead, with the sharply defined widow's peak in the middle of it, and those blue eyes under their lowering black brows! Tall, too, the way a woman ought to be. Then he perceived with increased astonishment that René had advanced to meet her and was conducting her to the witness-chair. Old Duke recognized her, too, and struggled to his feet as she passed, pawing at her dress.

The word spread to the street that the Judge's daughter was

going to testify for the defence and the crowd outside surged against the windows. Judge Peyton stammered noticeably as he administered the oath. For several seconds the girl kept her eyes fastened upon Old Duke. Then she raised them to Mr. Townsend and smiled faintly. René d'Auriac had not resumed his seat but remained hardly noticeable standing just beside her.

'Miss Peyton,' said Mr. Townsend, 'I regret having to put you to the embarrassment of being a witness, but your testimony is of vital importance. Do you recall the evening of the fourteenth of May?'

'I do—very well', she replied.

'Did you see Old Duke that night?'

'I did.'

'Where, if I may ask?'

Helen lowered her eyes once more to the dog's face.

'Shortly after ten, I saw him coming from the direction of Major d'Auriac's house toward the golf course.'

'Please go on.'

The girl dropped her head. It was not an easy thing to do. Old Duke thrust his nose toward her across the railing of the dock and wrinkled it affectionately.

'It was about ten o'clock,' she answered, 'and I had walked out to the golf course. It was moonlight, but there was a low mist on the meadow. The gate leading from Mr. Bullock's pasture was open and I walked through it on to the links. I could hear the sheep cropping the turf and the tinkle of their bells. I walked along the edge of the mist and came out on the little hill that overlooks the meadow pasture that used to belong to Major d'Auriac.'

She hesitated and looked away. The windows were black with heads, but the sheriff was too engrossed to pay any heed to them.

Judge Peyton was gazing at the girl in complete amazement. Helen out at night alone—when he supposed she was safe in bed!

'There is a clump of oaks up on the hill and an old wooden seat between two of the trunks. I sat down upon it. Here and there, where the mist was thinner, I could see the backs of the sheep. All of a sudden they began to run, first this way and then that. I could hear them bleating and squealing with fright. Then they all rushed pell-mell toward the open gate. But one of the sheep which was being chased by a dog ran back out into the moonlight, and I saw the dog leap at its throat and throw it to the ground. It was terrible!'

Helen closed her eyes as if to efface the recollection.

'What sort of dog was it?' asked Mr. Townsend.

'It was a huge, spotted carriage-dog', she replied. 'I had never seen it before. It ran away when Old Duke came.'

'Then Old Duke was there?'

'The spotted dog mauled the sheep until it was dead and then it must have heard something, for it stood stock still and looked toward Major d'Auriac's house and then dashed off into the mist again. It had gone when Old Duke got there. He smelled the dead sheep and pawed it, and was looking very intently into the mist when Mr. Evans came running up. I heard him speak to Old Duke and I saw the dog go up to him. He licked his hand. That was why—Oh, nobody could kill Old Duke!'

She uttered the words with such passionate tenderness that several in the audience answered involuntarily: 'No! No!'

The throng outside was pressing in through the door now, filling the aisles and crowding along the walls. Those on the rear benches were standing up on them in order to see over the heads of those in front and not to lose a word.

'Your honour, are you satisfied?'

Judge Peyton rubbed his damp forehead with his handkerchief.

'What were you doing out on the golf-links alone at that hour of the night?' he demanded.

'I was keeping an appointment', she answered, blushing furiously and covering her face with both her hands.

'With whom?' he asked sharply.

René d'Auriac stepped forward.

'With me, sir', he interposed. 'It was all my fault, sir. Something had happened in the afternoon and we—I—You see, sir, I had asked your daughter to marry me—and she was going to give me her answer—'

Major d'Auriac, fiery red, pushed his way forward. By this time most of the audience were on their feet. As a dog trial the affair was over.

'What did you mean, sir, by telling me you locked Old Duke in the library when you went to bed?' roared the Major at his son.

'I did', replied René. 'Only I didn't go to bed when you thought I did, sir.'

The Major paused helplessly. Then his eye caught sight of the Bullocks.

'You miserable scoundrel', he stammered. 'If I ever get—'

Judge Peyton banged with his gavel.

'Order in court!' he shouted. 'Be seated everybody! Mr. Townsend, have you any more questions?'

The crowd sank back, restoring a semblance of discipline.

'What was the matter to which you referred as having happened earlier in the afternoon?' inquired the old lawyer with a suppressed chuckle.

'Mr. René d'Auriac had knocked the younger Mr. Bullock into the water hazard', answered Miss Peyton.

'Bravo!' ejaculated the Major in spite of himself, although his world seemed upside down at the moment.

Judge Peyton looked bewilderedly from René to Helen, and thence to the Major. Inside his alpaca jacket his heart was thumping in a most disconcerting way. Indeed there was a moisture—perspiration or something—in his eyes that blurred his vision so that he could hardly see at all. Also there was unwonted impediment in his pharynx. But he cleared his throat with a brave show of authority, and, looking at where the Major ought to be, he said huskily:

'The fact that this witness is my own daughter renders it improper that I should take the case from the jury on the strength of her testimony. However, if they believe it, the defendant must be acquitted. I shall leave the case to them, but—unless they wish to do so—they need not leave their seats.'

The foreman looked around the box for any dissenting eye.

'We find the defendant not guilty', he announced. 'And on behalf of my fellow jurors and of the citizens of Valley Fair, I am bold to state that I hope the lady said "Yes".'

For answer, René stepped forward and took Helen's hand in one of his while with the other he patted the head of Old Duke, now once more a free and independent dog. There was a burst of applause inside the court, while a cheer arose from the square.

The Major had begun to act very queerly. In spite of the intense heat he appeared suddenly to have taken a cold, for he blew his nose loudly as he stepped toward the bench in front of the jury-box.

'Gentlemen,' he began in his customary stilted tones, 'I feel that my remarks this morning reflecting upon the—er—the integrity of the bench were entirely unjustified. Judge Peyton, I desire to apologize to you, sir, most humbly, sir, not only for my animadversions upon you here to-day, but, sir, for whatever I may have said regarding you in the past. I regret, sir—deeply regret—' His goatee quivered and he bit his lip.

On the bench Judge Peyton was struggling manfully to twist his face into a smile. Leaning forward, he stretched out both his hands to his old friend.

'Louis!' he choked.

The Major dashed the back of his hand across his eyes.

'Ranny!' he answered. 'What a pair of damned old fools we've been all these years.'

Just then Old Duke, whom some one had unloosed, as if desiring to share in the general rejoicing, jumped up between the two old men and laid his nozzle on the Major's shoulder.

'It was all my fault, Louis!' protested the Judge. 'I shouldn't have been so sensitive.'

'No, Ranny, it was mine!' insisted Major d'Auriac.

Two Friends

DAN RUSSELL

THE badger-earth was in the little delkin which lay between Cold Farm and the beechwood. It was a small earth and used only at odd times by the brocks. So on the evening when the keeper came with the report that a badger had been using the earth regularly, there was joy in the heart of Tom Conigar, the landlord of the Green Man. It would be an easy task to get a badger out of a small place like that, and there was not much danger of the terriers getting hurt. Conigar gathered his henchmen about him, and one July morning they set off for the earth with terriers and spades and a gallon jar of ale. No sooner was a terrier put into the main hole than he began to bay; the badger was at home.

The men stripped off their coats and began to dig in the direction of the dog's challenging voice. Every now and then they heard the agitated grunting of the badger as it charged the terrier. Very soon they were close to the sounds of combat. Conigar lay down and peered up the hole.

'Can't see nothin' ', he said. 'Here, Jess.'

The terrier backed out, bleeding from a mangled jaw.

'Now gie us the torch', said Conigar.

He directed the beam up the hole, and there, within four feet of him was the badger, a small sow. The long-handled tongs were pushed into the hole and the badger was dragged out and killed.

'Let's see if there's another', cried Conigar, and once more he peered up the tunnel.

'Well by gosh, look here', he shouted and reached in his arm. He hauled out a struggling cub.

'The old sow were usin' this earth as a nursery,' he grinned, 'us'll take this lil beggar alive.'

They put the little cub into a sack. He lay very quiet and still, scared of the noise and the men and the smell of his mother's blood.

The men returned to the village exulting in their luck and that night much ale was drunk in the bars of the Green Man. The frightened cub was produced and exhibited to the favoured few in the saloon bar. They crowded round and gazed at the terrified little creature.

'What have you got there?'—the Master of the Foxhounds had entered the bar unseen.

' 'Tis a badger-cub us got to-day, sir', replied Conigar.

'Poor little beggar', muttered the Master. 'I'll give you a pound for him.'

And so little Brock went home in the Master's car. He was put into an empty loose-box and a bowl of bread and milk was prepared for him. Eagerly he lapped it up and then returned to sleep upon the straw. Within a week he was quite reconciled to his new life and was as tame as a dog. Then one morning the Master arrived with a Cairn puppy.

'Here's a playmate for you', he said, and dropped the puppy into the loose-box.

Brock backed away and eyed the pup suspiciously. The puppy, friendly to all creatures, wagged his tail and bounded forward. Brock grunted and retreated to a corner. The puppy sat down, puzzled by this unsociable behaviour. Then he walked straight up and licked the badger with his pink tongue. Brock grunted again and sniffed at the little dog. Then he rolled over on his back in invitation to a game. So began a friendship that was to endure until death.

From that day the dog and the badger slept together in the loose-box. And all their waking hours were spent in each other's company. A strange sight it was to see the perky Cairn and the lumbering badger trotting round the stable yards and playing in the paddocks. Always it was the terrier who was the leader in their games and exploits. He would trot ahead with his impudent tail awave, while behind him lolloped Brock, grunting in protest at being hurried at such a rate.

Even when they arrived at the mature age of two years they did not quarrel. Rather did this strange friendship deepen. Did Jock the Cairn commit a crime and receive punishment, then Brock would comfort him. Did Brock do wrong, then it was Jock who would lick the chastened sinner with his tongue.

It was when this peculiar pair were two years old that there happened the strangest incident of all. Jock was small and cheeky, but Brock had grown until he was a powerful beast weighing some thirty-five pounds. A docile, amiable fellow who never lost his temper with the teasing terrier.

One day, Jock was in the yard alone. He was sniffing among the bales of hay in search of rats when he heard a patter of feet upon the stone flags. He turned to see a strange dog in the yard. It was the sheep-dog from the Home Farm, a big ugly beast, scarred from many battles. Little Jock's hackles went up as he marched to meet the intruder.

But before he could even bark the ugly brute darted forward and pinned him by the neck. Jock was game enough, but against this enormous foe he stood no chance. The big dog shook him like a rat and growled savagely. Jock lay limp and helpless in his jaws, dazed by the savage gripe. . . .

Brock was in the adjacent paddock, basking in the sun. Suddenly he heard the sounds of combat from the yard. He rose lazily to his feet and listened. He heard a savage worrying, and then high and clear he heard the voice of his friend calling for aid. Brock broke into a gallop, his hair stood out on end all round his body, and as he ran he roared, a deep rumbling sound infinitely more terrifying than the growling of a dog. Gone was the pleasant, domesticated creature which wandered freely round the yards; in its place was an angry badger, thirty-five pounds of fighting fury.

The big dog in the yard had nearly made an end of Jock when round the corner came a grey thunderbolt. Straight up to the struggling pair it charged like a roaring tornado. The bully received a blow in the side which knocked him sprawling. Before he could recover, a lean, arrowy head had darted down and Brock had his throat in that most terrible of all holds, the hold of a fighting boar-badger.

Deeper and deeper sank the long white tusks into the defenceless throat. The big dog plunged and threw himself about, but there was no breaking that terrible grip. The struggles of the dog grew weaker, and as they did so the iron jaws about his throat tightened until at last he lay dead. Only then did Brock relax his grip. He looked down and the angry fire left his sloe-black eyes.

He trotted over to where little Jock lay upon the ground and nuzzled him with his snout. The terrier's eyes opened and he whimpered his thanks. Then weakly he staggered to his feet. Brock came close to him and supported him with his shoulder, making little sounds of encouragement. Then very slowly the two friends walked back to their straw-covered sleeping bench.

Wapi the Walrus

JAMES OLIVER CURWOOD

PETER gave a cry of pleasure when the door opened and Dolores entered. He saw Wapi crowding in, and laughed.

'Pals already! I guess I needn't have been afraid for you. What a giant of a dog!'

The instant she appeared, Dolores forced upon herself an appearance of joyous excitement. She flung off her coat and ran to Peter, hugging his head against her as she told him swiftly what they were going to do. Fort Confidence was only one hundred and fifty miles away, and a garrison of police and a doctor were there. Five days on a sledge. That was all. And she had persuaded Blake, the trader, to help them. They would start now, as soon as she got him ready and Blake came. She must hurry. And she was wildly and gloriously happy, she told him. In a little while they would be at least on the outer edge of this horrible night, and he would be in a doctor's hands.

She was holding Peter's head so that he could not see her face, and by the time she jumped up and he did see it, there was nothing in it to betray the truth or the fact that she was acting a lie. First she began to dress Peter for the trail. Every instant gave her greater courage. This helpless, sunken-cheeked man with the hair greying over his temples was Peter, her Peter, the Peter who had watched over her, and sheltered her, and fought for her ever since she had known him, and now had come her chance to fight for him. The thought filled her with a wonderful exultation. It flushed her cheeks, and put a glory into her eyes, and made her voice tremble. How wonderful it was to love a man as she loved Peter! It was impossible for her to see the vivid contrast they made—Peter with his scrubby beard, his sunken cheeks, his emaciation, and she with her radiant, golden beauty. She was ablaze with the desire to fight. And how proud of her Peter would be when it was all over!

She finished dressing him and began putting things into their big dunnage sack. Her lips tightened as she made this preparation. Finally she came to a box of revolver cartridges and emptied them into one of the pockets of her under-jacket. Wapi, flattened out near the door, watched every movement she made.

When the dunnage sack was filled, she returned to Peter. 'Won't it be a joke on Captain Rydal!' she exulted. 'You see, we aren't going to let him know anything about it.' She appeared not to observe Peter's surprise. 'You know how I hate him, Peter dear', she went on. 'He is a beast. But Mr. Blake has done a great deal of trading with him, and he doesn't want Captain Rydal to know the part he is taking in getting us away. Not that Rydal would miss us, you know! I don't think he cares very much whether you live or die, Peter, and that's why I hate him. But we must humour Mr. Blake. He doesn't want him to know.'

'Odd', mused Peter. 'It's sort of—sneaking away.'

His eyes had in them a searching question which Dolores tried not to see and which she was glad he did not put into words. If she could only fool him another hour—just one more hour!

It was less than that—half an hour after she had finished the dunnage sack—when they heard footsteps crunching outside and then a knock at the door. Wapi answered with a snarl, and when Dolores opened the door and Blake entered, his eyes fell first of all on the dog.

'Attached himself, eh?' he greeted, turning his quiet, unemotional smile on Peter. 'First white woman he has ever seen, and I guess the case is hopeless. Mrs. Keith may have him.'

He turned to her. 'Are you ready?'

She nodded and pointed to the dunnage sack. Then she put on her fur coat and hood and helped Peter sit up on the edge of the bed while Blake opened the door again and made a low signal. Instantly Uppy and another Eskimo came in. Blake led with the sack, and the two Eskimos carried Peter. Dolores followed last, with the fingers of one little hand gripped about the revolver in her pocket. Wapi hugged so close to her that she could feel his body.

On the ice was a sledge without dogs. Peter was bundled on this, and the Eskimos pulled him. Blake was still in the lead. Twenty minutes after leaving the ship they pulled up beside his cabin.

There were two teams ready for the trail, one of six dogs and another of five, each watched over by an Eskimo. The visor of Dolores' hood kept Blake from seeing how sharply she took in the situation. Under it her eyes were ablaze. Her bare hand gripped her revolver, and if Peter could have heard the beating of her heart, he would have gasped. But she was cool, for all that. Swiftly and accurately she appraised Blake's preparations. She observed that in the six-dog team, in spite of its numerical superiority, the animals were more powerful than those in the five-dog team. The Eskimos placed Peter on the six-dog sledge, and Dolores helped to wrap him up warmly in the bearskins. Their dunnage sack was tied on at Peter's feet.

Not until then did she seem to notice the five-dog sledge. She smiled at Blake. 'We must be sure that in our excitement we haven't forgotten something', she said, going over what was on the sledge. 'This is a tent, and here are plenty of warm bearskins—and—and—' She looked up at Blake, who was watching her silently. 'If there is no timber for so long, Mr. Blake, shouldn't we have a big bundle of kindling? And surely we should have meat for the dogs!'

Blake stared at her and then turned sharply on Uppy with a rattle of Eskimo. Uppy and one of his companions made their exit instantly and in great haste.

K

'The fools!' he apologized. 'One has to watch them like children, Mrs. Keith. Pardon me while I help them.'

She waited until he followed Uppy into the cabin. Then, with the remaining Eskimo staring at her in wonderment, she carried an extra bearskin, the small tent, and a narwhal grub-sack to Peter's sledge. It was another five minutes before Blake and the two Eskimos reappeared with a bag of fish and a big bundle of shop-timber kindlings. Dolores stood with a mittened hand on Peter's shoulder, and bending down, she whispered:

'Peter, if you love me, don't mind what I'm going to say now. Don't move, for everything is going to be all right, and if you should try to get up or roll off the sledge, it would be so much harder for me. I haven't even told you why we're going to Fort Confidence. Now you'll know!'

She straightened up to face Blake. She had chosen her position, and Blake was standing clear and unshadowed in the starlight half a dozen paces from her. She had thrust her hood back a little, inspired by her feminine instinct to let him see her contempt for him.

'*You beast!*'

The words hissed hot and furious from her lips, and in that same instant Blake found himself staring straight into the unquivering muzzle of her revolver.

'*You beast!*' she repeated. 'I ought to kill you. I ought to shoot you down where you stand, for you are a cur and a coward. I know what you've planned. I followed you when you went to Rydal's cabin a little while ago, and I heard every-thing that passed between you. Listen, Peter, and I'll tell you what these brutes were going to do with us. You were to go with the six-dog team and I with the five, and out on the barrens we were to become separated, you to go on and be killed when you were a proper distance away, and I to be brought back—to Rydal. Do you understand, Peter dear? Isn't it splendid that we should have forced on us like this such wonderful material for a story!"

She was gloriously unafraid now. A pæan of triumph rang in her voice, triumph, contempt, and utter fearlessness. Her mittened hand pressed on Peter's shoulder, and before the weapon in her other hand Blake stood as if turned into stone.

'You don't know', she said, speaking to him directly, 'how near I am to killing you. I think I shall shoot unless you have the meat and the kindlings put on Peter's sledge immediately and give Uppy instructions—*in English*—to drive us to Fort Confidence. Peter and I will both go with the six-dog sledge. Give the instructions quickly, Mr. Blake!'

Blake, recovering from the shock she had given him, flashed back at her his cool and cynical smile. In spite of being caught in an unpleasant lie, he admired this golden-haired, blue-eyed slip of a woman for the colossal bluff she was playing. 'Personally, I'm sorry,' he said, 'but I couldn't help it. Rydal—'

'I am sure, unless you give the instructions quickly, that I shall shoot', she interrupted him. Her voice was so quiet that Peter was amazed.

'I'm sorry, Mrs. Keith. But—'

A flash of fire blinded him, and with the flash Blake staggered back with a cry of pain and stood swaying unsteadily in the starlight, clutching with one hand at an arm which hung limp and useless at his side.

'That time, I broke your arm', said Dolores, with scarcely more excitement than if she had made a bull's-eye on the Piping Rock Range. 'If I fire again, I am quite positive that I shall kill you!'

The Eskimos had not moved. They were like three lifeless, staring gargoyles. For another second or two Blake stood clutching at his arm. Then he said:

'Uppy, put the dog meat and the kindlings on the big sledge —and drive like hell for Fort Confidence!' And then, before she could stop him, he followed up his words swiftly and furiously in Eskimo.

'*Stop!*'

She almost shrieked the one word of warning, and with it a second shot burned its way through the flesh of Blake's shoulder, and he went down. The revolver turned on Uppy, and instantly he electrified into life. Thirty seconds later, at the head of the team, he was leading the way out into the chaotic gloom of the night. Hovering over Peter, riding with her hand on the gee-bar of the sledge, Dolores looked back to see Blake staggering to his feet. He shouted after them, and what he said was in Uppy's tongue. And this time she could not stop him.

She had forgotten Wapi. But as the night swallowed them up, she still looked back, and through the gloom she saw a shadow coming swiftly. In a few moments Wapi was running at the tail of the sledge. Then she leaned over Peter and encircled his shoulders with her furry arms.

'We're off!' she cried, a breaking note of gladness in her voice. 'We're off! And, Peter dear, wasn't it perfectly thrilling!'

A few minutes later she called upon Uppy to stop the team. Then she faced him, close to Peter, with the revolver in her hand.

'Uppy,' she demanded, speaking slowly and distinctly, 'what was it Blake said to you?'

For a moment Uppy made as if to feign stupidity. The revolver covered a spot halfway between his narrow-slit eyes.

'I shall shoot—'

Uppy gave a choking gasp. 'He said—no take trail For' Con'dence—go wrong—he come soon get you.'

'Yes, he said just that.' She picked her words even more slowly. 'Uppy, listen to me. If you let them come up with us—unless you get us to Fort Confidence—I will kill you. Do you understand?'

She poked her revolver a foot nearer, and Uppy nodded emphatically. She smiled. It was almost funny to see Uppy's understanding liven up at the point of the gun, and she felt a thrill that tingled to her finger-tips. The little devils of adventure were wide-awake in her, and, smiling at Uppy, she told him to hold up the end of his driving whip. He obeyed. The revolver flashed, and a muffled yell came from him as he felt the shock of the bullet as it struck fairly against the butt of his whip. In the same instant there came a snarling, deep-throated growl from Wapi. From the sledge Peter gave a cry of warning. Uppy shrank back, and Dolores cried out sharply and put herself swiftly between Wapi and the Eskimo. The huge dog, ready to spring, slunk back to the end of the sledge at the command of her voice. She patted his big head before she got on the sledge behind Peter.

There was no indecision in the manner of Uppy's going now. He struck out swift and straight for the pale constellation of stars that hung over Fort Confidence. It was splendid travelling. The surface of the arctic plain was frozen solid. What little wind there was came from behind them, and the dogs were big and fresh. Uppy ran briskly, snapping the lash of his whip and la-looing to the dogs in the manner of the Eskimo driver. Dolores did not wait for Peter's demand for a further explanation of their running away and her remarkable words to Blake. She told him. She omitted, for the sake of Peter's peace of mind, the physical insults she had suffered at Captain Rydal's hands. She did not tell him that Rydal had forced her into his arms a few hours before and kissed her. What she did reveal made Peter's arms and shoulders grow tense, and he groaned in his helplessness.

'If you'd only told me!' he protested.

Dolores laughed triumphantly, with her arm about his shoulder. 'I knew my dear old Peter too well for that', she exulted. 'If I had told you what a pretty mess we'd be in now, Peter! You would have insisted on calling Captain Rydal into our cabin and shooting him from the bed—and then where would we have been? Don't you think I'm handling it pretty well, Peter dear?'

Peter's reply was smothered against her hooded cheek.

He began to question her more directly now, and with his ability to grasp at the significance of things he pointed out quickly the tremendous hazard of their position. There were many more dogs and other sledges at Blake's place, and it was utterly inconceivable that Blake and Captain Rydal would permit them to reach Fort Confidence without making every effort in their power to stop them. Once they succeeded in placing certain facts in the hands of the Mounted Police, both Rydal and Blake would be done for. He impressed this uncomfortable truth on Dolores and suggested that if she could have smuggled a rifle along in the dunnage sack it would have helped matters considerably. For Rydal and Blake would not hesitate at shooting. For them it must be either capture or kill —death for him anyway, for he was the one factor not wanted in the equation. He summed up their chances and their danger calmly and pointedly, as he always looked at troubling things. And Dolores felt her heart sinking within her. After all, she had not handled the situation any too well. She almost wished she had killed Rydal herself and called it self defence. At least she had been criminally negligent in not smuggling along a rifle.

'But we'll beat them out', she argued hopefully. 'We've got a splendid team, Peter, and I'll take off my coat and run behind the sledge as much as I can. Uppy won't dare play a trick on us now, for he knows that if I should miss him, Wapi would tear the life out of him at a word from me. We'll win out, Peter dear. See if we don't!'

Peter hugged his thoughts to himself. He did not tell her that Blake and Rydal would pursue with a ten- or twelve-dog team, and that there was almost no chance at all of a straight get-away. Instead, he pulled her head down and kissed her.

To Wapi there had come at last a response to the great yearning that was in him. Instinct, summer and winter, had drawn him south, had turned him always in that direction, filled with the uneasiness of the mysterious something that was calling to him through the years of forty generations of his kind. And now he was going south. He sensed the fact that this journey would not end at the edge of the arctic plain and that he was not to hunt caribou or bear. His mental formulæ necessitated no process of reasoning. They were simple and to the point. His world had suddenly divided itself into two parts; one contained the woman, and the other his old masters and slavery. And the woman stood against those masters. They were her enemies as well as his own. Experience had taught him the power and the significance of firearms, just as it had made him understand the uses for which spears, and harpoons, and whips were made. He had seen the woman shoot Blake, and he had seen her ready to shoot at Uppy. Therefore he understood that they were enemies and that all associated with them were enemies. At a word from her he was ready to spring ahead and tear the life out of the Eskimo driver and even out of the dogs that were pulling the sledge. It did not take him long to comprehend that the man on the sledge was a part of the woman.

He hung well back, twenty or thirty paces behind the sledge, and unless Peter or the woman called to him, or the sledge stopped for some reason, he seldom came nearer. It took only a word from Dolores to bring him to her side.

Hour after hour the journey continued. The plain was level as a floor, and at intervals Dolores would run in the trail that the load might be lightened and the dogs might make better time. It was then that Peter watched Uppy with the revolver, and it was also at these intervals—running close beside the woman—that the blood in Wapi's veins was fired with a riotous joy.

For three hours there was almost no slackening in Uppy's

speed. The fourth and fifth were slower. In the sixth and seventh the pace began to tell. And the plain was no longer hard and level, swept like a floor by the polar winds. Rolling undulations grew into ridges of snow and ice; in places the dogs dragged the sledge over thin crust that broke under the runners; fields of drift snow, fine as shot, lay in their way; and in the eighth hour Uppy stopped the lagging dogs and held up his two hands in the mute signal of the Eskimo that they could go no farther without a rest.

Wapi dropped on his belly and watched. His eyes followed Uppy suspiciously as he strung up the tent on its whalebone supports to keep the bite of the wind from the sledge on which Dolores sat at Peter's feet. Then Uppy built a fire of kindlings and scraped up a pot of ice for tea-water. After that, while the water was heating, he gave each of the trace dogs a frozen fish. Dolores herself picked out one of the largest and tossed it to Wapi. Then she sat down again and began to talk to Peter, bundled up in his furs. After a time they ate and drank hot tea, and after he had devoured a chunk of raw meat the size of his two fists, Uppy rolled himself in his sleeping bag near the dogs. A little at a time Wapi dragged himself nearer until his head lay on Dolores' coat. After that there was a long silence broken only by the low voices of the woman and the man, and the heavy breathing of the tired dogs. Wapi himself dozed off but never for long. Then Dolores nodded, and her head drooped until it found a pillow on Peter's shoulder. Gently Peter drew a bearskin about her, and for a long time sat wide-awake guarding Uppy and baring his ears at intervals to listen. A dozen times he saw Wapi's bloodshot eyes looking at him, and twice he put out a hand to the dog's head and spoke to him in a whisper.

Even Peter's eyes were filmed by a growing drowsiness when Wapi drew silently away and slunk suspiciously out into the night. There were no yapping foxes here, forty miles from the coast. An almost appalling silence hung under the white stars, a silence broken only by the low and distant moaning the wind always makes on the barrens. Wapi listened to it, and he sniffed with his grey muzzle turned to the north. And then he whined. Had Dolores or Peter seen him him or heard the note in his throat, they too would have stared back over the trail they had travelled. For something was coming to Wapi. Faint, elusive, an indefinable breath in the air, he smelled it in one moment, and the next it was gone. For many minutes he stood undecided, and then he returned to the sledge, his spine bristling and a growl in his throat.

Wide-eyed and staring, Peter was looking back. 'What is it, Wapi?'

His voice roused Dolores. She sat up with a start. The growl had grown into a snarl in Wapi's throat.

'I think they are coming', said Peter calmly. 'You'd better rouse Uppy. He hasn't moved in the last two hours.'

Something that was like a sob came from Dolores' lips as she stood up. 'They're not coming', she whispered. 'They've stopped—and they're building a fire!'

Not more than half a mile away a point of yellow flame flared up in the the night.

'Give me the revolver, Peter.'

Peter gave it to her without a word. She went to Uppy, and at the touch of her foot he was out of his sleeping-bag, his moon-face staring at her. She pointed back to the fire. Her face was dead white. The revolver was pointed straight at Uppy's heart.

'If they come up with us—you die!'

The Eskimo's narrow eyes widened. The was murder in this white woman's face, in the steadiness of her hand, and in her voice. If they came up with them—he would die! Swiftly he gathered up his sleeping-bag and placed it on the sledge. Then he roused the dogs, tangled in their traces. They rose to their feet, sleepy and ill-humoured. One of them snapped at his hand. Another snarled viciously as he untwisted a trace. Then one of the yawning brutes caught the new smell in the air, the smell that Wapi had gathered when it was a mile farther off. He sniffed. He sat back on his haunches and sent forth a yelping howl to his comrades in the other team. In ten seconds the other five were howling with him, and scarcely had the tumult burst from their throats when there came a response from the fire half a mile away.

'My God!' gasped Peter under his breath.

Dolores sprang to the gee-bar, and Uppy lashed his long whip until it cracked like a repeating rifle over the pack. The dogs responded and sped through the night. Behind them the pandemonium of dog voices in the other camp had ceased. Men had leaped into life. Fifteen dogs were straightening in the tandem trace of a single sledge.

Dolores laughed, a sobbing, broken laugh that in itself was a cry of despair. 'Peter, if they come up with us, what shall we do?'

'If they overtake us,' said Peter, 'give me the revolver. It is fully loaded?'

'I have cartridges—'

For the first time she remembered that she had not filled the three empty chambers. Crooking her arm under the gee-bar, she fumbled in her pocket.

The dogs, refreshed by their sleep and urged by Uppy's whip, were tearing off the first mile at a great speed. The trail ahead of them was level and hard again. Uppy knew they were on the edge of the big barren of the Lacs Delesse, and he cracked his whip just as the off runner of the sledge struck a hidden snow-blister. There was a sudden lurch, and in a vicious up-shoot of the gee-bar the revolver was knocked from Dolores' hand—and was gone. A shriek rose to her lips, but she stifled it before it was given voice. Until this minute she had not felt the terror of utter hopelessness upon her. Now it made her faint. The revolver had not only given her hope, but also a steadfast faith in herself. From the beginning she had made up her mind how she would use it in the end, even though a few moments before she had asked Peter what they would do.

Crumpled down on the sledge, she clung to Peter, and suddenly the inspiration came to her not to let him know what had happened. Her arms tightened about his shoulders, and she looked ahead over the backs of the wolfish pack, shivering as she thought of what Uppy would do could he guess her loss. But he was running now for his life, driven on by his fear of her unerring marksmanship—and Wapi. She looked over her shoulder. Wapi was there, a huge grey shadow twenty paces behind. And she thought she heard a shout!

Peter was speaking to her. 'Blake's dogs are tired', he was saying. 'They were just about to camp, and ours have had a rest. Perhaps—'

'We *shall* beat them!' she interrupted him. 'See how fast we are going, Peter! It is splendid!'

A rifle-shot sounded behind them. It was not far away, and

involuntarily she clutched him tighter. Peter reached up a hand.

'Give me the revolver, Dolores.'

'No', she protested. 'They are not going to overtake us.'

'You must give me the revolver', he insisted.

'Peter, I can't. You understand. I can't. I must keep the revolver.'

She looked back again. The was no doubt now. Their pursuers were drawing nearer. She heard voices, the la-looing of running Eskimos, a faint shout which she knew was a white man's shout—and another rifle-shot. Wapi was running nearer. He was almost at the tail of the sledge, and his red eyes were fixed on her as he ran.

'Wapi!' she cried. 'Wapi!'

His jaws dropped agape. She could hear his panting response to her voice.

A third shot—over their heads sped a strange droning sound.

'Wapi,' she almost screamed, 'go back! Sick 'em, Wapi—*sick 'em—sick 'em—sick 'em!*' She flung out her arms, driving him back, repeating the words over and over again. She leaned over the edge of the sledge, clinging to the gee-bar. 'Go back, Wapi! *Sick 'em—sick 'em—sick 'em!*'

As if in response to her wild exhortation, there came a sudden yelping outcry from the team behind. It was close upon them now. Another ten minutes—

And then she saw that Wapi was dropping behind. Quickly he was swallowed up in the starlit chaos of the night.

'Peter', she cried sobbingly. 'Peter!'

Listening to the retreating sound of the sledge, Wapi stood a silent shadow in the trail. Then he turned and faced the north. He heard the other sound now, and ahead of it the wind brought him a smell, the smell of things he hated. For many hours something had been fighting itself toward understanding within him, and the yelping of dogs and the taint in the air of creatures who had been his slave-masters narrowed his instinct to the one vital point. Again it was not a process of reason but the cumulative effect of things that had happened and were happening. He had scented menace when first he had given warning of the nearness of pursuers, and this menace was no longer an elusive and unsizeable thing that had merely stirred the fires of his hatred. It was now a near and physical fact. He had tried to run away from it—with the woman—but it had followed and was overtaking him, and the yelping dogs were challenging him to fight as they had challenged him from the day he was old enough to take his own part. And now he had something to fight for. His intelligence gripped the fact that one sledge was running away from the other, and that the sledge which was running away was *his* sledge—and that for his sledge he must fight.

He waited, almost squarely in the trail. There was no longer the slinking, club-driven attitude of a creature at bay in the manner in which he stood in the path of his enemies. He had risen out of serfdom. The stinging slash of the whip and his dread of it were gone. Standing there in the starlight with his magnificent head thrown up and the muscles of his huge body like corded steel, the passing spirit of Shan Tung would have taken him for Tao, the Great Dane. He was not excited, and yet he was filled with a mighty desire—more than that, a tremendous purpose. The yelping excitement of the oncoming Eskimo dogs no longer urged him to turn aside to avoid their insolent bluster, as he would have turned aside yesterday or the day before. The voices of his old masters no longer sent him slinking out of their way, a growl in his throat and his body sagging with the humiliation and the rage of his slavery. He stood like a rock, his broad chest facing them squarely, and when he saw the shadows of them racing up out of the star-mist an eighth of a mile away, it was not a growl but a whine that rose in his throat, a whine of low and repressed eagerness, of a great yearning about to be fulfilled. Two hundred yards— a hundred—eighty—not until the dogs were less than fifty from him did he move. And then like a rock hurled by a mighty force he was at them.

He met the onrushing weight of the pack breast to breast. There was no warning. Neither men nor dogs had seen the waiting shadow. The crash sent the lead-dog back with Wapi's great fangs in his throat, and in an instant the fourteen dogs behind had piled over them, tangled in their traces, yelping and snarling and biting, while over them round-faced, hooded men shouted shrilly and struck with their whips, and from the sledge a white man sprang with a rifle in his hands. It was Rydal.

Under the mass of dogs Wapi, the Walrus heard nothing of the shouts of men. He was fighting. He was fighting as he had never fought before in all the days of his life. The fierce little Eskimo dogs had smelled him, and they knew their enemy. The lead-dog was dead. A second Wapi had disembowelled with a single slash of his inch-long fangs. He was buried now. But his jaws met flesh and bone, and out of the squirming mass there rose fearful cries of agony that mingled hideously with the bawling of men and the snarling and yelping of beasts that had not yet felt Wapi's fangs. Three and four at a time they were at him. He felt the wolfish slash of their teeth in his flesh. In him the sense of pain was gone. His jaws closed on a fore-leg, and it snapped like a stick. His teeth sank like ivory knives into the groin of a brute that had torn a hole in his side, and a smothered death-howl rose out of the heap. A fang pierced his eye. Even then no cry came from Wapi, the Walrus. He heaved upward with his giant body. He found another throat, and it was then that he rose above the pack, shaking the life from his victim as a terrier would have shaken a rat. For the first time the Eskimos saw him, and out of their superstitious souls strange cries found utterance as they sprang back and shrieked out to Rydal that it was a devil and not a beast that had waited for them in the trail. Rydal threw up his rifle. The shot came. It burned a crease in Wapi's shoulder and tore a hole as big as a man's fist in the breast of a dog about to spring upon him from behind. Again he was down, and Rydal dropped his rifle and snatched a whip from the hand of an Eskimo. Shouting and cursing, he lashed the pack, and in a moment he saw a huge, open-jawed shadow rise up on the far side and start off into the open starlight. He sprang back to his rifle. Twice he fired at the retreating shadow before it disappeared. And the Eskimo dogs made no movement to follow. Five of the fifteen were dead. The remaining ten, torn and bleeding—three of them with legs that dragged in the bloody snow—gathered in a whipped and whimpering group. And the Eskimos, shivering in their fear of this devil that had entered into the body of Wapi, the Walrus, failed to respond to Rydal's command when he pointed to the red trail that ran out under the stars.

At Fort Confidence one hundred and fifty miles to the south there was day—day that was like cold, grey dawn, the day one finds just beyond the edge of the Arctic night, in which the sun hangs like a pale lantern over the far southern horizon. In a log-built room that faced this bit of glorious red glow lay Peter, bolstered up in his bed so that he could see it until it faded from the sky. There was a new light in his face, and there was something of the old Peter back in his eyes. Watching the final glow with him was Dolores. It was their second day.

Into this world, in the twilight that was falling swiftly as they watched the setting of the sun, came Wapi, the Walrus. Blinded in one eye, gaunt with hunger and exhaustion, covered with wounds, and with his great heart almost ready to die, he came at last to the river across which lay the barracks. His vision was nearly gone, but under his nose he could still smell faintly the trail he was following until the last. It led him across the river. And in darkness it brought him to a door.

After a little the door opened, and with its opening there came at last the fulfilment of the promise of his dreams—hope, happiness, things to live for in a new, a white-man's world. For Wapi, the Walrus, forty years removed from Tao of Vancouver, had at last come home.

Blood Will Tell

DON MARQUIS

I AM a middle-sized dog, with spots on me here and there, and several different colours of hair mixed in even where there aren't any spots, and my ears are frazzled a little on the ends where they have been chewed in fights.

At first glance you might not pick me for an aristocrat. But I am one. I was considerably surprised when I discovered it, as nothing in my inmost feeling up to that time, nor in the treatment which I had received from dogs, humans or boys, had led me to suspect it.

I can well remember the afternoon on which the discovery was made. A lot of us dogs were lying in the grass, up by the swimming hole, just lazying around, and the boys were doing the same. All the boys were naked and comfortable, and no humans were about, the only thing near being a cow or two and some horses, and although large they are scarcely more human than boys. Everybody had got tired of swimming, and it was too hot to drown out gophers or fight bumblebees, and the boys were smoking grapevine cigarettes and talking.

Us dogs was listening to the boys talk. A Stray Boy, by which I mean one not claimed or looked out for or owned by any dog, says to Freckles Watson, who is my boy:

'What breed would you call that dog of yours, Freck?'

I pricked up my ears at that. I cannot say that I had ever set great store by breeds up to the time that I found out I was an aristocrat myself, believing, as Bill Patterson, a human and the town drunkard, used to say when intoxicated, that often an honest heart beats beneath the outcast's ragged coat.

'Spot ain't any *one* particular breed', says Freckles. 'He's considerably mixed.'

'He's a mongrel', says Squint Thompson, who is Jack Thompson's boy.

'He ain't', says Freckles, so huffy that I saw a mongrel must be some sort of disgrace. 'You're a link, link liar, and so's your Aunt Mariar', says Freckles.

I thought there might be a fight then, but it was too hot for any enjoyment in a fight, I guess, for Squint let it pass, only saying, 'I ain't got any Aunt Mariar, and you're another.'

'A dog', chips in the Stray Boy, 'has either got to be a thoroughbred or a mongrel. He's either an aristocrat or else he's a common dog.'

'Spot ain't any common dog', says Freckles, sticking up for me. 'He can lick any dog in town within five pounds of his weight.'

'He's got some spaniel in him', says the Stray Boy.

'His nose is pointed like a hound's nose', says Squint Thompson.

'Well,' says Freckles, 'neither one of them kind of dogs is a common dog.'

'Spot has got some bulldog blood in him, too', says Tom Mulligan, an Irish boy owned by a dog by the name of Mutt Mulligan. 'Did you ever notice how Spot will hang on so you can't pry him loose, when he gets into a fight?'

'That proves he is an aristocrat kind of dog', says Freckles.

'There's some bird dog blood in Spot', says the Stray Boy, sizing me up careful.

'He's got some collie in him, too', says Squint Thompson. 'His voice sounds just like a collie's when he barks.'

'But his tail is more like a coach dog's tail', says Tom Mulligan.

'His hair ain't though', says the Stray Boy. 'Some of his hair is like a setter's.'

'His teeth are like a mastiff's', says Mutt Mulligan's boy Tom. And they went on like that; I never knew before there were so many different kinds of thoroughbred dog. Finally Freckles says:

'Yes, he's got all them different kinds of thoroughbred blood in him, and he's got other kinds you ain't mentioned and that you ain't slick enough to see. You may think you're running him down, but what you say just *proves* he ain't a common dog.'

I was glad to hear that. It was beginning to look to me that they had a pretty good case for me being a mongrel.

'How does it prove it?' asked the Stray Boy.

'Well,' says Freckles, 'you know who the King of Germany is, don't you?'

They said they'd heard of him from time to time.

'Well,' says Freckles, 'if you were a relation of the King of Germany you'd be a member of the German royal family. You fellows may not know that, but you would. You'd be a swell, a regular high-mucky-muck.'

They said they guessed they would.

'Now, then,' says Freckles, 'if you were a relation to the King of Switzerland, too, you'd be just *twice* as swell, wouldn't you, as if you were only related to one royal family? Plenty of people are related to just *one* royal family.'

Tom Mulligan butts in and says that way back, in the early days, his folks was the Kings of Ireland; but no one pays any attention.

'Suppose, then, you're a cousin of the Queen of England into the bargain and your grand-dad was King of Scotland, and the Prince of Wales and the Emperor of France and the Sultan of Russia and the rest of those royalties were relations of yours, wouldn't all that royal blood make you *twenty times* as much of a high-mucky-muck as if you had just *one* measly little old king for a relation?'

The boys had to admit that it would.

'You wouldn't call a fellow with all that royal blood in him a *mongrel*, would you?' says Freckles. 'You bet your sweet life you wouldn't! A fellow like that is darned near on the level with a congressman or a vice-president. Whenever he travels around in the old country they turn out the brass band; and the firemen and the Knights of Pythias and the Modern Wood-men parade, and the mayor makes a speech, and there's a picnic and firecrackers, and he gets blamed near anything he wants. People kow-tow to him, just like they do to a swell left-handed pitcher or a champion prizefighter. If you went over to the old country and called a fellow like that a mongrel, and it got out on you, you would be sent to jail for it.'

Tom Mulligan says yes, that is so; his grand-dad came to this country through getting into some kind of trouble about the King of England, and the King of England ain't anywhere near as swell as the fellow Freckles described, nor near so royal, neither.

'Well, then,' says Freckles, 'it's the same way with my dog, Spot, here. *Any* dog can be full of just *one* kind of thorough-bred blood. That's nothing! But Spot here has got more different kinds of thoroughbred blood in him than any dog you ever saw. By your own say-so he has. He's got *all* kinds of thoroughbred blood in him. If there's any kind he ain't got, you just name it, will you?'

'He ain't got any Great Dane in him', yells the Stray Boy, hating to buckle under.

'You're a liar, he has, too', says Freckles.

The Stray Boy backed it, and there was a fight. All us dogs and boys gathered around in a ring to watch it, and I was more anxious than anybody else. For the way that fight went, it was easy to see, would decide what I was.

Well, Freckles licked that Stray Boy, and rubbed his nose in the mud, and that's how I came to be an aristocrat.

Being an aristocrat may sound easy. And it may look easy to outsiders. And it may really be easy for them that are used to it. But it wasn't easy for *me*. It came on me suddenly, the

L

knowledge that I was one, and without warning. I didn't have any time to practise up being one. One minute I wasn't one, and the next minute I was; and while, of course, I felt important over it, there were spells when I would get kind of discouraged, too, and wish I could go back to being a common dog again. I kept expecting my tastes and habits to change. I watched and waited for them to. But they didn't. No change at all set in on me. But I had to pretend I was changed. Then I would get tired of pretending and be downhearted about the whole thing, and say to myself, 'There has been a mistake. I am *not* an aristocrat after all.'

I might have gone along like that for a long time, partly in joy over my noble birth, and partly in doubt, without ever being certain, if it had not been for a happening which showed, as Freckles said, that blood will tell.

It happened the day Wilson's World's Greatest One Ring Circus and Menagerie came to our town. Freckles and me, and all the other dogs and boys, and a good many humans, too, followed the street parade around through town and back to the circus lot. Many went in, and the ones that didn't have any money hung around outside a while and explained to each other they were going at night, because a circus is more fun at night anyhow. Freckles didn't have any money, but his dad was going to take him that night, so when the parade was over him and me went back to his dad's drug store on Main Street, and I crawled under the soda water counter to take a nap.

Freckles's dad, that everyone calls Doc Watson, is a pretty good fellow for a human, and he doesn't mind you hanging around the store if you don't drag bones in or scratch too many fleas off. So I'm there considerable in right hot weather. Under the soda water counter is the coolest place for a dog in the whole town. There's a zinc tub under there always full of water, where Doc washes the soda water glasses, and there's always considerable water slopped on to the floor. It's damp and dark there always. Outdoors it may be so hot in the sun that your tongue hangs out of you so far you tangle your feet in it, but in under there you can lie comfortable and snooze, and when you wake up and want a drink there's the tub with the glasses in it. And flies don't bother you because they stay on top of the counter where soda water has been spilled.

    *   *   *   *

Circus day was a hot one, and I must have drowsed off pretty quick after lying down. I don't know how long I slept, but when I waked up it was with a start, for something important was going on outside in Main Street. I could hear people screaming and swearing and running along the wooden side-walk, and horses whinnying, and dogs barking, and old Tom Cramp, the city marshal, was yelling out that he was an officer of the law, and the steam whistle on the flour mill was blowing. And it all seemed to be right in front of our store. I was think-ing I'd better go out and see about it, when the screen doors crashed like a runaway horse had come through them, and the next minute a big yellow dog was back of the counter, trying to scrouch down and scrooge under it like he was scared and was hiding. He backed me into the corner without seeing me or knowing I was there, and like to have squashed me.

No dog—and it never struck me that maybe this wasn't a dog —no dog can just calmly sit down on me like that when I'm waking up from a nap, and get away with it, no matter *how* big he is, and in spite of the darkness under there I could see and feel that this was the biggest dog in the world. I had been dreaming I was in a fight, anyhow, when he crowded in there with his hindquarters on top of me, and I bit him on the hind leg.

When I bit him he let out a noise like a threshing machine starting up. It wasn't a bark. Nothing but the end of the world coming could bark like that. It was a noise more like I heard one time when the boys dared Freckles to lie down between the cattle guards on the railroad track and let a train run over him about a foot above his head, and I laid down there with him and it nearly deafened both of us. When he let out that noise I says to myself, 'Great guns! What kind of a dog have I bit?'

And as he made that noise he jumped, and over went the counter, marble top and all, with a smash, and jam into the show window he went, with his tail swinging, and me right after him, practically on top of him. It wasn't that I exactly intended to chase him, you understand, but I was rattled on account of that awful noise he had let out, and I wanted to get away from there, and I went the same way he did. So when he bulged through the window glass on to the street I bulged right after him, and as he hit the sidewalk I bit him again. The first time I bit him because I was sore, but the second time I bit him because I was so nervous I didn't know what I was doing, hardly. And at the second bite, without even looking behind him, he jumped clean over the hitch rack and a team of horses in front of the store and landed right in the middle of the road with his tail between his legs.

And then I realized for the first time he wasn't a dog at all. He was the circus lion.

Mind you, I'm not saying that I would have bit him at all if I'd a-known at the start he was a lion.

And I ain't saying I *wouldn't* 'a' bit him, either.

But actions speak louder than words, and records are records, and you can't go back on them, and the fact is I *did* bite him. I bit him twice.

And that second bite, when we came bulging through the window together, the whole town saw. It was getting up telephone poles, and looking out of second-story windows, and crawling under the sidewalks and into cellars, and trying to hide behind the town pump; but no matter where it was trying to get to, it had one eye on that lion, and it saw me chasing him out of that store. I don't say I would have chased him if he hadn't been just ahead of me, anyhow, and I don't say I wouldn't have chased him, but the facts are I *did* chase him.

The lion was just as scared as the town—and the town was so scared it didn't know the lion was scared at all—and when his trainer got hold of him in the road he was tickled to death to be led back to his cage, and he lay down in the far corner of it, away from the people, and trembled till he shook the wagon it was on.

But if there were any further doubts in any quarter about me being an aristocrat, the way I bit and chased that lion settled 'em forever. That night Freckles and Doc went to the circus, and I marched in along with them. And every kid in town, as they saw Freckles and me marching in, says:

'There goes the dog that licked the lion!'

And Freckles, every time anyone congratulated him on being the boy that belonged to that kind of a dog, would say:

'Blood will tell! Spot's an aristocrat, he is.'

And him and me and Doc Watson, his dad, stopped in front of the lion's cage that night and took a good long look at him.

He was a kind of an old moth-eaten lion, but he was a lion all right, and he looked mighty big in there. He looked so big that all my doubts come back on me, and I says to myself: 'Honest, now, if I'd *a-known* he was a lion, and that *big* a lion, when I bit him, *would* I have bit him, or would I not?'

But just then Freckles reached down and patted me on the head and said: 'You wasn't afraid of him, was you, old Spot! Yes, sir, blood will tell!'

The Black Godmother

JOHN GALSWORTHY

SITTING out on the lawn at tea with our friend and his retriever, we had been discussing those massacres of the helpless which had of late occurred, and wondering that they should have been committed by soldiery of so civilized a State, when in a momentary pause of our astonishment, our friend, who had been listening in silence, crumpling the drooping soft ear of his dog, looked up and said: 'The cause of atrocities is Fear. Fear's at the back of all crimes, and most follies.'

Knowing that his philosophical statements were always the result of concrete instance, and that he would not tell us what that instance was if we asked him—such being his nature—we were careful not to agree.

He gave us a look out of those eyes of his, so like the eyes of a mild eagle, and said abruptly: 'What do you say to this, then? . . . I was out in the dog-days last year with this fellow of mine, looking for Osmunda, and stayed some days in a village—never mind the name. Coming back one evening from my tramp, I saw some boys stoning a mealy-coloured dog. I went up and told the young devils to stop it. They looked at me in the injured sort of way that boys do, and one of them called out,

'It's mad guv'nor!' 'Nonsense!' I said. 'Get off with you!'
They took to their heels and the dog followed me. It was a
young leggy, mild-looking mongrel, cross—I should say—
between a brown retriever and an Irish terrier. There was froth
about its lips, and its eyes were watery; it looked indeed as if it
might be in distemper. I was afraid of infection for this fellow
of mine, and whenever it came too close shooed it away, till at
last it slunk off altogether. Well, about nine o'clock, when I was
settling down to write by the open window of my sitting-room
—still daylight, and very quiet and warm—there began that
most maddening sound, the barking of an unhappy dog. I
could do nothing with that continual 'Yap—yap!' going on;
and as it was too hot to shut the window, I went out to see if I
could stop it. The men were all at the pub, and the women just
finished with their gossip; there was no sound at all but the
continual barking of this dog, somewhere away out in the fields.
I travelled by ear across three meadows, till I came on a haystack by a pool of water. There was the dog sure enough—the
same mealy-coloured mongrel, tied to a stake, yapping, and
making frantic little runs on a bit of rusty chain; whirling
round and round the stake, then standing quite still, shivering.
I went up and spoke to it, but it backed into the haystack, and
there it stayed shrinking away from me, with its tongue hanging
out. It had been heavily struck by something on the head; the
cheek was cut, one eye half-closed, and an ear badly swollen. I
tried to get hold of it, but the poor thing was beside itself with
fear. It snapped and flew round so that I had to give it up, and
sit down with this fellow here beside me, to try and quiet it—a
strange dog, you know, will generally form his estimate of you
from the way it sees you treat another dog. I had to sit there
quite half an hour before it would let me go up to it, pull the
stake out, and lead it away. The poor beast, though it was so
feeble from the blows it had received, was still half frantic, and
I didn't dare touch it; and all the time I took good care that
this fellow here didn't come too near. Then came the question
what was to be done. There was no vet, of course, and I'd no
place to put it except my sitting-room, which didn't belong to
me. But looking at its battered head, and its half-mad eyes, I
thought: 'No trusting you with these bumpkins; you'll have to
come in here for the night!' Well, I got it in, and heaped two
or three of those hairy little red rugs landladies are so fond of,

up in a corner, and got it on to them, and put down my bread and milk. But it wouldn't eat—sense of proportion all gone, you see, fairly destroyed with terror. It lay there moaning, and every now and then it raised its head with a 'yap' of sheer fright, dreadful to hear, and bit the air, as if its enemies were on it again; and this fellow of mine lay in the opposite corner, with his head on his paw, full of dark thoughts. I sat up for a long time watching that poor beast, sick enough, and wondering how it had come to be stoned and kicked and battered into this state; and next day I made it my business to find out.' Our friend paused, scanned us a little angrily, and then went on: 'It had made its first appearance, it seems, following a bicyclist. There are some men, you know—save the mark —who, when their beasts get ill or too expensive, jump on their bicycles and take them for a quick run, taking care never to look behind them. When they get back home they say: "Hallo! where's Fido?" And there's an end! Well, this poor puppy gave up just as it got to our village; and, roaming about in search of water, attached itself to a farm labourer. The man —with excellent intentions, as he told me, himself—tried to take hold of it, but too abruptly, so that the startled puppy snapped at him. Whereon he kicked it for a dangerous cur, and it went drifting back towards the village, and fell in with the boys coming home from school. It thought no doubt that they were going to kick it too, and nipped one of them, who took it by the collar. Thereupon they hullabalooed and stoned it down the road to where I found them. Then I put in my little bit of torture, and drove it away, through fear of infection to my own dog. After that it seems to have fallen in with a man who told me: "Well, you see, he came sneakin' round my house, with the children playin', and snapped at them when they went to stroke him, so that they came running in to their mother, an' she called to me in a fine takin' about a mad dog. I ran out with a shovel and gave 'im one, and drove him out. I'm sorry if he wasn't mad, he looked it right enough; you can't be too careful with strange dogs." Its next acquaintance was an old stone-breaker, a very decent sort. "Well! you see," the old man explained to me, "the dog came smellin' round my stones, an' it wouldn' come near, an' it wouldn' go away; it was all froth and blood about the jaw, and its eyes glarin' green at me. I thought to meself, bein' the dog-days—I don't like the look o' you, you look funny! So I took a stone, an' got it here, just on the ear; an' it fell over. And I thought to meself: Well you've got to finish it, or it'll go bitin' somebody, for sure! But when I come to it with my hammer, the dog it got up—an' you know how it is when there's somethin' you've 'alf killed, and you feel sorry, and yet you feel you must finish it, and' you hit at it blind, you hit at it agen an' agen. The poor thing, it wriggled and snapped, an' I was terrified it'd bite me, an' some'ow it got away." ' Again our friend paused, and this time we dared not look at him.

'The next hospitality it was shown,' he went on presently, 'was by a farmer, who, seeing it all bloody, drove it off, thinking it had been digging up a lamb that he'd just buried. The poor homeless beast came sneaking back, so he told his men to get rid of it. Well, they got hold of it somehow—there was a hole in its neck that looked as if they'd used a pitchfork—and, mortally afraid of its biting them, but not liking, as they told me, to drown it, for fear the owner might come on them—they got a stake and a chain, and fastened it up, and left it in the water by the haystack, where I found it. I had some conversation with that farmer. "Yes," he said, "but who was to know? I couldn't have my sheep worried. The brute had blood on his muzzle. These curs do a lot of harm when they've once been blooded. You can't run risks." ' Our friend cut viciously at a dandelion with his stick. 'Run risks!' he broke out suddenly: 'That was it—from beginning to end of that poor beast's sufferings, fear, fear, fear! From that fellow on the bicycle, afraid of the worry and expense, as soon as it showed signs of distemper, to the man with the pitchfork—not one of them, I dare say, would have gone out of his way to do it a harm. But they felt fear, and so—by the law of self-preservation, or whatever you like, it all began—till, there the poor thing was, with a battered head and a hole in its neck, ravenous with hunger, and too distraught even to lap my bread and milk. Yes, and there's something uncanny about a suffering animal—we sat watching it, and we were afraid, looking at its eyes and the way it bit the air. Fear! It's the black godmother of all damnable things!'

Our friend bent down, crumpling and crumpling at his dog's ears. We, too, gazed at the ground, thinking of that poor lost puppy, and the horrible inevitability of all that happens, see-

ing men are what they are; thinking of all the foul doings in
the world, whose black godmother is Fear.

'And what became of the poor dog?' one of us asked at last.

'When', said our friend slowly, 'I'd had my fill of watching,
I covered it with a rug; took this fellow away with me, and
went to bed. There was nothing else to do. At dawn I was
wakened by three dreadful cries—not like a dog's at all. I
hurried down. There was the poor beast—wriggled out from
under the rug—stretched on its side, dead. This fellow of mine
had followed me in, and he went and sat down by the body.
When I spoke to him he just looked round and wagged his tail
along the ground, but would not come away; and there he sat
till it was buried, very interested, but not sorry at all.'

Our friend was silent, looking angrily at something in the
distance.

And we, too, were silent, seeing in spirit that vigil of early
morning: The thin, lifeless, sandy-coloured body, stretched on
those red mats; and this black creature—now lying at our feet
—propped on its haunches like the dog in 'The Death of
Procris', patient, curious, ungrieved, staring down at it with his
bright, interested eyes.

A Dog's Ghost

"GEOFF"

SNOW! snow! snow! For the last three days the air had been full of it; and yet, as I stood gazing out of the window, those eternal flakes came whirling in myriads, each one as if in gleeful pursuit of its predecessor. Not a sound broke the stillness outside, and here was I, landed at a small hotel, the only one in the little village of Andover, on the Tobique River, New Brunswick.

My employers had sent me up from St. John, with instructions to go back sixty-five miles from this place to the shanties of a 'jobber', who was getting out logs for us, and report.

'Well, mister,' said a voice behind me, which I recognized as that of mine host, 'there ain't much chance of further progress. Seems to me we're agoing to have a fall like that of '54, when the snow was thirteen feet deep on the level. A terrible place for blizzards this 'ere.'

And off he went, muttering away to himself and trying to get a puff or two of smoke from a black, played-out, old briar-pipe, which certainly for the last three days, as far as my knowledge went, had never left his lips, except at meal-times, and then only for a short interval.

Thoroughly disgusted at my delay, I turned away from the

171

window and sought consolation, after my host's lead, in the soothing effects of tobacco-smoke.

After dinner, things looked a bit brighter. The snow had nearly ceased falling, and far away in the north-west a patch of blue sky had made its appearance. The wind had sprung up and was momentarily increasing. The night turned out bitterly cold, with a bright moon, and the wind fell almost as quickly as it had risen.

The next morning I woke up with the sun streaming into my bedroom, and the temperature of the apartment about that of a refrigerator. I was soon undergoing the process of thawing out before the large dining-room stove, enjoying its cheerful influence, as the fire roared and crackled, and shed a ruddy glow from the many cracks in its ancient sides.

'Well,' said I to my host, 'how am I to get on now?'

'Must wait till the roads are broken', he replied.

'Can't!' I cried. But he only shrugged his shoulders.

Ten o'clock found me all ready for a start. After walking all day long, just stopping at a farm-house for a meal, I was pushing forward, thoroughly fagged out by such unusual exertion and exercise, and as far as I could judge from the description given me of the road, I judged that I was about three miles from my destination for the night. It was about eight o'clock, and the moon pierced through the shade of spruce trees that lined each side of the road, filling the path before me with shadows varied and grotesque. The wind, which had sprung up into a gentle breeze, sighed sadly through the trees, coming and going in a fitful manner. No sound but this broke the stillness; indeed so still was it that the creaking and soft 'whish' of my snow-shoes, slowly dragged along by wearied feet, seemed to be the echo of following footsteps, and, involuntarily, with suspicious eye, I would look over my shoulder, expecting to see, I knew not what. Only those who have experienced it can know the utter loneliness of being by one's self in a Canadian forest on a winter's night.

I tried whistling to throw off my nervousness, but to no effect. The whistle, through want of breath from exertion, ended in a nearly soundless gasp. And this sound again, although I knew it was caused by myself, seemed to come from a distance, and brought with it a suggestion of wolves.

Suddenly there came the short, sharp bark of a dog.

In an instant all my fears vanished, and with renewed energy I pushed forward. Ahead was a clearing, and one of those quaint and very old stone houses—probably built by some of the first settlers.

The house stood back from the road, in an open space of some few acres, backed by the dark dismal wood and a snake-fence.

Ahead of me on the road I distinguished clearly the figure of a dog, evidently the author of the bark I had heard. His long, white hair gleamed in the moonbeams like silver. I can yet see in my imagination the bright, phosphorescent-like light of his eyes as they turned towards me.

There was no light from the house, and, as I approached, the dog retreated over the snake-fence, taking up his stand on the cottage doorstep.

As I came nearer my spirits once more dropped to zero. The place was falling to pieces and evidently devoid of occupants. The dog stood in the doorway. I whistled to him and used all the usual terms of endearment to attract him to my side, but he made no advances, only standing there monotonously wagging his bushy tail, and every now and then giving tongue to another of those short, sharp barks which had at first attracted my attention. I left him, disgusted at his want of manners toward strangers, and pushed on discouraged. I looked back over my shoulder once or twice to see if he was following, but there was no evidence of his appearance.

At last lights gleamed out of the darkness ahead, and I emerged from the gloom of the woods into a large clearing. There stood a farm-house, hazy in the moonlight, with its long array of barns, stables, etc., the smoke lazily curling up from its chimney into the cold, clear sky, and the ruddy light from its window speaking of warmth and comfort within. It was not long before I was feasting upon a substantial supper.

My host, a tall man of herculean build, with sandy hair, long beard, and keen blue eyes, showed Scotch extraction in his high cheek-bones and broad accent. He sat over by the stove, contemplatively mending a piece of harness, and puffing away at a short clay pipe.

I found him a most agreeable companion, modest in his opinions, well read, and of an inquiring turn of mind. We discussed the lumbering prospects, the farming resources of that part of the country, etc., etc. Then, at last, our conversation drifted on to the subject of my day's walk, and incidently I mentioned the old, ruined house, and the meeting with that unfriendly Pomeranian dog.

I noticed his face grew more serious, and his answers to my inquiries haphazard and hardly to the point.

'That was no dog you saw', he said.

'What!' said I, 'no dog? Why, man, you must be mistaken. I saw him as distinctly as I now see you!'

He only shook his head slowly.

'It was a dog once,' he said, 'ten years ago, but it's the ghost of a dog now.'

Could anything be more preposterous—the ghost of a dog! Who ever heard of such a thing, thought I; and yet, in a moment flashed across my mind's eye the appearance of that animal, as he stood there on the dismantled doorstep of that lonely building, the moon pouring its rays down upon his long, white coat, and then, those uncanny phosphorescent, piercing eyes staring through his tangled mane.

'Yes,' my host continued, 'that was a dog ten years ago, but he died then, and he's a ghost now. Ah, there is a queer story in connection with that ghost dog, and if you'd like to hear it I'll tell it to you. Mind, I don't expect you to believe it; few do, but I know it to be true. S'pose you don't believe in ghosts? After hearing my story you shall judge for yourself whether that was a ghost dog or not.'

After this introduction he related the following:

Some fifteen years ago—I am thirty-five now—an aunt of mine who owned this property, died, leaving it to me. I then came up here for the first time to look over the place, and although it had been much neglected, it had the making of a snug little property, the land being first-rate. I determined to locate, and with a younger brother of mine came up here to live. In those days the ruined house you passed tonight was owned and inhabited by an old man named James Meikle.

He had been there since the earliest remembrances of any one living on the Tobique, and had owned a considerable amount of property round and about. This property by degrees he sold, but what became of the money got by these sales no one knew; he never seemed to go down to Andover, our nearest village, the only place from which he could send a deposit down to the bank, and he got the reputation of having fabulous wealth hidden away in that old house.

Certainly he could not spend much on himself, for he was always in rags, picking up any old thrown-off scraps of clothing he could find, and patching these into garments for himself as best he could. Then, as for food, old Meikle grew a few vegetables on that small patch of ground in front of his house, and these, together with what he could beg, borrow or steal from his neighbours, formed his subsistence.

I soon got to know the old chap, but could never get any conversation out of him more than a good-morning, so that I remained as much in ignorance about the man and his position as anyone else. No one, to my knowledge, had ever been in his cottage; he always scrupulously barred the door against all visitors. In those days he owned that white dog you saw tonight, a surly sort of animal enough, always ready to sneak up behind you, when you were passing and not on the lookout, grabbing the unwary by the leg, after the manner of such curs.

Ten years back the dog died; whether he was killed or not on account of these little civilities and habits of snapping, I can't say, but certain it is that the old man took the loss of his beast very much to heart. I saw him myself, happening to pass at the time, burying the poor remains beneath that spruce tree on the right of the house, with many tears and lamentations.

After this old Meikle kept more to himself than ever. Sometimes a month at a time would elapse between the intervals of my meeting him, though I used to pass his house almost every day.

So two years rolled by, the old man still keeping his seclusion, but in other respects, as an occasional glimpse of him told me, not materially changing in appearance. A dirtier old 'coon' I never saw in my life. His face, covered for the most part by a grizzled and matted beard, was almost as black as an Indian's and his whole appearance utterly neglected and forlorn.

One night, about eight years ago, I was returning from Andover, having been down to sell some hay. It was winter, and the roads in perfect condition. The moon shone bright, and not a breath of air stirred the frosty atmosphere. The horses, knowing they were near home, got along at a splendid pace, and the sleigh, lightened of its morning's load, simply flew over the road's frozen surface. I was all alone, heartily tired and hungry after my long drive. I consoled myself with thoughts of the cosy supper awaiting me beside a warm stove. Mary—that's my wife's name—and I had only been married two months. Just as we came out of the woods into Meikle's clearance, and were passing his old house, what was my surprise to see a white Pomeranian dog bound over the snake-fence and rush to the heads of my team, jumping up and barking furiously, as if in an attempt to stop them. The dog was an exact double of that formerly owned by Miekle, which as I told you had been killed two years before. I thought it very strange at the moment, but considered that the old man must have got another of the same breed.

The horses kept on trotting as fast as ever, being accustomed to dogs, and pawing at this one with their front hoofs as they stepped out.

At last, seeing, I suppose, that it was hopeless to try and stop us in this way, the animal came around to the side of the sleigh, leaping up and still continuing to bark, looking into my face with flashing intelligent eyes, and saying as plainly as a dog could say, that he had some news to impart.

I thought it singular and pulled up for a moment. As soon as the horses came to a stand he ceased barking, trotted a few yards back down the road, wagging his tail, then stopping, looking around as if expecting me to follow him. I have always had a great belief in the sagacity of animals, dogs in particular, and this chap showed so plainly that he wanted me to return the way I had come. I determined to indulge him out of mere curiosity to see what he was up to. So, turning the horses, I drove down towards old Meikle's place. The dog trotting on ahead seemed perfectly satisfied now, wagging his tail vigorously, and looking around every now and again as if to make certain that we were following.

When once more in the clearance and not more than fifteen yards from the cottage, my canine guide turned sharp to right, bounded over the snake-fence before the house and—completely disappeared.

I pulled up sharply, looking around in vain for the animal; he was nowhere to be seen. How he could so mysteriously have vanished from sight was altogether beyond my comprehension.

I got down and carefully examined the snow all around the place, but not a track could I discover on its light surface.

It was certainly very curious, and I must confess that I felt more than startled, if not actually afraid. The night, as I said, was perfectly calm, the only sound that disturbed its stillness was the panting of my tired horses and the throbbing of my own heart. Try as I might I could not stop its fast beating, nor conceal from myself the fact that I was at least very much startled. No light shone out from the cottage, and I concluded old Meikle must be in bed, and yet, another strange thing that struck me was that no smoke curled up from the rickety old chimney.

Could Meikle be away? I certainly had not seen him for over a month, but as I said just now, that was nothing unusual.

I shouted his name at the top of my voice. No response, only the sound of my own re-echoed through the woods and died away softly in the distance. Determining to return next day and find out both as to the old man and dog, I got into the sleigh and turned my horses' heads towards home. Hardly had they turned when the most anguished howl I ever heard in my life arose from the cottage, and echoing through the woods gradually died away in the distance, ending in a wail of abject misery.

The horses heard it, too, and, terrified out of their lives, plunged forward and bolted, never stopping until they had reached the door of their stables.

Never, as long as I live, shall I forget that furious gallop through the shadows of the woods. Thoroughly unnerved I attended to the wants of the horses, putting them into their stable and rubbing them down, endeavouring to the best of my ability to reassure them. Then, having given the beasts their supper, and seen that all was snug for the night, I barred the door and went into the house. My wife noticed my pale face and disturbed manner, but I thought it better not to tell her what had occurred till I had to some extent cleared up the mystery of the night.

Next morning the snow was falling gently in large flakes, covering as it were with a veil the landscape around.

My brother was still living with us then, but I had not seen him the night before. He laughed at the whole thing, saying

M

that my nerves were a bit unstrung by the fatigues of the day, and that no doubt old Meikle had a new dog which I had not seen before, and as for the howl, the animal was just begging to be let into the cottage, naturally not wanting to be left out in the cold all night, and the loneliness of the place, together with my nervousness, had made me imagine that this brute's howl was unlike any other dog's. Finally, as to there being no response to my call, old Meikle was in the first place deaf and probably never heard it, and in the second place was of such a kind as totally to disregard it if he had. Then the horses got tired of waiting, bolted—and I imagined the rest.

So my brother Andrew explained it away. But I myself thought otherwise, and at length persuaded him to agree to accompany me to Meikle's place. After breakfast we started on foot, the snow still falling, though lightly, and the day warm with a probability of brighter weather later on, betokened by the broken state of the clouds. A southerly wind blew gently through the woods, murmuring among the branches, the foliage was covered with a soft coating of the clinging snow, and every now and then a bird or a squirrel with sharp little 'chirp' in striking against the boughs would send down a shower of white feathers, leaving the branch trembling and dripping green in the soft light. Andrew chatted away gaily, laughing at what he called my 'vain imaginings' of the night before; but I remained silent, foreboding I knew not what.

At last we arrived, and saw the walls of the building standing out through the snow. We climbed the fence in front, and knee-deep in snow made our way up to the door. Here we knocked loudly, but no answer greeted us from within. We waited, then again and again hammered a summons on the wooden panel, but no one responded.

We tried the latch, but the door was locked. I climbed up to the window-sill and attempted to look in, but a piece of sacking hung on the inside obscured the view, the same with the window on the other side of the door.

At last we gave up our attempts on the front of the house and went around to the back, fully determined to run the risk of forcing an entrance. At the back there was one solitary window, open, and the sacking which covered this moved slowly backwards and forwards, swayed by the light wind. On examination we discovered one pane of glass broken in its frame, and to the jarred fragments still remaining in the putty a small piece of cloth adhered.

Here, then, was our chance of gaining an entrance. I noticed that Andrew rather hung back, and I certainly did not like going in first. For aught we could tell, Meikle inside might take us for robbers, and use his old flint-lock musket. I had sometimes seen him shooting birds around his garden in summer-time.

We listened—not a sound within. At last curiosity overcame prudence, and I drew aside the sacking and looked in. The room was small, faintly lighted, and apparently without the least bit of furniture. Here and there the rough boarding of the floor was pulled up, and a door opposite to the window, closed, evidently led into another apartment. Slowly and cautiously, followed by Andrew, I crept in. Cautiously we picked our way over the gaps in the flooring to the door on the opposite side, and here again paused and listened, but, reassured by the stillness of the farther room, I opened it. At first nothing could be made out, owing to the darkness, but after a time I could see what what might be a bed, a table and a chair. Slowly moving to the window, my foot slipped on something soft and I fell on my hands and knees.

At this moment Andrew tore down the sacking which covered the casement.

A cold, dim light stole in—and I see him now, in my mind's eye, standing there with staring eyes, gazing down at something just behind me. Good God! as I looked around what a sight met my eye. Lying there on the floor at my back was a human form, both arms thrown behind its head, surrounded by a dark pool of blood. Terrified, I rose to my feet, and there I saw the figure once more of that white dog standing in the doorway, as if to cut off our retreat. His eyes, ablaze with that unearthly fire, seemed to pierce my very soul.

Still looking at him, fascinated by those luminous orbs, his form gradually, very gradually, died away from sight, and a blast as of a piercing wind chilled me through and through. Spasmodically I turned my gaze again towards the face of that form on the floor, and recognized the features of old Meikle. A dark stain marked the side of his cheek from the forehead downwards, and now I could distinguish the gleaming blade of an axe, with its long handle upraised, embedded in the skull.

The fingers of his hands were entangled in his blood-matted hair, in a last death agony.

Andrew stood at the window like a statue, his features frozen into an expression of horror. Then with uncertain footsteps I moved towards the door leading out to the road, and finding the key in the lock turned it and threw it open. The familiar sound of my voice seemed once more to awaken my brother to his senses, and with one bound he was by my side, out in the daylight and 'neath the still falling snow.

Both of us were overcome by this awful scene. Certainly a murder had been committed, and we concluded that the best thing to do would be to go straight down to Andover and there report the affair to the authorities. Of course, as we would have to be gone all night, the facts must be concealed from my wife, as she and the servant girl would be alone and terribly frightened at the idea of their close proximity of that scene of blood with its attendant dog spirit. Having so arranged for our future course of action, we were about to start for home, both equally determined not to enter that cottage again on any account, when once more the quietude was broken by that awful howl I had heard the night before. In an instant I was over the fence and by Andrew's side.

The match dropped from his hands, and the pipe from his lips, his feet hardly seemed to touch the ground, as he disappeared up the road into the woods in rapid flight. I can assure you sir, I was not long after him.

The air was full of that terrible cry; and for months afterwards I would wake at night, sit up in bed and listen, imagining that I heard those anguished wails coming again through the stillness.

The rest of my story is soon told. The same day Andrew and myself drove down to Andover, going by a back road five miles out of our way to avoid that cottage, for neither of us would face the possibilities we might encounter in passing it.

The Andover people sent up a couple of constables, and a detective soon put in an appearance from St. John.

They discovered, beyond all question, that the poor old man was murdered—a thing Andrew and I could have told them from the first; but you know what the police are. The whole place had been ransacked, the flooring torn up, hearthstone lifted, and in fact everything turned upside down, in a search for his supposed hidden treasure. The body was buried by the side of the Pomeranian dog, under the spruce tree, and although by means of that piece of cloth which I told you we noticed on the jagged edge of the window-sill, and which the police would never have seen had not Andrew pointed it out to them, a man was traced to Woodstock, yet there all clue was lost, and the perpetrator of this awful deed has never yet been discovered. Nor was there any store of wealth found in the cottage, which was carefully searched, so that if there really had been any, the murderer must have come upon it, and carried off his ill-gotten gains with him.

Thus my host ended his story. 'But', said I, 'did none of the people engaged on the inquiry and around the cottage see anything of that dog?'

'Ah,' he replied hastily, 'I forgot to tell you. When we were burying poor old Meikle's remains, and had lowered the coffin into the grave, filled up the hole with earth and turned away, the burial service being over, it was evening, and six of us were doing the work, suddenly Mr. Sturder, the parson from Andover, happening to look back, said, "Who owns that dog over there?"

'We all turned around, and there sure enough was the white Pomeranian, standing on the freshly turned sods and looking towards us. The phosphorescent, glowing orbs that I so well remember fixed upon our little party—there is no earthly fire with which you can compare that light. And as our gaze was still riveted, dimmer and dimmer grew the brightness of those eyes, and more and more shadowy that white figure till it had totally disappeared. With a shiver we turned aside, and as our little party wound its way through the darkening woods to my house, you may be sure we kept very close together and repeatedly cast anxious glances behind us as I narrated to them the story of my experiences with the dog, hitherto concealed by Andrew and myself, for fear of the ridicule of our hearers. Since then never again, although the dog is often seen by strangers like yourself, and frequently by those living around here, has that agonized howl been heard.

'For my part, I think that the faithful animal, true even after death to its master, having succeeded in bringing to light that awful crime, now rests more content. If the perpetrator of the dark deed shall once again pass by, who can say what may happen?'

And as my host ceased speaking, a silence fell upon us, the old clock still ticked on with its monotonous stroke, and the sleeping infant's regular breathing came soft and hushed to our ears. The red glow from the coals shone out brightly through the stove door, and the lamp after one or two spasmodic flickers of light left us nearly in darkness. We relighted our pipes for a last whiff ere going to bed, our minds too full of that story to speak.

Fox Terrier or Something

BOOTH TARKINGTON

I HAD belonged to one dog, a brave, foolish, witty French gentleman, a black poodle, Gamin, and after an automobile killed him I preferred the loneliness to letting another dog usurp his place. But I was ill, and my nine-year old nephew, who lives across the street, thought I needed a little companion. He brought to my sick-room the largest, dirtiest, malest old tom-cat I had seen in years. 'It's a present for you', he explained. 'I thought you'd like her around while you're feeling bad.'

The cat went under the bed and made loud malignant sounds. 'Did somebody give her to you?' I asked.

'What?'

'Did she belong to you?'

'She was going across our yard a while ago and I just thought she'd make a good present for you, because you're not well. You'll like her. She's a mighty fine cat.'

'Had you ever seen her before she went across your yard a while ago?'

'I *think* so.' He reflected. 'I'm pretty sure I saw her one day, chasin' sparrows in the alley. Well—I just thought I'd give her to you. G'bye!'

He left the door open, and presently the cat went out in a threatening manner. There followed a coloured lady's free, frank shriek from the kitchen, the sound of metal hurtling against plaster, a slam of the back door, language—and silence. My gift was gone.

A week later I was convalescent, able to sit up, and my nephew called, leading a reluctant female dog by a string.

'Nellie told me the cat I gave you ran way', he said. 'So I found this dog for you. He's a mighty good dog.'

'What kind of a dog is it?' I asked. It was the first question anybody would have asked about that dog.

My nephew quoted an undeniable authority, coloured, employed by a relative.

'Earl says he's one of the best dogs he ever saw. Earl says he's almost a fox terrier or something.'

'Was he going across your yard when you found him?'

'No. He was out in the street. But Earl says he's certain he don't belong to anybody.'

I believed Earl to be right about this.

'Earl says this dog's lots of mighty good blood in him', continued my nephew. 'He says he's a young dog, too, and I hope you won't let him run away like you did the cat. I think Tricksie'd be a good name for him. You can train him to do tricks. Earl says he's a pup.'

And that very evening Tricksie proved Earl's eye for age to be accurate. After a hearty dinner in the kitchen he ate another upstairs—one bedroom slipper, parts of a pair of new shoes, and a small section of satin quilt. He was chastised, and after yawning, went to sleep upon the hearth. I perceived that he meant to remain.

The next day he wholly destroyed the pelt of a wildcat that a friend had sent me, and began work on the buttons of a divan. Punishment interested him only temporarily, and, emerging from a brief seclusion, he gallantly attacked a tigerskin. When detected, he had chewed both ears down to the roots and had plaster upon his nose. He looked up waggishly, and was shocked and horrified at the response he got.

A week later he developed the mange, and I sent him to a veterinary surgeon's hospital, where he remained for two months before a complete cure was pronounced. The day he returned he greeted me with an air of preoccupation, went immediately to the cellar, and had five pups.

Four were female, and from the standpoint of a person who likes to put a definite name to things, all were uneugenical. That is, the ruthless spirit who calls a spade a spade would have been put to it by these pups. One looked a little like an Airedale, and one looked a little like a Brazilian ant-eater, but the others were less definite. My nephew named them George, Frank, Alfie, Bob Son of Battle, and Caruso. Tricksie was as proud of them as if they had been real dogs, and although without previous experience, he proved himself to be one of the most capable mothers I have ever seen.

They remained in the cellar until he had weaned them, and then, by means of a sort of lottery, including cash prizes, they were given away. That is to say, not given, precisely. If you took a dog you got something for taking it; otherwise you would not have taken George, Frank, Alfie, Bob Son of Battle, or Caruso.

The coloured man who thus accepted Alfie was in a generous mood; he said, give him a dollar more and get Tricksie cured of the mange again, and he'd take him, too. He offered a good home.

The dollar was hurried to his hand and Tricksie to the veterinarian's hospital. Then I closed the house and went away and stayed six months.

Last week I came home, but I did not spend the first three nights there. A new cook went down into the cellar, returned hastily, vociferated, gave a fine acrobatic performance, and resigned. The cellar was alive. If you looked into it you saw it moving. It didn't matter where you looked, because all of it moved.

Fleas.

They are gone now. But this morning I received a bill for $41.75 from the veterinarian. Part of it was for curing Tricksie of the mange—again—but most of it was for board and lodging 'to date'; so I called up the coloured person whom I had be-dollared to accept him.

'I thought you were going to take that dog as soon as it was cured of the mange.'

'Yessuh. Is 'at dog well *a'ready*? Ain' nobody never *tell* me she's well. I go git 'er, boss. I git 'er nex' week.'

'Why can't you go to-day?'

'Boss, I got a good two-dollar job to-day. 'Cose if you willin' to fix me up so's I could let 'at job *go*—'

. . . When I feel that I am going to be ill again I shall try to get to some other town. There is an affectionate look in my nephew's eye that I do not like.

A Dog's Tale

MARK TWAIN

I

MY father was a St. Bernard, my mother was a collie, but I am a Presbyterian. This is what my mother told me; I do not know these nice distinctions myself. To me they are only fine large words meaning nothing. My mother had a fondness for such; she liked to say them, and see other dogs look surprised and envious, as wondering how she got so much education. But, indeed, it was not real education; it was only show: she got the words by listening in the dining-room and drawing-room when there was company, and by going with children to Sunday-school and listening there; and whenever she heard a large word she said it over to herself many times, and so was able to keep it until there was a dogmatic gathering in the neighbourhood, then she would get it off, and surprise and distress them all, from pocket-pup to mastiff, which rewarded

187

her for all her trouble. If there was a stranger he was nearly sure to be suspicious, and when he got his breath again he would ask her what it meant. And she always told him. He was never expecting this, but thought he would catch her; so when she told him, he was the one that looked ashamed, whereas he had thought it was going to be she. The others were always waiting for this, and glad of it and proud of her, for they knew what was going to happen, because they had had experience.

When she told the meaning of a big word they were all so taken up with admiration that it never occurred to any dog to doubt if it was the right one; and that was natural, because, for one thing, she answered up so promptly that it seemed like a dictionary speaking, and for another thing, where could they find out whether it was right or not? for she was the only cultivated dog there was.

By and by, when I was older, she brought home the word Un-intellectual, one time, and worked it pretty hard all the week at different gatherings, making much unhappiness and despondency; and it was at this time that I noticed that during that week she was asked for the meaning at eight different assemblages, and flashed out a fresh definition every time, which showed me that she had more presence of mind than culture, though I said nothing, of course. She had one word which she always kept on hand, and ready, like a life-preserver, a kind of emergency word to strap on when she was likely to get washed overboard in a sudden way—that was the word Synonymous. When she happened to fetch out a long word which had had its day weeks before and its prepared meanings gone to her dump-pile, if there was a stranger there of course it knocked him groggy for a couple of minutes, then he would come to, and by that time she would be away down the wind on another tack, and not expecting anything; so when he'd hail and ask her to cash in, I (the only dog on the inside of her game) could see her canvas flicker a moment—but only just a moment—then it would belly out taut and full, and she would say, as calm as a summer's day, 'It's synonymous with super-erogation', or some godless long reptile of a word like that, and go placidly about and skim away on the next tack, perfectly comfortable, you know, and leave that stranger looking profane and embarrassed, and the initiated slatting the floor with their tails in unison and their faces transfigured with a holy joy.

And it was the same with phrases. She would drag home a whole phrase, if it had a grand sound, and play it six nights and two matinées, and explain it a new way every time—which she had to, for all she cared for was the phrase; she wasn't interested in what it meant, and knew those dogs hadn't wit enough to catch her anyway. Yes, she was a daisy! She got so she wasn't afraid of anything, she had such confidence in the ignorance of those creatures. She even brought anecdotes that she had heard the family and the dinner guests laugh and shout over; and as a rule she got the nub of one chestnut hitched on to another chestnut, where of course, it didn't fit and hadn't any point; and when she delivered the nub she fell over and rolled on the floor and laughed and barked in the most insane way, while I could see that she was wondering to herself why it didn't seem as funny as it did when she first heard it. But no harm was done; the others rolled and barked too, privately ashamed of themselves for not seeing the point, and never suspecting that the fault was not with them and there wasn't any to see.

You can see by these things that she was of a rather vain and frivolous character; still, she had virtues, and enough to make up, I think. She had a kind heart and gentle ways, and never harboured resentments for injuries done her, but put them easily out of her mind and forgot them; and she taught her children her kindly way, and from her we learned also to be brave and prompt in time of danger, and not to run away, but face the peril that threatened friend or stranger, and help him the best we could without stopping to think what the cost might be to us. And she taught us not by words only, but by example, and that is the best way and the surest and the most lasting. Why, the brave things she did, the splendid things! She was just a soldier; and so modest about it—well, you couldn't help admiring her, and you couldn't help imitating her; not even a King Charles spaniel could remain entirely despicable in her society. So, as you see, there was more to her than her education.

II

When I was well grown at last, I was sold and taken away, and I never saw her again. She was broken-hearted, and so was

I, and we cried; but she comforted me as well as she could, and said we were sent into this world for a wise and good purpose, and must do our duties without repining, take our life as we might find it, live it for the best good of others, and never mind about the results; they were not our affair. She said men who did like this would have a noble and beautiful reward by and by in another world, and although we animals would not go there, to do well and right without reward would give to our brief lives a worthiness and dignity which in itself would be a reward. She had gathered these things from time to time when she had gone to the Sunday-school with the children, and had laid them up in her memory more carefully than she had done with those other words and phrases; and she had studied them deeply, for her good and ours. One may see by this that she had a wise and thoughtful head, for all there was so much lightness and vanity in it.

So we said our farewells, and looked our last upon each other through our tears; and the last thing she said—keeping it for the last to make me remember it the better, I think—was, 'In memory of me, when there is a time of danger to another do not think of yourself, think of your mother, and do as she would do.'

Do you think I could forget that? No.

III

It was such a charming home!—my new one; a fine great house, with pictures, and delicate decorations, and rich furniture, and no gloom anywhere, but all the wilderness of dainty colours lit up with flooding sunshine; and the spacious grounds around it, and the great garden—oh, greensward, and noble trees, and flowers, no end! And I was the same as a member of the family; and they loved me, and petted me, and did not give me a new name, but called me by my old one that was dear to me because my mother had given it me—Aileen Mavourneen. She got it out of a song; and the Grays knew that song, and said it was a beautiful name.

Mrs. Gray was thirty, and so sweet and so lovely, you cannot imagine it; and Sadie was ten, and just like her mother, just a darling slender little copy of her, with auburn tails down her back, and short frocks; and the baby was a year old, and plump and dimpled, and fond of me, and never could get enough of hauling on my tail, and hugging me, and laughing out its innocent happiness; and Mr. Gray was thirty-eight, and tall and slender and handsome, a little bald in front, alert, quick in his movements, businesslike, prompt, decided, unsentimental, and with that kind of trim-chiselled face that just seems to glint and sparkle with frosty intellectuality! He was a renowned scientist. I do not know what the word means, but my mother would know how to use it and get effects. She would know how to depress a rat-terrier with it and make a lap-dog look sorry he came. But that is not the best one; the best one was Laboratory. My mother could organize a Trust on that one that would skin the tax-collars off the whole herd. The Laboratory was not a book, or a picture, or a place to wash your hands in, as the college president's dog said—no, that is the lavatory; the laboratory is quite different, and is filled with jars, and bottles, and electrics, and wires, and strange machines; and every week other scientists came there and sat in the place, and used the machines, and discussed, and made what they called experiments and discoveries; and often I came too, and stood around and listened, and tried to learn, for the sake of my mother, and in loving memory of her, although it was a pain to me, as realizing what she was losing out of her life and I gaining nothing at all; for try as I might, I was never able to make anything out of it all.

Other times I lay on the floor in the mistress's workroom and slept, she gently using me for a footstool, knowing it pleased me, for it was a caress; other times I spent an hour in the nursery, and got well tousled and made happy; other times I watched by the crib there, when the baby was asleep and the nurse out for a few minutes on the baby's affairs; other times I romped and raced through the grounds and the garden with Sadie till we were tired out, then slumbered on the grass in the shade of a tree while she read her book; other times I went visiting among the neighbour dogs—for there were some most pleasant ones not far away, and one very handsome and courteous and graceful one, a curly-haired Irish setter by the name of Robin Adair, who was a Presbyterian like me, and belonged to the Scotch minister.

The servants in our house were all kind to me and were fond

of me, and so, as you see, mine was a pleasant life. There could not be a happier dog than I was, nor a gratefuller one. I will say this for myself, for it is only the truth: I tried in all ways to do well and right, and honour my mother's memory and her teachings, and earn the happiness that had come to me, as best I could.

By and by came my little puppy, and then my cup was full, my happiness was perfect. It was the dearest little waddling thing, and so smooth and soft and velvety, and had such cunning little awkward paws, and such affectionate eyes, and such a sweet and innocent face; and it made me so proud to see how the children and their mother adored it, and fondled it, and exclaimed over every little wonderful thing it did. It did seem to me that life was just too lovely to—

Then came the winter. One day I was standing a watch in the nursery. That is to say, I was asleep on the bed. The baby was asleep in the crib, which was alongside the bed, on the side next the fireplace. It was the kind of crib that has a lofty tent over it made of gauzy stuff that you can see through. The nurse was out, and we two sleepers were alone. A spark from the wood-fire was shot out, and it lit on the slope of the tent. I suppose a quiet interval followed, then a scream from the baby woke me, and there was that tent flaming up toward the ceiling! Before I could think, I sprang to the floor in my fright, and in a second was halfway to the door; but in the next half-second my mother's farewell was sounding in my ears, and I was back on the bed again. I reached my head through the flames and dragged the baby out by the waistband, and tugged it along, and we fell to the floor together in a cloud of smoke; I snatched a new hold, and dragged the screaming little creature along and out at the door and around the bend of the hall, and was still tugging away, all excited and happy and proud, when the master's voice shouted—

'Begone, you cursed beast!' and I jumped to save myself; but he was wonderfully quick, and chased me up, striking furiously at me with his cane, I dodging this way and that, in terror, and at last a strong blow fell upon my left fore leg, which made me shriek and fall, for the moment, helpless; the cane went up for another blow, but never descended, for the nurse's voice rang wildly out, 'The nursery's on fire!' and the master rushed away in that direction, and my other bones were saved.

The pain was cruel, but, no matter. I must not lose any time; he might come back at any moment; so I limped on three legs to the other end of the hall, where there was a dark little stairway leading up into a garret where old boxes and such things were kept, as I had heard say, and where people seldom went. I managed to climb up there, then I searched my way through the dark amongst the piles of things, and hid in the secretest place I could find. It was foolish to be afraid there, yet still I was; so afraid that I held in and hardly even whimpered, though it would have been such a comfort to whimper, because that eases the pain, you know. But I could lick my leg, and that did me some good.

For half an hour there was a commotion downstairs, and shoutings, and rushing footsteps, and then there was quiet again. Quiet for some minutes, and that was grateful to my spirit, for then my fears began to go down; and fears are worse than pains—oh, much worse. Then came a sound that froze me! They were calling me—calling me by name—hunting for me!

It was muffled by distance, but that could not take the terror out of it, and it was the most dreadful sound to me that I had ever heard. It went all about, everywhere, down there: along the halls, through all the rooms, in both stories, and in the basement and the cellar; then outside, and farther and farther away—then back, and all about the house again, and I thought it would never, never stop. But at last it did, hours and hours after the vague twilight of the garret had long ago been blotted out by black darkness.

Then in that blessed stillness my terrors fell little by little away, and I was at peace and slept. It was a good rest I had, but I woke before the twilight had come again. I was feeling fairly comfortable, and I could think out a plan now. I made a very good one; which was to creep down, all the way down the back stairs, and hide behind the cellar door, and slip out and escape when the iceman came at dawn, whilst he was inside filling the refrigerator; then I would hide all day, and start on my journey when night came; my journey to—well, anywhere where they would not know me and betray me to the master.

H

I was feeling almost cheerful now; then suddenly I thought, Why, what would life be without my puppy!

That was despair. There was no plan for me; I saw that; I must stay where I was; stay, and wait, and take what might come—it was not my affair; that was what life is—my mother had said it. Then—well, then the calling began again! All my sorrows came back. I said to myself, the master will never forgive. I did not know what I had done to make him so bitter and so unforgiving, yet I judged it was something a dog could not understand, but which was clear to a man and dreadful.

They called and called—days and nights, it seemed to me. So long that the hunger and thirst near drove me mad, and I recognized that I was getting very weak. When you are this way you sleep a great deal, and I did. Once I woke in an awful fright—it seemed to me that the calling was right there in the garret! And so it was; it was Sadie's voice, and she was crying; my name was falling from her lips all broken, poor thing, and I could not believe my ears for the joy of it when I heard her say,

'Come back to us,—oh, come back to us, and forgive—it is all so sad without our—'

I broke in with *such* a grateful yelp, and the next moment Sadie was plunging and stumbling through the darkness and the lumber and shouting for the family to hear, 'She's found, she's found!'

The days that followed—well, they were wonderful. The mother and Sadie and the servants—why, they just seemed to worship me. They couldn't seem to make me a bed that was fine enough; and as for food, they couldn't be satisfied with anything but game and delicacies that were out of season; and every day the friends and neighbours flocked in to hear about my heroism—that was the name they called it by, and it means agriculture. I remember my mother pulling it on a kennel once, and explaining it that way, but didn't say what agriculture was, except that it was synonymous with intramural incandescence; and a dozen times a day Mrs. Gray and Sadie would tell the tale to newcomers, and say I risked my life to save the baby's, and both of us had burns to prove it, and then the company would pass me around and pet me and exclaim about me, and you could see the pride in the eyes of Sadie and her mother; and when people wanted to know what made me limp, they looked ashamed and changed the subject, and sometimes when people hunted them this way and that way with questions about it, it looked to me as if they were going to cry.

And this was not all the glory; no, the master's friends came, a whole twenty of the most distinguished people, and had me in the laboratory, and discussed me as if I was a kind of discovery; and some of them said it was wonderful in a dumb beast, the finest exhibition of instinct they could call to mind; but the master said, with vehemence, 'It's far above instinct; it's *reason*, and many a man, privileged to be saved and go with you and me to a better world by right of its possession, has less of it than this poor silly quadruped that's foreordained to perish'; and then he laughed, and said, 'Why, look at me—I'm a sarcasm! bless you, with all my grand intelligence, the only thing I inferred was that the dog had gone mad and was destroying the child, whereas but for the beast's intelligence—it's *reason*, I tell you!—the child would have perished!'

They disputed and disputed, and *I* was the very centre and substance of it all, and I wished my mother could know that this grand honour had come to me; it would have made her proud.

Then they discussed optics, as they called it, and whether a certain injury to the brain would produce blindness or not, but they could not agree about it, and said they must test it by experiment by and by; and next they discussed plants, and that interested me, because in the summer Sadie and I had planted seeds—I helped her dig the holes, you know—and after days and days a little shrub or a flower came up there, and it was a wonder how that could happen; but it did, and I wished I would have told those people about it and shown them how much I knew, and been all alive with the subject; but I didn't care for the optics; it was dull, and when they came back to it again it bored me, and I went to sleep.

Pretty soon it was spring, and sunny and pleasant and lovely, and the sweet mother and the children patted me and the puppy good-bye, and went away on a journey and a visit to their kin, and the master wasn't any company for us, but we played together and had good times, and the servants were kind and friendly, so we got along quite happily and counted the days and waited for the family.

And one day those men came again, and said now for the test, and they took the puppy to the laboratory, and I limped three-leggedly along, too, feeling proud, for any attention shown the puppy was a pleasure to me, of course. They discussed and experimented, and then suddenly the puppy shrieked, and they set him on the floor, and he went staggering around, with his head all bloody, and the master clapped his hands and shouted:

'There, I've won—confess it! He's as blind as a bat!'

And they all said,

'It's so—you've proved your theory, and suffering humanity owes you a great debt from henceforth', and they crowded around him, and wrung his hand cordially and thankfully, and praised him.

But I hardly saw or heard these things, for I ran at once to my little darling, and snuggled close to it where it lay, and licked the blood, and it put its head against mine, whimpering softly, and I knew in my heart it was a comfort to it in its pain and trouble to feel its mother's touch, though it could not see me. Then it drooped down, presently, and its little velvet nose rested upon the floor, and it was still, and did not move any more.

Soon the master stopped discussing a moment, and rang in the footman, and said, 'Bury it in the far corner of the garden', and then went on with the discussion, and I trotted after the footman, very happy and grateful, for I knew the puppy was out of its pain now, because it was asleep. We went far down the garden to the farthest end, where the children and the nurse and the puppy and I used to play in the summer in the shade of a great elm and there the footman dug a hole, and I saw he was going to plant the puppy, and I was glad, because it would grow and come up a fine handsome dog, like Robin Adair, and be a beautiful surprise for the family when they came home; so I tried to help him dig, but my lame leg was no good, being stiff, you know, and you have to have two, or it is no use. When the footman had finished and covered little Robin up, he patted my head, and there were tears in his eyes, and he said, 'Poor little doggie, you SAVED *his* child.'

I have watched two whole weeks, and he doesn't come up! This last week a fright has been stealing upon me. I think there is something terrible about this. I do not know what it is, but the fear makes me sick, and I cannot eat, though the servants bring me the best of food; and they pet me so, and even come in the night, and cry, and say, 'Poor doggie—do give it up and come home; *don't* break our hearts!' and all this terrifies me the more, and makes me sure something has happened. And I am so weak; since yesterday I cannot stand on my feet any more. And within this hour the servants, looking toward the sun where it was sinking out of sight and the night chill coming on, said things I could not understand, but they carried something cold to my heart.

'Those poor creatures! They do not suspect. They will come home in the morning, and eagerly ask for the little doggie that did the brave deed, and who of us will be strong enough to say the truth to them: "The humble little friend is gone where go the beasts that perish." '

Don

ZANE GREY

IT has taken me years to realize the greatness of a dog; and often I have told the story of Don—his love of freedom and hatred of men—how I saved his life and how he saved mine—it never was told as I feel it now.

I saw Don first at Flagstaff, Arizona, where arrangements had been made for me to cross the desert with Buffalo Jones and a Mormon caravan en route to Lee's Ferry on the Colorado River. Jones had brought a pack of nondescript dogs. Our purpose was to cross the river and skirt the Vermilion Cliffs, and finally work up through Buckskin Forest to the north rim of the Grand Canyon, where Jones expected to lasso mountain lions and capture them alive. The most important part of our outfit, of course, was the pack of hounds. Never had I seen such a motley assembly of canines. They did not even have names. Jones gave me the privilege of finding names for them.

Among them was a hound that seemed out of place because of his superb proportions, his sleek dark smooth skin, his noble head, and great solemn black eyes. He had extraordinarily

long ears, thick-veined and faintly tinged with brown. Here
was a dog that looked to me like a thoroughbred. My friendly
overtures to him were unnoticed. Jones said he was part bloodhound and had belonged to an old Mexican don in southern
California. So I named him Don.

We were ten days crossing the Painted Desert, and pro-
tracted horseback riding was then so new and hard for me that
I had no enthusiasm left to scrape acquaintance with the dogs.
Still I did not forget and often felt sorry for them as they
limped along, clinking their chains under the wagons. Even
then I divined that horses and dogs were going to play a great
part in my Western experience.

At Lee's Ferry we crossed the Colorado and I was introduced
to the weird and wild canyon country, with its golden-red walls
and purple depths. Here we parted with the caravan and went
on with Jones' rangers, Jim and Emmet, who led our outfit
into such a wonderful region as I had never dreamed of. We
camped several days on the vast range where Jones let his
buffalo herd run wild. One day the Arizonians put me astride a
white mustang that apparently delighted in carrying a tender-
foot. I did not then know what I was soon to learn—that the
buffalo always chased this mustang off the range. When I rode
up on the herd, to my utter amaze and terror they took after
me and—but I am digressing, and this is a dog story.

Once across the river, Jones had unchained the dogs and let
them run on ahead or lag behind. Most of them lagged. Don
for one, however, did not get sore feet. Beyond the buffalo
range we entered the sage, and here Jones began to train the
dogs in earnest. He carried on his saddle an old blunderbuss
of a shotgun, about which I had wondered curiously. I had
supposed he meant to use it to shoot small game.

Moze, our black and white dog, and the ugliest of the lot,
gave chase to a jack rabbit.

'Hyar, you Moze, come back!' bawled Jones in stentorian
tones. But Moze paid no attention. Jones whipped out the old
shotgun and before I could utter a protest he had fired. The
distance was pretty far—seventy yards or more—but Moze
howled piercingly and came sneaking and limping back. It was
remarkable to see him almost crawl to Jones' feet.

'Thar! That'll teach you not to chase rabbits. You're a lion dog!' shouted the old plainsman as if he were talking to a human.

At first I was so astounded and furious that I could not speak. But presently I voiced my feeling.

'Wal, it looks worse than it is', he said, with his keen grey-blue eyes on me. 'I'm usin' fine birdshot an' it can't do any more than sting. You see, I've no time to train these dogs. It's necessary to make them see quick that they're not to trail or chase any varmints but lions.'

There was nothing for me to do but hold my tongue, though my resentment appeared to be shared by Jim and Emmett. They made excuses for the old plainsman. Jim said, 'He shore can make animals do what he wants. But I never seen the dog or hoss that cared two bits for him.'

We rode on through the beautiful purple sageland, gradually up hill, toward a black-fringed horizon that was Buckskin Forest. Jack rabbits, cottontails, coyotes and foxes, prairie dogs and pack rats infested the sage and engaged the attention of our assorted pack of hounds. All the dogs except Don fell victim to Jones' old blunderbuss; and surely stubborn Moze received a second peppering, this time at closer range. I espied drops of blood upon his dirty white skin. After this it relieved me greatly to see that not even Moze transgressed again. Jones' method was cruel, but effective. He had captured and subdued wild animals since his boyhood. In fact, that had been the driving passion of his life, but no sentiment entered into it.

'Reckon Don is too smart to let you ketch him', Jim once remarked to our leader.

'Wal, I don't know', responded Jones, dubiously. 'Mebbe he just wouldn't chase this sage trash. But wait till we jump some deer. Then we'll see. He's got bloodhound in him, and I'll bet he'll run deer. All hounds will, even the best ones trained on bear an' lion.'

Not long after we entered the wonderful pine forest the reckoning of Don came as Jones had predicted. Several deer bounded out of a thicket and crossed ahead of us, soon disappearing in the green blur.

'Ahuh! Now we'll see', ejaculated Jones, deliberately pulling out the old shotgun.

The hounds trotted along beside our horses, unaware of the

danger ahead. Soon we reached the deer tracks. All the hounds showed excitement. Don let out a sharp yelp and shot away like a streak on the trail.

'Don, come hyar!' yelled Jones, at the same time extending his gun. Don gave no sign he had heard. Then Jones pulled the trigger and shot him. I saw the scattering of dust and pine needles all round Don. He doubled up and rolled. I feared he might be badly injured. But he got up and turned back. It seemed strange that he did not howl. Jones drew his plunging horse to a halt and bade us all stop.

'Don, come back hyar', he called in a loud, harsh, commanding voice.

The hound obeyed, not sneakingly or cringingly. He did not put his tail between his legs. But he was frightened and no doubt pretty badly hurt. When he reached us I saw that he was trembling all over and that drops of blood dripped from his long ears. What a sombre sullen gaze in his eyes!

'See hyar,' bellowed Jones, 'I knowed you was a deer chaser. Wal, now you're a lion dog.'

Later that day, when I had recovered sufficiently from my disapproval, I took Jones to task about this matter of shooting the dogs. I wanted to know how he expected the hounds to learn what he required of them.

'Wal, that's easy', he replied curtly. 'When we strike a lion trail I'll put them on it—let them go. They'll soon learn.'

It seemed plausible, but I was so incensed that I doubted the hounds would chase anything; and I resolved that, if Jones shot Don again, I would force the issue and end the hunt unless assured there would be no more such drastic training methods.

Soon after this incident we made camp on the edge of a beautiful glade where a snowbank still lingered and a stream of water trickled down into a green swale. Before we got camp pitched a band of wild horses thudded by, thrilling me deeply. My first sight of wild horses! I knew I should never forget that splendid stallion, the leader, racing on under the trees, looking back at us over his shoulder.

At this camp I renewed my attempts to make friends with Don. He had been chained apart from the other dogs. He ate what I fetched him, but remained aloof. His dignity and distrust were such that I did not risk laying a hand on him then. But I resolved to win him if it were possible. His tragic eyes haunted me. There was a story in them I could not read. He always seemed to be looking afar. On this occasion I came to the conclusion that he hated Jones.

Buckskin Forest was well named. It appeared to be full of deer, the large black-tailed species known as mule deer. This species must be related to the elk. The size and beauty of them, the way they watched with long ears erect and then bounded off as if on springs, never failed to thrill me with delight.

As we travelled on, the forest grew wilder and more beautiful. In the park-like glades a bleached white grass waved in the wind and bluebells smiled wanly. Wild horses outnumbered the deer, and that meant there were some always in sight. A large grey grouse flew up now and then; and most striking of the forest creatures to fascinate me was a magnificent black squirrel, with a long bushy white tail, and tufted ears, and a red stripe down its glossy sides.

We rode for several days through this enchanting wilderness, gradually ascending, and one afternoon we came abruptly to a break in the forest. It was the north rim of the Grand Canyon. My astounded gaze tried to grasp an appalling abyss of purple and gold and red, a chasm too terrible and beautiful to understand all at once. The effect of that moment must have been tremendous, for I have never recovered from it. To this day the thing that fascinates me most is to stand upon a great height— canyon wall, or promontory, or peak—and gaze down into the mysterious colourful depths.

Our destination was Powell's Plateau, an isolated cape jutting out into the canyon void. Jones showed it to me—a distant gold-rimmed black-fringed promontory, seemingly inaccessible and unscalable. The only trail leading to it was a wild-horse hunter's trail, seldom used, exceedingly dangerous. It took us two days over this canyon trail to reach the Saddle— a narrow strip of land dipping down from the plateau and reaching up to the main rim. We camped under a vast looming golden wall, so wonderful that it kept me from sleeping. That night lions visited our camp. The hounds barked for hours. This was the first chance I had to hear Don. What a voice he had! Deep, ringing, wild, like the bay of a wolf!

Next morning we ascended the Saddle, from the notch of

which I looked down into the chasm still asleep in purple shadows; then we climbed a narrow deer trail to the summit of the Plateau. Here indeed was the grand wild isolated spot of my dreams. Indeed I was in an all-satisfying trance of adventure.

I wanted to make camp on the rim but Jones laughed at me. We rode through the level stately forest of pines until we came to a ravine, on the north side of which lay a heavy bank of snow. This was very necessary, for there was no water on the Plateau. Jones rode off to scout while the rest of us pitched camp. Before we had completed our tasks a troop of deer appeared across the ravine, and motionlessly they stood watching us. There were big and little deer, blue-grey in colour, sleek and graceful, so tame that to me it seemed brutal to shoot at them.

Don was the only one of the dogs that espied the deer. He stood up to gaze hard at them, but he did not bark or show any desire to chase them. Yet there seemed to me to be a strange yearning light in his dark eyes. I had never failed to approach Don whenever opportunity afforded, to continue my overtures of friendship. But now, as always, Don turned away from me. He was cold and sombre. I had never seen him wag his tail or whine eagerly, as was common with most hounds.

Jones returned to camp jubilant and excited, as far as it was possible for the old plainsman to be. He had found lion trails and lion tracks, and he predicted a great hunt for us.

The Plateau resembled in shape the ace of clubs. It was perhaps six miles long and three or four wide. The body of it was covered with a heavy growth of pine and the capes that sloped somewhat toward the canyon were thick with sage and cedar. This lower part, with its numerous swales and ravines and gorges, all leading down into the jungle of splintered crags and thicketed slopes of the Grand Canyon, turned out to be a paradise for deer and lion.

We found many lion trails leading down from the cedared broken rim to the slopes of yellow and red. These slopes really constituted a big country, and finally led to the sheer perpendicular precipices, three thousand feet lower.

Deer were numerous and as tame as cattle on a range. They grazed with our horses. Herds of a dozen or more were common. Once we saw a very large band. Down in the sage and under the cedars and in ravines we found many remains of deer. Jones called these lion-kills. And he frankly stated that the number of deer killed yearly upon the Plateau would be incredible to anyone who had not seen the actual signs.

In two days we had three captive lions tied up to pine saplings near camp. They were two year olds. Don and I had treed the first lion; I had taken pictures of Jones lassoing him; I had jumped off a ledge into a cedar to escape another; I had helped Jones hold a third! I had scratches from lion claws on my chaps, and—but I keep forgetting that this is not a story about lions. Always before when I have told it I have slighted Don.

One night, a week or more after we had settled in camp, we sat round a blazing red fire and talked over the hunt of the day. We all had our part to tell. Jones and I had found where a lioness had jumped a deer. He showed me where the lioness had crouched upon a little brushy knoll, and how she had leaped thirty feet to the back of the deer. He showed me the tracks the deer had made—bounding, running, staggering with the lioness upon its back—and where, fully a hundred paces beyond, the big cat had downed its prey and killed it. There had been a fierce struggle. Then the lioness had dragged the carcass down the slope, through the sage, to the cedar tree where her four two year old cubs waited. All that we found of the deer were the ragged hide, some patches of hair, cracked bones, and two long ears. These were still warm.

Eventually we got the hounds on this trail and soon put up the lions. I found a craggy cliff under the rim and sat there watching and listening for hours. Jones rode to and fro above me, and at last dismounted to go down to join the other men. The hounds treed one of the lions. How that wild canyon slope rang with barks and bays and yells! Jones tied up this lion. Then the hounds worked up the ragged slope towards me, much to my gratification and excitement. Somewhere near me the lions had taken to cedars or crags, and I strained my eyes searching for them.

At last I located a lion on top of an isolated crag right beneath me. The hounds, with Don and Ranger leading, had been on the right track. My lusty yells brought the men. Then the lion stood up—a long, slender, yellowish cat—and spat at me. Next it leaped off that crag, fully fifty feet to the slope below, and bounded down, taking the direction from which the men had come. The hounds gave chase, yelping and baying. Jones bawled at them, trying to call them off, for what reason I could not guess. But I was soon to learn. They found the lion Jones had captured and left lying tied under a cedar, and they killed it, then took the trail of the other. They treed it far down in the rough jumble of rocks and cedars.

One by one we had ridden back to camp that night, tired out. Jim was the last in and he told his story last. And what was my amazement and fright to learn that all the three hours I had sat upon the edge of the caverned wall, the lioness had crouched on a bench above me. Jim on his way up had seen her, and then located her tracks in the dust back of my position. When this fact burst upon me I remembered how I had first imagined I heard faint panting breaths near me somewhere. I had been too excited to trust my ears.

'Wal,' said Jones, standing with the palms of his huge hands to the fire, 'we had a poor day. If we had stuck to Don there'd have been a different story. I haven't trusted him. But now I reckon I'll have to. He'll make the greatest lion dog I ever had. Strikes me queer, too, for I never guessed it was in him. He has faults though. He's too fast. He outruns the other hounds, an' he's goin' to be killed because of that. Some day he'll beat the pack to a mean old Tom lion or a lioness with cubs, an' he'll get his everlastin'. Another fault is, he doesn't bark often. That's bad, too. You can't stick to him. He's got a grand bay, shore, but he saves his breath. Don wants to run an' trail an' fight alone. He's got more nerve than any hound I ever trained. He's too good for his own sake—an' it'll be his death.'

Naturally I absorbed all that Buffalo Jones said about dogs, horses, lions, everything pertaining to the West, and I believed it as if it had been gospel. But I observed that the others, especially Jim, did not always agree with our chief in regard to the hounds. A little later, when Jones had left the fire, Jim spoke up with his slow Texas drawl:

'Wal, what does he know about dawgs? I'll tell you right heah, if he hadn't shot Don we'd had the best hound thet ever put his nose to a track. Don is a wild strange hound, shore enough. Mebbe he's like a lone wolf. But it's plain he's been mistreated by men. An' Jones has just made him wuss.'

Emmet inclined to Jim's point of view. And I respected this

giant Mormon who was famous on the desert for his kindness
to men and animals. His ranch at Lee's Ferry was overrun with
dogs, cats, mustangs, burrows, sheep, and tamed wild animals
that he had succoured.

'Yes, Don hates Jones and, I reckon, all of us', said Emmet.
'Don's not old, but he's too old to change. Still, you can never
tell what kindness will do to animals. I'd like to take Don
home with me and see. But Jones is right. That hound will
be killed.'

'Now I wonder why Don doesn't run off from us?' inquired
Jim.

'Perhaps he thinks he'd get shot again', I ventured.

'If he ever runs away it'll not be here in the wilds', replied
Emmet. 'I take Don to be about as smart as any dog ever gets.
And that's pretty close to human intelligence. People have to
live lonely lives with dogs before they understand them. I
reckon I understand Don. He's either loved one master once
and lost him, or else he has always hated all men.'

'Humph! That's shore an idee', ejaculated Jim dubiously.
'Do you think a dog can feel like that?'

'Jim, I once saw a little Indian shepherd dog lie down on its
master's grave and die', returned the Mormon, sonorously.

'Wal, dog-gone me!' exclaimed Jim in mild surprise.

One morning Jim galloped in driving the horses pell-mell
into camp. Any deviation from the Texan's usual leisurely
manner of doing things always brought us up short with keen
expectation.

'Saddle up', called Jim. 'Shore thar's a chase on. I see a big
red lioness up heah. She must have come down out of the tree
whar I hang my meat. Last night I had a haunch of venison.
It's gone. . . . Say, she was a beauty. Red as a red fox.'

In a very few moments we were mounted and riding up the
ravine, with the eager hounds sniffing the air. Always over-
anxious in my excitement, I rode ahead of my comrades. The
hounds trotted with me. The distance to Jim's meat tree was a
short quarter of a mile. I knew well where it was and, as of
course the lion trail would be fresh, I anticipated a fine
opportunity to watch Don. The other hounds had come to
regard him as their leader. When we neared the meat tree,
which was a low-branched oak shaded by thick silver spruce,

Don elevated his nose high in the air. He had caught a scent even at a distance. Jones had said more than once that Don had a wonderful nose. The other hounds, excited by Don, began to whine and yelp and run around with nose to the ground.

I had eyes only for Don. How instinct he was with life and fire! The hair on his neck stood up like bristles. Suddenly he let out a wild bark and bolted. He sped away from the pack and like a flash passed that oak tree, running with his head high. The hounds strung out after him and soon the woods seemed full of a baying chorus.

My horse, Black Bolly, well knew the meaning of that medley and did not need to be urged. He broke into a run and swiftly carried me up out of the hollow and through a brown-aisled pine-scented strip of forest to the canyon.

I rode along the edge of one of the deep indentations on the main rim. The hounds were bawling right under me at the base of a low cliff. They had jumped the lioness. I could not see them, but that was not necessary. They were running fast towards the head of this cove, and I had hard work to hold Black Bolly to a safe gait along that rocky rim. Suddenly she shied, and then reared, so that I fell out of the saddle as much as I dismounted. But I held the bridle, and then jerked my rifle from the saddle sheath. As I ran toward the rim I heard the yells of the men coming up behind. At the same instant I was startled and halted by sight of something red and furry flashing up into a tree right in front of me. It was the red lioness. The dogs had chased her into a pine the middle branches of which were on a level with the rim.

My skin went tight and cold and my heart fluttered. The lioness looked enormous, but that was because she was so close. I could have touched her with a long fishing pole. I stood motionless for an instant, thrilling in every nerve, revelling in the beauty and wildness of that great cat. She did not see me. The hounds below engaged all her attention. But when I let out a yell, which I could not stifle, she jerked spasmodically to face me. Then I froze again. What a tigerish yellow flash of eyes and fangs! She hissed. She could have sprung from the tree to the rim and upon me in two bounds. But she leaped to a ledge below the rim, glided along that and disappeared.

I ran ahead and with haste and violence clambered out upon

a jutting point of the rim, from which I could command the situation. Jones and the others were riding and yelling back where I had left my horse. I called for them to come.

The hounds were baying along the base of the low cliff. No doubt they had seen the lioness leap out of the tree. My eyes roved everywhere. This cove was a shallow V-shaped gorge, a few hundred yards deep and as many across. Its slopes were steep with patches of brush and rock.

All at once my quick eye caught a glimpse of something moving up the opposite slope. It was a long red pantherish shape. The lioness! I yelled with all my might. She ran up the slope and at the base of the low wall she turned to the right. At that moment Jones strode heavily over the rough loose rocks of the promontory toward me.

'Where's the cat?' he boomed, his grey eyes flashing. In a moment more I had pointed her out. 'Ha! I see . . . Don't like that place. The canyon boxes. She can't get out. She'll turn back.'

The old hunter had been quick to grasp what had escaped me. The lioness could not find any break in the wall, and manifestly she would not go down into the gorge. She wheeled back along the base of this yellow cliff. There appeared to be a strip of bare clay or shale rock against which background her red shape stood out clearly. She glided along, slowing her pace, and she turned her gaze across the gorge.

Then Don's deep bay rang out from the slope to our left. He had struck the trail of the lioness. I saw him running down. He leaped in long bounds. The other hounds heard him and broke for the brushy slope. In a moment they had struck the scent of their quarry and given tongue.

As they started down Don burst out of the willow thicket at the bottom of the gorge and bounded up the opposite slope. He was five hundred yards ahead of the pack. He was swiftly climbing. He would run into the lioness.

Jones gripped my arm in his powerful hand.

'Look!' he shouted. 'Look at that fool hound! . . . Runnin' up hill to get to that lioness. She won't run. She's cornered. She'll meet him. She'll kill him. . . . Shoot her! Shoot her!'

I scarcely needed Jones' command to stir me to save Don, but it was certain that the old plainsman's piercing voice made me tremble. I knelt and levelled my rifle. The lioness showed red against the grey—a fine target. She was gliding more and more slowly. She saw or heard Don. The gunsight wavered. I could not hold steady. But I had to hurry. My first bullet struck two yards below the beast, puffing the dust. She kept on. My second bullet hit behind her. Jones was yelling in my ear. I could see Don out of the tail of my eye. . . . Again I shot. Too high! But the lioness jumped and halted. She lashed with her tail. What a wild picture! I strained—clamped every muscle, and pulled trigger. My bullet struck right under the lioness, scattering a great puff of dust and gravel in her face. She bounded ahead a few yards and up into a cedar tree. An instant later Don flashed over the bare spot where she had waited to kill him, and in another his deep bay rang out under the cedar.

'Treed, by gosh!' yelled Jones, joyfully pounding me on the back with his huge fist. 'You saved that fool dog's life. She'd have killed him shore. . . . Wal, the pack will be there pronto, an' all we've got to do is go over an' tie her up. But it was a close shave for Don.'

That night in camp Don was not in the least different from his usual sombre self. He took no note of my proud proprietorship or my hovering near him while he ate the supper I provided, part of which came from my own plate. My interest and sympathy had augmented to love.

Don's attitude toward the captured and chained lions never ceased to be a source of delight and wonder to me. All the other hounds were upset by the presence of the big cats. Moze, Sounder, Tige, Ranger would have fought these collared lions. Not so Don! For him they had ceased to exist. He would walk within ten feet of a hissing lioness without the slightest sign of having seen or heard her. He never joined in the howling chorus of the dogs. He would go to sleep close to where the lions clanked their chains, clawed the trees, whined and spat and squalled.

Several days after that incident of the red lioness we had a long and severe chase through the brushy cedar forest on the left wing of the Plateau. I did well to keep the hounds within earshot. When I arrived at the end of that run I was torn and blackened by the brush, wet with sweat, and hot as fire. Jones, lasso in hand, was walking round a large cedar under which

o

the pack of hounds was clamouring. Jim and Emmet were seated on a stone, wiping their red faces.

'Wal, I'll rope him before he rests up', declared Jones.

'Wait till—I get—my breath', panted Emmet.

'We shore oozed along this mawnin' ', drawled Jim.

Dismounting, I untied my camera from the saddle and then began to peer up into the bushy cedar.

'It's a Tom lion', declared Jones. 'Not very big, but he looks mean. I reckon he'll mess us up some.'

'Haw! Haw!' shouted Jim, sarcastically. The old plainsman's imperturbability sometimes wore on our nerves.

I climbed a cedar next to the one in which the lion had taken refuge. From a topmost fork, swaying to and fro, I stood up to photograph our quarry. He was a good-sized animal, tawny in hue, rather grey of face, and a fierce-looking brute. As the distance between us was not far, my situation was as uncomfortable as thrilling. He snarled at me and spat viciously. I was about to abandon my swinging limb when the lion turned away from me to peer down through the branches.

Jones was climbing into the cedar. Low and deep the lion growled. Jones held in one hand a long pole with a small fork at the end, upon which hung the noose of his lasso. Presently he got far enough up to reach the lion. Usually he climbed close enough to throw the rope, but evidently he regarded this beast as dangerous. He tried to slip the noose over the head of the lion. One sweep of a big paw sent pole and noose flying. Patiently Jones made ready and tried again, with similar result. Many times he tried. His patience and perseverance seemed incredible. One attribute of his great power to capture and train wild animals here asserted itself. Finally the lion grew careless or tired, on which instant Jones slipped the noose over its head.

Drawing the lasso tight, he threw his end over a thick branch and let it trail down to the men below. 'Wait now!' he yelled and quickly backed down out of the cedar. The hounds were leaping eagerly.

'Pull him off that fork an' let him down easy so I can rope one of his paws.'

It turned out, however, that the lion was hard to dislodge. I could see his muscles ridge and bulge. Dead branches cracked, the tree-top waved. Jones began to roar in anger. The men replied with strained hoarse voices. I saw the lion drawn from his perch and, clawing the branches, springing convulsively, he disappeared from my sight.

Then followed a crash. The branch over which Jones was lowering the beast had broken. Wild yells greeted my startled ears and a perfect din of yelps and howls. Pandemonium had broken loose down there. I fell more than I descended from that tree.

As I bounded erect I espied the men scrambling out of the way of a huge furry wheel. Ten hounds and one lion comprised that brown whirling ball. Suddenly out of it a dog came hurtling. He rolled to my feet, staggered up.

It was Don. Blood was streaming from him. Swiftly I dragged him aside, out of harm's way. And I forgot the fight. My hands came away from Don wet and dripping with hot blood. It shocked me. Then I saw that his throat had been terribly torn. I thought his jugular vein had been severed. Don lay down and stretched out. He looked at me with those great sombre eyes. Never would I forget! He was going to die right there before my eyes.

'Oh Don! Don! What can I do?' I cried in horror.

As I sank beside Don one of my hands came in contact with snow. It had snowed that morning and there were still white patches in shady places. Like a flash I ripped off my scarf and bound it round Don's neck. Then I scraped up a double hand-ful of snow and placed that in my bandana handkerchief. This also I bound tightly round his neck. I could do no more. My hope left me then, and I had not the courage to sit there beside him until he died.

All the while I had been aware of a bedlam near at hand. When I looked I saw a spectacle for a hunter. Jones, yelling at the top of his stentorian voice, seized one hound after the other by the hind legs and, jerking him from the lion, threw him down the steep slope. Jim and Emmet were trying to help while at the same time they avoided close quarters with that threshing beast. At last they got the dogs off and the lion stretched out. Jones got up, shaking his shaggy head. Then he espied me and his hard face took on a look of alarm.

'Hyar—you're all—bloody', he panted plaintively, as if I had been exceedingly remiss.

Whereupon I told him briefly about Don. Then Jim and

Emmet approached and we all stood looking down on the quiet dog and the patch of bloody snow.

'Wal, I reckon he's a goner', said Jones, breathing hard. 'Shore I knew he'd get his everlastin'.'

'Looks powerful like the lion has aboot got his too', added Jim.

Emmet knelt by Don and examined the bandage round his neck. 'Bleeding yet', he muttered, thoughtfully. 'You did all that was possible. Too bad! . . . The kindest thing we can do is to leave him here.'

I did not question this but I hated to consent. Still, to move him would only bring on more hæmorrhage and to put him out of his agony would have been impossible for me. Moreover, while there was life there was hope! Scraping up a goodly ball of snow I rolled it close to Don so that he could lick it if he chose. Then I turned aside and could not look again. But I knew that tomorrow or the following day I would find my way back to this wild spot.

The accident to Don and what seemed the inevitable issue weighed heavily upon my mind. Don's eyes haunted me. I very much feared that the hunt had reached an unhappy ending for me. Next day the weather was threatening and, as the hounds were pretty tired, we rested in camp, devoting ourselves to needful tasks. A hundred times I thought of Don, alone out there in the wild brakes. Perhaps merciful death had relieved him of suffering. I would surely find out on the morrow.

But the indefatigable Jones desired to hunt in another direction next day and, as I was by no means sure I could find the place where Don had been left, I had to defer that trip. We had a thrilling hazardous luckless chase, and I for one gave up before it ended.

Weary and dejected I rode back. I could not get Don off my conscience. The pleasant woodland camp did not seem the same place. For the first time the hissing, spitting, chain-clinking, tail-lashing lions caused me irritation and resentment. I would have none of them. What was the capture of a lot of spiteful vicious cats to the life of a noble dog? Slipping my saddle off, I turned Black Bolly loose.

Then I imagined I saw a beautiful black long-eared hound enter the glade. I rubbed my eyes. Indeed there was a dog coming. Don! I shouted my joy and awe. Running like a boy

I knelt by him, saying I knew not what. Don wagged his tail! He licked my hand! These actions seemed as marvellous as his return. He looked sick and weak but he was all right. The handkerchief was gone from his neck but the scarf remained, and it was stuck tight where his throat had been lacerated.

Later, Emmet examined Don and said we had made a mistake about the jugular vein being severed. Don's injury had been serious, however, and without the prompt aid I had so fortunately given he would soon have bled to death. Jones shook his grey old locks and said, 'Reckon Don's time hadn't come. Hope that will teach him sense.' In a couple of days Don had recovered and on the next he was back leading the pack.

A subtle change had come over Don in his relation to me. I did not grasp it so clearly then. Thought and memory afterward brought the realization to me. But there was a light in his eyes for me which had never been there before.

One day Jones and I treed three lions. The largest leaped and ran down into the canyon. The hounds followed. Jones strode after them, leaving me alone with nothing but a camera to keep those two lions up that tree. I had left horse and gun far up the slope. I protested; I yelled after him, 'What'll I do if they start down?'

He turned to gaze up at me. His grim face flashed in the sunlight.

'Grab a club an' chase them back', he replied.

Then I was left alone with two ferocious-looking lions in a piñon tree scarcely thirty feet high. While they heard the baying of the hounds they paid no attention to me, but after that ceased they got ugly. Then I hid behind a bush and barked like a dog. It worked beautifully. The lions grew quiet. I barked and yelped and bayed until I lost my voice. Then they got ugly again! They started down. With stones and clubs I kept them up there, while all the time I was wearing to collapse. When at last I was about to give up in terror and despair I heard Don's bay, faint and far away. The lions had heard it before I had. How they strained! I could see the beating of their hearts through their lean sides. My own heart leaped. Don's bay floated up, wild and mournful. He was coming. Jones had put him on the back trail of the lion that had leaped from the tree.

Deeper and clearer came the bays. How strange that Don should vary from his habit of seldom baying! There was something uncanny in this change. Soon I saw him far down the rocky slope. He was climbing fast. It seemed I had long to wait, yet my fear left me. On and up he came, ringing out that wild bay. It must have curdled the blood of those palpitating lions. It seemed the herald of that bawling pack of hounds.

Don espied me before he reached the piñon in which were the lions. He bounded right past it and up to me with the wildest demeanour. He leaped up and placed his forepaws on my breast. And as I leaned down, excited and amazed, he licked my face. Then he whirled back to the tree, where he stood up and fiercely bayed the lions. While I sank down to rest, overcome, the familiar baying chorus of the hounds floated up from below. As usual they were far behind the fleet Don, but they were coming.

Another day I found myself alone on the edge of a huge cove that opened down into the main canyon. We were always getting lost from one another. And so were the hounds. There were so many lion trails that the pack would split, some going one way, some another, until it appeared each dog finally had a lion to himself.

It was a glorious day. From far below, faint and soft, came the strange roar of the Rio Colorado. I could see it winding, sombre and red, through the sinister chasm. Adventure ceased to exist for me. I was gripped by the grandeur and loveliness, the desolation and loneliness of the supreme spectacle of nature.

Then as I sat there, absorbed and chained, the spell of enchantment was broken by Don. He had come to me. His mouth was covered with froth. I knew what that meant. Rising, I got my canteen from the saddle and poured water into the crown of my sombrero. Don lapped it. As he drank so thirstily I espied a bloody scratch on his nose.

'Aha! A lion has batted you one, this very morning', I cried. 'Don—I fear for you.'

He rested while I once more was lost in contemplation of the glory of the canyon. What significant hours these on the lonely heights! But then I only saw and felt.

Presently I mounted my horse and headed for camp, with Don

trotting behind. When we reached the notch of the cove the hound let out his deep bay and bounded down a break in the low wall. I dismounted and called. Only another deep bay answered me. Don had scented a lion or crossed one's trail. Suddenly several sharp deep yelps came from below, a crashing of brush, a rattling of stones. Don had jumped another lion.

Quickly I threw off sombrero and coat and chaps. I retained my left glove. Then, with camera over my shoulder and revolver in my belt, I plunged down the break in the crag. My boots were heavy soled and studded with hobnails. The weeks on these rocky slopes had trained me to fleetness and sure-footedness. I plunged down the sliding slant of weathered stone, crashed through the brush, dodged under the cedars, leaped from boulder to ledge and down from the ledge to bench. Reaching a dry stream bed, I espied in the sand the tracks of a big lion, and beside them smaller tracks that were Don's. And as I ran I yelled at the top of my lungs, hoping to help Don tree the lion. What I was afraid of was that the beast might wait for Don and kill him.

Such strenuous exertion required a moment's rest now and then, during which I listened for Don. Twice I heard his bay, and the last one sounded as if he treed the lion. Again I took to my plunging, jumping, sliding descent; and I was not long in reaching the bottom of that gorge. Ear and eye had guided me unerringly for I came to an open place near the main jump-off into the canyon, and here I saw a tawny shape in a cedar tree. It belonged to a big Tom lion. He swayed the branch and leaped to a ledge, and from that down to another, and then vanished round a corner of wall.

Don could not follow down those high steps. Neither could I. We worked along the ledge, under cedars, and over huge slabs of rock toward the corner where our quarry had disappeared. We were close to the great abyss. I could almost feel it. Then the glaring light of a void struck my eyes like some tangible thing.

At last I worked out from the shade of rocks and trees and, turning the abrupt jut of wall, I found a few feet of stone ledge between me and the appalling chasm. How blue, how fathomless! Despite my pursuit of a lion I was suddenly shocked into awe and fear.

Then Don returned to me. The hair on his neck was

bristling. He had come from the right, from round the corner of wall where the ledge ran, and where surely the lion had gone. My blood was up and I meant to track that beast to his lair, photograph him if possible, and kill him. So I strode on to the ledge and round the point of wall. Soon I espied huge cat tracks in the dust, close to the base. A well-defined lion trail showed there. And ahead I saw the ledge—widening somewhat and far from level—stretch before me to another corner.

Don acted queerly. He followed me, close at my heels. He whined. He growled. I did not stop to think then what he wanted to do. But it must have been that he wanted to go back. The heat of youth and the wildness of adventure had gripped me and fear and caution were not in me.

Nevertheless my sensibilities were remarkably acute. When Don got in front of me there was something that compelled me to go slowly. Soon, in any event, I should have been forced to that. The ledge narrowed. Then it widened again to a large bench with cavernous walls overhanging it. I passed this safe zone to turn on to a narrowing edge of rock that disappeared round another corner. When I came to this point I must have been possessed, for I flattened myself against the wall and worked round it.

Again the way appeared easier. But what made Don go so cautiously? I heard his growls; still, no longer did I look at him. I felt this pursuit was nearing an end. At the next turn I halted short, suddenly quivering. The ledge ended—and there lay the lion, licking a bloody paw.

Tumultuous indeed were my emotions, yet on that instant I did not seem conscious of fear. Jones had told me never, in close quarters, to take my eyes off a lion. I forgot. In the wild excitement of a chance for an incomparable picture I forgot. A few precious seconds were wasted over the attempt to focus my camera.

Then I heard quick thuds. Don growled. With a start I jerked up to see the lion had leaped or run half the distance. He was coming. His eyes blazed purple fire. They seemed to paralyse me, yet I began to back along the ledge. Whipping out my revolver I tried to aim. The gun wobbled. I dared not risk shooting. If I wounded the lion it was certain he would knock me off that narrow ledge.

So I kept on backing, step by step. Don did likewise. He stayed between me and the lion. Therein lay the greatness of that hound. How easily he could have dodged by me to escape along that ledge! But he did not do it.

A precious opportunity presented when I reached the widest part of the bench. Here I had a chance and I recognized it. Then, when the overhanging wall bumped my shoulder, I realized too late. I had come to the narrowing part of the ledge. Not reason but fright kept me from turning to run. Perhaps that might have been the best way out of the predicament. I backed along the strip of stone that was only a foot wide. A few more blind steps meant death. My nerve was gone. Collapse seemed inevitable. I had a camera in one hand and a revolver in the other.

That purple-eyed beast did not halt. My distorted imagination gave him a thousand shapes and actions. Bitter despairing thoughts flashed through my mind. Jones had said mountain lions were cowards, but not when cornered—never when there was no avenue of escape!

Then Don's haunches backed into my knees. I dared not look down but I felt the hound against me. He was shaking yet he snarled fiercely. The feel of Don there, the sense of his courage caused my cold thick blood to burst into hot gushes. In another second he would be pawed off the ledge or he would grapple with this hissing lion. That meant destruction for both, for they would roll off the ledge.

I had to save Don. That mounting thought was my salvation. Physically, he could not have saved me or himself, but this grand spirit somehow pierced to my manhood.

Leaning against the wall, I lifted the revolver and steadied my arm with my left hand, which still held the camera. I aimed between the purple eyes. That second was an eternity. The gun crashed. The blaze of one of those terrible eyes went out.

Up leapt the lion, beating the wall with heavy thudding paws. Then he seemed to propel himself outward, off the ledge into space—a tawny spread figure that careened majestically over and over, down—down—down to vanish in the blue depths.

Don whined. I stared at the abyss, slowly becoming unlocked from the grip of terror. I staggered a few steps forward to a wider part of the ledge and there I sank down, unable to stand longer. Don crept to me, put his head in my lap.

I listened. I strained my ears. How endlessly long seemed that lion in falling! But all was magnified. At last puffed up a sliding roar, swelling and dying until again the terrific silence of the canyon enfolded me.

Presently Don sat up and gazed into the depths. How strange to see him peer down! Then he turned his sleek dark head to look at me. What did I see through the sombre sadness of his eyes? He whined and licked my hand. It seemed to me Don and I were more than man and dog. He moved away then round the narrow ledge, and I had to summon energy to follow. Shudderingly, I turned my back on that awful chasm and held my breath while I slipped round the perilous place. Don waited there for me, then trotted on. Not until I had got safely off that ledge did I draw a full breath. Then I toiled up the steep rough slope to the rim. Don was waiting beside my horse. Between us we drank the rest of the water in my canteen, and when we reached camp night had fallen. A bright fire and a good supper broke the gloom of my mind. My story held those rugged Westerners spellbound. Don stayed close to me, followed me of his own accord, and slept beside me in my tent.

There came a frosty morning when the sun rose red over the ramparts of coloured rock. We had a lion running before the misty shadows dispersed from the canyon depths.

The hounds chased him through the sage and cedar into the wild brakes of the north wing of the Plateau. This lion must have been a mean old Tom for he did not soon go down the slopes.

The particular section he at last took refuge in was impassable for man. The hounds gave him a gruelling chase, then one by one they crawled up, sore and thirsty. All but Don! He did not come. Jones rolled out his mighty voice, which pealed back in mocking hollow echoes. Don did not come. At noonday Jones and the men left for camp with the hounds.

I remained. I had a vigil there on the lofty rim, alone, where I could peer down the yellow-green slope and beyond to the sinister depths. It was a still day. The silence was overpowering. When Don's haunting bay floated up it shocked me. At long intervals I heard it, fainter and fainter. Then no more!

Still I waited and watched and listened. Afternoon waned. My horse neighed piercingly from the cedars. The sinking sun began to fire the Pink Cliffs of Utah, and then the hundred miles of immense chasm over which my charmed gaze held dominion. How lonely, how terrifying that stupendous rent in the earth! Lion and hound had no fear. But the thinking, feeling man was afraid. What did they mean—this exquisitely hued and monstrous canyon—the setting sun the wildness of a lion, the grand spirit of a dog—and the wondering sadness of a man?

I rode home without Don. Half the night I lay awake waiting, hoping. But he did not return by dawn, nor through that day. He never came back.

Reunion

MAZO DE LA ROCHE

YOUNG Ffolkes sat on the deck of the ocean liner, his travelling rug wrapped neatly about his legs, a freshly lighted cigarette between his lips, and the latest crime novel on his lap. Its title, in snaky black letters on a canary ground, stared up at him: *Twice Murdered*.

But he could not get on with the book. He was too much excited, too much stirred by emotions of exhilaration and regret. He was going back to the place where he had been born and had spent all his life except the past two years, and his spirit strained forward to the old familiar scenes. Yet the two years he had spent in London had been the most full, the most expansive, of any he had known. He had made friends from whom it had been hard to part. He had found in London a new home—the great town had taken her colonial son to her heart with the simplicity of a village.

It was a man's town, he thought, looking back on London; and there he seemed to have reached his full manhood. He felt immeasurably older and more experienced than when he had left Canada. He had been promoted by his bank to a very

good post in their London office. He had done well there, and
now he was being returned to Canada to a still more
responsible post. Pretty fair going, he thought, for a fellow of
thirty.

The deck stewards came along with a trolley laden with cups
of hot bouillon. As the steward gave him his, he remarked
cheerily, 'Well, sir, Canada is preparing a grand welcome for
you. I've never seen finer weather.'

'Glorious', said Ffolkes. And glorious was the word for it.
After the coldest, wettest spring in many years, this effulgence
of blue and gold, these happy waves, this flowering spray made
crowded streets, jostling umbrellas, electrically lighted offices,
and piles of ledgers grotesque, almost impossible.

There was something very likeable about young Ffolkes.
Everyone on board seemed to know that he was going home
after two years in London, that he had no relatives living to
welcome him, and that he was looking forward, with touching
eagerness, to seeing a loved collie dog named Peter. Everyone
wondered whether or not the friends with whom Ffolkes had
left the dog would be willing to give him up. There was the
danger that they had become too greatly attached to it.

And there was the dog's side of the question to be considered.
It would be rather rough on him to be uprooted again, after
two years, especially as he was now living in a house with
children. Dogs were nearly always devoted to children. The
mothers on board gave Ffolkes practically no hope of winning
back his dog's love without the lure of children to help him.

But Ffolkes was scarcely cast down by their predictions.
The love between him and Peter had been too deep, the understanding between them too sensitive, to be lost, even after a
separation of two years. He pictured their reunion and in
imagination felt Peter's lithe, muscular body clasped against
his own, saw his wide grin showing his long red tongue and
superb teeth.

He showed his own teeth in a smile of satisfaction as he
sipped his bouillon; and the captain, strolling along the deck,
dropped into the vacant chair beside him and said, with his
tolerant twinkle, 'Thinking of Peter, eh?'

Young Ffolkes was abashed. He must be a nitwit, he
thought, to exhibit to the world a face that could be read at a

glance. He drew it peremptorily into the mould of gravity that had furthered his promotion in the bank, and answered, 'Oh, well, it's very nice to be going home.'

'And after all,' went on the captain, 'he's your greatest pal over here, isn't he?'

'Oh, rather!'

'He must be a beauty. Won prizes, you say. I should like to see him.'

In his pride of Peter, Ffolkes' gravity became very boyish. 'Why, look here,' he said, 'I have a photograph of him. I'll fetch it, if you like.'

The captain did like. He settled his stocky figure in the chair and picked up *Twice Murdered*.

In a few minutes Ffolkes returned with the framed photograph. He said, 'You can imagine I was pleased when they sent me this. It's a perfect picture of him. And those are the Pryce kids.'

The captain took the picture in his square brown hands and examined it. Across it was written, in large black letters, 'Joan and Kenneth, with their faithful friend, Peter.' He observed:

'Attractive kids.'

Ffolkes was disappointed. What the devil did he care whether or not Pryce's children were attractive? What he wanted was the captain's opinion of Peter.

Now he had it. 'He's a beauty. I don't think I've ever seen a grander head on a dog, but—'

'But what?' demanded Ffolkes.

'Well'—the captain spoke hesitatingly—'you have talked of his high spirits and his joy in life, but in the picture he looks rather spiritless to me.'

'Of course, it's only a picture. He probably hated being photographed. Most dogs do.'

The lady in the chair on Ffolkes' other hand could endure her curiosity no longer. 'Oh, do let me see! What an adorable picture! Oh, Mr. Ffolkes, it's your wonderful Peter!'

The lady, who was mother to the worst-spoiled child on board, declared that Peter would die of a broken heart, if he were separated from Joan and Kenneth.

Ffolkes brooded a good deal on these remarks. They somehow dulled the brightness of his anticipation. Or perhaps it was the heat and noise of the long train journey which succeeded the voyage. But when he reached the boarding house where he had spent six happy years and where he had brought Peter as a puppy, his spirits went up with a leap. He could scarcely wait to pay the taxi driver and see his luggage into the house, he was so anxious to take possession once more of the large room at the top.

Little change had taken place there since he had left. Of the seventeen ladies—to whom he had been, as the only male guest —the centre of attraction—sixteen remained. Mrs. Forrester had gone to live with a married daughter. But, it being the summer season, most of the ladies had gone to the agreeable places where they spent the hot months. Only ugly, kind, Mrs. Kane, hearty, loud-voiced Miss Hubbard, and pretty, white-haired, pink-cheeked Mrs. Slee remained. These three clustered about him in the drawing-room in a state approaching bliss. They had never hoped to have him back with them. With his departure something of the glamour of living had gone. Not that the ladies were in any way dissatisfied with their lots—the days passed very happily at Mrs. Dowling's. But they had enjoyed the presence of young Ffolkes in the house, and it seemed almost too good to be true that they had him back.

In his new position he could have afforded to keep up a good establishment of his own. That might come later. For the present he was satisfied to take up the threads of his life as he had left it, to enjoy the comfort of Mrs. Dowling's house and the good food provided by her cook.

Mrs. Dowling was as handsome as ever, he thought, as she stood smiling at him in his room after lunch. 'Now, what about Peter?' she asked. 'Are you going to get him back again?'

'Should you like to have him, Mrs. Dowling? Do you think the ladies would mind?'

'There isn't a soul in this house who wouldn't be glad to have Peter back', she said emphatically. 'Several of us went to the dog show last fall just to see him. He looked grand, but he didn't seem to have any use for his old friends, I must say. He looked sort of haughty and don't-care. I suppose you know he took a prize.'

'Yes, Mr. Pryce let me know. What I'm afraid of is that they won't want to give him up. But I think I have a right to ask for him, don't you?'

Mrs. Dowling became suddenly furious. 'Give him up? Give him up? I should think they would! You just lent him to them, didn't you? The glory they've had in taking prizes with him is more than enough for them, I should say.'

'Well, I'm glad you think so. There were people on board who felt that it would break Peter's heart to separate him from the children. What do *you* think about that?'

Mrs. Dowling felt very strongly that the Pryces had no claim whatever on Peter. All that young Ffolkes needed to do was to call at their house and request, politely but firmly, the return of his dog. Mrs. Dowling's establishment was waiting for Peter, just as it had waited for his master.

Ffolkes' sensations that night were that odd mingling of the familiar and the strange which one experiences after return from long absence. All about him was so familiar that he expected at any moment to hear Peter as a puppy snuffling in his basket, yet all was so strange that he felt at times that he was in a dream and would never see Peter again.

The next morning he went to the bank where Pryce was manager. He found that Pryce was attending a board meeting and would not return to the bank that day. At lunch time he called up Pryce's house and was told by a maid that the family had gone to their summer cottage for the week-end. No, the dog had not gone with them. He took up too much room in the car.

This was splendid luck, thought Ffolkes. He had not hoped for a chance of meeting Peter alone, without the beguilement of Joan and Kenneth to come between them. He called a taxi and went straight to Pryce's house.

It stood in a curving, tree-shaded street, and its front was secluded by large shrubs in white flower. A lawn sprinkler whirled its cool freshness on the grass. 'By George, it's been a nice home for Peter!' thought Ffolkes. 'I wonder if he'll be glad to see me.'

But he really did not wonder. He was confident of the furry torrent of love that would in a moment leap on him.

He opened the gate and strode eagerly along the brick-paved walk.

He heard a low growl, then stopped, profoundly surprised by

what he thought for a flash was the statue of a collie dog sitting on the balustrade beside the stone steps. It could scarcely be real—that rigid, immobile beauty! Then he knew that it was Peter.

He took three strides and had him in his arms. 'Peter! Peter, old man! Glad to have me back? Dear old pal!'

There was no more response than would have come from the statue he had first thought him to be. Yes there was a response, after all—a terrible one. He felt Peter's hackle rise under his hands!

Young Ffolkes stepped backward with an air almost ludicrously crestfallen. His arms fell to his sides. His jaw dropped. 'Peter', he said softly. 'Pete, old man! You can't have forgotten me! You simply can't! I'm Ffolkes—Ffolkes, your old pal! *Peter!*'

The last word was almost a cry, for now he saw that Peter did remember him! There was recognition in those remote hazel eyes. Remembrance—but no love. They looked through him, past him, with a dignity remote and unapproachable. The hair on the back of his neck settled into place. He ignored Ffolkes.

Ffolkes gave a sickly smile. He could not comprehend how such a weaning away could have taken place in two years. The understanding between him and Peter had been so complete. Peter was so intelligent.

Well, there was only one thing for it, and that was to win him back. Probably a day or two alone together would do the trick.

He tried to say comforting doggie things—Nice old fellow . . . good old boy—but the words stuck in his throat. Very quietly he took one of Peter's paws and held it in his hand, that firm muscular paw that had padded beside him many a happy mile on their holiday in the north. Peter allowed him to hold it. He looked down at Ffolkes' hand, then up into his face; and, to Ffolkes' mind, his look held not so much coldness as a terrible and abiding reproach. What had happened? How was he ever to find out? That look cut him to the quick.

He went to the door and rang the bell. A smart, matter-of-fact maid answered it. Ffolkes asked her to tell Mrs. Pryce that he had called to see Peter. Then: 'He seems very quiet', he remarked.

'He's always like that', the maid answered. 'He's a good, well-

P

behaved dog. But underneath he's got a mean streak. He's snapped at two or three people for no reason at all. I keep clear of him myself.'

'I suppose', said Ffolkes, 'he is devoted to the children.'

'Oh, I don't know about that. I don't think he cares for anyone but himself. You see, he's a show dog. He's won prizes and been fussed over. I guess it's made him conceited.'

New bewilderment was opening up before young Ffolkes. If only he could find out what it all meant! If only the girl were a more sympathetic person! Still, she seemed intelligent. He felt that if anyone could help him she could. He said:

'He's really mine, you know. At least, I think he's mine. But it must depend on what Mrs. Pryce feels about it. She has kept him for me for two years while I have been in England. I want him back most awfully. Do you think she will let me have him?' He looked anxiously into her eyes.

She became a little less matter-of-fact. 'Well,' she said judicially, 'I can't say. Madam is very proud of him. She likes to show him off and all that, but I do know he gave Master Kenneth an awful shaking-up once—that was before I came—and she's sort of nervous about leaving him with the children.'

'Then you wouldn't say that he's very fond of the children, would you?'

'As I've said before, I don't think he's fond of anyone but himself. He's a cold, proud dog, I'd say.'

When she had shut the door, he went down the steps and stood looking at Peter. He did not approach him again. Peter sat noble-looking and remote as though carved out of stone. He looked as though the goings or comings of no one on earth could affect him. He did not give Ffolkes a glance when he returned to his taxi.

'It is ridiculous', thought Ffolkes, 'to feel so awful about a dog. I expect that anyone with any sense would say that it is ridiculous. Yet I do feel awful. I feel as though the bottom had fallen out of things.' He threw himself back in a corner of the taxi and gave himself up to blackness.

But later on he called himself a fool for being depressed about Peter. What he had to do was to get him back, and all would be well. He was glad he had had that talk with the

maid; it was a relief to know that Peter had not given his heart
to young Kenneth, at any rate.

On Monday morning he found Pryce in his office at the end
of the marble-walled bank. He thought that Pryce was a little
embarrassed when they met. He supposed it was due to
reluctance to give up Peter. Ffolkes came straight to the point.

'I wish you would tell me what I said when I left Peter with
you. I can't for the life of me remember. Did I give him to you
outright? I must just throw myself on your mercy, but I do
want very much to have him back.'

Everything was different from what young Ffolkes had
expected. He had expected Peter to be half-mad with joy at
seeing him, and Peter had given him no faintest sign of love.
He had expected difficulty in getting the Pryces to give him up,
and he met with no opposition at all. Pryce said he thought his
wife would be quite willing to part with the collie. He was too
big for the city; he was too big for the car; and at their summer
cottage, he had a habit of absenting himself for days, which was
very worrying. Mrs. Pryce thought she would rather have a
dachshund. They were very fashionable just now.

Yet Pryce still remained embarrassed when Ffolkes expressed
his gratitude. He evidently had something on his mind; and
Ffolkes, with resentment in his heart, tried to get it out of him.
He asked questions about Peter's life in the past two years.
Pryce was noncommittal. The most he could be brought to say
was that Peter had not turned out to be so friendly as they had
expected and that he guessed he had given all his love to
Ffolkes before they had him. Yes he was pretty good with the
children. They had had a lot of fun with him. . . . Ffolkes
could take him away whenever he wanted.

It all seemed too good and too bad to be true.

'What have I taken on?' thought Ffolkes as, that very afternoon, he and Peter walked through the streets on their way to
Mrs. Dowling's. 'How is it going to end? Am I to have this
frozen statue for a companion, or am I going to be able to win
him back to what he was?' The first bitterness of his disappointment over, he was on his mettle. He would leave nothing un-
done that might help to bring the old prideful gaiety, the trust-
ful affection, back into Peter's eyes.

Peter stalked now, on his leash, neither straining forward nor
lagging behind, but accommodating his step to Ffolkes' with

disdainful submission. When other dogs approached him his hackle rose and he uttered a growl, low but so menacing that they slunk instantly away. During the long walk he gave no sign of interest in anything they passed.

The three guests at Mrs. Dowling's were enchanted to see how he had developed. He was as beautiful as a dream, declared Miss Hubbard; and indeed there was a strange dream-like quality about him, as though he were scarcely conscious of what went on. Mrs. Kane remembered how she had been the one to name him, and Mrs. Slee recalled how she had saved his life when, as a puppy, he had escaped into the street. They were rebuffed when he took no notice of them whatever, only submitting with an air of polite resignation to their fondling.

That night he slept in Ffolkes' room. Purposely Ffolkes had not taken him to it till bedtime. Now he paid no attention to him, allowing him to sense the once loved atmosphere for himself.

Ffolkes' heart quickened its beat as Peter stood motionless but with eager eyes in the middle of the room. His sensitive nostrils quivered. He sniffed every corner of the room. Then he gave a sharp whine and turned once again that look of terrible reproach on Ffolkes.

But that was the end of it. He had weakened, it seemed, for that moment only. When it was past he was once again remote and invulnerable. He seemed buried in a reverie from which nothing could rouse him.

Ffolkes was not yet disheartened. He remembered how, on a trip to the north country, Peter had attained the fullness of his doghood. How the shallow puppy brightness of his eyes had deepened to a steady glow of pride and confidence, how he had learned, it seemed, to read Ffolkes' very thoughts!

Ffolkes made up his mind to have a like holiday this year. He longed to see that wild and lovely country again, and his persistent hope led him to believe that in that noble solitude the wall that separated him and Peter would crumble.

He bought a car and a tent and arranged to go to the same spot where they had camped two years ago. Ffolkes felt very hopeful when he saw Peter standing, foursquare to the summer wind, on the seat of the car in the midst of the outing para-phernalia, his head high, his adroit nostrils sniffing the pure air.

In the north-land that air swept untainted over vast tracts of virgin country. Ffolkes had forgotten the great fine sweep of it.

He and Peter seemed the only inhabitants of a new and glorious world. Ffolkes, remembering his holidays of the past two years, pitied the people of those seaside resorts who swam, paddled beach boats, and rode on surfboards, never out of sight and sound of one another. At sunset he found the very spot where he had raised his tent on the former visit. He found traces of his old fires. He found the circular stove of flat stones which he had built, where he had cooked his fish. The same settler came to bring him bread and milk and vegetables.

He was hot and tired from the long drive. He could scarcely wait to strip off his clothes and plunge into the cool lake. He remembered how Peter, after his first puppyish hesitation, had swum beside him, glorying in this new freedom and intimacy.

He ran across the sand and out into the green depths. Peter stood on the shore.

'Peter! Peter! Pete, old man!' he shouted. 'Come on—it's simply great!'

But Peter viewed the forest, the lake, the tent pitched on the well-loved spot, with no more response than he had given to his reunion with Ffolkes. His plumed tail, which he had used to wave extravagantly in his joy, now drooped in majestic melancholy.

As Ffolkes came dripping out of the water he said aloud, forcing hope into his voice, 'Tomorrow—he will be himself tomorrow.'

That night he made a bed for Peter at the foot of his own couch of balsam boughs and army blankets, but the collie, after sniffing it, stalked out and curled up near the dying fire.

'He is a different dog', mourned Ffolkes. 'I can never win him back. He's lost.'

He could not help reproaching himself for the change that had come over Peter. He felt that he should have known more about the Pryces before leaving a sensitive dog with them. But they had seemed so kind and there had been the children for playmates.

It was long before he fell asleep. The strange noises of the forest crept closer, became more personal. Yet it was no forest noise that woke him from his first sleep, but terrible heart-rending howls—howls that gave voice to a despair long stifled. Ffolkes leaped from his bed and tore wildly at the flap of the tent.

Peter was sitting by the embers of the fire, his muzzle raised to the low-hanging stars, while out of his deep chest those anguished howls came in dreadful succession.

Ffolkes shouted to him. He ran and put an arm about him and stroked him. 'Peter, dear old fellow, what's wrong? Lord, if only I knew what you want!'

Peter hung his head as though ashamed of his outburst, and from that time their nights were undisturbed.

To Ffolkes the holiday was a failure, though the weather was perfect, the fish fairly shouldered one another out of the lake, and his own body became lithe and brown as an Indian's. He made the journey back to town with a heavy heart. Peter sitting beside him was a noble figure, his full ruff as white as the foam of the lake; but his spirit was still a prisoner in the remote world to which it had withdrawn.

One night, weeks later, as Ffolkes sat pulling at his pipe, an idea came to him about Peter, of whom he found himself thinking in every spare moment. He would take him to the Pryces' house and see what his reactions were to that house and those people. He might find out something. If there was psychology for human beings, why not for dogs?

The next afternoon he and Peter arrived at the house without warning. The maid told him that Mrs. Pryce and Joan were away for the day, that Pryce was expected at any moment. Only the little boy was in the house. Would Mr. Ffolkes come in?

Kenneth swaggered out to the veranda at that moment, important at being the one to receive Ffolkes. They shook hands, and then Kenneth took Peter by the collar and began to pull him about.

'Hallo!' he exclaimed. 'Aren't you an old silly! Don't you know me?'

Ffolkes' anger rose against the boy, but he forced himself to grin. 'I guess he's not likely to forget *you*, eh?' he said.

'I'll bet he won't', returned Kenneth, getting astride the submissive dog.

'I suppose you and Pete had lots of fun.'

Kenneth gave a grunt of assent as he joggled up and down on Peter. Then his face changed as the collie's hackle rose, and he got to his feet. 'Mother's glad you've taken him away', he said, pushing out his lips. 'She was afraid he'd go for me again.'

'Go for you!' grinned Ffolkes. 'What d'you mean, go for you? Surely he wouldn't do that!'

'Surely he would', affirmed Kenneth vigorously. 'They had the doctor for me. I wasn't really hurt. But Mother was scared.'

'No wonder!' Ffolkes kept the grin frozen on his face. 'I expect he got a good licking for that, eh?'

Some family instinct impelled Kenneth to deny this. 'No', he lied. 'But he should have had a good licking with a piece of rubber hose. That's what I said.'

'Of course he should!' Ffolkes' voice grew even heartier. 'What was it that made him go for you?'

'Why—why, I just drove him off his chair. The one that was yours. The old silly used to lie with his chin on the seat. I just jumped into it and drove him off, and then he went for me.' Kenneth stared glumly at Peter, sitting statuesque and aloof.

'I expect', said Ffolkes, oozing geniality, 'that you've had lots of fun teasing him, you and Joan. It's fun teasing dogs.'

Kenneth looked sly. 'Did we! You can bet we did! But the best fun of all was when we would put the record on.'

Ffolkes looked sly, too. 'Record?' he purred. 'What record?'

'Why, the one you made on Daddy's dictaphone. Don't you remember? You did it for us kids one night when you were here to dinner. Gosh, that was what made him wild! Oh, it was fun!' Kenneth rolled over on the swing couch in mirthful remembrance.

'Ha, ha, ha!' shouted Ffolkes, clenching his hands. 'That must have been fun! He'd go wild, eh?'

'Wouldn't he just! He'd fairly tie himself into knots, thinking you were really there. Then, when he found it was all a sell, he'd slink away looking as mean as anything.'

Ffolkes made hysterical chuckling sounds. 'I'd give a dollar', he said, 'to see that.'

Kenneth looked suddenly serious. 'Would you truly?'

'Would I? I'd give two dollars in a minute. It'd be such fun!'

'I'll do it! I'll do it before Dad comes.' Then the brightness went out of his face. 'But it's no go. He never showed off properly again, not after the—' He caught himself in time.

'The licking', supplemented Ffolkes. 'You see, I know all about it.'

Kenneth grunted sulkily, then he said, 'Well, anyhow, he's got you back now. He would care.'

'He doesn't like me much now. Perhaps he'd like the voice in the box better than the real master. Let's try him, Ken. Come along!'

He caught hold of Kenneth and pushed him toward the hall. As he felt that firm body in his hands, he saw suddenly before his mind's eye the livid title of the thriller he had been reading on board ship—*Twice Murdered*—and he grinned ferociously.

'Come, Peter!' he called. 'Come along, boy!'

In Pryce's study he slapped the two-dollar bill on the table.

Kenneth looked askance at the money. 'I didn't ask for it, did I? I'm not supposed to ask for money.'

'It's a gift', assured Ffolkes, and Kenneth pocketed it with dignity.

Ffolkes' heart pounded uncomfortably. Peter sat in rigid attention. He knew what Kenneth was going to do. He was going to call out from that mysterious box the voice that had once so driven him to desperation. He sat as hard as iron, his nerves tense to repel the onslaught. Ffolkes had slipped out into the passage.

Now came the familiar voice:

'Hallo—hallo, children! How are you? Pretty well, eh? What shall I say to you? Why, look here, I'll tell you—I've got a dog. A lovely dog, a Scotch collie. His name is Peter—Peter. He's a grand fellow, Peter is . . .'

Ffolkes came into the room. He did not just walk in, but he came as though in answer to the summons of his own voice. His arms were tense. His heart pounded in his side. His own voice took the words from the machine:

'Peter! Peter! I've got a lovely dog named Peter. A Scotch collie—my own Peter!'

Every hair of Peter's beautiful coat rose in an ecstasy of attention. A great change came over him. The chains of despair that had held him dropped from him, broken. His prison was demolished. He gave a succession of barks, almost savage in their release of his spirit, and circled about Ffolkes as though it were the first time he had seen him since his return. Then he leaped full upon him, his paws on Ffolkes' shoulders, almost knocking him down. Ffolkes clasped him close, and their bodies rocked together.

This was the sight that Pryce saw when he entered the room.

Czar of The High Sierras

EMMA-LINDSAY SQUIER

THIS is not really my story; it belongs to Uncle Blink, who told it to me. But bits of it are mine, because the story had for its setting the forests of the High Sierras, that belong to all who love them and who seek to understand them. It was to him that a wonderful experience was vouchsafed, and appeal for compassion and aid from woods creatures sorely hurt and friendless. And to Ranger Adair and me he told it, as we rode slowly up the steep trail of the rocky wall that shuts Yosemite in from the outside world.

Uncle Blink is not his name, of course; it is only the nickname I have given him. No ordinary name would fit him, I maintain, for he does not look upon the world with usual eyes. He sees things quite differently from other people I have known. He loves the woods and all things in them with a deep and quiet pleasure. And it is rarely he will tell of things he has seen or felt, because he dreads misunderstanding, or worse—a listener who does not care.

But on this warmly fragrant August day, as our horses slowly climbed the valley's wall, we talked, the three of us, of woods friends we had known. And through the long warm afternoon we crept higher, always higher. The dusty tang of sagebrush was in our nostrils, and the sweeter smell of pine trees. High above the valley's floor we reached the woods at last, and halted, looking down upon Half Dome, like the top of some great world rent in two by lightning and left among the clouds. In the distance we could see the shining Merced River, a slender thread of brightness, winding through the verdant meadows. And the far falls of Illilouet gleamed like a slender waving veil against the gaunt brow of the cliff.

It was very quiet there in the High Sierras. In soothing undertone we heard the murmur of the pines, and there was always the far-off babble of a little stream that clambered along a rocky bed. Now and then a bird note, faint as a star at sunrise, filtered down from lofty aisles of branches interlaced. But still there was silence, for the world, with its hurrying noises, its senseless clang and babble, was far, far away from us. We were wrapped around with sunlight and shadows, perfume of pine trees and azalea flowers. The horses sought the little stream and drank deeply, contentedly, while we lounged in our saddles, unwilling to break the beauty of the day with needless speech.

Then suddenly, from the nodding shadows of ferns and azalea bushes, there slipped a dusky shape, lithe and graceful, with pointed nose and plumy tail, roughly-furred flanks dotted with bits of twigs and clinging burrs.

'What is it,' I whispered to the Ranger, 'a coyote or a wolf?'

'Neither', he whispered back. 'A wild dog who has taken to the woods.'

It seemed almost incredible. For somehow there was no suggestion of domesticity in that silent, furtive creature, who slunk from out the bushes as a coyote would creep, alert to every sound or action, running toward the stream with head bent to the ground, sensitive nose sniffing at alien odours, pausing with one foot raised and curved under him.

He halted at the water's edge, saw us suddenly, and growled savagely, the hair along his back lifting into a rigid line of menace. But we were silent, watching him. And presently he drank, eyeing us sharply in suspicion, and when he had finished he gave us no second look, but slipped away into the protecting greenery whence he had emerged.

We stared after him silently, and presently the Ranger spoke.

'Funny things about dogs that go wild—it's usually because they've had a raw deal from human beings. Maybe they've been whipped or starved, or made to shift for themselves when they were puppies. Anyway, they seem to bear mankind a grudge. They are meaner than a coyote, more savage than a wolf. And once wild—they never go back. I've never known of a wild dog who went back to civilization or had anything to do with men.'

Uncle Blink spoke suddenly. 'I have', was all he said.

But I knew he had a story hidden, for there was in his eyes a reminiscent look as if he were seeing something which lay in the past, something strange, and dear to his heart. And presently, because we were silent, waiting for what he had to tell us, he began the story, as he knew it, of the Czar and Little Princess. And as he talked, we rode very slowly through the trail that was bordered by ferns and wild azaleas, ever higher, toward the wind-swept summit of the mountains.

The early history of the Czar and Little Princess he pieced together from the bits of comment and talk of guides and packers in the High Sierras. News from such a source, strange as it may seem, is hard to come by, especially when it seems to deal with sentiment or love for the out-of-doors. But once having heard of the outlaw collies who roamed in the mountains in company with a coyote band, Uncle Blink persisted in his questions concerning the two and learned at last the reasons for their flight from mankind.

The little town of Independence, in the state of California, lies at the gateway of the High Sierras. One goes from there in one day's pack journey up through Kearsarge Pass, twelve thousand feet above it, and then, in the flick of an eyelash, men and cities, and all the things of men, vanish as if they had never been. A new world lies beyond—peak upon peak, vastness without end—and the wind is fresh with the smells of un-touched places. There are tamaracks and firs, tiger lilies and snow flowers, glowing like patches of fire on barren rocks swept clean by scarcely-melted snows. There are snow-fed lakes cupped in gaunt hollows of rocky giant hands. They lie between the grim upstanding fingers of stone-like shreds of sky torn out of the heaven's floor. And it is here, in this wild country, that the Czar and Little Princess found freedom and kinship, and later, the shadow of slow and painful death.

Some five years before Uncle Blink came packing up into the High Sierras, an old man with his patient burros and his ramshackle camp wagon left at the outskirts of Independence, where the willows grow thickly beside the irrigating ditches, a lank and gangling collie dog, and a younger, woollier collie pup. The Czar and Little Princess were what he called them, and when he died from old age and hardship, he left friendless the only two friends he had ever known.

It seems that the people of the little town did not take kindly to the outcasts left so unexpectedly in their midst. No home opened to them; no kindly heart responded to their pleading eyes and eager, wagging tails. No one offered them the shelter of a fireside and the protection of a family name, and so the two orphans, bereft of the old man who had loved them, foraged as best they could, living on scraps and grudgingly given charity. At first they knew ill-treatment, felt the hard boots of drunken men, the rushing brooms of impatient housewives. They learned that all their friendly puppy ways were useless, that the world can be very hard and very cruel for friendless, masterless dogs.

But strangely enough, ill-treatment did not crush them, did not make them cringe or cower. They were made of higher, sterner metal than the other mongrels of the town who ran yelping from the sight of a broom or the gesture of a hand. They learned in time that no one wanted them. But still they went from door to door on daily foraging excursions. The Czar went boldly, as one who knew his worth. And beside him always went the Little Princess, more gentle, more appealing, but quick and vicious as he, if need be, to resent insult or abuse.

So for that long hot summer, and through a winter white with snow, they went their way. The Czar suffered no indignities to fall upon himself or the Little Princess whom he loved, either from men or the canine inhabitants of the town. His body took on magnificent proportions, and his fur held the smoky softness that spoke of royal ancestry. The Little Princess was never so large as he, but her body was supple and tawny, and she was the colour of the goldenrod. So they went their way from door to door in dignity and without fear. People looked at them askance and fed them, not knowing what else to do.

But in the springtime, when the Czar was two years old and

Little Princess some months younger, misfortune overtook the pair. There was in the town a man whose mind was bloated with importance, and whose heart was not the thing it should have been.

He owned a dog of great ferocity, and it was the man's boast that no other dog could conquer him. Now, he had marked the two collies, friendless but peaceable, who went their quiet way, asking of mankind only the barest necessities of life. And he hated them unreasoningly, even complaining to the powers that be that the dogs were a nuisance and should be destroyed. His complaint received scant attention, for every one knew that the Czar and Little Princess did no harm. They were not given to brawling with other dogs, neither were they dangerous to women or children. So the man determined to exterminate them in his own way. He set in the entrance of an unused barn a quantity of meat and succulent bones. And he toled the collies there by means of meat held just out of reach. When they reached the barn, Little Princess, always more on the alert and more suspicious than the Czar, would not go inside, for she vaguely suspected danger. But the Czar went on in. And the man followed and slammed the door. Little Princess stood with cocked ears, lifted forefoot, and blinking, worried eyes. Then she heard a savage snarl and the fighting growl of the Czar.

Inside the barn was great commotion. For the man had hidden his savage dog inside, and let him loose upon the unsuspecting collie.

There was a rush, and the bull-dog pinned the Czar down by his savage grip on the collie's throat. The man laughed aloud. But even as he laughed, the window darkened. The poised body of a massive collie stood framed there for an instant, a living picture of vengeance. Every hair of her smoky body stood erect. The white ruff about her neck was like the spreading decoration that a nobleman might wear; it stood out rigidly as if each hair were made of steel. Then she sprang, with the ease of a spring released. And full upon the body of the attacking bull-dog she crashed with all her strength.

No one knows what happened inside that unused barn. Only that after a while, the man staggered out, scarcely a man in looks, his clothing torn to shreds, his face and arms gashed and bleeding. The bull-dog was dead. Of the Czar and Little

Princess there was no sign. They had vanished utterly from sight. And though the man told a certain version of the story, tried to say that the collies had attacked him needlessly and killed his dog from wantonness, yet there were those who believed differently, and who were glad that the two had been triumphant.

Months passed. And now presently there began to filter down to the lowlands news and rumours of two wild dogs of the mountains, who shunned men as wild things shun them, who had a super-canine cunning, who were ruthless, brave, invincible. Later it was known that this same pair had attained leadership of a band of coyotes who dwelt high in the mountains. And sometimes the carcass of a sheep or cow would be found sacrificed to their appetites. Once a packer saw them at their kill and knew them for the Czar and Little Princess.

So the talk went round of the menace of the two. The hands of men were turned once more against them, and they were marked for death, labelled as outlaws, just prey for the gun of whomsoever should encounter them. But as if they knew the edict had gone forth, the two were doubly cunning. They took their savage band higher into the wind-swept Sierras, and though many plans were made to trap them, they were always unsuccessful.

This much of their story did Uncle Blink piece together, as in the ripening heat of August he with other men, packers, cooks, and guides, climbed up from the desert's dusty stretch, up through the Kearsarge Pass, up past the places where there were once trails made by men, into the country of windy peaks and great silences unmarred by man-made noises.

For ten days they had not crossed a human trail or seen the flaming of any camp fire save their own. They were high, almost above the timber line. The mountains rimmed them round barren and grey, and the snow upon the hoary peaks was like white hair upon the heads of old, old men. A fringe of tamaracks skirted their base, the great trees were twisted and stunted by the fury of winter winds and the burden of winter snows.

Here it was, just at evening, that Uncle Blink and all his party climbed down along steep trails that scarce gave footing to the ever-wary burros, to a little meadow where a lake lay sparkling in the ruddy glow of sunset. The meadow was softly verdant and sprinkled with tiger lilies that made soft red spots of colour like glowing embers scattered upon a carpet of green. A little stream came down to greet the lake, murmuring like a child who has come from a great distance and is glad to be at home. All along its grassy banks, Indian paintbrush flamed like elfin torches, and wild pansies bent down to dip their yellow faces in its rippling flow. The silence of the place was soft, yet mighty—a benediction, a warning, and a welcome.

The tarpaulins were flung down as a rest for weary bodies. The packers set up tents and relieved the patient burros of their load. Camp fires began to crackle as the dusk came swift and cold, and the sizzling smell of bacon mingled with the odour of wood smoke and tobacco. The light of the glowing sky went out suddenly, as if a great lamp had been exchanged for the glimmering candles of the stars. The lake grew black and full of mystery, and far sounds of night crept down from out the great ravines and groves of stunted tamaracks.

Then suddenly, high upon the darkly looming slopes, came the weird, unearthly yelping of a coyote band. The burros stirred uneasily, and the men were silent, listening to the tremulous chorus. All at once, in strange contrast to the uncanny, high-pitched call that trailed across the night, came the sharp authoritative barking of a dog. It had an honest homely ring to it, despite the background of eerie shrilling yelps. The men questioned each other in undertones, and the packers stood alert with ears keenly tuned to the sounds of the out-of-doors.

'The Czar and Little Princess', said the Veteran Guide softly. 'They are hungry—they and their coyote pack. The camp smells mighty good. I shouldn't be surprised if they paid us a visit before the night is over.'

The yelpings died away, swept into silence by the rushing of the night wind among the tamaracks. In the satisfaction of crisp bacon and coffee hot and fragrant, the men ate and drank and forgot the eerie chorus.

But later in the night, when the fire had burned to embers and the camp was shrouded in the silence of murmuring trees and the soft lapping of wind-ruffled waters, there came a great commotion, a sudden rush of swift, shadow-like forms, and a frenzy among the hobbled burros. It was the coyote band, fearful and skulking, yet emboldened by hunger. Down into the little valley they rushed, snapping up the remnants of supper, springing against the bags that held provisions. And in the lead two powerful animal bodies loomed against the darkness, wolf-like in size, but more shaggy and more graceful. The camp was filled with startled noises.

The packers snatched their guns; Uncle Blink seized his flashlight. Into the darkness he sent the stream of light, and there, in the white glare, stood revealed two collies, surprised for an instant into immobility by the sudden blinding flash. They stood with startled eyes that glinted blue-green in the glare. And there was, in their attitude, the suggestion of standing at bay, of expecting neither pity nor reprieve, yet of waiting staunch and unafraid.

'The Czar and Little Princess', came the voice of the Veteran Guide, but this time there was a grimness in his tone, and he made a motion with his gun.

Uncle Blink's hand struck suddenly at the weapon, and the shot went slanting harmlessly into the night. There was a muddled confusion of yelps, snarls, and a dog's authoritative bark—a leaping line of shadows that melted into the outer darkness—a far whimper trailing back through the night—and again there was silence, with only the hooting of an owl to dot the night with sound. The Veteran Guide looked upon Uncle Blink with accusing eyes. The other men spoke in disappointed tones of having failed in wounding or killing any of the robber crew or the dogs who were the leaders.

But Uncle Blink made no excuse for his action. 'They aren't bad—only hungry', was all he said.

Now the next day, and the next day, the party lingered in the meadow. And on the third morning, when all but Uncle Blink and the Veteran Guide had gone hunting in the mountains, the two of them sat talking where the little stream was racing. All at once the Guide pointed to the fringe of tamarack that bordered the mountain's gauntness. Something was moving slowly toward them from the shadow of the trees; two tawny bodies that crept and grovelled, heads with pointed muzzles that turned upward to whine pitifully—plumy tails that dragged in the dust.

The men stared amazed, half doubting the thing they saw. For it seemed incredible that those two outlaws—the Czar of

Q

the High Sierras, and his mate, Little Princess—should come of their own free will to man or the haunts of men; should come in clear daylight to the camp they had tried to plunder under the cover of night. The dogs paused at a distance, their tails curving dejectedly between their legs, their bodies cowering in an attitude of desperate fear. Yet there was something, too, in the little, hitching motions of their heads, which indicated a great need, a terrible calamity that had driven them to ask mercy of their enemy, man.

Uncle Blink stood up. He held out his hand to the distant pair. 'Come along, it's all right', he called, and as if they had understood his very words, the two came swiftly forward.

They came with little, whimpering, heartbreaking cries. And when they neared the men, they stopped and lay down, trembling, their heads upon their paws, their brown eyes dulled with misery, their tongues white-flecked and lolling.

Then Uncle Blink knew what had happened to the pair. For from eyes to nose, from dripping tongues to the white ruffles under their throats, they were enveloped in a deadly mask of porcupine quills—quills so closely, deeply driven that they hung bristling beads of black and white.

Uncle Blink and the Veteran Guide could picture the beginning of the tragedy. The two dogs, hungry—famished even—disregarding the instinct which makes all animals give the prickly brethren free passage in the woods. The rustling, lumbering coming of the porcupines, walking pigeon-toed like baby bears; the leap of the dogs; the startled flaring of the porcupines' quills. And then the agonized howls of the Czar and Little Princess as their jaws, buried for an instant in the mass of upstanding bristles, came away filled with the barbed needles of death. Porcupines do not throw their quills. But they can be released by a touch. And when the long slender needles enter the flesh of an animal enemy, they go deeper and even deeper, being barbed like tiny fishhooks. They may not be pawed out or broken off. They drill through flesh and marrow until slow death ends the torture.

And thus it was, upon this day, that Czar and Little Princess, knowing well their utter helplessness and the doom that lay before them, came again to seek from mankind the pity once denied them. Forgot their ancient grudge and came begging for assistance, even to the camp which they had sought to

plunder came the outlaw couple. But once there, in full sight
of men and at the mercy of men their old fear came upon them.
And so they crouched with their heads upon their paws, their
brown eyes mute and tortured, waiting for whatever the hearts
of these men should dictate.

Uncle Blink spoke to them again, kindly, reassuringly. And
when he stooped and held out his hands to them, they dragged
forward in timorous jerks and lay down before him, lifting
their bleeding faces upon his knees.

But when Uncle Blink tried to touch them, to pull out one
of the quills from Little Princess's throat, then they sprang
away yelping, and sat upon their haunches uttering desperate,
despairing howls. So he waited, still with hands outstretched,
speaking comfortingly, but making no move toward them. And
though the Czar wagged a feeble tail and moved as if to come,
it was Little Princess who came forward at last, crawling with
tremulous, reluctant hitches, until her head was upon his hand,
the poor pierced tongue lolling from between her trembling
jaws.

Slowly Uncle Blink put his free hand down past the pleading
eyes that watched his face. Then swiftly his fingers clutched at
a porcupine quill and drew it cleanly out. With a yelp of pain
Little Princess sprang away, and the Czar lifted his head and
howled. But the little collie lady came back again, writhing
under his hands, always with her eyes fixed steadfastly upon his
face. Again and again he pulled the quills, and each time she
leaped away, whimpered, and circled back to him. Until at
last, worn out with pain and terror, she lay panting at his feet,
her lovely body limp, her eyes tightly closed. And so she lay,
and suffered, and whimpered, until the long task was accomplished, and the quills were all pulled out.

The Guide, meantime, was ministering to Czar. But he,
bravest in the hunt, was weaker in endurance. At every pull he
flinched, and snapped, and wrenched himself away. Always he
would come back, even as Little Princess came, but though his
body trembled with a mighty effort to endure the pain, he
could not stand the torture that was necessary to free the quills
from his flesh. And when Uncle Blink had finished with the
Little Princess, and she lay with heaving flanks and grateful
exhausted eyes beside him, Czar was still in torment, for his

tongue and lips were embedded with the deadly quills so firmly fixed that fingers could not pull them. And Uncle Blink took out small pincers from his kit.

The tawny collie came to Uncle Blink willingly, eagerly, and put one massive paw upon his knee, promising with lovely, wretched eyes to do the best he could. But at the first touch the great jaws would snap together, and he would dart away, while Little Princess watched him anxiously, as if afraid that he would run away unrelieved.

Then Uncle Blink spread a tarpaulin upon the ground, and knelt and stretched his hand to Czar. He spoke to him, as a human being, telling him that he knew how great the pain must be, and that though the Czar had tried to stand the anguish, yet it was impossible that he should endure it quietly as was necessary.

'You must be tied', he said over and over. 'You must be tied so we can help you.'

And at last, as if the dog knew, and understood his words, he crept forward, trembling, lay down upon the canvas, suffered it to be wrapped about him, tied with ropes firmly knotted, and he never turned or whimpered, but endured the heavy wrappings, and the Little Princess watched him, whining softly for encouragement.

They put a stick between his jaws to hold them wide apart. And even this he allowed, though his eyes were wide and bloodshot. But when Uncle Blink again took the pincers and plucked at the hidden quills, he cried, and whined, and struggled, and he fought with frightful vigour.

At last the task was finished. The last quill was found and plucked, the knots were untied, the canvas unwound. And Czar, the outlaw collie, he who was the coyotes' leader, was free once more.

He stood up, shook himself, licked gingerly at his bleeding nose and jaws, brought a tawny paw up to rub the places where the quills had pierced his ears. The Little Princess came to him slowly, rested her slender nose on his neck, tenderly licked the wounds on his face. And presently they lay down together, exhausted, and Uncle Blink let them stay there, and brought them food and water.

That day and the next the Czar and Little Princess lingered, unwilling to leave the place where they had received solace for their hurts. Uncle Blink gave them such food as their poor sore mouths would let them eat. At night the Little Princess slept at the foot of his canvas cot, and Czar kept vigilant watch at the open door of the tent.

But on the second night, in the stillness and the darkness, when the stars were mirrored in the little lake so clearly that it seemed to be a meadow decked with sparkling flowers, then from the high wind-swept cliffs came a faint and eerie yelping. A high-pitched trailing call that swept across the darkness, echoed back from sleeping cliffs, died away into silence, and came again, insistent, mocking, tantalizing—the brethren of the wild calling to hearts newly tamed by kindness.

Czar heard the distant summons and growled, deep in his throat. Little Princess whimpered and stirred uneasily where she lay. But when Uncle Blink spoke softly and put out his hand into the darkness, he saw the blue-green flicker of her eyes and felt a soft wet tongue caress his fingers.

When morning came, the two had gone. Silently, and with no leave-taking at all. Uncle Blink was sorry, for he would have liked to take them back to civilization, to give them home and shelter.

Was that the end of the story, I asked him, as we rode. No, not quite, he answered me. It was perhaps a week later, and they had camped in several places, when one morning, he heard a whimper, familiar and pathetic. It was Czar, the lovely collie, who had trailed him and had found him. And he came up to him confidently, put his graceful head upon his knees, and spoke to him with little whines and brown eyes that beseeched him. What was wrong the others could not fathom. But Uncle Blink surmised the trouble and began to examine carefully the furry throat and ears, the jaws, and the sensitive tongue. He found there what he sought—a quill that he had overlooked when first he aided Czar. And this time the dog stood still, without twitch or shudder, and let him pull the hidden needle out from the place in his mouth where it had festered and gone deep.

The Czar stayed long enough to lick his hand, to gaze upon him with adoring brown eyes that all but spoke his gratitude. Then he dashed away into the sheltering greenery of the tamaracks, back to the Little Princess who awaited him, back to the coyote band who owned him king and leader. His tawny

leaping body was like the flicker of an autumn leaf. His plumy
tail was like a trail of smoke behind him.

We rode in silence for a little when Uncle Blink had told his
story. But all at once I spoke, for a three-needled pine cluster
had dropped down upon his saddle.

'Three wishes for you', I told him, as the Indians had told me
long ago in childhood. 'One for yourself, one for your companions, and one for absent friends. If you leave the pine
needles where they fall, the wishes will come true.'

He smiled at me, as is his way, and humoured my desire.
And when he spoke of 'absent friends'—

'Wish that the Czar and Little Princess may some time come
down from the mountains and live in friendship with people
who love them', I said eagerly.

Again he smiled, and pretended to scoff at my belief. But I
noticed that he did not brush the pine cluster from the saddle.
It clung there as if promising fulfilment.

And so the shadows lengthened as we rode into the forest.

Riquet

ANATOLE FRANCE

QUARTER day had come. With his sister and daughter,
Monsieur Bergeret was leaving the dilapidated old house in the
Rue de Seine to take up his abode in a modern flat in the Rue
de Vaugirard. Such was the decision of Zoé and the Fates.

During the long hours of the morning, Riquet wandered
sadly through the devastated rooms. His most cherished habits
were upset. Strange men, badly dressed, rude and foul-
mouthed, disturbed his repose. They penetrated even to the
kitchen, where they stepped into his dish of biscuit and his
bowl of fresh water. The chairs were carried off as fast as he
curled himself up on them; the carpets were pulled roughly
from under his weary limbs. There was no abiding-place for
him, not even in his own home.

To his credit, be it said, that at first he attempted resistance.
When the cistern was carried off he barked furiously at the
enemy. But no one responded to his appeal; no one encouraged
him, there was no doubt about it his efforts were regarded with
disapproval. Mademoiselle Zoé said to him sharply: 'Be

247

quiet!' And Mademoiselle Pauline added: 'Riquet, you are silly!'

Henceforth he would abstain from useless warnings. He would cease to strive alone for the public weal. In silence he deplored the devastation of the household. From room to room he sought in vain for a little quiet. When the furniture removers penetrated into a room where he had taken refuge, he prudently hid beneath an as yet unmolested table or chest of drawers. But this precaution proved worse than useless; for soon the pieces of furniture tottered over him, rose, then fell with a crash, threatening to crush him. Terrified, with his hair all turned up the wrong way, he fled to another refuge no safer than the first.

But these inconveniences and even dangers were as nothing to the agony he was suffering at heart. His sentiments were the most deeply affected.

The household furniture he regarded not as things inert, but as living benevolent creatures, beneficent spirits, whose departure foreshadowed cruel misfortunes. Dishes, sugar-basins, pots and pans, all the kitchen divinities; armchairs, carpets, cushions, all the fetishes of the hearth, its lares and its domestic gods had vanished. He could not believe that so great a disaster would ever be repaired. And sorrow filled his little heart to overflowing. Fortunately, Riquet's heart resembled human hearts in being easily distracted and quick to forget its misfortunes.

During the long absence of the thirsty workmen, when old Angélique's broom raised ancient dust from the floor, Riquet breathed an odour of mice and watched the flight of a spider; thus was his versatile mind diverted. But he soon relapsed into sadness.

On the day of departure, when he beheld things growing hourly worse and worse, he grew desperate. It seemed to him above all things disastrous when he saw the linen being piled in dark cases. Pauline with eager haste was putting her frock into a trunk. He turned away from her, as if she were doing something wrong. He shrank up against the wall and thought to himself: 'Now the worst has come; this is the end of everything.' Then, whether it were that he believed things ceased to exist when he did not see them, or whether he was simply avoiding a painful sight, he took care not to look in Pauline's direction. It chanced that as she was passing to and fro she noticed Riquet's attitude. It was sad: but to her it seemed funny, and she began to laugh. Then, still laughing, she called out: 'Come here! Riquet, come to me!' But he did not stir from his corner, and would not even turn his head. He was not then in the mood to caress his young mistress, and, through some secret instinct, through a kind of presentiment, he was afraid of approaching the gaping trunk. Pauline called him several times. Then, as he did not respond, she went and took him up in her arms. 'How unhappy we are!' she said to him. 'What is wrong then?' Her tone was ironical. Riquet did not understand irony. He lay in Pauline's arms, sad and inert, affecting to see nothing and to hear nothing. 'Riquet, look at me!' She said it three times and three times in vain. Then, pretending to be in a rage: 'Silly creature,' she cried, 'in with you': and she threw him into the trunk and shut the lid on him. At that moment her aunt having called her, she went out of the room, leaving Riquet in the trunk. He was seized with wild alarm; for he was very far from supposing that he had been playfully thrown into the trunk for a mere joke. Esteeming his situation about as bad as it could be, he was desirous not to make it worse by any imprudence. So he remained motionless for a few moments, holding his breath. Then he deemed it expedient to explore his dark prison. With his paws he felt the skirts and the linen on to which he had been so cruelly precipitated, endeavouring to find some way out of this terrible place. He had been thus engaged for two or three minutes, when he was called by Monsieur Bergeret, who had been getting ready to go out.

'Riquet! Riquet! Come for a walk on the quays, that is the land of glory. True, they have disfigured it by erecting a railway station of hideous proportions and striking ugliness. Architecture is a lost art. They have pulled down a nice-looking house at the corner of the Rue du Bac. They will doubtless put some unsightly building in its place. I trust that at least our architects may abstain from introducing to the Quai d'Orsay that barbarous style of which they have given such a horrid example at the corner of the Rue Washington and the Champs Elysées! . . . Riquet! Riquet! Come for a walk on the quays. That is the glorious land. But architecture has deteriorated sadly since the days of Gabriel and of Louis. . . . Where is the dog? . . . Riquet! Riquet?'

The sound of Monsieur Bergeret's voice was a great consolation to Riquet. He replied by making a noise with his paws, scratching frantically against the wicker sides of the trunk.

'Where is the dog?' her father asked Pauline as she was returning with a pile of linen in her arms.

'He is in the trunk, Papa.'

'What, in the trunk! Why is he there?' asked Monsieur Bergeret.

'Because he was silly', replied Pauline.

Monsieur Bergeret liberated his friend. Riquet followed him into the hall, wagging his tail. Then a sudden thought occurred to him. He went back into the room, ran up to Pauline and rubbed against her skirt. And not until he had wildly caressed her as evidence of his loyalty did he rejoin his master on the staircase. He would have felt himself deficient in wisdom and religious feeling had he failed to display these signs of affection to one who had been so powerful as to plunge him into a deep trunk.

In the street, Monsieur Bergeret and his dog beheld the sad sight of their household furniture scattered over the pavement. The removers had gone off to the public-house round the corner, leaving the plate-glass mirror of Mademoiselle Zoé's wardrobe to reflect the passing procession of girls, workmen, shopkeepers, and Beaux Arts students, of drays, carts and cabs, and the chemist's shop with its bottles and its serpents of Æsculapius. Leaning against a post was Monsieur Bergeret senior, smiling in his frame, mild, pale and delicate looking, with his hair ruffled. With affectionate respect the son contemplated his parent whom he moved away from the post. He likewise lifted out of harm's way Zoé's little table, which looked ashamed at finding itself in the street.

Meanwhile Riquet was patting his master's legs with his paws, looking up at him with sorrowing beautiful eyes, which seemed to say:

'Thou, who wert once so rich and so powerful, canst thou have become poor? Canst thou have lost thy power, O my master? Thou permittest men clothed in vile rags to invade thy sitting-room, thy bedroom, thy dining-room, to throw themselves upon thy furniture and pull it out of doors, to drag down the staircase thy deep armchair, thy chair and mine, for in it we repose side by side in the evening and sometimes in the morning too. I heard it groan in the arms of those tatterde-malions; that chair which is a fetish and a benignant spirit. Thou didst offer no resistance to the invaders. But if thou dost no longer possess any of those genii who once filled thy dwell-ing, if thou hast lost all, even those little divinities, which thou didst put on in the morning when getting out of bed, those slippers which I used to bite in my play, if thou art indigent and poor, O my Master, then what will become of me?'

THE MEDITATIONS OF RIQUET

I

Men, beasts and stones grow great as they come near and loom enormous when they are upon me. It is not so with me. I remain equally great wheresoever I am.

II

When my master places for me beneath the table the food which he was about to put into his own mouth, it is in order that he may tempt me and that he may punish me if I yield to temptation. For I cannot believe that he would deny himself for my sake.

III

The smell of dogs is sweet in the nostrils.

IV

My master keeps me warm when I lie behind him in his chair. It is because he is a god. In front of the fire-place is a hot stone. That stone is divine.

V

I speak when I please. From my master's mouth proceed likewise sounds which make sense. But his meaning is not so clear as that expressed by the sounds of my voice. Every sound that I utter has a meaning. From my master's lips come forth many idle noises. It is difficult but necessary to divine the thoughts of the master.

VI

To eat is good. To have eaten is better. For the enemy who lieth in wait to take your food is quick and crafty.

VII

All is flux and reflux. I alone remain.

VIII

I am in the centre of all things; men, beasts and things, friendly and adverse, are ranged about me.

IX

In sleep one beholdeth men, dogs, horses, trees, forms pleasant and unpleasant. When one awaketh these forms have vanished.

X

Reflection. I love my master, Bergeret, because he is powerful and terrible.

XI

An action for which one has been beaten is a bad action. An action for which one has received caresses or food is a good action.

XII

At nightfall evil powers prowl round the house. I bark in order that my master may be warned and drive them away.

XIII

Prayer. O my master, Bergeret, god of courage, I adore thee. When thou art terrible, be thou praised. When thou art kind be thou praised. I crouch at thy feet: I lick thy hands. When, seated before thy table spread, thou devourest meats in abundance, thou art very great and very beautiful. Very great art thou and very beautiful when, striking fire out of a thin splint of wood, thou changest night into day. Keep me in thine house and keep out every other dog. And thou, Angélique, the cook, divinity good and great, I fear thee and I venerate thee in order that thou mayest give me much to eat.

XIV

A dog who lacketh piety towards men and who scorneth the fetishes assembled in his master's house liveth a miserable and a wandering life.

XV

One day, from a broken pitcher, filled with water which was being carried across the parlour, water ran on to the polished floor. A thrashing must have been the punishment of that dirty pitcher.

XVI

Men possess the divine power of opening all doors. I by myself am only able to open a few. Doors are great fetishes which do not readily obey dogs.

XVII

The life of a dog is full of danger. If he would escape suffering he must be ever on the watch, during meals and even during sleep.

XIX

Invocation. O Fear, Fear august and maternal. Fear sacred

and salutary, possess me, in danger fill me, in order that I may void that which is harmful, lest, casting myself upon the enemy, I suffer for my imprudence.

XX

Vehicles there are which horses pull through the street. They are terrible. Other vehicles there are which move themselves breathing loudly. These are also fearful. Men in rags are detestable, likewise such as carry baskets on their heads or roll casks. I do not love children who utter loud cries and flee from and pursue each other swiftly in the streets. The world is full of hostile and dreadful things.

Tiddlywinks and the Train Wrecker

DOROTHY COTTRELL

MARY had brought Tiddlywinks home from school, 'as the parting gift of a dear friend'—although there were those who maintained that he was unquestionably the deed of an enemy.

Tiddlywinks was a terrier of the variety known as Australian. This means that he weighed about twenty pounds, was delightfully stocky of body and short of leg, with a long coat of silver-grey silk not trailing and effeminate, as are the coats of some terriers, but which gleamingly plumed his stubby tail and fell in wisps across his brown eyes.

He possessed a tremendous small dog's dignity, but had the misfortune to live in a big dog's world. Thus he supplied the main relaxation of the other, and larger, dogs of Grey Farm. For instance, he would be crossing the yard, with his two-inch tail very upright, his front feet moving with great dignity and his hind feet following them in a springy sort of fashion and slightly sideways, when Keela, the big sheep dog, would apparently say to Lad, her husband, 'Let's play a little football, dear!' And with the destroying charge of a locomotive they would bear down upon Tiddlywinks.

255

Sometimes he did not see them coming, and only realized they had come when he was sorting himself out of the dust and brambles. But for a long while, when he *did* see, he demonstrated much that 'lightning getaway' that its advertisers claim for 'Spinks Sparkling Gasoline which gives your accelerator acceleration'.

Keela and Lad particularly liked this as, when they caught him at high speed, he usually turned over three or four times.

So at last he learned not to run when he saw disaster overtaking him, but instead to sit down *hard*, shut his eyes, and howl for help.

This rather spoiled the big dogs' enjoyment. Still they could roll him over, and worry his stomach, and laugh at the way it made his legs revolve—or else have tugs of war with him.

It must not be thought that his misfortunes were not in part his own fault. He could have lived in the flower garden, into which the other dogs were not allowed to come. But he would go out beneath the gate, a difficult process in itself, which involved his lying flat, getting his head and front paws under, bulging himself out wide, and then frantically prying for leverage with his hind feet, to the accompaniment of violent wriggles of his tail. Just why he took so much trouble to reach the humiliations that awaited him on the outer side was hard to understand.

But, on seeing someone approaching the house or passing on the highway, he would tear down the path, fairly bursting with growls, push desperately beneath the gate—making it impossible to open whilst he was there—and get outside just in time for the big dogs to play catchers with him. . . . Under the very noses of the people he had sought to impress!

In all the household only Mary divined anything of the tragedy of his situation, the general consensus of family opinion being that he was 'a pest'. And indeed he usually was stuck under the gate when it should have been opened in a hurry, or in the way when Keela was bringing up her sheep, or scurrying past the cows just as they were having their 'cream milk' taken—so that they tossed their heads and refused to let it down.

At night he slept before Mary's door, and if Mrs. Grey tried to go in he made as much fuss as if she had been Mrs. Captain Kidd or Jack the Ripper!

When he bathed he never shook until he was somewhere wherein it would do great damage. Even Mrs. Grey agreed with Mary's father that 'a good home should be found' for him —a good home meaning a place as far away from Grey Farm as possible.

Mary said defensively: 'He has a noble heart—and some day he'll do something great that will surprise you all!'

Whereat instead of being bashful, Tiddlywinks merely growled a little, and spurned the earth, or set out for no place in particular to show the smaller dogs, for which he was always vainly seeking, what he would do to them if they didn't look out!

Grey Farm lay some five miles from Peddle, a little country town of New South Wales, lost in hills whose gentler slopes were close-cropped and green and set with huge ring-barked trees, and whose more precipitous places were still virgin brush tangles all veiled with matted, sweet-scented bush things. At the time of this tale 'Old Bolshy' Karaseff had just come out of the Peddle jail, wherein he had been confined for throwing a tomato at the mayor. Old Bolshy had once—so at least he said —been a Russian count, and had been sent to Siberia because he gave some grains of wheat to a starving peasant—instead of letting him go on starving according to the best Russian traditions. Anyway, he had been to Siberia—or if he hadn't he thought that he had, and that is assumably much the same.

It had turned him 'a little queer'. For instance, he said that we were all 'bourgeois', instead of admitting the obvious truth that we were simply dairy farmers and growers of turnips and carrots. He said we 'crawled' to kings, and licked the boots of princes, and were guilty of many other humiliating and indigestible practices.

When Old Bolshy came out of jail he was quieter than he had been, but once or twice John Grey said that he 'didn't like the look of him' as he went muttering and mumbling about. Still everyone secretly believes that things like murder, or incendiarism, or riot, which happen in other districts and lands, can't really happen in your own. Anyway, we said that 'Old Bolshy was looking black' and—forgot him.

It was, as recorded above, about five miles from the Grey place into Peddle—that is, it was five miles if you took the short

R

cut across the hills, and then chanced walking on the railway viaduct. (This latter act was illegal, but as the village constable went home by the viaduct every evening, nothing was done about it.)

On a clear, blowing day, Mary set out along the short cut with Tiddlywinks—running at the front end and bouncing behind—as her escort.

They crossed the cleared paddock and the wattle paddock and then went up into the lonely brush country of thicket and ravine.

Lyre birds were calling, and the girl found quite a bunch of wild violets, while Tiddlywinks frisked about and chased things and was generally important.

The sort of day when death, and evil, and hate, seem just silly words.

On top of the Big Hill—below which the deep railway cutting ran—they turned off to get some rosy waratah leaves . . . and wandered across to the top of the cutting.

Tiddlywinks looked over the edge and cocked his head and wriggled his tail interestedly. Mary looked over too.

About five hundred feet down lay the tracks, and a man was working at them. Or rather he was working at the bank on the far side.

There was something vaguely queer about his actions, and Mary tried to see what he was doing.

She knew that when the trains left Peddle they used to go slowly across the big viaduct, and then gather speed, and come singing their power song up the long grade, and be going, in the words of Driver MacTavish, 'like puffin', snortin' hell' when they came round the bend below the Big Hill. When she was a child she had once heard her father say that it was the 'perfect place for a wreck'.

Now, because of the intervening limbs, she could not get a good view of what the man was doing, and rather wanted to know.

So, instead of going on by the short cut, she climbed down breaking through the sweet white clematis wreaths, and holding by the young, springy, gum saplings. She went quietly and at last came out on the tracks.

She was not at all alarmed, but just curious; for it was an unusual thing to see a solitary man working away at an important cutting.

Tiddlywinks and Mary rounded the turn simultaneously and beheld Old Bolshy, inflamed of face and dripping with sweat, prying at the base of a great twenty-foot boulder!

The crazy aspect of the man, and the evil import of what he was doing, startled the girl, so that she gave a small exclamation of fright. . . . There could not be over half an hour's time until the express came thundering royally round the bend!

The man stood, swaying slightly, glaring with the frantic menace of unswervable purpose; then he ran at her savagely.

In his reddened eyes and general appearance of insanity she saw her danger, but she wanted to get past him and warn the train. So, instead of running back, she tried to spring past— and he caught her about the waist.

'Be still, you little fool, and you will not get hurt!' She knew it was a million to one chance against anyone's being within earshot. . . . But the express was coming in half an hour! She screamed, with the ringing clarity of healthy young lungs. Screamed so that the echoes shook back from the soft ravines, and a grey lyre bird darted across a rock.

Old Bolshy tried to put his huge dirty hand over her mouth, but she twisted free, matching her young strength against his crazed one. Again she screamed, and then he struck her in the face, and her world went out in darkness.

He flung her down, not on the lines, but beside them, with indifference as to what would be her fate in the crashing pile-up of speeding engine and carriages. Then he savagely kicked Tiddlywinks, who was trying to tear the leg of his trousers! And Tiddlywinks did his famous treble somersault.

Old Bolshy went on labouring at his work of destruction, his eyes lighted by a maniacal purpose that was almost holy.

Lion hearts are not everything in this world. Tiddlywinks set out to find his friend, the station master in Peddle, and bring him back suitably to avenge unbearable insult. He went with his front half running straight and low, his hind half bounding rather high and slightly crooked. Round the curve he fled, faster and faster on the down grade to the bridge. His ears flapped back, his grey eyebrows were tossed by the wind as he took the straight run on to the big viaduct.

All his life he had crossed the viaduct, or any other bridge, with infinite care that he did not break it by his great weight; stepping softly and high, that he might cause it as little shock as possible, and taking a long time to put a foot down when once he had raised it. But now he was not going to consider his personal safety.

There was a double set of tracks across the viaduct, so that if any of the townspeople were caught on its quarter-mile span by a train, they just stepped from one set to the other.

As Tiddlywinks came on to the viaduct at one end the express moved out from the Peddle station.

It came chuffing deliberately forward, wriggled its length slightly as it crossed the points, gathered pulsing momentum of piston, whistled self-importantly and rolled thunderously down toward the bridge . . . and Tiddlywinks!

The engine driver, looking ahead along the shining rails, saw, far down the bridge on the centre of his track, a small grey speck . . . a greyish-silver lump . . . a little fat dog, with its muzzle raised appealing to heaven, pouring forth inaudible wails. The engine driver had a schedule, but he had once possessed a dog of his own, a small dog whose death had left his world very bleak and empty.

The bridge shuddered and the lines cried as he applied the brakes. Passengers left their seats unexpectedly . . . iron ground on iron . . . the express had stopped!

Tiddlywinks sat firmly on his tail, wailing to the skies.

The engine driver had great faith in portents. 'There be more to it, mon, I tell thee, than meets the oie!' said Driver MacTavish to his fireman. ''Tisn't natural for a dog in possession o' his moind to sit fair in the way o' doom for no pourpose! If he didn' mean to stop of us why didn' he run on to the other tracks?' By this time they were standing beside the cause of the stop, and the speaker poked Tiddlywinks with a kindly foot. Tiddlywinks opened his eyes, and, finding himself living and help at hand, he looked desperately up at the men and the towering engine, then began to run agitatedly back to where he knew Mary was lying at the mercy of one of the many varieties of deadly peril that inhabited the world.

'He's mad', said the prosaic fireman.

'He's a warning!' said the engine driver firmly. 'Look at the lookin' back o' him! Look how he stopped us if it took his bonny wee loife!'

So it was that, instead of coming roaring and singing her power song round the turn to the great cutting, the express came chuffing gently in the wake of Tiddlywinks—who was running rather low in front and gallopng high and rather sideways behind.

. . . And they found a great hurtled mass of rock across the lines and an unconscious girl lying where the carriages would have piled above her; while a poor crazed creature waited with evil glee to see the destruction he had wrought.

'I would never have dreamed he had it in him!' said Mr. Grey, rather unsteadily, as he looked at Tiddlywinks, who swaggered uppishly about seeking for the other smaller dogs whom he never found! And on Tiddlywink's neck amidst the grey silk of his ruff hung glinting the Royal Humane Society's medal 'for the saving of human life'.

'You can never tell what's in a dog's heart', Mary's mother said softly. 'Think if we had sent him away . . . why, Mary would have been—'

But only the one who loved him best knew what had been in Tiddlywink's heart.

After she came out of the hospital, Mary had held his fat firmness of twenty-pound body very closely, while he rolled his whiskers and growled a little, and into one of his silver, lopping ears she had whispered:

'You thought it was Keela and Lad coming when you saw the horrid 'spress—didn't you, darling?'

But in her eyes this was no detraction, for even the bravest must at times sit on their tails and call for help.

S.P.C.A. Case 280,141

JOHN HELD, JR.

I'VE always been proud of the fact that I can take it. Yeah, any way it comes. I've been three days now with nothing to eat and no water. It don't mean a thing to me.

There ain't any of 'em my weight I can't win from. I can give 'em eight pounds and eat 'em up. I've done it so I know. Many's the time I've gone without eating for longer than three days. That's the way they train me for a fight. Makes me more vicious when I'm hungry. And Jeeze, do I eat 'em? Ask 'em. Go on and ask 'em. I know it's three days because I can see the light through the grating up on the sidewalk. It's come dark three times. The only light I've ever seen is through that grating.

We always fight at night. That's the only time He ever takes me out is when we're going to fight. He works me on a tread-mill to build up my strenck. I always know when there's going to be a fight because He feeds me plenty. Then every day on the mill, and that turns the heavy grub into big long muscles on my shoulders and quarters. Then I get starved to make me lean and vicious. I'm vicious all right without the starving part of it.

I eat 'em up, I do. I'm so mean that His brother had to feed me on a long pole when He was in stir. They got Him with a loft full of sacramental wine, then they railroaded Him before the wrong judge. A great bunch, the cops. Can't trust 'em. He pays plenty for protection and never knows whether He's going to get it or no. But I suppose that's part of the racket.

This fight game is a racket, too, but there's no paying for protection for fights. The cops say that fighting is cruel. Maybe it is, but it's my game and it's all I know. They have to be plenty quiet about where they hold the fights. We generally have 'em upstairs in the stables where they keep the horses that they rent to pedlars. They always bet lots of jack on our fights, so you see the better I can take it the more valuable I am to Him.

He's a great little guy. He can take it as well as I can. He always says He's ready. He never knows when He's going to get it in the back, which is the way His kind fight. He never packs a rod. He gets his work done for Him by the needle-workers and the hopheads. It ain't because He's yellow that He don't pack a rod, it's just that the cops are always trying to hang something on Him, but He never gives 'em a chanct.

I hate cops just like He does. I don't see why there has to be cops. They are against everything. There may be some good cops, but the general run of 'em are always coming 'round and asking personal questions or taking Him in to give Him the works, but He is a wise egg and never knows nothing. He's no squealer. Squealers don't live long in this district.

It seems like He's getting me ready for a fight, not feeding me or bringing me a drink for all this time. But there's something queer about it all. I haven't had the heavy feeding or any work on the treadmill. But I'm in fighting trim without it.

I sort of look forward to a good stiff battle. I'd like to get my teeth in one of those Long Island City babies right this minute. I'd tear him to shreds. I'm getting sick of the clank of my chain.

I'd sort of like to see Him. I like it when He comes down and runs His hands over my back and neck to see if I'm hard. Perhaps this is going to be a hard fight and He wants to get me extra vicious. Maybe He has made a big bet on me. He don't need to worry. I'll win for Him. I would like a drink of water. I've tried to lick the moisture off the basement wall, but there ain't much. But what the Hell, I'm tough enough to take it. I wish He would come down to see if I was hard. I don't know what's the matter with me, but I feel kind of creepy every time that cop walks across the grating up there. I can always tell cops' feet. There he is now. He's stopping. There's a second cop's feet. Now the second cop is talking.

'We don't need to worry about this Dago any more.'

The first cop says, 'What happened?'

Then the second one says, 'They took him for a ride.'

'Who?'

'Eddie the Wop.'

That's Him they are talking about. Him. He's Eddie the Wop.

'Yeah, they found him up outside of White Plains in the blue car.'

'Dead!'

'Deader than Hell. Six holes in the back of his curly head.'

Those cops are crazy. It can't be him. They wouldn't take Him for a ride. He's no squealer. Maybe it's just because I'm hungry that I'm hearing things. No. Here the cops come down the steps.

'The Captain told me to come over here and look things over. What's down here? Have you got your flashlight?'

Now they are flashing the light all round the basement. I'm growling, low, I always like to give 'em a chanct. But don't let 'em come too near. I'll eat 'em up. I always wanted a chanct to tear up a cop.

'Look out for the dog', one of 'em says.

'Jesus, he looks like a nasty one', says the other one.

'Shall I let him have it?' asks the first one as he takes out his gat.

'Hell, no, if you shoot him you'll have to make out a report. I'll phone the S.P. Let them do the dirty work.'

Then they both go back up to the sidewalk and go away. Then He wasn't starving me for a fight. He's dead. He won't come down and chain me in the mill again. I'll never see Him no more. Jeeze, I wish I could break this chain, I'd go up and tear those cops to ribbons. I'll bet it was a cop that done it to

Him. I'll bet it was. I'd like to get my teeth into that yellow quitter.

I wish there was a weak link in my chain so I could kink it and get loose. They have left the door open. If I could get off this chain I could go out there on the street and tear a few cops to pieces. I'd get even with them for putting Him on the spot.

He won't come down here with His friends no more to show them how vicious I am. That was fine sport. I would lunge on my chain and curl back my lips and show my sharp teeth and roar. And then He would pretend to give me the boot and I would pretend to go into a mad rage. His friends would be scared stiff. That won't happen no more.

I wish I could get a little sleep, but the hunger pains keep me awake. My mouth is dry and sticky. I'd like a drink to cool my tongue. I wonder what will happen to me now that He's gone. Jeeze, time goes slow now that I know He won't ever come again. I wish that cop had let me have it. Then I would be dead the same as Him.

Now there's somebody else coming down the steps. Another one come to look around, I suppose. Yeah, it's a cop all right. He's in a uniform. Maybe I can chew this one up. He's coming right over to me. He ain't afraid like the others were. I'll get him.

But he smells of dog. There's something wrong here. He's in uniform, and he smells of dog and he ain't afraid of me! I guess this guy must be all right. Now he's undoing my chain. He's leading me out, and I'm going up the steps into the daylight. This is the first time I've ever been out in daylight. Now he's unfastening the doors of a car that's built like a cage. He's putting me in. There's straw on the floor of the cage, and there's been dogs in here. I wonder where we're going. It must be O.K. because he wasn't afraid of me.

Brown Wolf

JACK LONDON

SHE had delayed because of the dew-wet grass, in order to put
on her rubbers, and when she emerged from the house found
her waiting husband absorbed in the wonder of a bursting
almond-bud. She sent a questioning glance across the tall grass
and in and out among the orchard trees.

'Where's Wolf?' she asked.

'He was here a moment ago.' Walt Irvine drew himself away
with a jerk from the metaphysics and poetry of the organic
miracle of blossom, and surveyed the landscape. 'He was running a rabbit the last I saw of him.'

'Wolf! Wolf! Here, Wolf!' she called, as they left the clearing and took the trail that led down through the waxen-belled
manzanita jungle to the country road.

Irvine thrust between his lips the little finger of each hand and
lent to her efforts a shrill whistling.

She covered her ears hastily, and made a wry grimace.

'My! for a poet, delicately attuned and all the rest of it, you can make unlovely noises. My ear-drums are pierced. You out-whistle—'

'Orpheus.'

'I was about to say a street arab', she concluded severely.

'Poesy does not prevent one from being practical—at least it doesn't prevent *me*. Mine is no futility of genius that can't sell gems to the magazines.'

He assumed a mock extravagance, and went on:

'I am no attic singer, no ballroom warbler. And why? Because I am practical. Mine is no squalor of song that cannot transmute itself, with proper exchange value, into a flower-crowned cottage, a sweet mountain meadow, a grove of red-woods, an orchard of thirty-seven trees, one long row of black-berries, and two short rows of strawberries, to say nothing of a quarter of a mile of gurgling brook. I am a beauty merchant, a trader in song, and I pursue utility, dear Madge. I sing a song, and, thanks to the magazine editors, I transmute my song into a waft of the west wind sighing through our redwoods, into a murmur of waters over mossy stones that sings back to me another song than the one I sang and yet the same song wonderfully—er—transmuted.'

'Oh, that all your song transmutations were as successful!' she laughed.

'Name one that wasn't.'

'Those two beautiful sonnets that you transmuted into the cow that was accounted the worst milker in the township.'

'She was beautiful—' he began.

'But she didn't give milk', Madge interrupted.

'But she *was* beautiful, now, wasn't she?' he insisted.

'And here's where beauty and utility fall out', was her reply. 'And there's the Wolf!'

From the thicket-covered hillside came a crashing of under-brush, and then, forty feet above them, on the edge of the sheer wall of rock, appeared a wolf's head and shoulders. His braced fore paws dislodged a pebble, and with sharp-pricked ears and peering gaze he watched the fall of the pebble till it struck at their feet. Then he transferred his gaze and with open mouth laughed down at them.

'You Wolf, you!' and 'You blessed Wolf!' the man and woman called out to him.

The ears flattened back and down at the sound, and the head seemed to snuggle under the caress of an invisible hand.

They watched him scramble backward into the thicket, then proceeded on their way. Several minutes later, rounding a turn in the trail, where the descent was less precipitous, he joined them in the midst of a miniature avalanche of pebbles and loose soil. He was not demonstrative. A pat and a rub around the ears from the man, and a more prolonged caressing from the woman, and he was away down the trail in front of them, gliding effortlessly over the ground in true wolf fashion.

In build and coat and brush he was a huge timber wolf; but the lie was given to his wolfhood by his colour and marking. There the dog unmistakably advertised itself. No wolf was ever coloured like him. He was brown, deep brown, red brown, an orgy of browns. Back and shoulders were a warm brown that paled on the sides and underneath to a yellow that was dingy because of the brown that lingered in it. The white of the throat and paws and the spots over the eyes were dirty because of the persistent and ineradicable brown, while the eyes themselves were twin topazes, golden and brown.

The man and woman loved the dog very much; perhaps this was because it had been such a task to win his love. It had been no easy matter, when he first drifted in mysteriously out of nowhere to their little mountain cottage. Footsore and famished, he had killed a rabbit under their very noses and under their very window, and then crawled away and slept by the spring at the foot of the blackberry bushes. When Walt Irvine went down to inspect the intruder, he was snarled at for his pains, and Madge likewise was snarled at when she went down to present, as a peace offering, a large pan of bread and milk.

A most unsociable dog he proved to be, resenting all their advances, refusing to let them lay hands on him, menacing them with bared fangs, and bristling hair. Nevertheless, he remained, sleeping and resting by the spring, and eating the food they gave him after they had set it down at a safe distance and retreated. His wretched physical condition explained why he lingered; and when he had recuperated, after several days' sojourn, he disappeared.

And this would have been the end of him so far as Irvine and his wife were concerned, had not Irvine at that particular time been called away into the northern part of the State. Riding along on the train, near to the line between California and Oregon, he chanced to look out of the window and saw his unsociable guest sliding along the wagon road, brown and wolfish, tired yet tireless, dust-covered and soiled with two hundred miles of travel.

Now, Irvine was a man of impulse, a poet. He got off the train at the next station, bought a piece of meat at a butcher shop, and captured the vagrant on the outskirts of the town. The return trip was made in the baggage-car, and so Wolf came a second time to the mountain cottage. Here he was tied up for a week and made love to by the man and woman. But it was very circumspect love-making. Remote and alien as a traveller from another planet, he snarled down their soft-spoken love-words. He never barked. In all the time they had him he was never known to bark.

To win him became a problem. Irvine liked problems. He had a metal plate made on which was stamped: 'RETURN TO WALT IRVINE, GLEN ELLEN, SONOMA COUNTY, CALIFORNIA.' This was riveted to a collar and strapped about the dog's neck. Then he was turned loose, and promptly disappeared. A day later came a telegram from Mendocino County. In twenty hours he had made over a hundred miles to the north, and was still going when captured.

He came back by Wells-Fargo Express, was tied up three days, and was loosed on the fourth and lost. This time he gained southern Oregon before he was caught and returned. Always, as soon as he received his liberty, he fled away, and always he fled north. He was possessed of an obsession that drove him north. The homing instinct, Irvine called it, after he had expended the selling price of a sonnet in getting the animal back from northern Oregon.

Another time the brown wanderer succeeded in traversing half the length of California, all of Oregon, and most of Washington before he was picked up and returned collect. A remarkable thing was the speed with which he travelled. Fed up and rested, as soon as he was loosed he devoted all his energy to getting over the ground. On the first day's run he was known to cover as much as a hundred and fifty miles, and after that he would average a hundred miles a day until caught. He always arrived back lean and hungry and savage, and always departed fresh and vigorous, cleaving his way northward in response to some prompting of his being that no one could understand.

But at last, after a futile year of flight, he accepted the inevitable and elected to remain at the cottage where first he had killed the rabbit and slept by the spring. Even after that, a long time elapsed before the man and woman succeeded in patting him. It was a great victory, for they alone were allowed to put hands on him. He was fastidiously exclusive, and no guest at the cottage ever succeeded in making up to him. A low growl greeted a stranger's approach; if he had the hardihood to come nearer, the lips lifted, the naked fangs appeared, and the growl became a snarl—a snarl so terrible and malignant that it awed the stoutest of them, as it likewise awed the farmers' dogs, that knew ordinary dog-snarling but had never heard wolf-snarling before.

He was without antecedents. His history began with Walt and Madge. He had come up from the south, but never a clue did they get of the owner from whom he had evidently fled. Mrs. Johnson, their nearest neighbour and the one who supplied them with milk, proclaimed him a Klondike dog. Her brother was burrowing for frozen pay-streaks in that far country, and so she constituted herself an authority on the subject.

But they did not dispute her. There were the tips of Wolf's ears, obviously so severely frozen at some time that they would never quite heal again. Besides, he looked like the photographs of the Alaskan dogs they saw published in magazines and newspapers. They often speculated over his past, and tried to conjure up (from what they had read and heard) what his Northland life had been. That the Northland still drew him they knew; for at night they sometimes heard him crying softly; and when the north wind blew and the bite of frost was in the air, a great restlessness would come upon him and he would lift a mournful lament which they knew to be the long wolf-howl. Yet he never barked. No provocation was great enough to draw from him that canine cry.

Long discussion they had during the time of winning him, as to whose dog he was. Each claimed him, and each proclaimed loudly any expression of affection made by him. But the man had the best of it at first, chiefly because he was a man. It was patent that Wolf had had no experience with women. He did not understand women. Madge's skirts were something he never quite accepted. The rustle of them was enough to set him a-bristle with suspicion, and on a windy day she could not approach him at all.

On the other hand, it was Madge who fed him; also it was she who ruled the kitchen, and it was by her favour, and her favour alone, that he was permitted to come within that sacred precinct. It was because of these things that she bade fair to overcome the handicap of her garments. Then it was that Walt put forth special effort, making it a practice to have Wolf lie at his feet while he wrote, and, between petting and talking, losing much time from his work. Walt won in the end, and his victory was most probably due to the fact that he was a man, though Madge averred that they would have had another quarter of a mile of gurgling brook, and at least two west winds sighing through their redwoods, had Walt properly devoted his energies to song-transmutation and left Wolf alone to exercise a natural taste and an unbiased judgement.

'It's about time I heard about those triolets', Walt said, after a silence of five minutes, during which they had swung steadily down the trail. 'There'll be a cheque at the post-office, I know, and we'll transmute it into beautiful buckwheat flour, a gallon of maple syrup, and a new pair of rubbers for you.'

'And into beautiful milk from Mrs. Johnson's beautiful cow', Madge added. 'Tomorrow's the first of the month you know.' Walt scowled unconsciously, then his face brightened and he clapped his hand to his breast pocket.

'Never mind. I have here a nice beautiful cow, the best milker in California.'

'When did you write it?' she demanded eagerly. Then, reproachfully, 'And you never showed it to me.'

'I saved it to read to you on the way to the post-office, in a spot remarkably like this one', he answered, indicating with a wave of his hand a dry log on which to sit.

A tiny stream flowed out of a dense fern-brake, slipped down a mossy-lipped stone, and ran across the path at their feet. From the valley arose the mellow song of meadow larks, while about them, in and out, through sunshine and shadow, fluttered great yellow butterflies.

Up from below came another sound that broke in upon Walt reading softly from his manuscript. It was a crunching of heavy feet, punctuated now and again by the clattering of a displaced stone. As Walt finished and looked to his wife for approval, a man came into view around the turn of the trail. He was bareheaded and sweaty. With a handkerchief in one hand he mopped his face, while in the other hand he carried a new hat and a wilted starched collar which he had removed from his neck. He was a well-built man, and his muscles seemed on the point of bursting out of the painfully new and ready-made black clothes he wore.

'Warm day', Walt greeted him. Walt believed in country democracy, and never missed an opportunity to practise it.

The man paused and nodded.

'I guess I ain't used much to the warm', he vouchsafed half-apologetically. 'I'm more accustomed to zero weather.'

'You don't find any of that in this country', Walt laughed.

'Should say not', the man answered. 'An' I ain't here a-lookin' for it, neither. I'm tryin' to find my sister. Mebbe you know where she lives. Her name's Johnson, Mrs. William Johnson.'

'You're not her Klondike brother,' Madge cried, her eyes bright with interest, 'about whom we've heard so much?'

'Yes'm, that's me', he answered modestly. 'My name's Miller, Skiff Miller. I just thought I'd s'prise her.'

'You are on the right track, then. Only you've come by the footpath.' Madge stood up to direct him, pointing up the canyon a quarter of a mile. 'You see that blasted redwood? Take the little trail turning off to the right. It's the short cut to her house. You can't miss it.'

'Yes'm, thank you, ma'am', he said.

He made tentative efforts to go, but seemed awkwardly rooted to the spot. He was gazing at her with an open admiration of which he was quite unconscious, and which was drowning, along with him, in the rising sea of embarrassment in which he floundered.

'We'd like to hear you tell about the Klondike', Madge said. 'Mayn't we come over some day while you are at your sister's? Or, better yet, won't you come over and have dinner with us?'

'Yes'm; thank you ma'am', he mumbled mechanically. Then he caught himself up and added, 'I ain't stoppin' long. I got to be pullin' north again. I go out on tonight's train. You see, I've got a mail contract with the Government.'

When Madge had said that it was too bad, he made another futile effort to go. But he could not take his eyes from her face. He forgot his embarrassment in his admiration, and it was her turn to flush and feel uncomfortable.

It was at this juncture, when Walt had just decided it was time for him to be saying something to relieve the strain, that Wolf, who had been away nosing through the brush, trotted wolf-like into view.

Skiff Miller's abstraction disappeared. The pretty woman before him passed out of his field of vision. He had eyes only for the dog, and a great wonder came into his face.

'Well, I'll be durned!' he enunciated slowly and solemnly.

He sat ponderingly on the log, leaving Madge standing. At the sound of his voice, Wolf's ears had flattened down, and his mouth had opened in a laugh. He trotted slowly up to the stranger and first smelled his hands, then licked them with his tongue.

Skiff Miller patted the dog's head, and slowly and solemnly repeated, 'Well, I'll be durned!'

'Excuse me, ma'am', he said the next moment; 'I was just s'prised some, that was all.'

'We're surprised too', she answered lightly. 'We never saw Wolf make up to a stranger before.'

'Is that what you call him—Wolf?' the man asked.

Madge nodded. 'But I can't understand his friendliness toward you—unless it's because you're from the Klondike. He's a Klondike dog, you know.'

'Yes'm', Miller said absently. He lifted one of Wolf's fore legs and examined the footpads, pressing them and denting them with his thumb. 'Kind of soft', he remarked. 'He ain't been on trail for a long time.'

'I say,' Walt broke in, 'it is remarkable the way he lets you handle him.'

Skiff Miller arose, no longer awkward with admiration of Madge, and in a sharp, businesslike manner asked, 'How long have you had him?'

But just then the dog, squirming and rubbing against the

S

newcomer's legs, opened his mouth and barked. It was an explosive bark, brief and joyous, but a bark.

'That's a new one on me', Skiff Miller remarked.

Walt and Madge stared at each other. The miracle had happened. Wolf had barked.

'It's the first time he ever barked', Madge said.

'First time I ever heard him, too', Miller volunteered.

Madge smiled at him. The man was evidently a humourist.

'Of course,' she said, 'since you have only seen him for five minutes.'

Skiff Miller looked at her sharply, seeking in her face the guile her words had led him to suspect.

'I thought you understood', he said slowly. 'I thought you tumbled to it from his makin' up to me. He's my dog. His name ain't Wolf. It's Brown.'

'Oh, Walt!' was Madge's instinctive cry to her husband.

Walt was on the defensive at once.

'How do you know he's your dog?' he demanded.

'Because he is', was the reply.

'Mere assertion', Walt said sharply.

In his slow and pondering way Skiff Miller looked at him, then asked, with a nod of his head toward Madge:

'How d'you know she's your wife? You just say, "Because she is", and I'll say it's mere assertion. The dog's mine. I bred 'm an' raised 'm, an' I guess I ought to know. Look here, I'll prove it to you.'

Skiff Miller turned to the dog. 'Brown!' His voice rang out sharply, and at the sound the dog's ears flattened down as to a caress. 'Gee!' The dog made a swinging turn to the right. 'Now mush on!' And the dog ceased his swing abruptly and started straight ahead, halting obediently at command.

'I can do it with whistles', Skiff Miller said proudly. 'He was my lead dog.'

'But you are not going to take him away with you?' Madge asked tremulously.

The man nodded.

'Back into that awful Klondike world of suffering?'

He nodded and added, 'Oh, it ain't so bad as all that. Look at me. Pretty healthy specimen, ain't I?'

'But the dog! The terrible hardship, the heart-breaking toil, the starvation, the frost! Oh, I've read about it and I know.'

'I nearly ate him once, over on Little Fish River', Miller volunteered grimly. 'Gettin' a moose that day was all that saved 'm.'

'I'd have died first!' Madge cried.

'Things is different down here', Miller explained. 'You don't have to eat dogs. You think differently just about the time you're all in. You've never been all in, so you don't know anything about it.'

'That's the very point', she argued warmly. 'Dogs are not eaten in California. Why not leave him here? He is happy. He'll never want for food—you know that. He'll never suffer from cold and hardship. Here all is softness and gentleness. Neither the human nor nature is savage. He will never know a whip-lash again. And as for the weather—why, it never snows here.'

'But it's all-fired hot in summer, beggin' your pardon', Skiff Miller laughed.

'But you do not answer', Madge continued passionately. 'What have you to offer him in that Northland life?'

'Grub, when I've got it, and that's most of the time', came the answer.

'And the rest of the time?'

'No grub.'

'And the work?'

'Yes, plenty of work', Miller blurted out impatiently. 'Work without end, an' famine, an' frost, an' all the rest of the miseries—that's what he'll get when he comes with me. But he likes it. He is used to it. He knows that life. He was born to it an' brought up to it. An' you don't know anything about it. You don't know what you're talking about. That's where the dog belongs, and that's where he'll be happiest.'

'The dog doesn't go', Walt announced in a determined voice. 'So there is no need of further discussion.'

'What's that?' Skiff Miller demanded, his brows lowering and an obstinate flush of blood reddening his forehead.

'I said the dog doesn't go, and that settles it. I don't believe he's your dog. You may have seen him sometime. You may even sometime have driven him for his owner. But his obeying the ordinary driving-commands of the Alaskan trail is no demonstration that he is yours. Any dog in Alaska would obey you as he obeyed. Besides, he is undoubtedly a valuable dog, as dogs go in Alaska, and that is sufficient explanation of your desire to get possession of him. Anyway, you've got to prove property.'

Skiff Miller, cool and collected, the obstinate flush a trifle deeper on his forehead, his huge muscles bulging under the black cloth of his coat, carefully looked the poet up and down as though measuring the strength of his slenderness.

The Klondiker's face took on a contemptuous expression as he said finally, 'I reckon there's nothing in sight to prevent me takin' the dog right here an' now.'

Walt's face reddened, and the striking-muscles of his arms and shoulders seemed to stiffen and grow tense. His wife fluttered apprehensively into the breach.

'Maybe Mr. Miller is right', she said. 'I am afraid that he is. Wolf does seem to know him, and certainly he answers to the name of "Brown". He made friends with him instantly, and you know that's something he never did with anybody before. Besides, look at the way he barked. He was just bursting with joy. Joy over what? Without doubt at finding Mr. Miller.'

Walt's striking-muscles relaxed, and his shoulders seemed to droop with hopelessness.

'I guess you're right, Madge', he said. 'Wolf isn't Wolf, but Brown, and he must belong to Mr. Miller.'

'Perhaps Mr. Miller will sell him', she suggested. 'We can buy him.'

Skiff Miller shook his head, no longer belligerent, but kindly, quick to be generous in response to generousness.

'I had five dogs', he said, casting about for the easiest way to temper his refusal. 'He was the leader. They was the crack team of Alaska. Nothin' could touch 'em. In 1898 I refused five thousand dollars for the bunch. Dogs was high then, anyway; but that wasn't what made the fancy price. It was the team itself. Brown was the best in the team. That winter I refused twelve hundred for 'm. I didn't sell 'm then, an' I ain't a-sellin' 'm now. Besides, I think a mighty lot of that dog. I've been lookin' for 'm for three years. It made me fair sick when I found he'd been stole—not the value of him, but the—well, I liked 'm like hell, that's all, beggin' your pardon. I couldn't believe my eyes when I seen 'm just now. I thought I was dreamin'. It was too good to be true. Why, I was his wet-nurse. I put 'm to bed snug every night. His mother died, an' I brought 'm up on condensed milk at two dollars a can when I couldn't afford it in my own coffee. He never knew any mother but me. He used to suck my finger regular, the darn little cuss —that finger right there!'

And Skiff Miller, too overwrought for speech, held up a forefinger for them to see.

'That very finger', he managed to articulate, as though somehow it clinched the proof of ownership and the bond of affection.

He was still gazing at his extended finger, when Madge began to speak.

'But the dog', she said. 'You haven't considered the dog.'

Skiff Miller looked puzzled.

'Have you thought about him?' she asked.

'Don't know what you're drivin' at', was the response.

'Maybe the dog has some choice in the matter', Madge went on. 'Maybe he has his likes and desires. You have not considered him. You give him no choice. It has never entered your mind that possibly he might prefer California to Alaska. You consider only what you like. You do with him as you would with a sack of potatoes or a bale of hay.'

This was a new way of looking at it, and Miller was visibly impressed as he debated it in his mind. Madge took advantage of his indecision.

'If you really love him, what would be happiness to him would be your happiness also', she urged.

Skiff Miller continued to debate with himself, and Madge stole a glance of exultation to her husband, who looked back warm approval.

'What do you think?' the Klondiker suddenly demanded.

It was her turn to be puzzled. 'What do you mean?' she asked.

'D'ye think he'd sooner stay in California?'

She nodded her head with positiveness. 'I am sure of it.'

Skiff Miller again debated with himself, though this time aloud, at the same time running his gaze in a judicial way over the mooted animal.

'He was a good worker. He's done a heap of work for me. He never loafed on me, an' he was a joe-dandy at hammerin' a raw team into shape. He's got a head on him. He can do everything but talk. He knows what you say to him. Look at 'm now. He knows we're talkin' about him.'

The dog was lying at Skiff Miller's feet, head close down on paws, ears erect and listening, and eyes that were quick and eager to follow the sound of speech as it fell from the lips of first one and then the other.

'An' there's a lot of work in 'm yet. He's good for years to come. An' I do like him. I do like him!'

Once or twice after that Skiff Miller opened his mouth and closed it again without speaking. Finally he said:

'I'll tell you what I'll do. Your remarks, ma'am, has some weight in them. The dog's worked hard, and maybe he's earned a soft berth an' has got a right to choose. Anyway, we'll leave it up to him. Whatever he says goes. You people stay right here settin' down. I'll say good-bye and walk off casual like. If he wants to stay he can stay. If he wants to come with me, let 'm come. I won't call 'm to come and don't you call 'm to come back.'

He looked with sudden suspicion at Madge, and added, 'Only you must play fair. No persuadin' after my back is turned.'

'We'll play fair', Madge began, but Skiff Miller broke in on her assurances.

'I know the ways of women', he announced. 'Their hearts is soft. When their hearts is touched they're likely to stack the cards, look at the bottom of the deck, and lie like the devil— beggin' your pardon, ma'am. I'm only discoursin' about women in general.'

'I don't know how to thank you', Madge quavered.

'I don't see as you've got any call to thank me', he replied. 'Brown ain't decided yet. Now, you won't mind if I go away slow? It's no more'n fair, seein' I'll be out of sight inside a hundred yards.'

Madge agreed, and added, 'And I promise you faithfully that we won't do anything to influence him.'

'Well, then, I might as well be gettin' along', Skiff Miller said in the ordinary tones of one departing.

At this change in his voice Wolf lifted his head quickly, and still more quickly got to his feet when the man and woman shook hands. He sprang up on his hind legs, resting his fore paws on her hip, and at the same time licking Skiff Miller's hand. When the latter shook hands with Walt, Wolf repeated his act, resting his weight on Walt and licking both men's hands.

'It ain't no picnic, I can tell you that', were the Klondiker's last words, as he turned and went slowly up the trail.

For the distance of twenty feet Wolf watched him go, himself all eagerness and expectancy, as though waiting for the man to turn and retrace his steps. Then, with a quick, low whine, Wolf sprang after him, overtook him, caught his hand between his teeth with reluctant tenderness, and strove gently to make him pause.

Failing in this, Wolf raced back to where Walt Irvine sat, catching his coat-sleeve in his teeth and trying vainly to drag him after the retreating man.

Wolf's perturbation began to wax. He desired ubiquity. He wanted to be in two places at the same time, with the old master and the new, and steadily the distance between them was increasing. He sprang about excitedly, making short, nervous leaps and twists, now toward one, now toward the other, in painful indecision, not knowing his own mind, desiring both and unable to choose, uttering quick, sharp whines, and beginning to pant.

He sat down abruptly on his haunches, thrusting his nose upward, the mouth opening and closing with jerking movements, each time opening wide. These jerking movements were in unison with the recurrent spasms that attacked the throat, each spasm severer and more intense than the proceeding one. And in accord with jerks and spasms the larynx began to vibrate, at first silently, accompanied by the rush of air expelled from the lungs, then sounding a low, deep note, the lowest in the register of the human ear. All this was the nervous and muscular preliminary to howling.

But just as the howl was on the verge of bursting from the full throat, the wide-open mouth was closed, the paroxysms ceased, and he looked long and steadily at the retreating man. Suddenly Wolf turned his head and over his shoulder just as steadily regarded Walt. The appeal was unanswered. Not a word nor a sign did the dog receive, no suggestion and no clue as to what his conduct should be.

A glance ahead to where the old master was nearing the

curve of the trail excited him again. He sprang to his feet with a whine, and then, struck by a new idea, turned his attention to Madge. Hitherto he had ignored her, but now, both masters failing him, she alone was left. He went over to her and snuggled his head in her lap, nudging her arm with his nose— an old trick of his when begging for favours. He backed away from her and began writhing and twisting playfully, curveting and prancing, half rearing and striking his fore paws to the earth, struggling with all his body, from the wheedling eyes and flattening ears to the wagging tail, to express the thought that was in him and that was denied him utterance.

This, too, he soon abandoned. He was depressed by the coldness of these humans who had never been cold before. No response could he draw from them, no help could he get. They did not consider him. They were as dead.

He turned and silently gazed after the old master. Skiff Miller was rounding the curve. In a moment he would be gone from view. Yet he never turned his head, plodding straight onward, slowly and methodically, as though possessed of no interest in what was occurring behind his back.

And in this fashion he went out of view. Wolf waited for him to reappear. He waited a long moment, silently, quietly, without movement, as though turned to stone—withal stone quick with eagerness and desire. He barked once, and waited. Then he turned and trotted back to Walt Irvine. He sniffed his hand and dropped down heavily at his feet, watching the trail where it curved emptily from view.

The tiny stream slipping down the mossy-lipped stone seemed suddenly to increase the volume of its gurgling noise. Save for the meadow-larks, there was no other sound. The great yellow butterflies drifted silently through the sunshine and lost themselves in the drowsy shadows. Madge gazed triumphantly at her husband.

A few minutes later Wolf got upon his feet. Decision and deliberation marked his movements. He did not glance at the man and woman. His eyes were fixed up the trail. He had made up his mind. They knew it. And they knew, so far as they were concerned, that the ordeal had just begun.

He broke into a trot, and Madge's lips pursed, forming an avenue for the caressing sound that it was the will of her to send forth. But the caressing sound was not made. She was impelled to look at her husband, and she saw the sternness with which he watched her. The pursed lips relaxed, and she sighed inaudibly.

Wolf's trot broke into a run. Wider and wider were the leaps he made. Not once did he turn his head, his wolf's brush standing out straight behind him, his speed not once lessened. He cut sharply across the curve of the trail and was gone.

The Dog

IVAN TURGENIEV

'BUT if you once admit the existence of the supernatural, and that it can enter into the ordinary affairs of everyday life, allow me to ask what scope is left for the exercise of reason?'

And so saying, Anthony Stephanich crossed his arms.

Anthony Stephanich was a Councillor to the Minister in some department or other, and this circumstance, joined with those of his possessing a grave bass voice, and of his speaking with great precision, rendered him an object of universal consideration. He had just been compelled, as his detractors phrased it, to accept the Cross of St. Stanislaus.

'There can be no doubt of that', said Skorevich.

'It is impossible to dispute it', said Cinarevich.

'I assent entirely', said the master of the house, Phinoplentoff, in his thin little voice.

Now there was a short, plump, bald, middle-aged little man who was sitting silent close to the stove, and he suddenly said,—

'I confess that I don't agree with you, for something which was certainly supernatural once happened to me myself.'

Everybody looked at him, and there was a pause. The little

man in question was a small landed proprietor in Kalouga who had only come to live at St. Petersburg a short time before. He had once been in the hussars and lost his money at play, resigned his commission, and returned to cultivate cabbages at his native village. Recent events had greatly reduced his income, and he had come to town in order to try and obtain some small employment. For this object he had none of the ordinary means of success, nor influential acquaintances, but he placed great confidence in the friendship of an old comrade in his regiment, who had certainly become a great personage, how or why nobody knew, and whom he had once helped to thrash a card-sharper. Besides this, he was a great believer in his own luck, and, as a matter of fact, his confidence turned out not to have been misplaced. After some days he was appointed inspector of certain government factories. The place was a good one, it stood rather high, and did not call for the exercise of any striking talents even if the factories in question had existed anywhere except upon paper, or if it had been settled what was to be manufactured in them when they did exist. But then they formed part of a new scheme of administrative economy.

Anthony Stephanich was the first to speak.

'Surely, my dear sir, you cannot mean seriously to tell us that you ever met with anything supernatural; I mean, any departure from the laws of nature.'

'Yes, I did', said the 'dear sir', whose name was Porphyry Capitonovich.

'A departure from the laws of nature', sharply repeated Anthony Stephanich, who had evidently got hold of a favourite phrase.

'Quite so; just as you are kind enough to express it', said the little man.

'This is very extraordinary. What do you think, gentlemen?'

Anthony Stephanich had tried to put on a sarcastic expression, but had failed; or, to be more exact, had given his features an expression such as would have been produced by perceiving a bad smell. He turned to the gentlemen from Kalouga and continued——

'Could you be so kind as to give us some details of such a strange occurrence?'

'Do you want to hear about it?' said the gentleman. 'All right.'

He got up, went to the middle of the room, and began.

'You may possibly know, gentlemen, or more probably you don't, that I possess a small property in the district of Kozelsk. I used to get something from it once upon a time, but, as you may well conceive, it brings me in nothing now, except business and quarrels. However, I don't want to talk politics. Well, on this property I had a small farm with a kitchen-garden to match, a pond with tench in it, divers buildings, and among others a little house for myself. I am not married. One fine day, six years ago, I came home rather late. I had been dining with one of the neighbours, but I assure you I was all right so far as that went. I took off my clothes, got into bed, and blew out the candle. I had hardly blown it out when I heard something move underneath the bed. I wondered what it could be. At first I thought it was mice. But it wasn't mice. I could hear it scratching and walking about and shaking itself. It was obvious that it was a dog, but I couldn't think what dog it could be. I hadn't got one. So I thought that it must be a stray one. I called the servant and scolded him for being careless, and letting a dog get hidden under the bed. He asked, "What dog?" I answered him, "How should I know?" It was his business to prevent that sort of thing happening. He stooped down with the candle and looked under the bed. He said there was not any dog there. I looked underneath myself, and sure enough there was no dog there. I stared at him, and he began to grin. I called him a fool, and said the dog must have slipped out and got away when he opened the door, that he had been half asleep and hadn't noticed it. I asked if he thought that I had been drinking? However, I did not await the reply which he was about to make, but told him to clear out. When he was gone, I curled myself up, and I heard nothing more that night.

'However, the night afterwards the whole thing began again. I had hardly put the candle out when I heard the beast shake itself. I called the servant again. He looked under the bed. There wasn't anything there. So I sent him away again, and put out the candle the second time. Then I heard the dog again. There couldn't be any doubt about it. I could hear it breathe. I could hear it biting at its own coat and hunting for fleas, so I called the man to come again, without bringing a candle. He came, and I told him to listen. He said he heard. I couldn't see him, but I knew by the sound of his voice that he was frightened. I asked him how he could explain it. He said it was the Evil One. I told him to hold his stupid tongue, but we were both pretty frightened. I lighted the candle, and then there was no more dog and no more noise. I left the candle burning all night, and whether you like to believe it or not, I assure you that the same thing went on every night for six weeks. I got quite used to it, and I used to put out the candle, because light prevents my sleeping, and I did not mind the thing, as it didn't do me any harm.'

'You are certainly brave', said Anthony Stephanich, with a smile of mingled pity and contempt. 'One can see that you have been a trooper.'

'I certainly shouldn't be afraid of you, at any rate', answered Porphyry Capitonovich, with a decided ring of the soldier in his tone. 'Anyhow, I'll tell you what happened. The same neighbour with whom I had dined before came to dine with me in turn. He took pot-luck with me, and I won fifteen roubles from him afterwards. He looked out into the night, and said he would have to be going. However, I had a plan, and I asked him to stay and sleep, and try and win his money back the next day. He considered, and then he agreed to stay. I had a bed made up for him in my own room. We went to bed and smoked and talked and discussed women, as men do. At last I saw that Basil Basilich put out his light and turned his back toward me, as much as to say *Schlafen Sie wohl*. I waited a little, and then I put out my own candle, and before I had time to think the game began. The beast did more than move; he came out from under the bed, and walked across the room. I could hear his feet on the wooden floor. He shook himself, and then there was a thump. He knocked against a chair, which was standing beside Basil Basilich's bed. Basil called out to me quite naturally, in his ordinary voice, to ask me if the dog that I had got was a pointer. I told him that I hadn't got any dog, and never had had. He asked me what the noise was then? I told him to light his candle and see. He asked me again if it wasn't a dog. Then I heard him turn round. He told me I was joking; and I told him I was not.

'After this I heard him scraping away with a match while the dog was scratching itself. Suddenly the match struck, and there was nothing to be seen or heard. Basil Basilich stared at me, and I stared at him. He asked me what all the nonsense was. I told him that if you made Socrates and Frederick the Great put their heads together over it, they couldn't explain it; and I told him all about it. He jumped out of bed like a scalded cat, and wanted to have his carriage called, to go away at once. I wanted to argue with him, but he only made more noise. He told me there must be some curse upon me, and that nothing would make him stay. I got him more or less quiet at last, but he insisted on having a bed in another room, and a light all night.

'When he was having his tea in the morning, he was calmer, and he gave me his advice to go away from home for some days, and then, perhaps, the thing would come to an end.

'He was a decidedly clever man, and I had great respect for his acumen. He got round his mother-in-law quite amazingly. He got her to accept letters of exchange, and she was as tame as a sheep. She made him commissioner for the administration of all her property. Fools don't do that sort of thing with their mothers-in-law. However, he was in a bad temper when he went away for I won a hundred more roubles from him, and he was cross. He told me I was behaving unthankfully towards him. How on earth could the luck be my fault? But I did as he advised, and I started for the town the same day. I knew an old man there who kept an inn, and who was a Dissenter, and it was to his house that I went. He was a little old creature, and a bit snappish, because he had lost his wife and all his children, and he was alone. He couldn't bear the smell of tobacco, and dogs were his particular horror. Rather than see a dog in his rooms he would have left the house. "Behold", he would say, "the all-holy Virgin, who is graciously pleased to hang inside my room, and then how could I allow the unclean brutes to come sniffing in there." Of course it is want of education. As far as I am concerned, I am content that everybody should use the common sense that God gives him. That's my Gospel.'

'You seem to be a philosopher', said Anthony Stephanich, with the same smile as before.

Porphyry Capitonovich made a slight movement of the eyebrows, and also moved his moustache a little. He said:

'As to my being a philosopher, no proof has yet been adduced, but I teach philosophy to other people.'

This made everybody look at Anthony Stephanich. We expected some startling reply, or at least a glance of scathing indignation. We were mistaken. The smile of the Ministerial Councillor changed from one of contempt to one of indifference. He yawned; he changed the position of his feet. There was nothing more.

'Well,' said Capitonovich, 'I took up my quarters in this old man's house; for the sake of his acquaintance with me, he put me in his own room, and made himself up a bed behind a screen. It wasn't a good room, at its best, and it was hot and stuffy beyond all belief. Everything was sticky, and the flies were all over the place. In one corner there was a cupboard full of old holy pictures covered with tarnished plates[1] all bulging out. There was a smell of oil and drugs like a chemist's shop. There were two pillows on the bed, and black beetles ran out if you touched them. For want of something to do I drank more tea than I wanted, and then, beastly as the place was I got into bed. I could hear the old Dissenter on the other side of the screen sighing and groaning and mumbling his prayers. Then he went to sleep. It wasn't long before he began snoring. I listened to him. He began gently, and then it got worse and worse. I became irritated. It was a long time since I put out my own light, but it was not dark, because there was a lamp burning in front of the holy pictures. It was this that put me out. I got out of bed as quietly as I could, walked barefoot to the lamp, and blew it out. Nothing happened. So I thought it was all right, and got back into bed again. But I was hardly in before I heard the old story again. The dog was scratching and shaking himself—the whole thing as before. I lay still in bed, listening to see what would happen next. My landlord woke up. I heard him call out, "Sir, what's the matter; have you put out the lamp, sir?" I made no answer, and I heard him get out of bed and say, "What's the matter? What's the matter?—dog—dog—the d—d Niconian."[2] I called to him not to put himself out, but to come to me, as something very odd was happening. He emerged from behind his screen with

[1] That is, the sheaves of metal in relief put by Russians over sacred pictures, with space cut out to show the flesh parts.

[2] That is, the Dissenter is complaining of the narrator as a follower of Nicon, Patriarch of Moscow, the reformer of the Russian Church, whose changes in that body are the cause of the Dissent of the class of Non-conformists here indicated.

the end of an unbleached wax taper in his hand. Such a figure I had never seen—his fierce eyes and hairy figure, with the hair growing even in his ears, were just like a badger. On his head he had a white felt hat; his white beard went down to his girdle, and over his chest he had a waistcoat with brass buttons. His feet were thrust into a pair of old furred slippers, and he diffused around him a pervading odour of gin. In this guise he proceeded to the holy pictures, before which he crossed himself three times with his two forefingers.[1] Then he relighted the lamp, crossed himself again, and having done so, turned round to me, and said in a thick voice,—

' "Well, what's the matter?"

'I told him the whole story. He did not utter a syllable; he scratched his head. When I had done, he sat down, still silent, on the foot of my bed. Here he proceeded to scratch his stomach and the nape of his neck, and to rub himself. But still he never uttered a word. At last I said to him,—

' "Well, Theodoulos Ivanovich, I want to know what you think about it. Don't you think it's a temptation of the Evil One?"

'The old man looked at me.

' "Temptation of the Evil One!" said he. "You think that, do you? It would be all very well in your own tobacco reek,[2] but how about this house? This house is an holy place. A temptation of the Evil One? If it is not a temptation of the Evil One, what is it?"

'Then he sat silent, thinking and scratching himself. At last he said to me, though not very distinctly, because the hair got into his mouth—

' "Go to Belev. There's only one man that I know of that can help you. He lives at Belev. He is one of our people. If he likes to help you, so much the better for you. If he does not like, you've got nothing more to do."

'I asked him how I could find the man.

' "I'll tell you," said the Nonconformist, "but, after all, why

---

1 All this relates to the peculiarities of the Russian Noncomformists, who object to cutting the beard, and in making the sign of the Cross join the thumb with the fourth and little finger, extending the index and the middle finger, whereas members of the Established Church join the thumb, index, and middle finger, and bend the fourth and little finger towards the palm.

2 The Dissenters object on conscientious grounds to tobacco-smoking.

should it be a temptation of the Evil One? It's a vision; it may become even a revelation, but you're not up to all that. That's beyond you. Well, now, try to get to sleep, with God the Father and His Christ watching over you. I am going to burn some incense. We will think about it tomorrow. You know that second thoughts are almost always best."

'In the morning, accordingly, we took counsel together, although he had nearly choked me in the night with his incense. The address which he gave me was this. When I got to Belev I was to go into the square and to ask at the second shop on the right hand for a certain Prochorovich, and give him a letter. The letter was a scrap of paper on which was written, "In the Name of the Father, and of the Son, and of the Holy Ghost. Amen. To Sergius Prochorovich Pervoushine. Trust this man. Theodoulus Ivanovich. Send some cabbages, and praised be God's Holy Name." I thanked my old Dissenter, and forthwith ordered a carriage, and went to Belev. My argument was, "This thing in the night has not done me any harm yet, but it's very tiresome, and it's not the thing for a man like me or an officer." What do you think?'

'And you went to Belev?' said Phinoplentoff.

'Yes, I went there straight. When I got to the square, I asked at the second shop on the right for Prochorovich. They told me he was not there. I asked where he lived, and they told me, in his own house in the suburb on the Oka. I accordingly crossed the Oka, and found the house in question, which might more fitly have been described as a shanty. I found a man in a darned blue shirt, with a torn cap, working among cabbages, with his back to me. I came up to him and said, "Are you so and so?" He turned round, and I give you my word of honour, I never saw such a pair of eyes. He was old, he had no teeth, his face was as small as one's hand, and he had a beard like a he-goat.

'"Yes," he said, "I am he. What can I do to serve you?"

'"There", said I, and gave him the letter.

'He stared hard at me, and then said,—

'"Be pleased to come into my room, I am not able to read without glasses."

'We went into his room. It was a perfect kennel, bare and wretched, and with hardly space enough in which to turn round. On the wall there was a sacred picture, as black as coal,

T

with black heads of Saints with gleaming whites to their eyes. He pulled out the drawer in an old table, took out a pair of spectacles mounted in iron, fixed them upon his nose and read the letter, after which he fixed his eyes on me through the spectacles.

' "Have you need of me?"

' "Yes."

' "Well, tell me what it is. I am listening."

'He sat down, took out of his pocket an old checked pocket-handkerchief, full of holes, and spread it upon his knees. Me he never invited to sit down. He fixed upon me a look of power and dignity which might have become a Senator or a Minister of the Government. To my amazement I suddenly found myself seized with an emotion of terror. My heart seemed to sink within my shoes. Then he averted his gaze. This seemed to be enough, and when I had recovered myself a little, I told him my story. He said nothing, but frowned and bit his lips. Then, with an air of majesty and dignity, he slowly asked me my name, my age, who had been my parents, and whether I was married or single. After I told him this, he bit his lips and frowned again; then he held up one finger, and said, "Cast yourself down before the holy images of the pure and helpful Saints, Sabbatius and Zosimus of the Solovetsky."[1]

'I threw myself down flat upon my face, and I might almost as well have remained lying there, such was the awe and fear with which this man inspired me. I would have done anything that he told me. Gentlemen, I see that you are laughing at me, but I assure you that I didn't feel anything like laughing. At last he said—

' "Get up, sir, it is possible to help you. What has been sent to you is not a punishment, but a warning, that means to say that you are in danger, but, fortunately for you, there is some one praying for you. Go to the market-place and buy a young

[1] "The Solovetsky Monastery in the Coenobium on an island in the White Sea named Solovki. It was first founded by St. Sabbatius in A.M. 6728 (A.D. 1220), in the time of the religious prince, Basil Basilivich. After his death St. Zosimus renewed the Coenobium, and enclosed it with a wall and collected a community." . . . This monastery is greatly revered among Russian Dissenters on account of the resistance of the larger number of the community to the changes made by Nicon, and the terrible cruelties and death to which many of them were subjected in consequence. (The Patriarch and the Tzar, by the late Mr. Palmer, Vol. II., p. 439-459).

dog, keep it always with you both day and night; your visions will stop, and, moreover, you will find the dog useful."

'Heaven seemed to open before me. His words filled me with gladness. I bowed profoundly to him, and was turning to go away when it struck me that I ought to give him something. I took out a three-rouble note, but he pushed it away with his hand and said:

' "Give it to a chapel or to the poor; things like this are not paid for."

'I bowed before him again, down to his very girdle, and walked off straight to the market-place. As I reached the shops, the first thing I saw was a man in a long grey gabardine, carrying a liver-coloured dog about two months old. I asked the man to stop and tell me the price of his dog. He said, "Two roubles", and I proposed to give him three. He thought I was mad, but I gave him the bank-note to hold in his teeth while he carried the dog for me to my carriage. The coachman was soon ready, and I was at home the same evening. I kept the dog on my knees the whole time, and when he whined I called him my treasure. I gave him food and water, and had straw brought up to my room and made him a bed there. When I had blown the candle out and found myself in the dark, I wondered what was going to happen, but nothing happened. I began to feel quite bold, and called on the unseen power to begin its usual performance, but there was no response. Then I called in my servant and asked him if he could hear anything, but he could hear nothing either.'

'Was that the end of it?' said Anthony Stephanich, but without sneering.

'It was the end of the noises,' said Porphyry Capitonovich, 'but it was not the end of the whole story. The dog grew, and became a large, strong setter. He showed an extraordinarily strong attachment to me. There is very little sport down in our part of the world, but whenever I took him out with me I always found it good. I used to take him all about with me. Sometimes he started a hare, or a partridge, or a wild duck, but he never went far from me. Wherever I went, he came too. I took him with me even when I went to bathe. A lady of my acquaintance wanted to turn him out of the drawing-room one day. We had a downright battle. I ended by breaking the affected creature's windows for her. Well, one fine day in summer there was the worst drought that I have ever known. There was a sort of haze in the air. Everything was burnt up. It was dark. The sun was like a red ball, and the dust was enough to make one sneeze. The earth gaped with cracks. I got tired of staying in the house, half-undressed, with shutters shut, and as it got a little cooler I made up my mind to go and call on a lady who lived about a verst off. She was a kind-hearted woman, still pretty young, and always smart. She was a little original, but that is rather an advantage in women than otherwise. I got to the steps of her door most frightfully thirsty, but I knew that Nymphodora Semenovna would pick me up with whortleberry-water and other refreshments. I had my hand on the door-handle, when I suddenly heard a tremendous row, and children shrieking, on the other side of a cottage, and in an instant a great red brute, that at first I did not see was a dog, made straight for me with his mouth open, his eyes red, and his hair all up. I had hardly gasped when it flew full at my chest. I almost had a fit. I shall never forget the white teeth and the foaming tongue close to my face. In an instant my own dog flew to my rescue like a flash of lightning, and hung on to the other's neck like a leech. The other one choked, snapped, and fell back. I opened the door, and jumped into the hall. I did not know where I was. I threw myself against a door with all my strength and yelled for help—while the two dogs fought upon the steps. The whole house was roused. Nymphodora ran out with her hair down. There was a lull in the noise, and I heard somebody call out to shut the gate. I peeped through the door. There was nothing on the steps, but men were running about the court seizing logs of wood as if they were mad themselves. I saw an old woman poke her cap out of a dormer window, and heard her call out that the dog had run down through the village, and I went out to look for mine. Presently he came into the court, limping, and hurt, and bloody. I asked what on earth was the matter, for there was a crowd gathered as if there had been a fire. They told me it was one of the Count's dogs that had gone mad, and that it had been about since the day before. This was a Count who was a neighbour of mine, and who had all sorts of strange dogs.

'I was in an awful fright, and I went to a looking-glass to see if I had got hurt. There was nothing, thank God, but I looked as green as grass, and Nymphodora Semenovna was lying on the sofa sobbing like a hen clucking. No wonder, too. It was her nerves, and her kind-heartedness. When she came to a little she said to me in an hollow voice—

' "Are you still alive?"

' "Yes," I said, "I am still alive. My dog saved me." She said—

' "What a noble thing! Did the mad dog kill him?"

' "No," said I, "he is not killed, but he is very much hurt."

'She answered, "Then he ought to be shot at once."

'I told her I would not. I was going to try to cure him.

'Then the dog himself came and scratched at the door, and I at once let him in.

' "Oh, what are you doing?" she said, "he will bite us all."

'I said, "Forgive me; it does not come out all at once like that."

'She said, "How can you? You have gone off your head."

'I said, "Nymphodora, do be quiet and talk sense", but she called out to me to go away with my horrid dog.

'I said I was going to go.

'She said, "Go away at once, don't stay a moment. Go away; you're a brute. Never you dare to see me again. I daresay you have got hydrophobia, too."

'I said, "All right, but just be good enough to let me have the carriage; there might be danger if I walked all the way back."

'She stared at me. "You can have the carriage or anything that you want, if only you will go away at once. Just look at its eyes."

'She bolted out of the room, and hit one of the maids whom she met, and then I heard her taken ill next door. You can take it as what you like, but Nymphodora Semenovna and I were never friends again from that day onwards, and the more I think about it the more I feel that if it was for nothing else, I ought to be thankful for that to my dog to my dying day. I ordered the carriage and took the dog home with me in it. When I got home I examined him and washed his wounds. I thought the best thing I could do would be to take him next day to the wise man of the country. He was an astonishing old man. He mumbles something or other over water. Some people say he puts snakes' slime into it. He gives it you to drink, and it makes you all right at once. I thought that I would get myself bled at the same time. Bleeding is a good thing for fits. Of course you ought not to be bled in the arm, but in the dimple.'

'Where is the dimple?' asked Phinoplentoff, timidly.

'Do you not know? It is the place under the hand, at the end of the thumb, where you put the snuff when you want to take a good lot of it. See. That is the right place to be bled, you can see that for yourself. The blood that comes out of the hand is the vein blood. In the other place it is the silly blood. Doctors don't know about those sort of things. The Germans know nothing about it. Farriers do it a great deal. They are very good at it. They just put their scissors there and give them a tap with the hammer, and the whole thing is done. The night came on while I was thinking about it, and it was time to go to bed. So I went, and of course, I kept the dog with me; but I don't know whether it was the heat or the shock that I had had, or the fleas, or what I was thinking about, but I could not get to sleep. I got restless. I drank water, I opened the window. I got the guitar and played the Moujik of Koumarino with Italian variations. But it would not do. I thought it was the room that I could not stand, so I took a pillow and two sheets and a coverlet and went across the garden, and made myself a bed in the hay under the shed. I was more comfortable there. It was a calm night. Every now and then there was a little breath of air that touched you on the face, like a woman's hand. The fresh hay smelt good, like tea. The crickets sang in the apple trees. Every now and then you'd hear a hen quail clucking, and you felt that she was happy in the dew beside her mate. The sky was quite still. The stars were shining, and there were little light clouds, like flakes of cotton wool, that hardly changed.

'Well,' continued Porphyry Capitonovich, 'I lay down, but I didn't get to sleep. I kept thinking, and especially about presentiments, and what that man Prochorovich had said to me, when he told me to look out for squalls, and now how such an extraordinary thing had happened. I could not understand it. It was impossible to understand it. All of a sudden the dog jumped up and whined. I thought his wounds were hurting him. Then the moon kept me awake. Do you not believe me? I assure you it did. The moon was straight in front of me, round, and flat, and big, and yellow, and I thought that she was there to tease me. I put out my tongue at her. Did she want to know what I was thinking about? I turned over, but I felt her upon my ear, and upon the back of my neck. It was like rain all over me. I opened my eyes again. The moon showed every little point of grass, every little twig in the hay, every little spider's web, as if it was cut out sharp, and she said, "There you are, look at it." There was nothing more to be done. I rested my head upon my hand and looked. I have strong eyes and I could not sleep. The gate of the shed was wide open and I looked through. One could see the country for five versts. It was patchy, clear in some places and dark in others, as is the case in moonlight. I was looking out over it when I thought I saw something moving a long distance off. Then I saw something pass quickly much nearer. Then I saw a dark figure leap. It had come much nearer then. I wondered if it was a hare. I supposed so, and it was coming nearer. Then I saw it was bigger than a hare. It came out of the shadow on to the meadow, which lay quite white in the moonlight, and the thing moved upon it like a great black spot. Evidently it was some kind of wild beast—a fox, perhaps, or a wolf. My heart began to beat. But what was there to be afraid of? There are plenty of beasts that run about at night. My curiosity overcame my fear. I got up and rubbed my eyes, when all of a sudden I turned cold as if ice had been put down my back. The shadowy creature grew larger and darted in at the gate of the yard. I then saw that it was an enormous brute with a great head. It shot past like a bullet, then stopped and began to snuff. It was the mad dog. I could neither move nor cry. It bounded in at the door of the shed with sparkling eyes, howled, and leaped upon me as I lay upon the hay. At that moment my own dog sprang forward wide-awake. The two beasts fought and fell. I don't remember what followed. I only remember that I fell over them somehow in a heap, escaped through the garden, and got to my own bedroom. When I recovered myself a little, I woke up the whole house, and we all armed ourselves and sallied out. I got a sword and a revolver. I had bought the revolver just after the emancipation of the serfs, for reasons which I need not mention, and a bad one it was. I missed two shots out of every three. We went to the shed with burning sticks; we went forward and shouted, but we could not hear anything. At last we went in, and there we found my dog lying dead and the other disappeared.

'I am not ashamed to tell you that I cried like a child.

'I knelt down and kissed the body of the poor beast who had saved my life twice, and I was there still when my old house-keeper Prascovia came and said to me, "What's the matter with you? To get into such a state about a dog, God forgive you. You ought to be ashamed of yourself, and you'll catch cold." It is true I had hardly anything on. "If the dog has got killed to save your life, it is an honour for him." I did not agree with Prascovia, but I went back to the house. As to the mad dog, it was shot by a soldier the next day, which must have been provi-dential, as the soldier had never fired off a gun before, although he possessed a medal for having been one of the saviours of the country in 1812. Now, gentlemen, that is why I told you that something supernatural had once happened to me.'

With these words, Porphyry Capitonovich was silent and filled his pipe. We all looked at one another without speaking. At last Phinoplentoff said, 'No doubt you lead an holy life, and this is a reward,'—but here he stopped short, for he saw that Porphyry got red in the face.

'But if you once admit the existence of the supernatural,' said Anthony Stephanich, 'and that it can enter into the ordinary affairs of every-day life, allow me to ask what scope is left for the exercise of reason?'

Nobody had anything to answer.

The Dog That Knew Too Much

B. W. CHANDLER

AFTER seein' Wilkins 'and over the best part of a week's wages
at the police-court this mornin' I shall never 'ave another word
to say against my dog for bein' a bit of a fool. In my spare time
I 'ave tried long and patient to learn 'im a trick or two, but the
most I 'ave ever got 'im to do is to stand on 'is 'ind legs with a
chair at 'is back. Now it stops at that. No more eddication. I
keep 'im simple and ignorant; it's safer. The Wilkinses' misfortune to-day is owin' to the 'igh-flown eddication of their dog
Podger by Mrs. Wilkins.

They 'ad Podger at six weeks old, and, not 'avin' chick nor
child, Mrs. Wilkins begun talkin' to 'im like a baby. The
things she's taught that dog to do and the things 'e's picked up
'isself watchin' 'er would fill a book. 'E'll sit in the kitchen
while she's scrubbin' the bedroom, and she's no need to keep
runnin' up and down stairs to look in the oven, because Podger
'ollers to 'er if 'e smells a smell of burnin'. She told my wife
that, if she 'appens to be a bit late with the dinner and 'as only
just put the pertaters on when the factory 'ooter goes, she's only

got to give the word to Podger, and 'e'll run and meet Wilkins as 'e turns the corner on 'is bicycle and pitch a yarn to 'im about a rat 'e's found round the chicken-house, and 'e'll keep Wilkins out in the garden interested and pleasant until Mrs. Wilkins calls out that everythin's gettin' cold.

When the Muzzlin' Order come in force in our area Mrs. Wilkins went nearly mad. She bought Podger the comfortablest muzzle she could lay 'ands on, and she explained to 'im every time she put it on 'im that it was the law and she couldn't 'elp 'erself, and 'e mustn't on no account go outside the door without it. 'e understood every word right enough, but 'e 'ated the muzzle and 'e begun slippin' off without it. One day Wilkins caught 'im not a 'undred yards from the police-station and carried 'im back 'ome under 'is mackintosh and give 'im a bit of 'is mind when 'e got 'im indoors.

'A muzzle as big as a bird-cage as don't scrape your nose nowhere, and you tryin' your best to get me 'auled up before the magistrates and fined ten bob, you varmint!' 'e 'ollered, shakin' the muzzle in Podger's face, while Podger 'ung 'is 'ead and shivered and looked miserable.

Mrs. Wilkins whipped a Treasury note out of 'er purse.

'Put that in your pocket, Albert, in case', she said to Wilkins. 'I saved it up to buy a blouse, but I'll go in rags sooner than 'ear the dog bullied.'

Wilkins was rather ashamed of 'isself and 'e wouldn't lay a finger on the note. But Mrs. Wilkins wouldn't touch it to take it back agen. 'No,' she said, 'there's the money ready', and she stuck it on the shelf be'ind Wilkins's 'baccy-jar, and, whenever Wilkins lugged Podger 'ome and begun shakin' the muzzle at 'im and speakin' 'arsh, she'd snatch up the note and offer it to 'im, and Wilkins 'adn't any more to say.

Then one afternoon the worst 'appened. A policeman brought Podger 'ome, 'e being caught without 'is muzzle. Mrs. Wilkins invited the officer into the parlour and begged 'im to take a seat, and was as polite as you please to 'im, and fetched the muzzle and asked if it was the pattern 'e approved of, and explained 'ow seldom Podger stirred a inch further than the doorstep without it, and asked 'im to scold Podger for doin' so this mornin' and obligin' 'im to be at the trouble of bringin' 'im 'ome, and begged 'im to forgive a poor dumb animal just this once.

Mrs. Wilkins 'asn't 'er equal as a soft sodderer. The constable done what she asked 'im willin' and pitched into Podger louder than Wilkins ever 'ad, and she listened to 'im without a word. 'e was just goin' to wish 'er 'Good day', and it's my belief they would never 'ave 'eard another breath about it, when that officious dog crept across the room to the shelf, shoved 'is nose be'ind the 'baccy jar and sidled up to the policeman with the ten bob note in 'is mouth.

That done it. It was brought out in the evidence this mornin'. The constable described 'ow 'e 'ad 'urled back Podger's bribe with scorn, and the magistrates expressed their deep disgust at the Wilkinses' crafty attempt to corrupt a officer of the law in the execution of 'is duty and fined 'em two pound ten.

Give me a fool for a dog.

The Strike at Tiverton Manor

WALTER A. DYER

NORMALLY, when left to his own devices, the dog tends to revert to savagery and to become a selfish, treacherous, skulking, revengeful, murderous brute. Under fair conditions he is, as everyone knows, the noblest of all God's dumb creatures, often shaming man himself by his devotion and courage.

It is human companionship that makes the difference. It is intimate human companionship, with the touch of kindness and the human voice, that calls forth the cardinal canine virtues.

It was constant association with John Dayton that made Prince Otto what he was. He had many remarkable attributes, as you shall see, but what he might have become without Professor Müller and John Dayton can only be surmised. It is only a question of motive, sometimes, which separates the hero from the fiend.

Prince Otto's parents were of noble German blood and had been brought to America in 1910, when the German shepherd breed first began to gain widespread popularity in this country. The Prince himself was born late in the same year at Müller's Kennels in Connecticut, a fat, fuzzy puppy, full of life and mischief.

Müller's were not ordinary kennels. His advertisement read:

Training school for police dogs. German and Belgian sheep-dogs. Dogs trained for police, military, and life-saving service, and as watchdogs for private estates.

Visitors came from far and near to see Müller's star performers climb ladders, leap through windows, execute high dives into an artificial lake, and attack a much padded attendant who impersonated an escaping criminal. And because there were people who knew enough to admire the wonderful agility and intelligence of Müller's dogs, the professor found a ready sale for his youngsters, and prospered.

Müller owed much of his success to hard-won experience, for there are things to be learned about dogs which only long association with them can make clear. But the professor possessed more than experience; he was gifted by nature with that sympathy and understanding which begets confidence and obedience and a ready response in the canine race. He loved his dogs.

From the first, Prince Otto had been one of the quickest to learn and the best loved of all Müller's puppies. The master early recognized in him a lurking strain of fearless, wolfish savagery and cunning, but this only called forth the greater care in his training, for it is such traits that go to the making of the most efficient police dogs. Every day the professor made a special point of spending an hour or two with his puppies, playing with them, talking to them, teaching them the rudiments of obedience, familiarizing them with human comradeship and with the meaning of human words.

One day in April, 1913, when Prince Otto was in his third year, a distinguished personage visited the Müller Kennels. G. Howard Tiverton, Esq., had bought a tract of land and two or three homesteads on the north shore of Long Island and had converted them into a great estate. On a bluff commanding a superb view of the Sound and the Connecticut shore beyond he had erected a Colonial dwelling of red brick with a white-pillared façade on the waterside, and had named it, with the millionaire's usual modesty, Tiverton Manor.

Lawns and terraces, stretched down to the water front, where bathhouses and a private boat landing were hidden behind the willows, and four or five acres about the house were transformed by a landscape gardener into a magnificent park, with gardens, a little lake, and great masses of flowering shrubs among the trees, all enclosed in a nine-foot iron fence running down to the water on each side and broken by three or four imposing gateways of wrought iron. Then Mr. Tiverton had moved into the manor house and had set his gangs of Italian workmen the task of converting the rest of the estate into a great wooded park, with roadways and waterways and bridle paths traversing it in every direction.

Public police protection being somewhat inadequate in the immediate vicinity, Mr. Tiverton had organized a little band of private watchmen, and he now purposed to add to this force one of Professor Müller's famous dogs. It was quite evident to him that they differed materially in character from the affectionate pointers and setters he had known and loved, and he was a bit puzzled by their alert aggressiveness. But softness was not what he was looking for now, and as soon as he laid eyes on Prince Otto he marked him for his own.

'Dot dog,' said the professor, swelling with pride, 'he is der finest of dem all yet. I haf raised him mit my own hands and I know. If I had vished to show him he could have beaten dem all. Look at dose eyes, dose shoulders, Mr. Tiverton!'

Prince Otto was indeed a superb specimen of his breed. He was large and powerful, with the springy muscles and tense sinews of a trained athlete. His coat was harsh and a bit grizzled and his erect, forward-pointing ears and sharp nose gave his head a formidable, wolfish expression. But one could not long avoid a contemplation of his eyes. Almost human they were in their keen intelligence—large, clear, fearless eyes, with none of the mournful pathos of the St. Bernard's and none of the trivial smartness of the fox terrier's.

An exclamation of sincere admiration escaped Mr. Tiverton's lips, the admiration of the connoisseur. He laid his hand on Prince Otto's head, and the Prince, with a glance at the professor, submitted to the homage with dignity but without the slightest sign of either annoyance or pleasure, for that was his way with men whom he did not know.

And so Professor Müller sold Prince Otto to the millionaire, for he got his top price, and that was his business. But when the purchase was concluded and Mr. Tiverton had driven off in his car, the stolid German took Prince Otto out of sight behind the kennels and fell upon his neck and whispered things into his ear that made the big dog lick his hand and whimper softly.

Hans Bruno, one of Müller's assistants, personally conducted Prince Otto across the Sound on a ferryboat and thence by motor to Tiverton Manor. The Prince was perplexed and unhappy, and, though not frightened, was nervous and uneasy. His conductor had his hands full, and people on the ferryboat kept at a respectful distance. One good lady was heard to remark that there ought to be a law prohibiting people from bringing such awful brutes into public places.

It was fortunate for all concerned that John Dayton was a born lover of dogs. No high-born collie or cur of low degree ever approached the high iron fence within John's range of vision that he did not smile at and speak to. Consequently, when John was summoned to meet the newcomer, he approached Prince Otto with the broadest of grins. Ignoring Hans Bruno completely he addressed Prince Otto volubly and without reserve.

'So you're the pup, are you?' he bawled. 'Pup, is it? You're a horse. We'll hitch you to a wagon and make you haul gravel, that's what we'll do with you. You great big beauty! Give us your paw.'

John bent down close to Otto's terrible jaws and held out his hand. Hans Bruno was a bit anxious as to how the Prince would accept such familiarity from a total stranger, but the dog merely regarded John watchfully and did nothing.

Prince Otto had been taught many things, but parlour tricks were not among his accomplishments. He did not understand John Dayton's outstretched hand, but he did understand the look in his eyes and the tone of his voice. Dogs are remarkably quick to recognize fear or dislike in men, and their opposites. When John straightened up and laid his hand kindly on the dog's head, Otto lifted his face and gently returned the pressure, which, if John had but known it, was a tremendous concession.

The result was that when they turned toward the stables, Prince Otto, who had long known Hans without greatly loving him, followed John.

Hans remained at Tiverton Manor for a few days, instructing John Dayton, who was the night watchman and was to have charge of Prince Otto. The dog, his devotion to John growing daily, took to his new duties readily enough. For the most part he had only to accompany the watchman on his tours of inspection, to come to heel when called, and to investigate dark corners and suspicious noises.

One other friend Prince Otto had. There was at the house a jolly round-faced Polish girl named Mary, her other name being an unused and unpronounceable superfluity. One evening, while the Prince was enjoying a little freedom before the duties of the night began, he cut his foot on a bit of glass and came limping across the lawn, stopping now and then to lick the bleeding paw. Warm-hearted Mary saw him and, forgetful of the servants' tales of the beast's ferocity, she hurried out to him.

'Poor dog,' she crooned, 'what matter wid foot?'

Prince Otto paused and surveyed her impersonally as she approached. She fell upon her knees and he suffered her to lift his foot and wipe it with her handkerchief.

'Oh, poor dog!' said she, looking compassionately into his eyes.

She took him by the collar and led him to John who washed the cut with peroxide and bandaged the foot with adhesive tape.

'All right now', said Mary, patting him. Otto touched her hand with his moist nose, and they were friends.

Prince Otto's first real adventure took place in October. It was about two o'clock in the morning and John and the dog were completing their third tour of inspection.

'It's a dark night, Otto', said John. 'It's a dark night, and I shouldn't be s'prised if it rained before day.'

Otto drew close so that he brushed the watchman's leg as they covered the familiar ground.

Suddenly John felt the dog's form stiffen and heard him sniff the air. Then Otto crept stealthily forward toward the rear of the garage. John felt for his revolver, clutched his stick, and followed. There was a rush, a cry of fear, and when John came up and snapped on his flashlight, he found a terrified man sitting on the ground with Otto holding him by the elbow. The dog had not closed his teeth on the arm; he merely held the sleeve. But it was enough, and the man quite willingly allowed John to lock him up.

In the morning the culprit was haled before Mr. Tiverton. He proved to be a Pole who lived in the village not far away, and though he was unable, in his broken English, to give a satisfactory account of himself, he appeared to have done no damage, and he was so thoroughly frightened that Mr. Tiverton decided he had been sufficiently warned and punished, and allowed to go free. But Prince Otto had won his spurs.

One or two other such encounters thoroughly established Otto as a trusted member of the private police force of Tiverton Manor, and by the following spring the master of the estate would not have accepted a thousand dollars for him.

In April several changes were made in the organization at the Manor, and Mr. Tiverton sent for John Dayton.

'John,' said he, 'I'm making some changes here, and I think I can let you go on days now if you like.'

John fidgeted with his cap.

'Thank you, sir,' said he, 'but I think I'd rather stay on nights, if you don't mind, sir.'

'Why,' said Mr. Tiverton in surprise, 'I thought you were anxious to get the daylight job. It's pleasanter, of course.'

'I know, sir', replied the watchman. 'I did want to go on days, and the wife wanted it, too. It's very kind of you, sir, but I think I'd rather stay on nights, if it's all the same to you, sir.'

'What's made you change your mind, John?'

The watchman stammered a little and grew red under his coat of tan.

'It's the Prince, sir', said he. 'You see a new man mightn't be able to manage him. Not everyone can, sir.'

Mr. Tiverton stood thinking for a moment, and then a twinkle came into his eyes.

'What if I should put you both on days?' he asked. 'You and the Prince?'

John Dayton looked up with quick gratitude, and then looked down again.

'But the dog is most needed at night, sir', said he.

U

'Well,' replied Mr. Tiverton, 'there are more where he came from.'

And so the matter was decided. Mike Donohue, a strapping young policeman from Brooklyn who had one eye injured in service, was engaged as night watchman. He had been on the dog squad in Flatbush and appeared to be an ideal man for the place. Then Hans Bruno appeared with Fritz, another of Professor Müller's powerful young German shepherd dogs.

There was trouble at the outset. The Prince growled and snarled and barked and whined, tugged at his chain and begged John Dayton to let him get at this intruder. The newcomer was hardly less anxious to have it out, but the two dogs were too valuable to risk an encounter, and Hans Bruno was sent back to Connecticut with the unsatisfied Fritz, and Prince Otto was left in undisputed possession of Tiverton Manor.

The following week Hans reappeared with Gretchen, a female, somewhat smaller than Otto or Fritz, but swift and sagacious.

John Dayton was anxious; but both Hans and Donohue assured him that no dog of breeding would attack a female of his species unprovoked, and such proved to be the case. John led Otto to the stables where Gretchen was temporarily housed. Both dogs bristled a little and appeared to be on their guard, but there was no snarling, no rush to the attack. Otto was allowed to walk slowly up to the newcomer. He sniffed at her doubtfully, then with interest, Gretchen drawing back a bit nervously. Then Prince Otto turned away, dissatisfied but peaceable, and Donohue and Gretchen were installed as joint guardians of the night.

One more incident remains to be recorded before the tragedy which upset the summer peace of Tiverton Manor. Mary, the Polish girl, while returning to the manor through the woods one day, was accosted by Tony Rampetto, one of the Italian labourers about the place. Tony had forced his attentions upon Mary before, but she had hitherto been able to repulse him good-naturedly. Now he had her at a disadvantage. The spot where he met her was secluded; no one was about.

The Italian with flashing eyes barred the girl's path and demanded that she hear him.

'I love you!' he cried. 'You shall marry me! You shall not get away this time. I have you.'

Mary drew back frightened, and started to run; but Tony grasped her wrist. He drew her toward him roughly. She struggled valiantly, for she was young and strong, but she was no match for the Italian. He drew her tighter until his dark eyes and gleaming teeth were close to her face.

Mary drew back her head with an effort and screamed. Tony clapped a dirty hand over her mouth, but it was too late. A crashing sound was heard, as of someone dashing through the woods. Tony looked quickly over his shoulder, and then dropped Mary just in time to throw up his arm and guard his throat against the sharp fangs and mighty jaws of Prince Otto.

The dog knew whose cry had pierced the air; he remembered his friend. He lost no time in indecision but hurled his huge bulk straight at the Italian, snarling angrily. Otto, his teeth missing their mark, was carried several paces beyond by his own impetus, and before he could turn Tony had drawn a long, wicked-looking knife.

But Otto had little knowledge of knives and no fear of them. Again he rushed, and so quickly that Tony had no time to strike. He was crushed back, with one arm raised to guard his face and throat, and the other flung beside him, his hand still clutching the knife.

Mary, her courage restored by the unexpected appearance of an ally, had struggled to her feet and now, catching sight of the gleaming blade, ground it into the soft earth with her heel.

Otto, had he not been trained to restraint in the use of his teeth, might have killed the Italian now. As it was, Tony was fighting desperately for his life, his eyes wild with terror and his breath coming in painful gasps.

John Dayton, wondering why Otto had not answered to his whistle, and hearing the sounds of conflict, came hurrying up. Seizing Otto by the collar he commanded the dog to draw back, and the animal obeyed. Tony, leaping to his feet, did not wait for further developments but took to his heels through the woods.

'I shouldn't have let him get away,' commented John, 'but I think he will trouble you no more.'

He loosed his hold on Otto's collar and the dog, though evidently eager to give chase, restrained himself. John took the now hysterical Mary by the arm and helped her back to the house, while Otto, walking by her side, lifted his head and gazed with troubled eyes into her face.

Whether Tony Rampetto was at the bottom of the trouble which broke out in July is not known. There was no good cause for it. Mr. Tiverton paid his men regularly, and though he demanded hard, steady work from them he was not an unreasonable taskmaster. Some disturbing influence got to work among them, and on July 14th they went on a strike.

There were about forty, all told, who left their work and placed Tiverton Manor in a state of siege. Not only the Italian labourers, but several of the stablemen and others joined in the strike.

At first Mr. Tiverton was disposed to make light of the matter, and took steps to fill the vacant places promptly; but the men who came to take the jobs of the strikers were roughly handled and driven off. Grocers and butchers were not allowed to come to the house and no one was permitted to leave.

The second night of the affair the boat landing was wrecked and the motor boat put out of commission. Then, when Mr. Tiverton, thoroughly angry, undertook to telephone to the county seat for assistance, he found that his wires had been cut. So he locked the great gates of the estate and armed such of his men as had remained loyal, and grimly waited.

On the eighteenth a boat appeared offshore and hailed the Manor. Mr. Tiverton was summoned.

'What's the trouble?' asked the man in the boat.

Briefly Mr. Tiverton explained. One of the strikers appeared at the water front, just outside the fence, with a shotgun, and the boat made off. But the intercepted tradesman had reported the unusual state of affairs. The sheriff would soon be notified and relief brought, and the men became doubly savage as they began to realize the utter folly of their action.

On the morning of the nineteenth a mob of some thirty cursing, gesticulating men appeared at the main gateway of Tiverton Manor, armed with various weapons. They were a silly, shouting, motley crowd, but dangerous for that very reason.

Johnson, the coloured lad who sometimes acted as chauffeur and who had had charge of the boats, was on guard. Unable to understand the broken English of the Italians, and frightened by their threatening attitude, he retired to give the alarm.

One of the men who had had some experience in blasting blew out the big lock with a stick of dynamite, and when John Dayton and Prince Otto appeared a few minutes later the men were just rushing back and were throwing wide the big iron gates.

John drew his revolver and held his ground in the roadway. Beside him stood the great handsome young dog, his majestic head held high, his clear eyes gleaming, every muscle tense and quivering.

At the sight of this determined man and his formidable comrade, the mob, cowards at heart, paused. John, fearing more for Otto than for himself, ordered the dog to heel, and Otto crouched reluctantly by his side. It was plainly John Dayton's task to spar for time, and he opened parley.

'What do you want?' he demanded.

A tall fellow, with his shirt open at his great hairy breast, stepped forward with lowering brows. He was armed with a revolver and appeared to be a sort of leader.

'We want that Tiverton', he said with an oath.

'You can't see him', said John.

'Can't, hey?' retorted the man with a sneer, and the crowd edged closer. Otto's hair was standing up straight along his back and he was growling ominously.

'First, drop that gun', commanded the man.

John, though he knew it would hardly serve the cause if he put himself in the way of being shot, resolved to hold his ground a little longer. He stood still and did not reply.

The tall man took a step or two forward, scowling angrily, and the others crowded close beside and behind him.

'Drop it!' ordered the leader, raising his own weapon. There were sounds of hurrying footsteps up by the house and the resounding bark of Gretchen. The men were becoming impatient. John's eyes were fixed upon his chief antagonist, but his ears were strained for the sound of approaching motors. There was another forward movement of the mob. John's attention was so closely engaged that he did not observe Prince Otto rise slowly and menacingly beside him.

John stood in silence, and still the tall man forbore to use his weapon. But there was a sudden swirl in the mob and Tony

Rampetto broke out in front, cursing shrilly in Italian. His eyes were fixed upon Prince Otto and his face was distorted with anger and hatred. He raised a big pistol he carried and fired point-blank at the Prince.

The action was like setting a spark to a powder train. With a yell the strikers started forward as though to brush the feeble defence from the path.

John Dayton raised his arm and fired twice over the heads of the mob. At the first shot they wavered; at the second they halted. Then there was another report and a bullet sang by John Dayton's ear.

'At them, Otto!' he cried, forgetting his resolve to remain coolly on the defence.

The dog needed no second bidding. Instantly his great, powerful body shot across the intervening space as if propelled by giant springs, his fearsome fangs bared and the snarl of battle in his throat. The mob fell back before his fierce onslaught, the more cowardly fighting to escape. The brawny leader went down at the first rush, his cheek torn open by Otto's fangs. Tony Rampetto drew his deadly knife, but Otto seized him by the shoulder and shook him as a terrier shakes a rat. Again and again the fearless dog charged. They dared not fire in the confusion and they were powerless against this unleashed fury.

Tony and the leader rose and ran for the gate, and the others followed pell-mell, Otto leaping madly on their backs and biting their legs.

John Dayton suddenly found himself supported by the rest of the little garrison. Mr. Tiverton came up, shouting orders, Mike Donohue appeared, half dressed, with Gretchen tugging wildly at her chain and crying to be loosed. They rushed to the gateway and the retreat of the mob strikers became a rout.

Then came the welcome sound of motors chugging up the hill. Mr. Tiverton met the first one, containing the sheriff and part of his posse. The automobiles went off in hot pursuit of the fugitives, and the dust of battle cleared from the gateway of Tiverton Manor.

But on the grass of the roadside John Dayton was bending over a silent form. Tony Rampetto's shot had gone home; his revenge was complete. Prince Otto had fought his last great fight with a bullet in his lung.

Tenderly they lifted him, Mr. Tiverton and Donohue and John, and carried him up to the house. They laid him on soft cushions on the white-pillared porch and brought water to moisten his poor fevered tongue.

Social distinctions were all forgotten on that porch. Mrs. Tiverton and her daughter, who had remained in their rooms, pale and frightened, during the shooting, came out to hear the story. Nora the cook was there, and Charles the butler, and the maids. Donohue stood apart with the perplexed Gretchen, and bit his lips. Johnson, the coloured boy, frankly wept. Mary burst forth and flung herself beside the dying dog with wild lamentations, and Miss Tiverton took the girl's head on her silken lap and comforted her. Mr. Tiverton was on his knees with his arm about the shaking shoulders of John Dayton, who hid his face in his hands and said no word.

Slowly the brave dog's eyes opened for the last time and looked about him. All were hushed; it was like a benediction. He lifted his head slightly with a pitiful little effort, and then fell weakly back and breathed no more.

Peace broods over Tiverton Manor. The breeze sighs softly in the great maple and horse chestnuts that shade its stately porch. At the foot of the green velvety terraces the waters of the Sound lap musically at the gravelly beach.

At night Mike Donohue and Gretchen make their hourly rounds in silent companionship, and on each tour they stop beside the great entrance gate where a little mound is just visible in the shadow of the rhododendrons and a white stone gleams in the moonlight.

Here Lies
PRINCE OTTO
A German Shepherd Dog
Æt. 3 Years, 8 Months

A NOBLE GENTLEMAN
A BRAVE WARRIOR
A FAITHFUL COMRADE

'Greater love hath no man than this, that
a man lay down his life for his friends'

A bsence

COLETTE

THE seamstress who goes out by the day does not really enjoy coming to my house. 'Of course it is healthy, almost woodsy,' she admits, 'but just a little too lonely. Still, what can you expect? It's Auteuil.'

For that complaint there is no help. I do not argue. But in Auteuil the snow stays spotless. Though it may make a Switzerland of our little ramparts, though the early sunshine gilds the infield of our track and tingles the bark of the budding elderberries, for my little Dorcas we are still Auteuil, and the tree-studded earth-works, manned only by children and nurses, for her are always 'the redoubt', dark with a twilight mystery, romantic, fearsome.

'How lonesome you must get out here,' she said to me the other day, 'without your husband and your little girl.'

I did not answer, and she added softly, thinking she had offended me, 'But you have the animals for company. They're so faithful, and that does cheer one up.'

I might have answered, 'Yes, they are faithful, but just for that reason sometimes they can't cheer me up.'

Ah, loyal friends, you hold a mirror at my heart! Our bulldog, I know, misses the little playmate she left behind in the country, but not to the final canine depth of spurning food and play. Spartan that she is, she never gives up and never whines; she hides her bruised paw and the scars of battle. She bears her bereavement with the same stolidity, till she is misled by the shadow of some passing child; then she dashes off. A little later, back she saunters—and it is hard to look into the eyes of a dog to whom mankind has lied.

The Persian, old but never older, the colour of a pale violet, is on the watch. At mealtimes she crouches on the table, always in the corner by the empty chair, yet at every masculine foot-step she forgets her lofty timidity and is gone to greet the prodigal. She picks her way alone across the Avenue to the Police Station. And so beautiful is she, so Orientally con-descending, that they treat her as a queen.

The Sergeant himself returned her in his arms. 'She meows a lot,' he said, 'but we know she isn't hungry. Wonder what she wants?'

As for the unswerving shepherd—there is a one-man dog above such temptations. She doesn't have to range or sniff; she knows. Two years ago she was a tiny puppy, and I marvel how she could reach in two short years a certainty so scornful, so ascetic almost. Hope deferred has no more secret for her than for me. As she lies by my chair, hardly breathing, her very repose has a meaning. 'I am not resting,' it says, 'but waiting.'

An overcoat never fools her, she never jumps at the doorbell; she knows and waits. The bulldog will blunder into the empty room and start to say hello.

'What!' she will seem to exclaim. 'He's not back yet?'

But not the sheep dog. Sometimes the sight of a long-legged stranger reminds her of her heart's own choice. Her eyes blazing inside their dark jungle, she softly thumps her tail, smiling at her memories. But the smile is to herself.

Then one day, without warning, her master did come walk-ing home. Far off, out of sight, she knew. A cry of anguish, and she tore the leash from my hands. Like a Fury, she outran me, —she would have knocked me down if she must—for it was she who had to hug him first, and I could only be the second.

The Mugger and the Shadow

R. G. KIRK

I LOOKED up from my book.

'Who's there?' I called.

But no one answered. Yet there was no mistaking it—the sound of laboured breathing. It came distinctly, through the doors that lead out from the library to the covered porch. Low down, too; almost level with the brick floor outside. Only the bottom panels of the doors are wood, the balance glass. Yet I could see no one.

'Who's there?' I asked again. And got an answer this time, hoarse and gruff.

I got up and went over to the door.

'What do you want?'

And I got another answer—hoarser, gruffer.

'Well,' I gruffed back, brave as a water-cracker, 'who do you think you're scaring, wuffing around all over the place? Come right in!' And I swung back the door.

Blood and destruction and the ground torn up! What came in might have scared a stouter heart than mine. Only I was used to it. It was like this every time The Shadow drifted through our neighbourhood. In limped The Mugger, grime from nose to tail, and bleeding, like Markos Bozzaris, at every vein. One holy mess, that bulldog. On him was every outward sign of an unholy beating. But with the Mugger's breed you mustn't go by outward signs. Slashed to a gory fare-thee-well, The Mugger looked up at me with that crocodile trap of his spread wide in a happy smile of victory. This was the sixth unmerciful hide-ripping, he had taken from The Shadow; but, as in every other case, he thought he'd won the fight. Perhaps he had. It's how the heart looks, not the hide. At any rate, I knew the signs. The Shadow had once more passed through.

The Shadow was the terror of our suburb; a big, wolf-like, wolf-cruel cross-breed. Nobody knew who owned him. No one knew whence he came. But come he did, at intervals, through our community, and nearly always left small children mourning; bewailing some pet creature that lay still and bloody, in his trail.

There was a dainty-footed little goat two doors below us named Philomel—from her voice. She was a gamester, that one, and she might, with her hard head and flying hoofs, have held The Shadow off, had she been free, till help arrived. But the children found her dead between the shafts of her small wagon by the tree to which she had been tied.

And just across the street from us were Antony and Cleopatra, man and wife, the most devoted, grandest, waddlingest, quackingest pair of ducks that ever kept their own and neighbour gardens free of snails; both murdered in cold blood on their own lawn, and left there; not even carried off for food.

Pet bunnies, kittens, even a parrot, put out on his stand to catch the sunlight on his gorgeous burnishings; and then, at last, our next-door neighbour, Doctor Philbin's puppy, Midnight Dan; all murdered by The Shadow, who always picked some gentle creature, smaller, weaker than himself. He almost got The Mugger.

I came upon their first encounter just in time. The Mugger still was standing, wide-braced to the onslaught, as bulldogs often will, and trying valiantly for his hold. But he was swaying from the loss of blood. He wasn't much more than a baby then and fine game for The Shadow, who was cutting him to ribbons. Before long one of those swift rushes would have knocked The Mugger over, turned his throat up. But I got there in time:

It was his first fight, and he took a beating in it, poor little happy-go-lucky, rollicking bull pup, that would have broken the courage and ruined the trusting friendliness of almost any dog. But The Mugger was a bulldog. He had had a splendid time and was genuinely sorry when I had to come along and spoil the party. And the whole world was as much his friend after that murderous business as before. With one exception. A dog who makes old Sourmug his foe has made a foe for good. He isn't much of a starter, and, to tell the truth, he looks a poor bet up the back stretch and around the turns; but he is one grand little finisher and I think he knows it, for he always sticks for that, no matter how tough the going may be.

And so each time thereafter that The Shadow visited our neighbourhood The Mugger galloped gaily into him and got a lovely beating. At first The Shadow liked it, although he was surprised and puzzled, always, to see The Mugger coming in to get it. But The Shadow was delighted to oblige. The Mugger was good hunting. He was smaller, infinitely slower; and The Shadow soon found that the squat dog couldn't punish with that undershot, bull-baiting jaw of his. He took a fiend's delight in cutting up The Mugger.

No doubt of it, he could have killed the bulldog, had he had the nerve. But after slashing in and out a while, impossible to put a hold on as the thing from which we named him, he'd realize again that the way to overturn his low-set, broad-braced enemy wasn't written in the book. And The Mugger grew, as a good bulldog will, more unupsettable every day. Also the loose skin at his dew-lapped throat grew into better and better protection for the life streams beneath. And most discouraging of all, as battle followed battle, The Shadow found his foeman coming in for more with fiercer, stronger rushes, no matter how the combat went. Slowly it dawned upon The Shadow that how the fight is going does not make one bit of difference to a bulldog.

And so at each succeeding time they fought, a streak of saffron started creeping, just a little earlier, up The Shadow's backbone. And he'd quit a little sooner each time, sneering as he danced away, jeering at the bloody Mugger as he plugged hopelessly, ridiculously after him till he was out of sight. Each time The Mugger's victory grew less Pyrrhic. But just the same, when he came limping from our porch into the library, wagging the whole back end of him in triumph, after his sixth encounter with The Shadow, he was largely mincemeat.

'Uh-huh!' I said to him. 'Your old friend, eh? I see he ran you through the sausage grinder again. Some time you're coming out real wiener meat. Why don't you get some sense in that thick head? I think he'd call it quits right now if you'd stop sailing into him.'

But Mugger only wriggled joyously.

'More dog-gone' fun!' he snuffled. 'Come on now. Let's get this disinfecting nonsense over!' And he led the familiar way up to the bathroom.

And as he lay there on the floor, all chewed to rags again, and took his cleaning up without a whimper, I felt the old grim hope rise in me that some day he would get his enemy *cul-de-sac*. And as I worked on The Mugger I kept wondering whose kids The Shadow would leave wailing this trip through.

Halfway finished with my job, the phone rang.

'Lie still there, Mugs', I said, and closed the door on him as I went out.

It was Doctor Philbin, next door, on the wire.

'You, Griff?' he asked.

I said, 'Yes'.

'Your dog all right?'

There was something in his voice.

'Doctor!' I cried. 'Not Midnight Dan this time!'

'Yep!' said Doctor Philbin. 'Sure tough on my kids.'

He was speaking shortly. Something in his voice, was right. It was telling me that this thing wasn't only tough on his three kids.

'Your old Mugs', said Philbin. 'Just wanted to be sure he was O. K. Went to the rescue, he did. Got there ahead of me. But he was too late, too. I had a gun. I've had it laid out for that brute. But I couldn't let him have it. The Mugger was right on him all the time, and when he ran took after him too close. Came back all right, eh? You can fix him up yourself? Fine. Called up a vet myself and had him bring a dog out, so we could do a blood transfusion; but Dan checked out before he got here. No chance anyhow. So long, Griff. We'll get that damned hyena, mind me. Come over when you can.'

Midnight Dan. He was a wonderful English sheepdog puppy, all woolly-woolly, and no tail at all, and the most marvellous way of moving that you ever saw. Only a youngster, but he had a fund of common sense quite beyond that of any other dog I've met; and a gentleness of disposition not to be outmatched even by a bulldog's. It took the little folks, both Philbin's and our own, a year to shake that dreadful sorrow off.

I went upstairs again. There on the tiles, lay The Mugger, patiently waiting for the balance of his disinfection. And as I finished it I thought about that lovely bobtail sheepdog puppy—and more than once of what a beautiful language French is. *Cul-de-sac*. In a closet with The Mugger, and the door locked; through slashing Mugger, and no place to run. Down a dry well with The Mugger. But best of all, 'küd sak!' *In the bottom of a bag!* With Mugger!

But there came an evening, not two months after Midnight Dan was murdered, when the twitch of a finger would have decided that The Mugger never was to avenge the slaughters of poor Philomel, and Antony and Cleopatra, and all the other helpless ones, and Dan; nor to even up, in the bottom of a bag, that cruel butchering he'd taken as a little pup, and all the rest that followed. One night, coming home after a leisurely drive, we were surprised to see the light turned on in our garage. Hurrying in, we found The Mugger, wagging his back end, and looking with expectant interest up into the muzzle of an automatic which a policeman was sighting at his head. Beside them was our neighbour, Doctor Philbin, kneeling by a still form on the floor.

Steve was the quicker, both with wit and body. I went for the officer. But Steve—Stephanie, my wife—got to the dog before I reached the man. A swift, wise move, with risk ignored. My rushing at the officer would not have stopped his trigger finger —would not have knocked his hand aside in time. But he did not dare shoot at the dog with her so swiftly running to him.

Steve snatched the heavy bulldog up into her arms.

'What happened?' I cried then, moving to bring the two of them behind me. 'My God! It's old Eph Joppey, Steve! Philbin! How bad is he? Who did this?'

For now I saw that the floor of our garage was splashed with dark, glistening spots, and I recognized the quiet form beside which Doctor Philbin knelt, working with a bandage at the throat, which was soaked through with crimson.

'Who did it?' That was the officer of the law. 'The garage doors and windows all were shut when we got here. And when we went inside, the doctor and I, there was the poor old black man on the floor, and this bulldog beside him.'

And the officer, a tall, broad-backed young fellow, with a good jaw, shuddered.

'Who did it is no mystery', he said. 'You folks ought to know.' Then, grimly, 'Stand aside, will you, please? Put him down, lady. Go in the house and leave this to us men. I know how. He'll never know what hit him. Stand aside, will you? Lady, put him down!'

But Steve, you bet your last round iron dollar, didn't put The Mugger down. She only held him that much tighter up against her. And The Mugger, perfectly content, hung limp, and utterly relaxed, making no struggle. Steve's arms were locked around his barrel chest, beneath his forelegs, and he shoved his black nose back toward Steve's face, snuffling bulldog affection. How any man could think that Mugs had done that dreadful thing I could not understand. But then the officer didn't know bulldogs. Why, even Doctor Philbin, who loved Mugs . . .

He got up from his knees and walked to where we stood, a tense, determined group.

'It looks bad, Griff', he said to me; then added, all too hastily —'for Eph. He's lost a lot of blood for one so old. His head, too, hit the concrete floor when he went down. I've done all I can do right now. Have you a cot? We mustn't move him. An hour ought to tell. If he has rallied then, I'll take him to the hospital.'

He looked toward Steve then, who still stood behind me hugging the bulldog tight. Steve never quite forgave him for not overpowering that officer, twice his size and Irish, and taking his gun away when he threatened Mugs with death before we came. Philbin saw accusation in her eye, and turned to me again. He couldn't give his damning evidence to her.

'I can't believe it, Griff,' he said to me, 'but it's exactly as the officer says. Sam Talford's little girl had a fall that knocked her out this evening. They were half crazy when they called me. When I was getting out my car I heard, it seemed to me, a terrifying, savage growl come from your dark garage. But it was thundering then, and so I wasn't sure. I glanced back as I started out my drive and a flash of lightning showed both your garage doors shut. But there were the Talfords waiting, and I couldn't stop.

'Sam's little girl had come around, however, by the time I got there; so I hurried back. Just as I turned in your place the officer here came riding by, so I stopped him, and he came along. We opened up the doors together. There was the upset feed pan as you see it; and Eph stretched out in blood. And there was Mugger. I'm sorry, and I can't believe it, Griff,' said Philbin, 'but that's how it was.'

I knew that he was sorry, giving that terrible testimony. He loved Mugs, and his youngsters joined our own in many a fearless, joyful mauling of the bulldog.

'I'm sorry, Mrs. Griffith', Philbin said again, forcing himself to face my wife this time. 'I thought immediately just what you and Griff are thinking now; about the murderous brute that finished little Dan. But even a shadow can't pass through latched doors. There was only old Eph and The Mugger. The officer looked all about. I know how sweet he's always been. I've watched the youngsters safely pull and haul and pester past all endurance. But,' said Doctor Philbin from a troubled heart, 'that's how it was.'

Then the officer spoke again.

'Why make it tough for me?' he said. 'Be good citizens, you two. I got to do it. Put him down, lady. I know how. He'll never know what hit him.'

I couldn't blame the officer.

'Sweet', Doctor Philbin had just said. He must have looked sweet to that officer. The Mugger at his best must look, to most folks, just about as harmless as a crocodile. In fact The Mugger got his name after that famous one that waited at the ford in Kipling's perfect tale, *The Undertakers*. Appropriately, too; for there is something undeniably reptilian about a good bull-dog's head. No doubt of it, old Mugger's style of beauty had in large measure the crocodilian charm that wins blue ribbons for his kind. And his voice, too, was the typical bulldog voice—

only more so. He very seldom spoke—but when he did! It was a petrifying thing! Partly thick, choking snarl, partly hoarse bellow, and much, we fondly felt convinced, like the voice of the mugger-at-the-ford, which was like the sound of something soft breaking in two.

One hard-boiled-looking customer was The Mugger. I could not blame the officer—the scene set as it was. He was a man that you could get to like, it even seemed to me—this black-browed, blue-eyed, motorcycle cop.   His name, I found out afterward, was O'Malley, Pat Aloysius, if you will believe it.

I racked my brains for some defence for Mugger; but could find none. The Mugger's only defence that night was character, and people do not know the character of old Sourmug. They only know his reputation. They do not know he got the reputation centuries ago, and has long since outlived it. They do not know that he, to-day, is that thing which is just as rare as it is male—a perfect gentleman. Strong, but no bully. Brave, but no bravo. Like Bayard: without fear and without reproach. The Mugger never pulled poor old Eph Joppey down.

So, officer of the law or not, no man was going to blow The Mugger's brains out. And certainly, officer of the law or not, no man was going to put a hand on Steve to take the bulldog from her. This I resolved, because I just had seen a little squaring back of the shoulders of this tall, broad-backed, good-jawed young fellow. He was about to take steps to put the law into action. He had an ordinance to back him—that I knew. He was entirely within his rights in using his judgement—and the gun. But just the same. . . . Well, just the same, The Mugger hadn't done it!

And so something unpleasant was about to happen. For the officer put one shoulder forward, as a man about to step aggressively. And then Steve spoke.

I heard first her little gasp, as one gasps who has, after much brain racking, come suddenly on the solution of an ugly problem.

Leave it to Steve. More times than once in fifteen years, while the brain, so called, of her helpmate, more or less, has been hitting on one cylinder in the well-known block, she has come through.

v

The phrase was one which we had used so often speaking of The Shadow and The Mugger.

'*Cul-de-sac!*'

And instantly I had it. The whole thing was before me in a flash, as though I actually had seen it. When later, it was all described, I found that I had made a mental picture of it that was almost perfectly correct. I knew absolutely, without the slightest trace of a doubt whatever, exactly where to look for that one who had done this dreadful thing. Where else but in the bottom of the bag?

I said to Officer O'Malley, 'You can put your gun up now. You'll never need it for the one that did this job.'

He hesitated.

So Steve, to show him that we knew, put down The Mugger, and gave him a shove right at the very muzzle of that automatic.

'Go over there, you lamb,' she said, 'and show the officer your weapons. Open his mouth, and look in, will you, Officer?'

The Mugger galloped over to O'Malley. O'Malley didn't know that the ferocious scowl that wrinkled Mugger's villainous black muzzle was an ingratiating smile. He didn't know but what the dog was going to try to eat him. But just the same O'Malley put aside his gun and kneeled. He must have felt sure from this gesture of my wife's, in sending Mugger to him, that we knew something that he didn't. So he kneeled and reached out for that terrible charging head, and put it on his thigh, and opened those great jaws, and looked inside. A man, I'd call O'Malley, who thought that squat brute fresh from murderous attack.

'See', I said. 'Undershot. Nose set back, so he could breathe while he kept his hold on the bull's soft nose. His lower fangs don't meet his upper ones. They're out in front of them half an inch. In spite of reputation, he's a rotten fighter, all but his heart. He can't slash. The only way he can hold, even, is with a deep-mouthed grip. He could choke a man to death if he got such a hold. But this poor black man wasn't hurt that way. Why, man, the bulldog loves old Eph.'

But I saw now that I no longer had to argue for The Mugger. Conviction was upon O'Malley. And it wasn't his examination of The Mugger's war tools that convinced him of the bulldog's innocence. He works fast, The Mugger. His alligator lower

jaw once on your thigh, and you're a goner! For his ears are
velvety, and the wrinkled mug of him is soft, and his heart-
warming snuffle of universal friendship warmer still.

'And I'd have done it', Officer O'Malley said. 'Had you folks
got here fifteen seconds later, I'd have had it done.'

He rubbed around behind The Mugger's ears. And Mugger
stood in motionless delight and let him rub. He might not
know bulldogs, this officer of the law, but dogs in general he
evidently knew. There is that place, you know, behind the
ears. . . .

'But who did do it then?' said O'Malley. 'We shut the doors.
Nothing got out. And nothing's in. Only the five—the six
of us.'

'You looked in our old car standing over there?' I asked him.

'Yes. Even there.'

'Beneath it?'

'Sure. Dark there; but you can see clear under to the other
side. Look for yourself.'

But I knew where to look.

Eph Joppey is the handy man about our neighbourhood. He
is as sweet and gentle an old soul as ever God chose to clothe
in black. That day had brought him to our place in his rounds
about our suburb. He was to do a little gardening, lawn mowing, washing out the garage, odd jobs; and feeling as safe with
him about as though he had been some trusted Southern
mammy, Steve had left the household in his care. Our neighbourhood had been suffering as outlying districts do, too far
from car lines and the talkies, from scarcity of house help. And
Steve, who needed a vacation from our kids, had consented to a
nice long twilight drive, with dinner and the theatre to end it.

'Mind you, Eph. Bedtime is half past eight', my wife had
told him.

'Sho, ma'am', Eph had assured her. 'I'll shoo 'em off to covers
early, ma'am.'

'And don't forget to feed The Mugger', I said, as we drove
away. 'Make it late this evening. I gave him a good big shot of
what's good for him this morning, and I don't want him to eat
till ten or later. Keep him in the garage. Don't let him out
when I'm away.'

Poor old Eph had not forgotten. The Mugger's upset dinner

pail lay on the floor beside old Eph when Doctor Philbin and the officer found him. I can see Eph coming down our drive with that pan of steaming dinner for The Mugger in his hands. And I can see, out from the shadow of our hedge, that other Shadow slink. The smell of savoury rump stew was in the air, and had it been The Mugger back of Eph, his black nose would have been tilted up so high, sniffing those heavenly delights, that he would almost have tilted over backward.

But this dark shadow, slinking after Eph, went nose down, smelling at old Eph's heels was a scent more significant to that shadow. Weakness, timidity, senility, defencelessness; humans, with their dull noses, cannot smell these things, but a dog . . . Here was a weaker one—good hunting. There came the unexpected, freezing snarl!

Eph wheeled about in sudden fright, and automatically let go a feeble kick. Then followed wolf play; a cruel game, partly sheer evil, partly mere amusement. A game of shadowy dashings in and leapings out, of nipping this old carrier of savoury meat, of harrying this weak one. It soon would have the muchdesired effect of panic. Another nip or two, another little slash, and he would run, dropping the pan in which good rump stew steamed. And soon he ran. But he did not drop The Mugger's dinner. Instead, he held it close up to him as he ran. It was The Mugger's dinner, made with fine pride and care, by old Eph's hands. It wasn't any other dog's.

His uppermost concern was to get doors between himself and this thing that came slipping in and out between his futile kicks as shrewdly and as swiftly as a rapier; and that bit into his old legs just as keenly. But he had also in mind, as he ran with stiff steps down our drive, the friendly presence shut inside our garage; the burly, honest-hearted, bull-strong presence that might very well be counted on to come careering, roaring, headlong into action on the side of one he loved.

Eph got the door unlatched and partly open; but as he tried to squeeze through narrowly, blocking other entrance, the leaping shadow hit him in the back, and tumbled him inside, and sprang in after him. He fell, holding the dish of meat as he went down, trying to save the scatterment of its greasy contents over the smooth cement that he had lately cleaned.

And as he fell he got the throat wound. Whether with intent or not, whether by calculation or miscalculation, a poniard point sank easily through to where, beneath a poor protection of age-wasted tissues, old Eph's life flowed close by.

I could see it all. More than old Eph could ever tell, for his head struck the concrete, and blackness that seemed death ended the scene for him as he went down with hot fangs at his throat. But I know what happened after that.

Rain began to fall. The same rain through which Steve and I then were leisurely driving home. It streamed in glistening streaks across the dark open doorway of our garage. And then a puff of the rising wind that slanted those bright streaks blew shut and latched the door.

But this I pictured also, and I know it's right: Just as the door began to swing—bright lightning. And a thunderbolt! Real lightning it was, flashing in a rainy heaven. But the roaring thunderbolt that struck, in our garage, was flesh and blood! A thunderbolt death-headed, brindle-hided. It hit its target full and fair, and knocked it sprawling, sliding, clawing. And then, remorseless, joyous, struck again.

I saw it all the minute Steve said, '*Cul-de-sac!*'

That roaring charge had knocked The Shadow under our old car. And under our old car, forgotten by Doctor Philbin, indistinguishable in the shadows cast by one bulb overhead, there is—the bottom of a bag. Agatha, who is our old car, and who is constantly in need of surgical attention, always stands over it, roofing it. A repair pit.

We rolled our old car clear of the repair pit.

There was silence.

It's not a deep repair pit. An active dog could easily get out, even with old Agatha over it. A spring, a hooking of strong pasterns on the edge, a little scramble of back legs, and it is done. The Mugger, who is squat and heavy, did it. But The Mugger, when he did it, was unhindered. There was no enemy to drag him back into the bottom of the bag to honest battle. He had no enemy.

O'Malley stayed, The Mugger's head upon his thigh until the ambulance arrived for Eph. Then he stood up and looked at Mrs. Griffith.

He said, 'I hope it's all right, lady.'

Steve said, 'Indeed, indeed yes, Officer. It's quite all right. You do right when you do what you think is right.'

'Thanks', said O'Malley.

He straightened stiffly then, and touched his cap. I knew that I could like him. He smiled at us a little grimly as he stood, with heels together. But his salute was not for me, and it was not for Steve. It was a gesture of respect such as one gentleman without fear may offer to another.

There came then, presently, the put-put-put of Officer O'Malley's engine going down our drive. At which, as at a challenge, The Mugger opened up his alligator trap to tell a cock-eyed world that the motorcycle had not been designed, nor ever would be, that could outbark him. Then he looked at the burden white-clad men were carrying so carefully out of our garage, and he shut his eager mouth without a sound. It was a gesture of consideration such as might be expected from a gentleman without reproach.

Jupiter

STEFAN ZWEIG

I SHALL never forget the picture he made as he stood there on the edge of the canal, he, the criminal, the monster, looking on the work he had done. Heaven knows we were none of us rational at that moment, with the horror that gripped us; and yet I can recall thinking that I knew how he felt, that I knew what was passing in that vengeful little brain of his—that extraordinary brain.

But let me try, if only for myself, to reconstruct the whole story.

When I retired some eight years ago, my wife and I decided to look for a quite home in the country. We found the place we wanted near a little town called Dover in upper New York state. An old canal ran through the section; a century ago it had been busy with the barge traffic of the time; then the railways came, traffic dwindled, the lock caretakers were dismissed, and now its atmosphere of desertion made it romantic and mysterious.

Here, on the crest of a hill a few miles out from town, over-looking the canal, was the home we bought. Sitting on our garden terrace at the water's edge, we could see the house, the trees, the garden and meadows reflected in the smooth surface of the stream. We were not entirely isolated, for there was another house fairly similar to ours a few hundred yards away.

Not long after we moved in, a pretty, slender woman, hardly more than twenty-eight or twenty-nine, came over one morning and introduced herself—Mrs. Sturgis, our neighbour. Her eyes were intelligent and kind, her manner attractive, and we were soon talking as if we had known each other for years. Mr. Sturgis, it seemed, worked in Buffalo, and although it was a journey of an hour and a half for him every morning and night on the train, he did not mind it because of the beauty of the country here.

Her manner of speaking of him struck me as rather strange, I remember thinking—as if she did not miss him and yet as if at the same time she was devoted to him.

A few days later, on a Saturday morning, we were starting out for a walk along the canal when we heard footsteps behind us, and a tall, strongly built man came up and offered his hand. He was Roger Sturgis, he had heard of us from his wife, and seeing us pass just then, he had come down to say hallo. Wasn't it a glorious morning! Didn't we think it was the most beauti-ful spot on earth? Could we imagine anyone living in a city, when there was a place like this?

He talked with such enthusiasm, such fluency, that you had hardly a chance to get a word in edgewise; but this allowed me to have a good look at him. He was perhaps thirty-five, a huge ox of a man, six feet anyway, with great broad shoulders. What good nature! He went on talking and laughing without pause. He gave out so strong a feeling of happiness, of utter content-ment, that one was carried away against one's will. Both of us were stimulated by him and delighted to think that such a jovial fellow was our neighbour.

But this enthusiasm did not last. There was nothing to be said against Roger Sturgis. He was kind, sympathetic, helpful —a decent, trustworthy man. And yet—

The truth was, he became intensely difficult to bear because he was so boisterously, overwhelmingly and permanently cheerful. Everything was for the best in this best of all possible worlds. His house was perfect. His wife was perfect. His garden was perfect; and the pipe he smoked was the very best pipe ever made.

Never, before I met Roger Sturgis, could I have dreamt that such good qualities could exhaust you and drive you almost to despair.

I began to understand now the strange contradiction in his wife's manner of speaking of him. He loved her passionately, as he loved passionately everything he owned. I have never seen such tenderness as he lavished on her; the pride he took in showing her off bordered on the embarrassing. She felt this, but what could she do about it? You cannot quarrel with such supreme devotion!

As we talked about it, my wife and I began to think that what the Sturgises needed was a child. And it seemed, my wife told me, that Mrs. Sturgis had wanted children, that this was the great disappointment of their married life. They had expected a child in the first year of their marriage, in the second and in the third. After eight years, they had given up hope.

It was at about this time that Betty went to visit an old friend of hers in Rochester. When she returned, she had what she thought was an excellent suggestion. Her friend owned a female bull terrier that had given birth to a litter of adorable puppies. Betty had refused one for us, feeling that we could not take care of it properly, but thought that it might make a wonderful pet for Mrs. Sturgis.

I agreed, and that night I asked them if they would like it.

Mrs. Sturgis was silent—she was always silent when he was there—but he accepted with enthusiasm. Certainly! Why hadn't he thought of it before? What a marvellous idea! He couldn't thank me enough.

Two days later, the puppy arrived, a comical, lovable little thing, all loose skin and big paws, pure white, a perfect specimen.

The result was not at all what we expected.

Our intention had been to provide a companion for her, but it was Sturgis who took possession of the dog. It was not long before he was telling me on every occasion that there had never been such a dog, a more intelligent one, a more beautiful one, a bull terrier of terriers, a king of his race.

It seems incredible now, the effect this new passion produced in Roger Sturgis. Sometimes we'd hear a noisy barking in their house. It wasn't Jupiter. It was Sturgis, lying prone on the floor, carrying on as if he were a child, playing with his pet. I swear the dog's diet gave him far more concern than his own. I know that once when a newspaper mentioned typhoid in an adjoining county, Jupiter was given bottled water to drink.

Yet there was an advantage to it, in that Sturgis' preoccupation with the bull terrier spared his wife and us some of his exuberance. He would play with Jupiter for hours, never wearying, taking him off on long walks; and Heaven knows it did not make Mrs. Sturgis jealous. Her husband had found a new shrine at which to worship, and for her it was a blessed relief.

All this time, Jupiter was growing, the wrinkles in his coat filling out with hard, tough flesh, his chest broadening, his legs thickening, his great long jaws becoming more massive.

I admit that he was a most handsome animal, sleek, groomed, combed. And at first he was a good-natured one. But this began to change. Imperceptibly, then more and more quickly. He was intelligent and observant, and it was not difficult for him to perceive that his master—his slave, rather—adored him, overlooked any misdemeanour. The result was inevitable.

Disobedient? Jupiter was far more than disobedient. He became tyrannical. He would not tolerate anything in the house centring around anyone else. If there were visitors and he was outside, he would hurl himself against the door, shaking it under his great weight, confident that Sturgis would leap up to open it. Then he would enter without so much as a glance at the guests, jump on the sofa, the best piece of furniture, and lie there, aloof, bored, proud.

Whenever he was called, he would make Sturgis wait. He would not feed himself if Sturgis was there; Sturgis had to coax him into it. And although during the days he would behave more or less as any normal dog—running in the meadows, chasing chickens, digging, exploring—as soon as the time came for Sturgis' return from the city his attitude changed completely. He would lie back lazily on the sofa, not glancing at Sturgis as he came in, not responding with so much as a wag of his tail to the man's hearty, 'Hallo there, Jupe! Good old Jupe!'

He was the despot, more and more confident of his power.

He discovered an amusing and perverse new game. It was the habit of some poor people in a little settlement not far away to bring their clothes in baskets to wash them in the canal. Jupiter knew the days when they came. He would steal down on them and, at the proper moment, charge at the baskets and with a butt of his great head send them flying into the canal; and then off he would go, his jaws open as if in laughter, his little pinkish eyes flashing, defying the washer-women to catch him—as if, even if they had caught him, they could do anything, for he was as powerful as a horse. In the end, they went elsewhere, and Jupiter had one more proof of his omnipotence.

A year went by. Jupiter was in his prime, a huge beast, impudent and overbearing, cunning in his special art—for art it was—of humiliating his slavish master.

Then the new day came.

For the past week or so Mrs. Sturgis had given us the impression that she was avoiding anything worthy of being called a conversation. Betty and I could not help noticing this sudden diffidence, and one afternoon she made up her mind to face it.

'Judith,' she said, 'I'm much older than you and I haven't any reason to feel shy, so I'm going to break the ice. If we've done anything to offend you, I do wish you'd tell me what it is.'

Mrs. Sturgis stammered, hesitated, and then came out with it: After nine years of married life, she thought she would never be a mother, but now—well, she had gone to the doctor and he had confirmed it: yes, she was to have a child. Imagine her joy!—but somehow she couldn't bring herself to tell her husband; she was almost afraid of the violence of his reaction! We knew what he was like. So she had been wondering—would it be possible—would we mind very much if we had a talk with him and prepared the ground?

Of course we were delighted. I left a note for Sturgis asking him to come over the moment he returned from town. And at six-thirty that afternoon, there he was, brimful of that extraordinary vitality.

'Roger,' I said, 'I'm going to ask you a funny question. If

you had one wish, for anything in the world, what would you want?'

Half-serious, half-laughing, Sturgis shook his head.

'What would I wish for? Why—'

'Surely there's something!'

'What's the joke?'

'I'm serious. Come on, what do you want above all else?'

He grinned. 'Why,' he said, 'I'm darned if I know what I'd wish for! After all, I've got everything I want—my wife, my house, my job, my—' He was going to say 'my dog', but thought better of it; he knew how we felt about that infernal beast.

'Then how about Mrs. Sturgis?' I said. 'What do you think she'd want?'

He looked at me in bewilderment. 'What could she possibly want?'

'Perhaps something more than a dog.'

At last he understood. His eyes opened so wide that we saw the whites. With one bound he was out of his chair, through the door and scrambling over the lawn and the garden fence, and we heard the door of his house slam.

We both laughed. We weren't surprised by his reaction.

But someone else was surprised—someone who, lying lazily on the sofa, with half-closed eyes, was waiting for the evening homage that he had come to think was his due. Someone who was waiting for the man to enter, to kneel beside him, to pat him. Someone who was waiting to ignore that homage.

But what was this? Without a word of greeting, the man rushed past into the bedroom, and Jupiter heard the talking and laughing and crying that went on and on and on. Jupiter, the tyrant, the smug, the proud—ignored!

An hour passed. The maid brought him his food. Contemptuously, he turned aside. He growled at the maid. They would see that he was not going to be snubbed! But this evening, no one seemed to realize that he had refused his food. There was Sturgis talking to his wife without interruption, overwhelming her with anxious advice and affection. Jupiter was too proud to force his way to his master's attention. Curled up in a corner, he waited.

He waited in vain.

The next morning Sturgis rushed by him again without a look. And he had the same experience that night, the following morning, the following night. Day after day.

He was intelligent, but this was beyond him. He became nervous and irritable. He would not approach Sturgis; not he. It was Sturgis who must return to his senses, who must come to him.

In the third week, Jupiter went lame. In normal circumstances Sturgis would have rushed for the vet, but now neither he nor anyone else noticed the limp, and Jupiter, in exasperation, had to give it up. A few days later he attempted a hunger strike—such was his intelligence, his subtlety. But no one worried. For two full days he refused his meals heroically. For all anyone seemed to care, he might starve himself to death.

Finally his animal hunger was stronger than his will power— yes, I say his will power, and I mean it, for I knew that dog— and he ate again, but I am sure, without enjoyment.

He grew thinner. He walked in a different way. Instead of swaggering around, insolently, he half crawled. His coat formerly brushed lovingly every day, lost its silky shine. His pinkish little eyes were puzzled. When you met him, he actually lowered his head so that you would not see his eyes and hurried by.

All his tricks, his fasting, his limping, were to no avail. Something was, and remained, changed in this house that he had ruled. What distinguishes the animal mind from the human is that the former is limited to past and present; it cannot imagine the future. And so Jupiter, with all his intelligence, could do no more than sense with agony and despair that something was growing and preparing itself in the house, something invisible, something that was against him—this enemy, this fiend, this thief!

Months later, he reached the end—or if not exactly the end, something like it. If he had been a human, I think he would have committed suicide. He vanished. He was gone for three full days. Not until the evening of the third did he turn up once more—dirty, hungry, looking as though he had been in a fight. In his raging, impotent fury he must have attacked every strange dog he had come across. But he came back, as a man would come back after touching the bottom depths. Perhaps, perhaps by now—

But new humiliations awaited him. No one to greet him.
No one to welcome him home. The maid would not even let
him in the house!

Actually, this was more than justified, for Mrs. Sturgis' time
had come, and the house was full of busy people. Sturgis had
an intense sentimental desire to have the baby born in their
home, and since the local hospital was crowded then anyway,
the doctor had consented. So the doctor was there, and a nurse,
and Mrs. Sturgis' mother, and my wife and I.

And Roger Sturgis. Face flushed, trembling with excitement,
getting in everyone's way, he waited.

Outside the front door, Jupiter waited too.

What were they doing in there? He heard voices, the
splashing of water, the tinkling of glass and metal. What was
happening was beyond his comprehension, but instinctively he
felt that it was *It*—It, the thing that had caused his downfall,
his humiliation. It, the invisible, the infamous, cowardly
enemy. It was now going to appear, and as soon as that door
was opened, It would not escape!

His powerful muscles were tensed. He crouched, waiting.

Of all this, we in the house of course had no idea. Betty and
I were delegated by the doctor to keep Sturgis in the living-
room. Because of his enormous capacity for emotion, it was a
harrowing job. But at last the good news came—a girl—and
some time later the bedroom door opened and the nurse
appeared with the little bundle.

The doctor followed smiling.

'Well, Mr. Sturgis!' he said. 'Go ahead! Hold her in your
arms for a minute and tell us how it feels to be a father!'

Trembling, the big man reached out his arms and the nurse
put the baby in them and he looked down at her with tears on
his cheeks.

The doctor was putting on his gloves. 'Everything's all right',
he said. 'Nothing to worry about, so I'll be getting along.'

Bidding us good-bye, he opened the front door.

In that split second, something shot past between his legs.
Jupiter was there in the room.

His eyes were on Sturgis; his little pinkish eyes were on the
bundle in his master's arms, and he knew, I know he knew,
that this was It. With a raging cry, he charged.

So sudden and fierce was the attack that the great strapping man staggered under the violence of it and fell against the wall. At the last moment he tried instinctively to save the child by raising it above his head. Betty was nearest him. She seized the bundle and thrust it at the nurse, who was in the bedroom door. She pushed the nurse into the bedroom and swung the door shut with all her might.

Now Sturgis had recovered his balance, and with a fury as savage as the dog's he threw himself on Jupiter. Chair and tables crashed to the floor. The doctor and I at last came to our senses, and picking up anything we could lay our hands on we battered the animal into unconsciousness. We bound him with rope and dragged him from the room to the lawn outside.

Sturgis was swaying like a drunken man. His coat had been ripped and we noticed now—what he was not even aware of, himself—that blood was dripping down his right arm. The doctor got him into the other bedroom, undressed him and attended to the gash Jupiter's teeth had left. Then, exhausted physically and emotionally, Sturgis fell asleep.

But what was to be done with Jupiter?

'Shoot him', I said, but the doctor objected. The dog must be put under observation; he might be hydrophobic, in which case Sturgis would require treatment. And so Jupiter, tightly bound, still only half conscious, was driven off in the doctor's car.

We heard later that the Pasteur test showed no signs of hydrophobia and that the dog seemed to be quiet and well behaved. Sturgis, once his adoring master, of course never wished to see him again. The doctor happened to learn that a hardware man in town was looking for a watchdog; he was told about Jupiter and offered to take him.

So he vanished from our horizon. Before long, none of us, even Sturgis, ever thought of him.

For now, needless to say, Sturgis had a new idol, infinitely more precious, on which he lavished all his passion and tenderness. Every day, every hour, every minute, he discovered new delights in his beautiful little baby. He could hardly stand to tear himself away in the morning to go to his office, and half a dozen times each day he would call up to see how she was. Every night when he returned he brought some new toy—a rattle, a teething ring, a thousand and one gadgets. His adoration was complete.

As I have said, none of us thought of Jupiter, a bad dream forgotten—until one night I was forcibly reminded of his existence.

For some reason I could not get to sleep. At last I got up, put on my robe, went into the kitchen and warmed some milk and drank it. Passing through the living room on my way back to bed, I saw through the window how lovely the night was, and for a while I stood there looking out. Behind a veil of thin silvery clouds the moon sailed high, and each time the clouds fell from its face the whole garden shimmered as though beneath a blanket of driven snow. There was not a sound. I felt that if a leaf had dropped from a tree I would have heard it fall. . . .

It gave me a start when in this great milky silence I noticed something moving along the hedge that separated our property from the Sturgises'.

It was Jupiter.

He crept forward slowly, his belly almost touching the ground. It was as if he had come to reconnoitre, to spy out the land, very cautiously, very stealthily, moving with none of that brash swaggering self-assurance that had been his. Instinctively I leaned out the window to see him better. My elbow brushed against a flower pot on the sill and knocked it to the ground. With one noiseless bound the huge dog leaped into the darkness. There was the garden again, empty, shimmering.

I closed and barred the window.

Yet the next morning, it seemed silly. He was only a dog, not a rational thing, a thinking being; not a wolf, a tiger, a beast of prey! So I did not mention what I had seen to the Sturgises. But when a few days later I was working in the garden and saw their maid hanging out the baby's clothes on the line, I went over and asked her if she had seen Jupiter lately.

She said she had not told Mrs. Sturgis, not wanting to upset her, but a week ago she had had a strange experience. She had taken the baby out in its carriage when a car had passed them on the road. The moment the car went by, she heard an angry barking. Looking up, she had caught a glimpse of a big white dog sitting beside the driver. It was a commercial car, a delivery truck—'Hardware', it said on the side.

Who else but Jupiter? What other explanation than that he had seen the carriage, the maid, the baby, recognized them and barked his hatred?

Now I did feel afraid. The dog had not forgotten. I had happened to see him one night. How many other nights had he returned and crept spying round the house?

'If you ever see him,' I said to the maid, 'you must tell Mr. Sturgis at once, or if he isn't home, tell me. The next time I'm in town I'll warn the hardware man that he must keep the dog leashed.'

But I asked myself: Is it possible for a dog to remember so bitterly, so vividly? Human rivalry is one thing, but this was a dumb animal, with a new master, new surroundings, and he had been there for months now. Could a dog remember so long?

Perhaps not the ordinary domestic pet, good old Rover or Jack or Sport. But this was not an ordinary dog. This dog had been spoiled. He had been given a ridiculous amount of attention and worship, and suddenly it had all been taken away. This dog was intelligent, with a warped, bitter intelligence. I hated him, but the fact that I thought of him in that way—a way in which I would never expect to think of an animal—showed that I respected his intelligence, that I admitted it.

What should I have done? Told the police my fears? Asked to have the dog put out of the way? Perhaps so; perhaps I was to blame; but at times it did seem absurd, and I could fancy the police laughing at me—'What is this, a dog, or a master criminal?'—and the hardware man saying, 'Why, he's a good dog, a fine watchdog; he's valuable; he was given to me and I don't want to give him up.'

So I did nothing. I worried about it and thought this way and that way and in the end did nothing, and the days passed, and we came to that Sunday, the final unforgettable day.

We had gone over to the Sturgises' that beautiful Sunday afternoon. We were sitting talking on the lower terrace, from which the slope of the hill descends to the canal. Near by, on this level ground, stood the baby carriage, and, needless to say, Sturgis kept interrupting our conversation to call attention to

w

the baby, to go over and wiggle his fingers at her and smile and talk.

By and by Mrs. Sturgis called to us from the house, a hundred feet or so above the lower terrace. 'Come on,' she said, 'the tea's on the table. Hurry, or the toast will get cold.' We went first; Sturgis lingered. We were in the house and sitting down by the time he came in. Mrs. Sturgis poured and we talked of the weather and the roses and so on until, as always, Sturgis returned to his favourite subject.

'The baby's asleep. You know, it's wonderful how well behaved she is. Never wakes us at night, none of this crying or—'

'Is she in the sun?' Mrs. Sturgis asked.

'Just a little; it's good for her. I would have brought her up here but I thought the movement might wake her.'

'You left her on the terrace?' I asked. I had assumed that he had wheeled the carriage up.

'Yes. Why? She's sleeping, you know, and I thought—'

I was uneasy. He sensed it. He half rose, looking at me. It was as if that tremendous all-devoted love of his for the child gave him the power to read the thought that was not even fully formed in my mind.

'Oh, Roger, sit down and finish your tea', Mrs. Sturgis said. 'Really, you're worse than an old woman the way you worry!'

She was smiling. He was not. I was looking at him and he at me, and although I tried to dismiss the thought from my mind, I couldn't. He did not sit down. Something, I do not know what, perhaps some slight sound, even from that far away, drew him to the door. And we heard his awful, anguished exclamation.

It was not loud but it was, I think, the most horrible noise I have ever heard, a choking convulsive sound, the last sound a man might make dying in agony.

'For God's sake, what is it?' I cried.

It was as if, from the horror of what he saw, Sturgis could not move. We shoved back our chairs, rushed to his side. That movement released him from the trance. He tore the door open and leaped across the veranda.

The baby carriage was no longer on the terrace.

Then I saw it. It was in the canal. It had rolled down the slope and into the water. It was still upright and floating, by some miracle, but as we looked—and this happened only in seconds, even as we still tried to comprehend what we saw—it slowly began to turn on its side, to sink.

And Jupiter stood on the bank.

He, Jupiter, the great white beast. He who, in the days when he ruled this house, had amused himself by dashing down to the canal and butting the baskets of laundry into it, pushing them down the slope with his powerful muscles. He stood and watched the carriage sinking, he the victor, he who had triumphed at last.

The carriage turned over. There was a flutter of white sheets, of arms and legs waving, and the child rolled out of the carriage into the water.

Then I saw the dog's great muscles go tense. I saw him throw himself into the canal. It was only a few feet out from the bank. His tremendous jaws opened, and the child lay in his grasp. The jaws were gentle. Jupiter thrust himself back and dragged the baby up on the bank. And now Sturgis reached it. He grabbed the child in his arms and hugged her. He saw that she breathed, that she was safe.

The dog stood looking at them, at the master who had worshipped him and the enemy who had destroyed that worship, the enemy in his master's loving arms, the enemy that he had restored to his one-time master's arms.

Sturgis knelt. I saw his face working. He knelt, hugging the baby, but he looked now not at her but at the dog. I saw him stretch a hand toward the dog. I heard what he said:

'Jupiter.'

The hand was reached out to stroke the dog. The dog stood still.

'Come here—old Jupiter.'

Jupiter turned and went away, and Roger Sturgis was left alone with his child.

I know who was the victor.

The Making of Silly Billy

ERNEST THOMPSON SETON

HE was the biggest fool-pup I ever saw, chuck full of life and spirits, always going at racing speed, generally into mischief, breaking his heart if his master did not notice him, chewing up clothing, digging up garden stuff, going direct from a wallow in the pigsty to frolic in the baby's cradle, getting kicked in the ribs by horses and tossed by cows, but still the same hilarious, rollicking, good-natured, energetic fool-pup, and given by common consent the fit name of Silly Billy.

It was maddening to find that he had chewed up one's leather glove, but it was disarming to have the good-natured little idiot come wagging his whole latter end south of the short ribs, offering the remaining glove as much as to say that 'one that size was enough for anyone'. You *had* to forgive him, and it did not matter much whether you did or not, for the children adored him. Their baby arms were round his neck as much of the time as he could spare from his more engrossing duties.

Every member of the family loved Silly Billy, but they wished from the bottom of their hearts that he might develop at least a glimmer of dog common sense. He was already past the time when, with most bull-terriers, puppyhood ended; yet for his destined place among his master's hunting dogs, he, it was judged, was not yet ripe enough.

Bob Yancy was a hunter, a professional—and his special line was killing bears, mountain lions, lynxes, wolves and other such things classed as varmints, for whose destruction the State pays a bounty. Much of this hunting was done on the high level of 'the chase', but, as a rule, the mountains were too rough. The game either ran off altogether, or, by crossing some impossible barrier, got rid of the hunters and then turned on the dogs to scatter them to flight.

That was the reason for the huge bear traps that were hanging in Yancy's barn. Those formidable objects would not actually hold the bear a prisoner; but they would hold him back so that the hunters, even on foot, could overtake the victim.

The dogs, however, were the interesting part of the pursuit. Three kinds were needed. Exquisite trailers, whose noses could follow with sureness the oldest, coldest trail; swift runners for swift game; and intelligent fighters. The fighters had of course to be brave, but intelligence was more important; for the dogs were expected to nip at the bayed quarry from behind and spring back from his counter blow, rather than to close at final grips.

Thus there were bloodhounds, greyhounds and a bulldog in the Yancy pack. Most of the pack had marked personality. There was Croaker, a small bitch with an exquisite nose and a miserable little croak for a bay. You could not hear her fifty feet away, but fortunately Big Ben was madly in love with her; he followed her everywhere and had a voice like the bell for which he was named.

Then there was Old Thunder, a very brave dog, with a fine nose. He was a combination of all good gifts and had been through many fights. Though slow and feeble now, he was respected by dogs and men.

The bulldog is more conspicuous for courage than discretion, so that the post of bulldog to the pack was often open—the last bulldog had been buried with the bones of their last grizzly. But Yancy had secured a new one, a wonder. He was the product of a long line of fighting bulldogs. And when the new incumbent of the office arrived it was a large event to all the hunters. He was no disappointment, but a perfect beast of the largest size. Surly, savage beyond his kind, the hunters at Yancy's knew at once that they had a fighting treasure in the Terrible Turk.

It was with some misgiving that he was turned loose on the ranch. He was so unpleasant in his manner. He made no pretence of hiding his sense of contemptuous superiority, and the pack seemed to accept him at his own value. Clearly, they were afraid of him. Only Silly Billy went bounding in hilarious friendliness to meet the great one; and a few minutes later flew howling with pain to hide and whimper in the arms of his little mistress. Of course, in a world of brawn the hunters had to accept this from their prize fighter, and see in it a promise of mighty deeds to come.

In the two weeks the Terrible Turk had quarrelled with nearly every hound in the pack. There was only one indeed that he had not actually injured. That was old Thunder. There was a certain dignity about Thunder that even a dog respected, and, in this case, without any actual conflict, the Terrible Turk retired and the onlookers hoped that this augured for a kindly spirit they had not hitherto seen in him.

October was glowing on the hills when word came that Old Reelfoot, a famous cattle-killing grizzly, had reappeared in the Arrow-bell Cattle Range and was up to his old tricks, destroying live stock in a perfect mania for destruction. There was a big reward offered for Reelfoot. Besides, there was really a measure of glory attached to his destruction, for every hunter in the country for several years back had tried to run the great grizzly down, and tried in vain.

Bob Yancy was ablaze with hunting ardour when he heard the news. His only dread was that some rival might forestall him. It was a spirited procession that left the Yancy Claim that morning, headed for the Arrow-bell Ranch. Everything was in fine shape for the hunt, and we were well away when a disconcerting element was tumbled in among us. With many a yap of glee, there came bounding that fool bull-terrier, Silly Billy.

Bob yelled 'Go Home' till he was hoarse. Silly Billy would only go off a little way and look hurt; then make up his mind that the boss was only fooling and didn't mean a word of it, and start again. He steered clear of the Terrible Turk, but otherwise occupied a place in all parts of the procession practically all of the time.

No one wished him to come, no one was willing to carry him back, there was no way of stopping him, so Silly Billy came, self-appointed, to a place on the first bear hunt of the season.

That afternoon the party arrived at the Arrow-bell Ranch and the expert bear man was shown the latest kill—a fine heifer, barely touched. The grizzly would surely come back for his next meal. Yes, an ordinary grizzly would, but Reelfoot was an extraordinary animal. Just because it was bear fashion to come again soon, he might not return for a week. Yancy set a big trap by this kill, also seeking out the kill of a week gone by, five miles away, and setting by that another gaping pair of grinning cast-steel jaws. Then all retired to the hospitable ranch house.

He who knows the grizzly will not be surprised to hear that that night brought the hunter nothing and the next was blank. But the third morning showed that the huge brute had come in craftiness to his older kill. The place of the trap was vacant, log and all were gone, and all around were signs of an upset, many large tracks, so many that scarcely any were clear, but farther on we got the sign most sought, the 13-inch track of a monster grizzly and the bunch on the right paw stamping it as Reelfoot's trail.

I had seen the joy blaze in Yancy before, but never like now. Letting the dogs run free, he urged them on with whoops of 'Sick him, boys!' It was Croaker that first had the real trail, Big Ben was there to let the world know, then Thunder endorsed the statement. All the pack knew Thunder's voice and his judgement was not open to question. They left their different tracks, and flocked behind the leader, baying deep and strong at every bound, while the Turk came hurrying after and Silly Billy tried to make amends in noise for all he lacked in judgement.

Away we went, the bawling pack our guides. Many a long

detour we had to make to find a horseman's road, for the country was a wilderness of rocky gullies. But we kept on, and within an hour the dinning of the pack, in a labyrinth of fallen trees, announced the bear—at bay.

No one who has not seen it can understand the feeling of such an hour. The quick dismount, the tying of the nerve-tense horses, the dragging forth of guns, the swift creep forward, the vital questions, How is he caught? By one toe that will give? Or firmly by one leg? Is he free to charge as far as he can hurl the log? Or is he stalled in trees and helpless?

Creeping from trunk to trunk we went, and once the thought flashed up, 'which of us might not come back alive?'

'Look out now, don't get too close', said Yancy. 'Log and all he can cover fifty feet while you make ten, and, I tell you, he won't bother about the dogs if he gets a chance at the men. He knows his game.'

The first peep, but it was a disappointment. There was the pack, bounding, seething, yelling, and back of some brush was some brown fur, that was all. But suddenly the brush swayed, and forth rushed a shaggy mountain of flesh, a tremendous grizzly—and charged at his tormentors, who scattered like flies when one strikes at a swarm of them.

But the log on the trap caught on a stump and held him.

This is the moment of all in the hunt. This is the time when you gauge your hounds. There was Old Thunder baying, tempting the bear to charge, but ever with an eye to the safe retreat. There were the greyhounds yapping and nipping at his rear; there in the background wisely waiting, reserving his power for the exact time was the Terrible Turk; and here and there, bounding yapping, insanely busy, was Silly Billy, dashing into the very jaws of death again and again, but saved by his ever restless activity, and proud of the bunch of bear's wool in his teeth.

Round and round they went as Reelfoot made his short furious charges, and even Turk kept back, baying gloriously, but biding his time for the very moment. And whatever side Old Thunder took, there Turk went too, and Yancy rejoiced for that meant that the fighting dog had also good judgement and was not over rash.

The fighting and baying swung behind a little bush. Yancy shouted to all to 'Keep back.' He knew the habits of the bear, and the danger of coming into range. But the shout of warning attracted the notice of the bear and straight for Bob he charged.

Many a time before had Yancy faced a bear, and now he had his gun, but, perched on a small and shaky rotten log, he had no chance to shoot, and, swinging for a clearer view, upraised his rifle with a jerk—an ill-starred jerk—for under it the rotten trunk cracked, crashed, went down; and Bob fell sprawling, helpless in among the tumbled logs, and now the grizzly had him in his power.

We were horror-held. We dared not fire, the dogs and the man himself were right in line. The pack closed in. Their din was deafening. They sprang on the huge, haired flanks; they nipped the soggy heels, they hauled and held and did their best, but they were as flies on a badger or as rats on a landslide. The brushwood switched, the small logs cracked, as he rushed, and Yancy would be in a moment more smashed with that fell paw.

In a flash Old Thunder saw the only way. The veteran of the pack ceased all half-way dashing at flank or heel. He leaped at the great bear's throat—but one swift sweep of that deadly paw and he went reeling back, bruised and shaken. He rallied, rushed as though he knew how much depended on him, when the mighty warrior Turk, the hope and valour of the pack, long holding back, sprang forward and fastened with all his strength. On the bear? No! *On poor Old Thunder,* wounded battered, winded—downed—seeking to save his master. On him the bulldog fastened with a grip of hate. This was what he had waited for. This was the time of times that he took to vent his pent-up, jealous rage. He dragged Thunder down to hold him strangling in the brushwood.

The bear had freedom now to wreak revenge. But from the reeling, yapping pack there sprang a small white flash of fury, not for the monster's heel, not for his flank or his massive shoulder, but for his face, the only place where a dog could count in such a sudden stand. Gripped as by an iron vice above the monster's eye, the huge head jerking back and forth made the little beast go flapping like a rag; but the dog hung on. The bear reared up to claw his antagonist. It was Silly Billy.

Bob scrambled to his feet and escaped. The huge brute seized the whirling white body in his paws—like stumps of trees—as a cat might seize a mouse, gripped and wrenched him; tore his own flesh, and hurled the pup like a bundle far aside. Then, wheeling for a moment, the grizzly paused to seek the bigger foe, the man. The pack recoiled. Four rifles rang. Reelfoot's elephantine bulk sank limp. Instantly Turk, the dastard traitor Turk, closed bravely on the dead brute's haunch and fearlessly tore out the hair. The pack sat lolling back, the battle done.

Bob Yancy's face was set. He had seen it nearly all, and we supplied the rest. Billy was wagging his whole latter end, in spite of some red-stained slashes on his ribs. Bob greeted him affectionately: 'You dandy! It's the finish that shows up the stuff a beardog is made of, an' I tell you there ain't nothing too good in Yancy's Ranch for *you*.'

'And you,' he said to the Turk, 'Come here.' He took off his belt, put it through the collar of the Terrible Turk and led him to one side. A rifle cracked. Yancy kicked leaves and rubbish over the body of what had once been a big, strong bulldog.

Heading all on the front of Yancy's saddle in triumphal procession homeward, was Silly Billy, the hero of the day, his white coat stained with red, his body stiff and sore, but his exuberant spirits little abated. He probably did not fully understand the feelings he had aroused but he did know that he was having a glorious time and that at last the world was responding to the love he had so bounteously squandered on it.

Riding in a pannier on a packhorse was Old Thunder. In a few weeks he fully recovered from the combined mauling he got from the bear and the Turk.

Billy himself was as fit as a fiddle within a month, and when half a year later he had shed his puppy ways, his good dog sense came forth in strength. Brave as a lion he had proved himself, full of life and energy, affectionate, true as steel, and within two years he was leader of the Yancy pack. They do not call him Silly now, but 'Billy, the pup that made good'.

The Pedlar's Dog

PAUL VETTERLI

FOR days he had been running around loose. He looked hungry and disreputable. At night he sneaked up to the houses and dung heaps, looking for scraps. During the day he wandered around in the woods or crouched wearily in the bushes.

Invariably he gave the impression of being tortured by a bad conscience. With his curly fur all matted, and the grey skin stretched taut over a skeleton of bones and ribs sunken in deeply at the flanks, he was unpleasant to look upon. The restlessness in his eyes aroused suspicion. He was considered nothing more than a cur and a vagabond—the pedlar's dog.

Even while his master was still alive, Grey, as everyone called him, hadn't been liked particularly. The scorn people had for his master was extended to him, too, only the more so since, it was thought, he did not display even toward his master the attachment and fidelity habitual in dogs. This strange and quite openly flaunted indifference of his made him seem disgusting and repulsive to those whose concept of the dog was identified with tail-wagging tenderness and cringing submission.

There were some who considered him a beast of prey in disguise and honestly believed that 'wild' blood coursed in his veins. Rumour had it that one of his ancestors had actually been a Russian wolf, with which some cynologist had made crossbreeding experiments in an effort to produce an especially keen work dog. Thus, irrespective of whether he was in harness, pulling the cart loaded with all kinds of goods cross country, or lounging around free, Grey was always burdened with this suspicion of his secret tie to the wild.

Only one man trusted the dog, and trusted him wholly—his master. As an itinerant pedlar and odd job man, who was often enough sick, he led a dreary existence. He did not demand tenderness and demonstrative outbursts from his four-legged companion. All he wanted was a comrade. Or perhaps he needed only a helper to take care of the chores. And the four-legged one proved both reliable and willing. That is why the pedlar called him True.

Now his master was no longer there—he was dead. One morning when True, as was his wont, nuzzled against the hand hanging over the edge of the bed to wake his master, the hand was immobile and cold.

Never again did the familiar voice address him. His ears listened in vain. His eyes sought in vain. His delicate nostrils tested each corner and each current of air, searching for the scent of him. He felt: his master was no longer around, was gone. A great distance had suddenly interposed itself between him and his lord.

Then alien hands took him over. He was put on a chain. Food was placed before him. No, he wasn't to go hungry, in those few days he still had left to live. After all, he was one of God's creatures. A dog! He probably hadn't had an easy time of it. Was supposed to have changed masters several times.

Immediately after the death of the pedlar they had asked around in the village if someone wanted to take Grey. If not, the state police would be given the job of doing away with him. This latter course was universally approved. After all, it was no more than a matter of a cur without a master, and since nobody wanted him, nobody came forward as his protector.

Silent, as if the senses formerly so acute had been dulled by sickness, True lay at the end of his chain. There was a great deal of discussion as to whether or not the dog was aware of his approaching end. His apathy was cited as much in proof of this possibility as against it. Only when he tore his collar one day and ran away were they all in agreement. Then there was no doubt any longer: Grey had known what was in store for him, that was why he had fled.

From that day on he remained invisible. But people heard about him. Bad things, very bad things. He was supposed to have jumped through the half-open kitchen window of a farm-house one night, to have emptied a bowl of milk and torn apart a loaf of bread. The raiding of a chicken coop was also, rightly or wrongly, held against him. A cat was found mangled in a field.

'Grey is the murderer!' they all swore.

When the mayor's dog returned from a foray with bloody haunches and torn ears, naturally suspicion again fell on only the one—on the renegade. He was roundly cursed. No respite at all should have been granted him after the demise of the pedlar, since they had known full well what sort of a beast hid under that grey pelt. Now he was a menace to everybody.

Within a few days, under the tremendous pressure of fate, a dismal change had indeed taken place in the dog. As if the departure of the only one who had meant him well had been sufficient to make him lose all other contact with the rest of mankind, he had fled. From the accustomed surroundings of hut and hearth he had saved himself in the dark vastness of the forest. More swiftly than any other of his kind he found his way about in his new surroundings. Hidden forces, ties to the wild days aeons distant, mysteriously passed on from wolf to dog and from generation to generation, awoke in him, enriching his instinct and determining his actions. In his poor dog's brain a recognition of freedom dawned.

No collar choked him any longer. No clanking chain burdened his legs with its iron weight. Where he had formerly lain on straw, he rested now on old dry leaves. Four walls had offered him protection against rain and wind. Now, in the middle of a thicket, sheltered by the crown of a tree, he felt no less snug.

But the stomach! The hunger! At regular intervals, twice a

day, he had received the necessary food from his master. Seldom had he suffered want. But now? During the third night he sneaked up to the houses of man and found his food there—milk and bread. But torturing fear drove him off before he had filled his empty stomach. Then he found courage to approach once again, trusting the darkness; confronted with closed doors and windows, he dug around in the garbage heap, gorging on carrion.

Then the scent of a cat stung his nostrils. Like a fox sneaking up on a nibbling hare, he stalked his prey. With the knowledge of his forebear, the wolf, with his ability to jump and hold, he seized the fleeing cat, crushing her spine just below the neck. Revolted, he swallowed a few bites.

This event was decisive. The brief chase after the booty, the lucky catch, the scent of blood, all of it directed Grey's course to the hunt. He gained confidence in the speed of his legs, the impact of his attack and the power of his jaws. Thus the last tie to mankind was severed; the bondage the dog soul had inhaled along with the scent of the food dish was extirpated.

With even less effort than his cousins in the tundras, Grey secured his daily fare. Rabbits, hares, roes and roebucks lived in the forest. Away from the frightened, cowering fawn he chased the doe, the mother. Silently he tracked her spoor. Noiselessly he tore her down.

Complaints rose from all around. Particularly at the head gamekeeper's lodge. There the deer losses were reported. And there they didn't merely curse, they acted. With all the means available to forestry, with poisoned bait, with traps and guns, the zealous officials, concerned about their game, advanced against the monster. Battues and other hunts were arranged. They surrounded thickets, sneaked along the edges of the forests, sat for days on end in clearings near carefully planted carrion and recently killed game. Tireless hunters spent moonlit nights on high perches. No one thought of rest as long as this grey devil was rampant. The work of years of gamekeeping was at stake. Various authorities and hunter's clubs offered prizes for the killing of the killer. But all efforts seemed in vain.

No one understood how that could be. The superstition of some of the Nimrods vied with the tall tales of others in an effort to correctly interpret the mysterious causes of this phenomenon and to make it comprehensible to the laymen at the inn.

Then a particularly clever fellow hatched out a last possible plan to outwit the freebooter. In the hut of the dead pedlar they looked for his clothes, his smock, his trousers, the shoes and socks he had worn at the end. All his was bundled together and carried into the woods. Cutting through the forest, the schemer dragged the bundle along on the ground over the entire route, until he reached his concealed perch, near which he left it. Then he climbed up to his lookout and waited, gun in hand. Now and then he whistled a little tune that always ended in the song of the oriole. He had heard this tune so often coming from the lips of the pedlar that he could not fail to imitate it.

Would the dog remember? Di-ta-diddle-i-ey! Softly and caressingly the mating call of the oriole sang through the woods, as if the singer had only love in mind.

Grey was dozing—a creature sleeping through the day so as to be ready for the hunt at night. But now, even at dusk, hunger drove him from his den. Yawning, thrusting out his open jaw, he rose. A comfortable stretching of the supple body, a springy rocking of the hindquarters, a short, wild switching of the tail—then he set out. From the clearing he followed a deer run through the high timber. His trail crossed the wood road. There his step was halted, his course barred. He stopped in his tracks, sniffing. Thus was he accustomed to stand stock-still when his nose detected the presence of game. But now there was a different scent in the air. Greedily he sucked it in, as if to carry the message to his heart, the news of one who has suddenly returned from afar, and is once again near.

A trembling ran through his entire body. A brightness, as if lit from within, shone in his eyes.

His nose close to the ground, he followed the spoor, hastily, ever more hastily. Now it jubilated in his ears: Di-ta-diddle-i-ey! His heart leapt ahead and dragged his body along, irresistibly, out of all the wildness and its laws, into destruction.

A hail of shot descended upon Grey, followed immediately by yet another crash of lightning and lead and thunder that struck him down—close to the bundle.

The dog's name was True.

Moses

WALTER D. EDMONDS

I

IT was a long climb. The scent was cold, too; so faint that when he found it behind the barn he could hardly trust himself. He had just come back from Filmer's with a piece of meat, and he had sat down behind the barn and cracked it down; and a minute later he found that scent reaching off, faint as it was, right from the end of his nose as he lay.

He had had the devil of a time working it out at first, but up here it was simple enough except for the faintness of it. There didn't appear to be any way to stray off this path; there wasn't any brush, there wasn't any water. Only he had to make sure of it, when even for him it nearly faded out, with so many other stronger tracks overlaying it. His tail drooped, and he stumbled a couple of times, driving his nose into the dust. He looked gaunt when he reached the spot where the man had lain down to sleep.

The scent lay heavier there. He shuffled round over it, sifting the dust with an audible clapping of his nostrils to work out the pattern the man had made. It was hard to do, for the dust didn't take scent decently. It wasn't like any dust he had ever come across either, being glittery, like mica, and slivery in his nose.

But he could tell after a minute how the man had lain, on his back, with his hands under his head, and probably his hat over his eyes to shield them from the glare which was pretty dazzling bright up this high, with no trees handy.

His tail began to cut air. He felt better, and all of a sudden he lifted up his freckled nose and let out a couple of short yowps and then a good chest-swelled belling. Then he struck out up the steep going once more. His front legs may have elbowed a little, but his hind legs were full of spring and his tail kept swinging.

That was how the old man by the town entrance saw him, way down below.

The old man had his chair in the shadow of the wall with a black and yellow parasol tied to the back of it as an extra insurance against the sun. He was reading the Arrivals in the newspaper, the only column that ever interested him; but he looked up sharply when he heard the two yowps and the deep chest note that, from where he sat, had a mysterious floating quality.

It was a little disturbing; but when he saw a dog was the cause he reached out with his foot and shoved the gate hard, so that it swung shut and latched with a sound like a gong. Only one dog had ever come here, and that sound had been enough to discourage him; he had hung around for a while, though, just on the edge, and made the old man nervous.

He said to himself that he wasn't going to watch this one, anyway, and folded the paper in halves the way the subway commuter had showed him and went on with the Arrivals.

x

After a while, though, he heard the dog's panting coming close and the muffled padding of his feet on the marble gate stone. He shook the paper a little, licked his thumb, and turned over half a sheet and read on through the Arrivals into the report of the Committee on Admissions. But then, because he was a curious old man, and kind-hearted, noticing that the panting had stopped—and because he had never been quite up to keeping his resolves, except once—he looked out of the gate again.

The dog was sitting on the edge of the gate stone, upright, with his front feet close under him. He was a rusty-muzzled, blue-tick foxhound, with brown ears, and eyes outlined in black like an Egyptian's. He had his nose inside the bars and was working it at the old man.

'Go away', said the old man. 'Go home.'

At the sound of his voice the hound wrinkled his nose soberly and his tail whipped a couple of times on the gate stone, raising a little star dust.

'Go home', repeated the old man remembering the dog that had hung around before.

He rattled the paper at him, but it didn't do any good. The dog just looked solemnly pleased at the attention, and a little hopeful, and allowed himself to pant a bit.

'This one's going to be worse than the other', the old man thought, groaning to himself as he got up. He didn't know much about dogs anyway. Back in Galilee there hadn't been dogs that looked like this one—just pariahs and shepherds and the occasional Persian greyhound of a rich man's son.

He slapped his paper along the bars; it made the dog suck in his tongue and move back obligingly. Peter unhooked his shepherd's staff from the middle crossbar, to use in case the dog tried to slip in past him, and let himself out. He could tell by the feeling of his bare ankles that there was a wind making up in the outer heavens and he wanted to get rid of the poor creature before it began really blowing round the walls. The dog backed off from him and sat down almost on the edge, still friendly, but wary of the shepherd's staff.

'Why can't the poor dumb animal read?' thought Peter, turning to look at the sign he had hung on the gatepost.

The sign read:

```
          TAKE NOTICE

                 NO
              DOGS
           SORCERERS
        WHOREMONGERS
           MURDERERS
           IDOLATERS
             LIARS
           WILL BE
           ADMITTED
```

When he had put it up, he thought it might save him a lot
of trouble; but it certainly wasn't going to help in the case of
this dog. He expected he would have to ask the Committee on
Admissions to take the matter up; and he started to feel annoyed with them for not having got this animal on the list
themselves. It was going to mean a lot of correspondence and
probably the Committee would send a memorandum to the
Central Office suggesting his retirement again, and Peter liked
his place at the gate. It was quiet there, and it was pleasant for
an old man to look through the bars and down the path, to
reassure the frightened people, and, when there was nothing
else to do, to hear the winds of outer heaven blowing by.

'Go away. Go home. Depart', he said, waving his staff; but
the dog only backed down on to the path and lay on his wish-
bone with his nose between his paws.

II

Peter went inside and sat down and tried to figure the
business out. There were two things he could do. He could
notify the Committee of the dog's arrival, or he could give the
information to the editor. The Committee would sit up and
take notice for once if they found the editor had got ahead of
them. It would please the editor, for there were few scoops in

Heaven. And then, as luck would have it, the editor himself came down to the gate.

The editor wasn't Horace Greeley or anybody like that, with a reputation in the newspaper world. He had been editor of a little country weekly that nobody in New York, or London, or Paris had ever heard of. But he was good and bursting with ideas all the time. He was now.

'Say, St. Peter,' he said, 'I've just had a swell idea about the Arrivals column. Instead of printing all the "arrivals" on one side and then the "expected guests" on the other, why not just have one column and put the names of the successful candidates in upper-case type? See?' He shoved a wet impression under Peter's nose and rubbed the back of his head nervously with his ink-stained hand. 'Simple, neat, dignified.'

Peter looked at the galley and saw how simple it would be for him, too. He wouldn't have to read the names in lower-case at all. It would make him feel a lot better not to know. Just check the upper-case names as they came to the gate.

He looked up at the flushed face of the editor and his white beard parted over his smile. He liked young, enthusiastic men, remembering how hard, once, they had been to find.

'It looks fine to me, Don', he said. 'But the Committee won't like losing all that space in the paper, will they?'

'Probably not', the editor said ruefully. 'But I thought you could pull a few wires with the Central Office for me.'

Peter sighed.

'I'll try', he said. 'But people don't pay attention to an old man, much, Don. Especially one who's been in service.'

The editor flushed and muttered something about bums.

Peter said gently, 'It doesn't bother me, Don. I'm not ashamed of the service I was in.' He looked down to his sandals. He wondered whether there was any of the dust of that Roman road left on them after so long a time. Every man has his one great moment. He'd had two. He was glad he hadn't let the second one go. 'I'll see what I can do, Don.'

It was a still corner, by the gate; and, with both of them silently staring off up the avenue under the green trees to where the butterflies were fluttering in the shrubbery of the public gardens, the dog decided to take a chance and sneak up again.

He moved one foot at a time, the way he had learned to do behind the counter in the Hawkinsville store, when he went prospecting towards the candy counter. These men didn't hear him; and as the men didn't take any notice, he gumshoed over he had time to sniff over the gatepost thoroughly. It puzzled him! and as the men didn't take any notice, he gumshoed over to the other post and went over that, too.

It was queer. He couldn't smell dog on either of them and they were the best-looking posts he had ever come across. It worried him some. His tail drooped and he came back to the gate stone and the very faint scent on it, leading beyond the gate, that he had been following so long. He sat down again and put his nose through the bars, and after a minute he whined.

It was a small sound, but Peter heard it.

'That dog', he said.

The editor whirled round, saying, 'What dog?' and saw him.

'I was going to let you know about him, only I forgot', said Peter. 'He came up a while ago, and I can't get rid of him. I don't know how he got here. The Committee didn't give me any warning and there's nothing about him in the paper.'

'He wasn't on the bulletin', said the editor. 'Must have been a slip-up somewhere.'

'I don't think so', said Peter. 'Dogs don't often come here. Only one other since I've been here, as a matter of fact. What kind of a dog is he anyway? I never saw anything like him.' He sounded troubled and put out, and the editor grinned, knowing he didn't mean it.

'I never was much of a dog man', he said. 'But that's a likely-looking foxhound. He must have followed somebody's scent up here. Hi, boy!' he said. 'What's your name? Bob? Spot? Duke?'

'Say', said the editor. 'Why don't I put an ad. in the Lost and Found? I've never had anything to put there before. But you better bring him in and keep him here till the owner claims him.'

'I can't do that', said Peter. 'It's against the Law.'

'No dogs. Say, I always thought it was funny there were no dogs here. What happens to them?'

'They get removed', said Peter. 'They just go.'

'That don't seem right', the young editor said. He ruffled his back hair with his hand. 'Say, Saint,' he asked, 'who made this law anyway?'

'It's in Revelations. John wasn't a dog man, as you call it. Back in Galilee we didn't think much of dogs, you see. They were mostly pariahs.'

'I see', said the editor. His blue eyes sparkled. 'But say! Why can't I put it in the news? And write an editorial? By golly, I haven't had anything to raise a cause on since I got here.'

Peter shook his head dubiously.

'It's risky', he said.

'It's a free country', exclaimed the editor.   'At least nobody's told me different. Now probably there's nothing would mean so much to the owner of that dog as finding him up here. You get a genuine dog man and this business of passing the love of women is just hooey to him.'

'Hooey?' Peter asked quietly.

'It just means he likes dogs better than anything. And this is a good dog, I tell you. He's cold-tracked this fellow, whoever he is, Lord knows how. Besides, he's only one dog, and look at the way the rabbits have been getting into the manna in the public garden. I'm not a dog man, as I said before, but believe me, Saint, it's a pretty thing on a frosty morning to hear a good hound high-tailing a fox across the hills.'

'We don't have frost here, Don.'

'Well,' said the editor, 'frost or no frost, I'm going to do it. I'll have to work quick to get it in before the forms close. See you later.'

'Wait', said Peter. 'What's the weather report say?'

The editor gave a short laugh.

'What do you think? Fair, moderate winds, little change in temperature. Those twerps up in the bureau don't even bother to read the barometer any more. They just play pinochle all day, and the boy runs that report off on the mimeograph machine.'

'I think there's a wind making up in the outer heavens', Peter said. 'When we get a real one, it just about blows the gate stone away. That poor animal wouldn't last a minute.'

The editor whistled. 'We'll have to work fast.' Then suddenly his eyes blazed. 'All my life I wanted to get out an extra. I never had a chance, running a weekly. Now, by holy, I will.'

He went off up the avenue on the dead run. Even Peter, watching him go, felt excited.

'Nice dog', he said to the hound; and the hound, at the deep gentle voice, gulped in his tongue and twitched his haunches. The whipping of his tail on the gate stone made a companionable sound for the old man. His beard folded on his chest and he nodded a little.

III

He was dozing quietly when the hound barked.

It was a deep, vibrant note that anyone who knew dogs would have expected the minute he saw the spring of those ribs; it was mellow, like honey in the throat. Peter woke up tingling with the sound of it and turned to see the hound swaying the whole hind half of himself with his tail.

Then a high loud voice shouted, 'Mose, by Jeepers! What the hell you doing here, you poor dumb fool?'

Peter turned to see a stocky, short-legged man who stuck out more than was ordinary, both in front and behind. He had on a grey flannel shirt, and blue denim pants, and a pair of lumberman's rubber packs on his feet, with the tops laced only to the ankle. There was a hole in the front of his felt hat where the block had worn through. He wasn't, on the whole, what you might expect to see walking on that Avenue. But Peter had seen queer people come to Heaven and he said mildly, 'Do you know this dog?'

'Sure', said the stout man. 'I hunted with him round Hawkinsville for the last seven years. It's old Mose. Real smart dog. He'd hunt for anybody.'

'Mose?' said Peter. 'For Moses I suppose.'

'Maybe. He could track anything through hell and high water.'

'Moses went through some pretty high water', said Peter. 'What's your name?'

'Freem Brock. What's yours?'

Peter did not trouble to answer, for he was looking at the hound; and he was thinking he had seen some people come to Heaven's gate and look pleased, and some come and look shy, and some frightened, and some a little shame-faced, and some satisfied, and some sad (maybe with memories they couldn't leave on earth), and some jubilant, and a whole quartette still singing 'Adeline' just the way they were when the hotel fell on their necks in the earthquake. But in all his career at the gate he had never seen anyone express such pure, unstifled joy as this rawboned hound.

'Was he your dog?' he asked Freeman Brock.

'Naw', said Freem.' He belonged to Pat Haskell.' He leaned his shoulder against the gatepost and crossed one foot over the other. 'Stop that yawping', he said to Mose, and Mose lay down, wagging. 'Maybe you ain't never been in Hawkinsville', he said to Peter. 'It's a real pretty village right over the Black River. Pat kept store there and he let anybody take Mose that wanted to. Pretty often I did. He liked coming with me because I let him run foxes. I'm kind of a fox hunter', he said, blowing out his breath. 'Oh, I like rabbit hunting all right, but there's no money in it. . . . Say,' he broke off, 'you didn't tell me what your name was.'

'Peter', said the old man.

'Well, Pete, two years ago was Mose's best season. Seventy-seven fox was shot ahead of him. I shot thirty-seven of them myself. Five crosses and two blacks in the lot. Yes, sir, I heard those black foxes had got away from the fur farm and I took Mose right over there. I made three hundred and fifty dollars out of them hides.'

'He was a good dog, then?' asked Peter.

'Best foxhound in seven counties', said Freem Brock. He kicked the gate with his heel in front of Mose's nose and Mose let his ears droop. 'He was a fool to hunt. I don't see no fox signs up here. Plenty rabbits in the Park. But there ain't nobody with a gun. I wish I'd brought my old Ithaca along.'

'You can't kill things here', said Peter.

'That's funny. Why not?'

'They're already dead.'

'Well, I know that. But it beats me how I got here. I never did nothing to get sent to this sort of place. Hell, I killed them farm foxes and I poached up the railroad in the *preserve*. But I never done anything bad.'

'No', said St. Peter. 'We know that.'

'I got drunk, maybe. But there's other people done the same before me.'

'Yes, Freem.'

'Well, what the devil did I get sent here for, Pete?'

'Do you remember when the little girl was sick and the

town doctor wouldn't come out at night on a town case, and you went over to town and made him come?'

'Said I'd knock his teeth out', said Freem, brightening.

'Yes. He came. And the girl was taken care of', said Peter.

'Aw,' Freem said, 'I didn't know what I was doing. I was just mad. Well, maybe I'd had a drink, but it was a cold night, see? I didn't knock his teeth out. He left them in the glass.' He looked at the old man. 'Jeepers', he said. 'And they sent me here for that?'

Peter looked puzzled.

'Wasn't it a good reason?' he asked. 'It's not such a bad place.'

'Not so bad as I thought it was going to be. But people don't want to talk to me. I tried to talk to an old timber-beast named Boone down the road. But he asked me if I ever shot an Indian, and when I said no he went along. You're the only feller I've seen that was willing to talk to me', he said, turning to the old man. 'I don't seem to miss likker up here, but there's nowhere I can get to buy some tobacco.'

Peter said, 'You don't have to buy things in Heaven.'

'Heaven?' said Freeman Brock. 'Say, is that what this is?' He looked frightened all at once. 'That's what the matter is. I don't belong here. I ain't the kind to come here. There must have been a mistake somewhere.' He took hold of Peter's arm. 'Listen', he said urgently. 'Do you know how to work that gate?'

'I do', said Peter. 'But I can't let you out.'

'I got to get out.'

'Peter's voice grew gentler.

'You'll like it here after a while, Freem.'

'You let me out.'

'You couldn't go anywhere outside', Peter said.

Freem looked through the bars at the outer heavens and watched a couple of stars like water lilies floating by below. He said slowly, 'We'd go somewhere.'

Peter said, 'You mean you'd go out there with that dog?'

Freem flushed.

'I and Mose have had some good times', he said.

At the sound of his name, Mose's nose lifted.

Peter looked down at the ground. With the end of his shepherd's staff he thoughtfully made a cross and then another overlapping it and put an X in the upper left-hand corner. Freem looked down to see what he was doing.

'You couldn't let Mose in, could you, Pete?'

Peter sighed and rubbed out the pattern with his sandal.

'I'm sorry', he said. 'The Committee don't allow dogs.'

'What'll happen to the poor brute, Pete?'

Peter shook his head.

'If you ask me,' Freem said, 'I think this is a hell of a place.'

'What's that you said?'

Peter glanced up.

'Hallo, Don', he said. 'Meet Freem Brock. This is the editor of the paper', he said to Freem. 'His name's Don.'

'Hallo', said Freem.

'What was that you said about Heaven being a hell of a place?' asked the editor.

Freem drew a long breath. He took a look at old Mose lying outside the gate with his big nose resting squashed up and sideways against the bottom crossbar; he looked at the outer heavens, and he looked at the editor.

'Listen', he said. 'That hound followed me up here. Pete says he can't let him in. He says I can't go out to where Mose is. I only been in jail twice', he said, 'but I liked it better than this.'

The editor said, 'You'd go out there?'

'Give me the chance.'

'What a story!' said the editor. 'I've got my extra on the Avenue now. The cherubs will be coming this way soon. It's all about the hound, but this stuff is the genuine goods. Guest prefers to leave Heaven. Affection for old hunting dog prime factor in his decision. It's human interest. I tell you it'll shake the Committee. By holy, I'll have an editorial in my next edition calling for a celestial referendum.'

'Wait', said Peter. 'What's the weather report?'

'What do you think? Fair, moderate winds, little change in temperature. But the Central Office is making up a hurricane for the South Pacific and it's due to go by pretty soon. We got to hurry, Saint.'

He pounded away up the Avenue, leaving a little trail of star dust in his wake.

Freem Brock turned on Saint Peter.

'He called you something', he said.

Peter nodded.

'Saint.'

'I remember about you now. Say, you're a big shot here. Why can't you let Mose in?'

Peter shook his head.

'I'm no big shot, Freem. If I was, maybe—'

His voice was drowned out by a shrieking up the Avenue.

'Extry! Extry! Special Edition. Read all about it. Dog outside Heaven's Gate. Dog outside . . .'

A couple of cherubs were coming down the thoroughfare, using their wings to make time. When he saw them, Freem Brock started. His shoulders began to itch self-consciously and he put a hand inside his shirt.

'My gracious', he said.

Peter, watching him, nodded.

'Everybody gets them. You'll get used to them after a while. They're handy, too, on a hot day.'

'For the love of Pete', said Freem.

'Read all about it! Dog outside Heaven's Gate. Lost Dog waiting outside . . .'

'He ain't lost!' cried Freem. 'He never got lost in his life.'

' "Committee at fault",' read Peter. 'Thomas Aquinas isn't going to like that', he said.

'It don't prove nothing', said Freem.

'Mister, please', said a feminine voice. 'The editor sent me down. Would you answer some questions?'

'Naw', said Freem, turning to look at a young woman with red hair and a gold pencil in her hand. 'Well, what do you want to know, lady?'

The young woman had melting brown eyes. She looked at the hound. 'Isn't he cute?' she asked. 'What's his name?''

'Mose', said Freem. 'He's a cute hound all right.'

'Best in seven counties', said Peter.

'May I quote you on that, Saint?'

'Yes', said Peter. 'You can say I think the dog ought to be let in.' His face was pink over his white beard. 'You can say a hurricane is going to pass, and that before I see that animal blown off by it I'll go out there myself—I and my friend Freem. Some say I'm a has-been, but I've got some standing with the public yet.'

The girl with red hair was writing furiously with a little gold glitter of her pencil. 'Oh', she said.

'Say I'm going out too', said Freem. 'I and Pete.'

'Oh', she said. 'What's your name?'

'Freeman Brock, Route 5, Boonville, New York, U.S.A.'

'Thanks', she said breathlessly.

'How much longer before we got that hurricane coming?' asked Freem.

'I don't know', said the old man, anxiously. 'I hope Don can work fast.'

'Extry! Owner found. Saint Peter goes outside with hound, Moses. Committee bluff called. Read all about it.'

'How does Don manage it so fast?' said Peter. 'It's like a miracle.'

'It's science', said Freem. 'Hey!' he yelled at a cherub.

They took the wet sheet, unheeding of the gold ink that stuck to their fingers.

'They've got your picture here, Pete.'

'Have they?' Peter asked. He sounded pleased. 'Let's see.'

It showed Peter standing at the gate.

'It ain't bad', said Freem. He was impressed. 'You really mean it?' he asked. Peter nodded.

'By cripus,' Freem said slowly, 'you're a pal.'

Saint Peter was silent for a moment. In all the time he had minded Heaven's Gate, no man had ever called him a pal before.

IV

Outside the gate, old Mose got up on his haunches. He was a weather-wise dog, and now he turned his nose outwards. The first puff of wind came like a slap in the face, pulling his ears back, and then it passed. He glanced over his shoulder and saw Freem and the old man staring at each other. Neither of them had noticed him at all. He pressed himself against the bars and lifted his nose and howled.

At his howl both men turned.

There was a clear grey point way off along the reach of the wall, and the whine in the sky took up where Mose's howl had ended.

Peter drew in his breath.

'Come on, Freem', he said, and opened the gate.

Freeman Brock hesitated. He was scared now. He could see that a real wind was coming, and the landing outside looked almightly small to him. But he was still mad, and he couldn't let an old man like Peter call his bluff.

'All right', he said. 'Here goes.'

He stepped out, and Mose jumped up on him, and licked his face.

'Get down, darn you', he said. 'I never could break him of that trick', he explained shamefacedly to Peter. Peter smiled, closing the gate behind him with a firm hand. It's gong-like note echoed through Heaven just as the third edition burst upon the Avenue.

Freeman Brock was frightened. He glanced back through the bars and Heaven looked good to him. Up the Avenue a crowd was gathering. A couple of lanky, brown-faced men were in front. They started towards the gate.

Then the wind took hold of him and he grasped the bars and looked outward. He could see the hurricane coming like an express train running through infinity. It had a noise like an express train. He understood suddenly just how the victim of a crossing accident must feel.

He glanced at Peter.

The old Saint was standing composedly, leaning on his staff with one hand, while with the other he drew Mose close between his legs. His white robe fluttered tight against his shanks and his beard bent sidewise like the hound's ears. He had faced lack of faith, in others; what was worse, he had faced it in himself; and a hurricane, after all, was not so much. He turned to smile at Freem. 'Don't be afraid', he said.

'O.K.', said Freem, but he couldn't let go the gate.

Old Mose, shivering almost hard enough to rattle, reached up and licked Peter's hand.

One of the brown-faced men said, 'That's a likely-looking hound. He's the one I read about in the paper?'

'Yep', said Freem. He had to holler now.

Daniel Boone said, 'Let us timber-beasts come out with you, Saint, will you?'

Peter smiled. He opened the gate with a wave of his hand, and ten or a dozen timber-beasts—Carson, Bridger, Nat Foster —all crowded through, and started shaking hands with him and Freeman Brock. With them was a thin, mild-eyed man.

'My name's Francis', he said to Freem when his turn came. 'From Assisi.'

'He's all right', Daniel Boone explained. 'He wasn't much of a shot, but he knows critters. We better get holt of each other, boys.'

It seemed queer to Freem. Here he was going to get blown to eternity and he didn't even know where it was, but all of a sudden he felt better than he ever had in his life. Then he felt a squirming round his legs and there was Mose, sitting on his feet, the way he would on his snowshoes in cold weather when they stopped for a sandwich on earth. He reached down and took hold of Mose's ears.

'Let her blow to blazes', he thought.

She blew.

The hurricane was on them. The nose of it went by, sweeping the wall of silver. There was no more time for talk. No voices could live outside Heaven's gate. If a man had said a word, the next man to hear it would have been some poor heathen aborigine on an island in the Pacific Ocean, and he wouldn't have known what it meant.

The men on the gate stone were crammed against the bars. The wind dragged them bodily to the left, and for a minute it looked as if Jim Bridger were going, but they caught him back. There were a lot of the stoutest hands that ever swung an axe in that bunch holding on to Heaven's gate, and they weren't letting go for any hurricane—not yet.

But Freem Brock could see it couldn't last that way. He didn't care, though. He was in good company, and that was what counted the most. He wasn't a praying man, but he felt his heart swell with gratitude, and he took hold hard of the collar of Mose and felt the licence riveted on. A queer thing to think of, a New York State dog licence up there. He managed to look down at it, and he saw that it had turned to gold, with the collar gold under it. The wind tore at him as he saw it. The heart of the hurricane was on him now like a million devils' fingers.

'Well, Mose', he thought.

And then in the blur of his thoughts a dazzling bright light came down and he felt the gate at his back opening and he and Peter and Francis and Daniel and the boys were all drawn back into the peace of Heaven, and a quiet voice belonging to a quiet man said, 'Let the dog come in.'

'Jesus', said Freem Brock, fighting for breath, and the quiet man smiled, shook hands with him, and then went over and placed his arm around Peter's shoulders.

V

They were sitting together, Freem and Peter, by the gate, reading the paper in the morning warmth, and Peter was having an easy time with the editor's new type arrangement. 'Gridley,' he was reading the upper-case names, 'Griscome, Godolphin, Habblestick, Hafey, Hanlon, Hartwell, Haskell . . .''

'Haskell', said Freem. 'Not Pat?'

'Yes', said Peter. 'Late of Hawkinsville.'

'Not in big type?'

'Yes.'

'Well, I'll be . . . Well, that twerp. Think of that. Old Pat.'

Peter smiled.

'By holy', said Freem. 'Ain't he going to be amazed when he finds Mose up here?'

'How's Mose doing?'

'He's all right now', said Freem. 'He's been chasing the rabbits. I guess he's up there now. The dew's good.'

'He didn't look so well, I thought', Peter said.

'Well, that was at first', said Freem. 'You see, the rabbits just kept going up in the trees and he couldn't get a real run on any of them. There, he's got one started now.'

Peter glanced up from the paper.

Old Mose was doing a slow bark, kind of low, working out the scent from the start. He picked up pace for a while, and then he seemed to strike a regular knot. His barks were deep and patient.

And then, all of a sudden, his voice broke out—that deep, ringing, honey-throated baying that Freem used to listen to in the late afternoon on the sand hills over the Black River. It went away through the public gardens and out beyond the city, the notes running together and fading and swelling and fading out.

'He's pushing him pretty fast', said Freem. 'He's going to get pretty good on these rabbits.'

The baying swelled again; it came back, ringing like bells. People in the gardens stopped to look up and smile. The sound of it gave Peter a warm tingling feeling.

Freem yawned.

'Might as well wait here till Pat Haskell comes in', he said.

It was pleasant by the gate, under the black and yellow parasol. It made a shade like a flower on the hot star dust. They didn't have to talk, beyond just, now and then, dropping a word between them as they sat.

After a while they heard a dog panting and saw old Mose tracking down the street. He came over to their corner and lay down at their feet, lolling a long tongue. He looked good, a little fat, but lazy and contented. After a minute, though, he got up to shift himself around, and paused as he sat down, and raised a hind leg, and scratched himself behind his wings.